Penelope Douglas is a *New York Times*, *USA Today*, and *Wall Street Journal* bestselling author. Their books have been translated into more than twenty languages and include The Fall Away Series, The Devil's Night Series, and the standalones: *Misconduct*, *Punk 57*, *Birthday Girl*, *Credence*, and *Tryst Six Venom*.

They live in New England with their husband and daughter.

Visit Penelope Douglas online:
www.penelopedouglasauthor.com
www.facebook.com/PenelopeDouglasAuthor
www.twitter.com/pendouglas

ALSO BY PENELOPE DOUGLAS...

Stand-Alones
Misconduct
Punk 57
Birthday Girl
Credence
Tryst Six Venom

The Devil's Night Series
Corrupt
Hideaway
Kill Switch
Conclave
Nightfall
Fire Night

The Fall Away Series
Bully
Until You
Rival
Falling Away
Aflame
Adrenaline
Next to Never

The Hellbent Series
(Fall Away Spin-Off/in progress)
Falls Boys
Pirate Girls
Quiet Ones
Night Thieves
Parade Alley
Fire Falls

PIRATE GIRLS

PENELOPE DOUGLAS

PIATKUS

PIATKUS

First published in 2024 by Penelope Douglas
Published in Great Britain in 2024 by Piatkus

1 3 5 7 9 10 8 6 4 2

Copyright © 2024 by Penelope Douglas
Cover Design © 2024 by Hang Le
Formatting and Proofreading by Allusion Publishing

The moral right of the author has been asserted.

*All characters and events in this publication, other than those
clearly in the public domain, are fictitious and any resemblance
to real persons, living or dead, is purely coincidental.*

All rights reserved.
No part of this publication may be reproduced, stored in a
retrieval system, or transmitted in any form or by any means, without
the prior permission in writing of the publisher, nor be otherwise circulated
in any form of binding or cover other than that in which it is published
and without a similar condition including this condition being
imposed on the subsequent purchaser.

A CIP catalogue record for this book
is available from the British Library.

ISBN 978-0-349-43577-0

Printed and bound in Great Britain
by Clays Ltd, Elcograf S.p.A.

Papers used by Piatkus are from well-managed forests
and other responsible sources.

Piatkus
An imprint of
Little, Brown Book Group
Carmelite House
50 Victoria Embankment
London EC4Y 0DZ

An Hachette UK Company
www.hachette.co.uk

www.littlebrown.co.uk

PLAYLIST

"Beneath the Serene" by Mercury's Antennae
"BORN DARK" by Holy Wars
"Caterwaul" by ...And You Will Know Us by the Trail of Dead
"Deadly Valentine" by Charlotte Gainsbourg
"debbie downer" by LØLØ, Maggie Lindemann
"(Don't Fear) The Reaper" by Pierce The Veil
"driver's license" by Olivia Rodrigo
"Gravedigger" by MXMS
"HONEY" by LUNA AURA
"Jealous Sea" by MEG MYERS
"Keep the Streets Empty for Me" by Fever Ray
"Luci" by ZAND
"Magic" by Olivia Newton-John
"Movies" by Weyes Blood
"Seize the Power" by YONAKA
"Slip To The Void" by Alter Bridge
"The Collapse" by Adelita's Way
"Victim" by Halflives
"you broke me first" by Tate McRae

In addition to playlists, all of my stories
come with Pinterest mood boards.
Please enjoy *PIRATE GIRLS*'s board
(https://www.pinterest.com/penelopedouglas/
pirate-girls-2024/) as you read!

AUTHOR'S NOTE

The Hellbent Series is a spin-off of the Fall Away Series. These are the kids' stories.

Reading *Fall Away* is helpful but not necessary. The parents do appear a lot, as well as references to their past storylines, so if you wish to read those first, the order is *BULLY, UNTIL YOU, RIVAL, FALLING AWAY, AFLAME,* and *NEXT TO NEVER.*

FALLS BOYS (Hellbent #1) is **strongly encouraged** before you read *PIRATE GIRLS*. There is an ongoing mystery playing out in the background. I do try to bring you up to speed in this story, but you'll have the best experience reading *FALLS BOYS* first. Just a warning.

And if you'd love to read all the times the characters in this series appeared before this series started, go here-> https://pendouglas.com/2022/02/28/get-ready-for-hellbent/

Again, none of this is necessary, but if you'd like to experience the whole world, *BULLY* is where you can start. Enjoy!

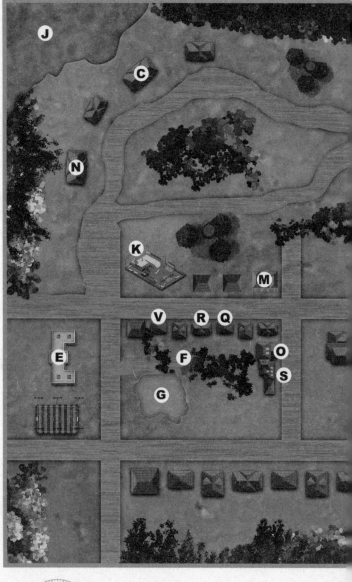

A. JARED'S HOUSE   F. EAGLE POINT PARK
B. TATE'S HOUSE   G. FISH POND
C. MADOC'S HOUSE   H. CEMETERY
D. JULIET'S HOUSE   I. THE LOOP
E. HIGH SCHOOL   J. MINES OF SPAIN

*This map is a loose representation of Shelburne Falls to give you a basic idea of the placement of homes and points of interest. There are more streets and businesses than what the map includes.

SHELBURNE FALLS

L

P

T

I

H

U

A   **B**   Toward
Weston

K. SKATE PARK
L. BLACKHAWK LAKE
M. JT RACING
N. QUINN'S HOUSE
O. QUINN'S BAKERY

P. BLACKHAWK SUMMER CAMP
Q. BOWLING ALLEY
R. MOVIE THEATER
S. TBD
T. THE DIETRICH HOUSE

U TBD
V. TBD

"You have to fight twice—once against your fear
and once against your enemy."
— Carolyn Keene,
Captive Witness (Nancy Drew Mystery Stories #64)

HELLBENT SERIES

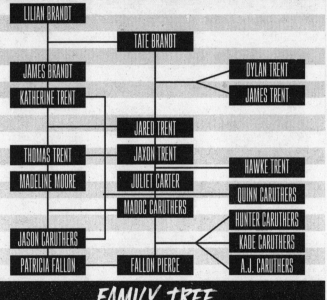

LILIAN BRANDT

TATE BRANDT

JAMES BRANDT

KATHERINE TRENT

DYLAN TRENT

JAMES TRENT

JARED TRENT

THOMAS TRENT

JAXON TRENT

MADELINE MOORE

JULIET CARTER

HAWKE TRENT

MADOC CARUTHERS

QUINN CARUTHERS

HUNTER CARUTHERS

JASON CARUTHERS

KADE CARUTHERS

PATRICIA FALLON

FALLON PIERCE

A.J. CARUTHERS

FAMILY TREE

To Aunt Carol, who read Bully
and asked, "Where the hell are their parents?"

They're now the parents!

PIRATES

CHAPTER ONE

Dylan

I lock eyes on Aro, willing her not to say it.

"You're half an hour late," she tells me.

Yeah, duh.

I cross the parking lot, speed-walking up to her as she waits near one of our school's rear entrances. The lights from the football stadium brighten the night sky off to my right, and an announcer's voice booms so loudly I can't make out what he's saying. But the crowd cheers anyway. I swipe my hand under my chin, wiping off the mud, and tuck my keys in the pocket of my filthy motorcycle jacket.

My cousin's girlfriend lowers her voice as I approach the door. "Your dad thinks I went to get you," she says.

I pull out a metal nail file, Aro moving to the side as I grab the door handle and start working the lock. I need to clean up before my parents come out of the stadium. I have a change of clothes in my gym locker. If my dad sees the dirt all over me...

I glance at her. "You didn't tell him where I was, did you?"

1

She hoods her brown eyes and locks her jaw, and I realize I've insulted her. She wouldn't rat me out. It's code.

"Good." I nod and continue working. "Just don't say *anything* if he asks."

"He's going to know," she fires back. "If I don't respond, it's because I don't want to lie, and he knows that."

I jiggle the nail file and then twist. "Well, you *can* lie…"

It's always an option, of course. He can't ground her.

I guess he can try to force my uncle Jax—his brother— to ground her, since she and her two siblings live with him and his wife next door to us. But Jax won't do that. Aro stopped being a child long before she should have, and Jax understands that better than most.

I grip the tool, twisting and jiggling some more, but then I feel the heat of her stare.

I look over, meeting very different eyes this time. Darker.

I shake my head, completely fed up with myself. She loves her life here. My dad is her boss. She lives in his brother's house. She dates my cousin, Hawke. She goes to school with me. Her brother and sister are thriving in our community…

I'm asking her to disrespect all of that.

"That wasn't okay." I pause. "I'm sorry."

Her left eyebrow arches, and she holds out for a moment more before finally giving in. "It's fine." She sighs. "Last year I was kicking your ass. This year, I'm the only one you tell all of your secrets."

Kicking my ass…what?

She smiles smugly. "You're so lucky to have me, aren't you?"

I am. I adore her.

But she did not kick my ass…

2

I jam and jiggle the tool in my hand, trying to muscle it.

If we hadn't been pulled off each other during that fight...

The thin edge of the nail file cuts into my hand as I try to pry the lock.

Nearly all of my cousins are guys. I know how to wrestle, thank you.

But then...the file snaps in two, half of it still lodged in the lock.

I dart my eyes over to Aro, a groan expelling from my lungs as my shoulders slump.

She rolls her eyes and moves in. "Seriously, get out of the way."

I step off to the side and watch her pull out her key ring full of carefully hidden little tools from her misspent youth. Digging my broken nail file out of the lock, she inserts a small tension wrench. Holding it with one hand, she finds another little thingy and slides that into the doorknob.

I'm glad I asked her to meet me here. She's taught me how to do this three times, but I still struggle. I should've just gone home to clean up, but Rivalry Week starts tonight. I need to be here.

Her eyes flash to my hand. "You're bleeding."

I look down, seeing blood spread over the long bone of my index finger.

I graze my chin again and hold my hand up, seeing a few thin crimson lines. Yeah, that wasn't mud I felt before. It's going to be hard to hide that.

She works the lock, and I can tell she's biting her tongue. She knows I fell off my bike, while I was training illegally and without permission tonight, and that my face is bleeding, because I took off my helmet while I was racing.

"What happens if you get injured and you're all alone out there?" she asks.

I check my phone, seeing two missed calls from my dad. I tuck it back into my pocket. "You've faced people with guns. Alone," I point out. "This is nothing."

"And what happened with the first person to make me feel like I was never going to be alone again?" she asks, meaning my cousin, Hawke. "I straddled him."

I pinch my eyebrows together. "Ugh."

"In your old car..." she taunts, and I hear a click.

"Christ." I growl under my breath. "Move."

I shove her out of the way and pull out her key chain, tossing it back at her and opening the door.

Hawke is a year older than me, so he's been alive every single moment of my life. I knew him before he noticed girls at all. Before he had muscles.

I don't care to hear about him doing things that will give me unwelcome mental images. But as my friend, she wants to talk to me about her boyfriend sometimes, and it's ew-y.

I enter the empty school, the hallway dark and quiet, and she follows me in, slamming the door. The music and cheers pounding from the stadium seep in, but only as a distant thrum as light from the moon and the football field spill through the overhead windows.

I start walking, Aro's unusually calm voice falling in behind me. "And I don't look at facing people with guns as something that was smart," she reminds me. "I did what I had to do, you know?"

I throw her a soft smile. *I know.*

She came from Weston, the dark and dilapidated mill town across the river where all the area's young criminals live, because police don't go there. It sits less than ten miles away, but it's another world from Shelburne Falls. Their newest building is from the turn of the century—the one before last, I mean—and you'd be lucky to find two working street lamps in a row.

But even if she grew up with the advantages I've had, she still wouldn't appreciate people telling her she can't have what she wants.

"And I have to do this," I explain.

I have to train, even if it's on my own. This town thinks they know who I am, because they know who my parents are, but no one really wants me to be me. They don't see me. They see a Trent.

We walk, and I pull off my jacket and boots, leaving a mud trail down the hallway.

I gesture to room fifty-eight as we pass. "That's the room where my mom cried and told my dad in front of the whole class how much she missed him..."

Aro's heard all the stories from when me and my cousins' parents went to school here.

We keep going. "And that's the lunchroom where Uncle Madoc asked her to prom," I chirp, walking by the windows of the newly renovated cafeteria.

We arrive at the gym, and I wave my hand to the door on the right. "And that's the locker room where my dad punched him afterward."

And then I stop, turning and jerking my chin at the locker with the number 1622 on it, sitting in full view of everyone who passes by. "And that's the locker where the cell phone was found."

It sits, along with two others, in a display case with trophies, championship banners, old photos, swim ribbons, newspaper clippings of successful alumni (including, not only my parents, but Madoc, the Mayor, and Aunt Juliet, the novelist), and some vintage clothing items. The exhibit spans nearly twelve feet down the long wall.

I stare at the chipped yellow lockers, number one-six-two-two on the left.

"How do you know that's the one?" she asks.

I don't blink, and I don't look at her. "Hawke hacked some old school records when I asked."

The metal corners are rusted where the paint has worn away, and dents and scratches are scattered across every square inch from the vents to below the handle.

More than twenty years ago, my parents lifted that handle to discover my dad's stolen cell phone that Nate Dietrich used to make my mother believe my dad had posted a video of them having sex.

That was the locker of his partner in crime, Piper Burke, and it didn't register with the administration when they decided to install new ones last year and save a few of the old for a nostalgic showcasing of the school's history, but it did with my step-cousin, Kade. He didn't want this locker trashed, so he made sure it was one of the artifacts preserved in this long glass case I have to walk past several times every day.

A lot of people saw that video all those years ago, and they had kids who are here now. It hasn't been forgotten, and while no one would dare say a word to my parents, the secret that's not really a secret still slowly fills any space I walk into like a ship filling with water.

I doubt Kade thought of that, though. All he cares about is that Nate and Piper had a kid, and that kid just started high school here this year. The sins of the father and all that...

And I know the video wasn't my parents' fault, but their shadow falls everywhere.

I glance at Aro and then walk over, pushing open the women's locker room door. "This entire town revolves around my family, this school orbiting them the most." I drop my jacket on a bench and kick off my boots. "My father

6

thinks I'll be a target as a motorbike racer. Not just because I'm a girl, but also because I'm his daughter. He doesn't want me to be taunted like I still am at this school from time to time over my parents' bullshit back in the day."

Make no mistake. My dad knows and regrets the reputation he made for himself when he was my age.

But his mistake is thinking it's *my* burden to bear.

I turn to her, whipping off my shirt and opening my jeans. "You know why my dad thinks it's my responsibility to lay low and not invite scrutiny because I already get so much for his life?" I ask her. "Because I'm a girl." I turn away and head for the showers in my bra and underwear, grabbing a towel off the rack. "When the time comes, he won't tell my brother he can't race motorcycles if he wants to."

He'd love for James to share his interests, but I'm the one who needs to be shielded.

Whipping open the shower curtain, I step inside and start the water. I hold my hand under, checking the temperature as I hang my towel on a hook.

Aro leans in, pressing both hands on each side of the stall. "I'm going to tell you a secret."

I cast my eyes up to her.

"Parents have far less control than you think they do, Dylan." She smiles a little. "There's a limit to how much and how hard they'll fight you before they just give up. If that's what you want."

No. I don't want them to give up. That's not...

But she pulls the curtain closed and leaves me to clean up.

I tear off the rest of my clothes, hearing the locker room door echo shut as she leaves. I pull my hair out of my ponytail, wetting it under the spray.

She's right. I know she is. I learned a long time ago that my parents would fold pretty easily on a lot of things with just a little resistance from me.

My father does not want me racing motorcycles, though. It's the one hill he won't descend.

I smooth my hand over the top of my head, seeing mud drip off my body, down to a pool around my feet as I quickly wash and shampoo.

However, I don't want to go as far as Aro's telling me I can.

Yeah, I can race, and he'll scream or try to put me behind lock and key, but eventually I'll find a way around him until he just gives up, both of us destroying our relationship—the respect and the trust—in all of the turmoil. I'll tear my house apart, distress my mom and my brother... I don't want my dad to just give in.

I want him to train me.

My head pounds, and I growl under my breath, shaking off all the noise in my brain.

I slam down the lever, shutting off the water, and grab my towel. I wrap it around me and exit the stall, finding clean clothes from the gym locker that I share with Aro.

The dull vibration of the music outside stops, but the walls are too thick to hear if an announcer is speaking or if the crowd is cheering.

I glance at the clock high to my left. *Eight-nineteen.*

We have to be there by nine.

I pull on the change of clothes, some clean sneakers, and my black varsity jacket that I love, because it has orange and black stripes around the cuffs and around the trim at the waist and collar. They're our school colors and no one else has this jacket. I scored it at a thrift shop when I was ten, and I've saved it all this time, waiting to fit into it.

Sticking my keys in my pocket and my phone in the back of my jeans, I brush out my hair and swipe it up into a ponytail. Wrapping my muddy gear in a towel, I stuff the bundle in my locker—which Aro won't appreciate when she opens it for gym class in the morning, but I can't risk my dad seeing it.

I start to head out, but instead, I veer through the coach's office, peering out her windows and down to the stadium below.

Everyone's still there. *Good*. I don't try to find my dad in the stands, I'll just tell him I was here the whole time. He can't prove I wasn't.

I push up the sleeves of my jacket and gaze down at the pep rally, confetti and the remnants of the massive broken banner that the football team crashes through when they burst onto the field scattered all over the turf. The marching band twists and turns in formation behind the cheer team flashing and shaking their pom poms high above their heads.

The football players stand on a platform, dressed in their jeans and jerseys as the head coach speaks at the podium. Kade Caruthers, as always, stands in the center of the lineup, chin raised, and I can almost see the ghost of the smile that always plays on his lips.

But...his green eyes are zoned in and sharp, which I know even if I can't see them clearly from here, because I've known him my whole life. And this? Being awesome and alpha and feeding a crowd? This is his fucking job.

I assume I've missed most of the festivities for the night, but I've seen it before. Every year. Always the same Sunday in October that kicks off Rivalry Week.

Which technically lasts *two* weeks.

The second week is the official story. Parade, pranks, football, dance... Yay, fun. Looks great on the school's Instagram page.

But the first week is just as exciting. Like a pre-game. Something to warm our blood, so it's nice and hot for the showdown on the field. Parties, *illegal* pranks, and the prisoner exchange. One of my favorite parts.

For the next two weeks, the Shelburne Falls Pirates, the St. Matthew's Knights, and the Weston Rebels will exchange one student. House them, feed them, take them to school...

At the end of the two weeks, we release the prisoners back to their respective student bodies, usually unharmed.

Sometimes they do a lot of damage while they're here, though.

The guy Weston sent us last year got two girls pregnant during his two weeks here, so that was interesting.

This year promises to be no less exciting, because more than a year ago, one of our own turned on us—switched schools. He'll be standing opposite of the team he once played for on this field very soon. Kade can't wait to face him.

It's all he thinks about. And talks about.

I watch as the coach invites Kade up to the podium. He gives his dynamite smile that he gets from his dad, and that makes all the girls feel like their hearts are filled with bubbles, but I can't hear what he's saying. By the way the crowd cheers, though, I can guess.

Kill!

Kill some more.

Kill everything and kill everyone.

Roar.

It laces all of his words and actions, because Kade's pride is at stake. His brother is the turncoat who enrolled at St. Matthew's, one of our rivals.

Kade has to win.

Pulling out my phone, I scroll the same text thread I've reread a hundred times.

I wish you would've stayed. Are you up?

He never responded.

Hunter.

Kade's twin.

He made an appearance last Thanksgiving, but he mostly stayed anywhere I wasn't. He hung out with his dad and mine for a while in the garage, then he moved to the kitchen with his mom and Addie, their former housekeeper, and then he walked outside, playing with his and Kade's little sister, A.J., for a while. He didn't talk much. Almost like we were all strangers to him and didn't share a thousand memories together.

It was so uncomfortable. Our dads are stepbrothers, and they were best friends long before that. I grew up with Hunter.

But I can't say his leaving, and transferring schools, was entirely a surprise. He and Kade had always been at odds while growing up, and one day Hunter just broke.

But why did he leave me too? He didn't meet my eyes once when he came for Thanksgiving.

And he didn't stay long. Without a word, he was gone. Back to his grandfather's house an hour away, and St. Matt's, his new school. I scroll, seeing a picture I sent him of a movie poster.

New Fast *movie tonight at eight! I'm sneaking in your favorite candy.*

I hoped that maybe in a dark theater where we didn't have to talk, he might just come and sit, and maybe we could smile and laugh a little.

He never showed.

I ate your candy, I texted him the next day.

Months passed, and I got the hint. He didn't want to talk.

Fine, then.

He had my number. I tried. If he wants to be friends again, he knows where I am.

But there were days that I couldn't ignore.

Happy Birthday!!

I wrote in August on his and Kade's eighteenth birthday, accompanied by a celebratory GIF.

He didn't text back. He leaves the *Read* receipts on, though. Kade says it's because Hunter wants us to know that he's deliberately ignoring us. I think it's because he wants us to know that he's okay. If there's no indication that communications are getting through, then we'll come looking for him. He wants that even less than our texts.

Kade had a pool party for his birthday and had all of his friends tag Hunter in pictures, because Kade wanted his twin to know he was living the high life without him.

That's when Hunter deleted his social media.

Hawke and his girlfriend are going to Chicago for a concert. I'm tagging along. Wanna meet up?

I sent that a few weeks ago. Maybe on his turf, without the reminders of home, he'd want to see me? Fat chance. The only way I really see him anymore is through pictures, when his parents see him and post on their own profiles.

He was in St. Matthew's alumni magazine last May, just a picture of current students, including him, hunched over lab tables. He was working alone. I didn't show Kade the picture.

I look down and see the text I started to type out last week when I found out what Kade was planning for tonight.

I nee—

But I'd stopped typing, because why should I warn him? What have I gotten from Hunter or Kade Caruthers for my loyalty?

I raise my eyes, seeing Kade look up at me. My heart skips the tiniest beat. He's looking at me. I know, because the only thing he ever notices about me anymore is my absence. That's when I matter.

Backing away from the podium, he lets the coach finish up, and then he throws up his arms at me like "why isn't your ass in the bleachers hanging on my every word like the rest of our family?"

I fold my arms over my chest and bring a hand up, feigning a yawn. His smile widens, and I can see his body shake with a chuckle.

"Fuck it." I tuck my phone into my pocket again. I'll go tonight, because I'm bored. Not because I'm curious.

Leaving the locker room, I jog back down the hallway, past the display case, the men's locker room, and the cafeteria. If I can get out of here before the rally ends, I can get home, grab my car, and be gone again before my dad sees me. Or my muddy motorcycle.

As soon as I push through the door and step outside, though, I see my father leaning against my bike. I pause mid-step, my stomach sinking instantly.

He stands twenty-five yards away, his legs crossed at the ankles and his hands resting in the pockets of his black bomber jacket. He stares at me.

I flit my eyes left and right, hearing the thundering sound of people descending the steel bleachers as the event ends. I don't see my mom yet.

Chin up, I walk toward him. I'll handle it like I always do.

But as soon as I get close enough to speak, he stops me before I can get the words out.

"Give me your bike keys," he says, holding out his hand.

I open my mouth.

"Now," he barks.

People are spilling out of the stadium, and I know he won't listen. Not tonight. I grab my keys out of my jacket pocket and hand them over.

"And it wasn't Aro who told me," he points out.

I didn't think it was.

He stands up straight, digging in his eyebrows. "I know how to use an app, thank you."

"You're tracking me?"

"You leave me no choice!" he growls, heat rising in his angry eyes. "I'll need to find your body when you break your damn neck."

"You and Mom were racing at my age."

"Not motorcycles."

Right. That's fine then. He gets to decide the amount of danger that's acceptable.

He walks around my bike, inspecting the condition. I narrow my eyes. "You train Noah."

His protégé from Colorado who's only a few years older than me.

My dad doesn't reply, simply squats down to check the tires.

"I want you to train me." I catch myself shifting on my feet and stop. "I want on your team."

He rises, his eyes zeroing in on me as he rounds the bike.

"Will you say no to James, too, when he gets older?" I blurt out.

He knows I'm right. He knows he doesn't have an argument. He won't tell his son no.

He stops in front of me, unblinking. "I love you," he says. "You and me have been in sync since the day you were born." And he holds up his two fingers, twisting them around each other, because until recently, we were that close. "But like me, you do not think. You're reckless, irresponsible, and you do *not* listen. I am not going to let you fuck up like I did—getting caught up in bad scenes and bad influences and risking your life before you've grown up."

I stare at him for a split-second before I start shaking my head. Just like I told Aro. I have to make myself smaller just because I'm not a guy. It's not fair.

"You can't stop me."

I say the words out loud before I can contain them, and I watch his spine go steel-rod straight. "What did you say?"

His gaze pierces my skin, and I feel like I'm sinking into the pavement.

He comes in close. "Say it again," he tells me, leaning in. "I didn't hear you."

I drop my eyes, clenching my teeth.

"Say it again."

I dart my eyes up at him. "When I graduate, I'm going to do it anyway, with or without you." I keep my tone in check this time. "You can wish me luck and pray I survive, or you can train me and make sure I'm the best."

I'm not trying to dare him. I'm just telling him how it is. It's going to happen.

But to my surprise, he just smiles. "When you graduate?" he repeats. "Hell, you almost scared me. That's seven-and-

15

a-half months away." He opens his jacket and makes a show of dropping my bike keys into the inside pocket. "Plenty of time for you to forget how to ride a bike at all."

I watch him turn, images of the next seven months with no motorcycle flooding my head and making me feel like I can't breathe.

Dammit.

He starts to leave, but my mother is there, and I can tell by the look she passes between my dad and me, she just heard that.

Stepping up to her, he cups her chin, brushing her jaw with his thumb. "I'll grab James and take her bike. We'll meet you two at home."

She nods, and he leaves, heading back into the stadium. People stream out and cars start up as everyone goes home, but I'm not leaving. He got my keys, so it can't get much worse for me.

I turn and lean back onto my bike as my mom rests next to me. "Let me tell you something about your dad, honey." She folds her arms over her chest, and I glance down at her hands that are always soft despite washing them a hundred times a day at the hospital. "Jared Trent is the love of my life," she says, "but sometimes...he needs to be handled."

Yeah. She and my dad have been in love since they were ten. She's also fought with him a lot more than anyone too.

I twist my lips to the side a little. "Can't you handle him for me?"

"No." She shakes her head, but I hear her amused tone. "This is a lesson most never learn. Some people aren't going to believe what you can do until you do it. You're not reckless. You're not irresponsible. You're you. Make him see it."

I know she agrees with my dad to some extent. She worries about my safety.

But she also knows this is who I am, and it won't change.

My dad loves me. My mom loves me *and* likes me, and some days I think that's cooler.

"Dylan," someone calls.

I look over my shoulder, seeing Kade with his friends Dirk and Stoli, and...Jessica. Kade's most recent girlfriend—a senior like me. They approach his black truck.

He tips his head, gesturing to me. "Let's go."

The prisoner exchange.

I start to leave, but I hear my mom's voice behind me. "Ten o'clock."

Normally, my curfew is nine on a school night, but the next two weeks will be an exception.

I toss her a wave and head for Kade's truck, but I continue on, not stopping. "I'll grab my car," I tell him. It's a hike to my house, but once I'm in my Mustang, I'll probably still beat him to the prisoner exchange with the way I drive. "I'll follow you."

"Why?" he asks.

"Because I'm sick of your back seat."

Drawing in a deep breath, he arches a brow and turns to Jessica, looking at her in the passenger seat through his driver's side window. He gives her a little shrug. "Babe, please?"

I sigh. "Don't do me any favors."

Jesus. That's not what I meant. *Back seat* was really more of a metaphor.

"I want you in the goddamn truck," he orders me. "Now."

And for a split-second, I feel like someone's fisting my collar.

Lips tight, Jessica climbs over Stoli, shoves open her door, and hops down out of her seat.

I stalk over to the passenger side.

"Lucky for you," she taunts as I swing around the door. "I love his back seat."

I grip the door hard, but I don't reply. Looking up, I see Stoli still sitting in the front, too, his deep brown hair expertly coiffed as he stares at his phone.

"Out," I tell him, so he can hear me through his earbuds.

I know I'm not more important than his girlfriend—or the one before her or the one before her—but I am more important than everyone else. I'm not Kade's crew. I'm family, even if we're not related by blood.

Rolling his eyes, Stoli slides out and jumps down, both of them climbing in the back seat with Dirk. Hauling myself up into the raised cab, I slam the door and fasten my seat belt as Kade fires up the engine. Music spills out of the speakers, always too loud for anyone to speak, which is what he prefers. I turn it down, and he punches the gas, the truck speeding out of the parking lot.

No one talks, but I see light from Dirk's phone screen glowing out of the corner of my eye, behind me. His cologne fills the cab, and I'm always grateful for it, because it covers up the scent of sweat and the slightly sweet tinge, no doubt from Kade's fruit-flavored condoms that I found in the center console once.

I pick at one of my fingernails. "You think Hunter will be there?"

Kade just shrugs. "Either way, we'll get him."

I can't help but smile to myself. *Soooo confident*. Hunter hasn't given us an inch in over a year only to be forced home tonight. He'd have to be an idiot to not anticipate Kade's move.

"What?"

I look over, seeing Kade watching me. I lose the smile and turn away. "Nothing."

I feel the three behind us, acting like they're not listening as two scroll through their phones and Stoli tips back his flask that I can't see. I hear the liquid slosh, though.

"What happened to your face?" Kade asks.

Leaning back in his seat, one hand on the wheel, he takes my jaw with the other and turns my face to look at the scratches. Warmth spreads under my skin.

"It's fine," I murmur.

My chin stings, but I don't check to see if it's still bleeding. It can't be too bad. My parents didn't notice.

"You're going to get hurt," he says.

I pull away, turning forward again. "I said it's fine."

"And then you'll be in traction for six months," he goes on, "learning how to walk again, forget about racing..."

I turn to look at him, but my tone is as calm as when I order breakfast. "Stop."

With the number of dumb things he does, his argument has no ground with me.

But Stoli chimes in from behind. "He's right, Dylan. If your dad told you no, then—"

"Hey, shut up," Kade barks, eyeing his friend in the rearview mirror. "This is family business. Don't talk to my cousin like that."

I scratch my eyebrow, but it doesn't really itch. Stoli closes his mouth, and everything in the truck silences.

I used to love it when Kade got territorial like that. It made me feel like I was important. He doesn't do it much anymore. Not since his and Hunter's falling out last year.

I don't even know what happened that night. In the blink of an eye, everything changed, and it wasn't even all that dramatic. They'd always been combative. I was used to it.

But no one expected Hunter to finally leave.

Maybe we should've seen it coming. I missed it.

"Hey." Kade ruffles my hair like he would a little cousin. "I'm just worried about you, okay?" He lowers his voice. "Men in those scenes won't treat you right. I don't want you around that shit."

I gaze over at him, my anger softening. He said it quietly, because it was hard for him to say at all. I wish he was like that more.

But then he notices something on his fingers and scrunches up his face, looking at where he touched my head as he wipes his hand on his jeans. "Is that mud?"

I must've missed a spot.

I lower my eyes to my lap, instead asking, "Do you ever watch me ride?"

I don't know where the question came from, but it just occurred to me.

"What?" he asks.

I look at him, his blond hair always styled like a vintage Ralph Lauren ad, and the blush across his cheeks making his skin look more golden than it actually is. He looks like that all the time now, with the weather being crisp and him outside as much as possible.

"When I used to race the Loop in my car," I explain. "Did you watch?"

His mouth opens and closes as he faces the road, and he finally shrugs. "Yeah." He nods. "Yeah, of course, I've seen you race. Why would you ask that?"

He never watches. He shows up, mingles at the track, sneaks beers behind the merch tents with his friends....

I have to watch his games. He never watches me ride.

He turns up the music, and I look out the window, trees flying past as their leaves rain down around us.

Kade, Hawke, my father... My senior year should be incredible, but my throat feels as narrow as a straw.

Moonlight gleams across the river down below to my right, and I peer out the window, over the cliff, to the sparse lights of Weston. Silos from abandoned mills rise high in the black sky, while the occasional old lamp around a warehouse still glows. A light will pop on up on a hill or in some alley, while others will fizz out, and I smile to myself because Aro explained they're motion activated. Security lights to keep delinquents from invading private property or deserted businesses. She brought me out here one night to watch the movement of the constant illegal invaders as they leave a trail of motion-activated lights in their wake. It was kind of funny, because not once, no matter how brightly they broadcasted their presence in places they weren't supposed to be, I never saw one blue or red light of a cop car.

Kade stops the truck in the middle of the three-way intersection. St. Matthew's heads toward us from the road ahead, and Weston will come over the bridge to our right. There won't be any other cars this time of night.

Leaving the engine running and the headlights on, he opens his door. "Let's go," he tells us.

Players from St. Matthew's, the wealthy suburb of Chicago and Hunter's school for the past year, walk to meet us, while Stoli, Dirk, and I flank Kade. Jessica stays in the truck.

"Kade Caruthers." Beck Valencourt grins, walking over with his crew. "How's it going over in Shitburne Falls?"

Kade laughs. "You know who my grandfather is, right? They would never find your body."

Beck flashes him a genuine smile—knowing of Kade's retired gangster grandpa and the stories surrounding him. He's used to Kade's jibe. They know each other well, and they better not be giving us Beck as a prisoner, because Kade and he will be frat bros in a year. Kade won't want to haze him, and I enjoy that part of Rivalry Week, actually.

School-sanctioned bullying? Why not? It's the one time everyone at your school is finally on the same side. The enemy of my enemy is my friend...

They shake, coming in for a quick hug.

"Will we see you on the slopes this year?" Beck asks him.

"You bet." Kade nods. "Iron Mountain."

"Hell yeah."

Kade glances over at the St. Matthew's cars parked opposite ours. I look, too, searching the profiles of the people inside.

"I can try to accommodate your request," Beck says, holding out his hands. "You just can't have my girlfriend."

Kade chuckles. "Actually, I just want a football player."

"I knew that about you."

"Shut up," Kade spits out.

The Weston crew, led by Farrow Kelly, approach from the right, exiting the two-lane bridge.

An entourage tails him, two guys and two girls, all about a foot shorter than he is. His blond hair is pushed back under a backward baseball cap, the short sleeves of his black T-shirt frayed. His blue eyes dance as they meet mine, and I look away.

Aro defected from them. She's a Pirate now. He's going to make someone pay for that.

Plus, he and his friends invaded Kade's house on Grudge Night several weeks ago. I'm still aggravated.

"It's only for two weeks," Kade continues talking to Beck. "You'll get him back in almost the same condition."

"Well, we want Trent." Beck points to me. "Agree to that and we'll give you a player." He gives me a grin. "We want to see what she can do on our track."

I narrow my eyes. "I don't want to go to St. Matt's." I throw Beck a look. "They're stuck up."

He laughs.

And I'm not forcing myself on Hunter. He doesn't want to see me.

But Kade replies, "You can have her."

I jerk my head right, glaring.

You can have her. Just that easy?

"Just give us Hunter," he tells Beck. "If Hunter comes here, she can go there."

My eyes burn. This is why he wanted me to come tonight. To pawn me off.

But Beck looks confused as he glances to the friend at his side and then back to Kade. "Hunter? Your brother?"

Kade is quiet.

"Hunter checked out weeks ago," Beck explains. "He's not attending St. Matt's this year."

He's not at St. Matt's? I process for a second and then I almost smile.

I warned Kade.

Kade takes a step closer to his friend. "What do you mean?"

"Yeah," Beck tells him. "I don't know what to tell you. He's a loss. Definitely. And he left us high and dry, short a tackle at the last minute too. But don't you worry." He smiles wide. "We'll be ready."

"What the hell are you talking about?" Kade tenses. "Where did he go?"

"I had assumed he went home."

I see Kade turn to me out of the corner of my eye, probably thinking I might've heard something from Hunter, but I haven't. I have no doubt Hunter's okay. Just one step ahead of us, as usual. His parents and his grandfather, Ciaran, probably let him go to Chile or Poland or somewhere else far away to study abroad for the semester. Funny they didn't say anything, though.

"Can we still have Trent?" Beck asks.

I hold my breath.

Kade shakes his head. "Fine, whatever."

Seriously? Like I'm not even here....

I'm not going to St. Matthew's.

And I'm not going to make it home by curfew, either.

I step forward, giving all my attention to Farrow Kelly, unable to believe what I'm doing. "You guys have an extra motorcycle?"

Kade jerks his head toward me.

Farrow's mouth lifts in a smile as he looks me up and down, a Green Street tattoo etched on his neck. "Yeah, but we don't have a track, honey. Can you handle it?"

"I can handle it," I reply immediately.

I know where they like to race. Phelan's Throat. A closed road full of potholes and fallen trees that makes a steep climb with an even steeper down slope. If I can show my dad that I can race it, he'll train me.

Even if it's just so no one else does.

"Can I be your prisoner?" I ask.

"Dylan," Kade grits out.

But I ignore him. "I need to get out of here for a couple of weeks," I tell Farrow.

Farrow chuckles, looking to Kade. "Did I really just get this lucky?" But he switches his attention back to me before Kade can answer. "Daddy gonna be okay with this, Baby Trent?"

"Do you care?"

If he's afraid of my father, he won't admit it in front of everyone.

But he'll take me. I'm perfect payback for Aro.

"We don't trade women to Weston," Dirk states.

But Farrow is already pulling out handcuffs and binding

my wrists in front of me as a dark-haired young woman with three roses inked on the back of her left hand rips off a piece of duct tape and plants it over my mouth. It's all a part of the ceremony of being a prisoner.

She smiles at me. "This won't be fun, honey. Brace yourself."

My stomach dives, and air pours in and out of my nose.

They shove over a guy with chestnut brown hair in exchange—I think his name is Stellan—as another one pulls me by the chain between the cuffs and leads me away with Farrow and the two young women.

"Dylan, goddammit," Kade growls. "You're going to get hurt."

He says the same words he said five minutes ago about racing.

I resist the urge to look back at him as we cross the bridge, because he sounds almost angry enough to come and take me back.

Would I let him? I might've before. Kade liked to tug, and his pull was always strong.

Hunter was kind.

Kade gave his attention sparingly.

I always thought Hunter would be there.

Kade was so loud sometimes, I couldn't hear anything else.

Hunter only took off his headphones to hear me.

But Hunter is gone, and I don't know why Kade wants me around. The only thing that feels good anymore is racing.

Chimes pierce the air as all four Weston students flip coins over the edge of the bridge and into the water below.

Pay to pass.

An offering to the girl still locked in the car at the bottom of the river.

Legend has it, she was from Shelburne Falls too. The only other female we traded.

And Weston never gave her back. That's why we don't trade women anymore.

Until me. Until tonight.

They push me into an old pickup truck, Farrow driving in the front with me sandwiched between the two girls in the back. He starts the engine, and we speed off, away from the docks and the warehouses, and I try to smile behind my tape. Two weeks, on my own, doing *my* thing, and not at the beck and call of anyone else.

When my dad or Kade look for me, I won't be there for once.

My phone dings with a notification, and I reach into my pocket, struggling with my cuffed hands to pull it out.

Swiping open the screen, I see a text from Hunter. My heart skips a beat.

That...was a mistake.

PIRATES

CHAPTER TWO

Dylan

I study the words.

What is he talking about?

Is he...

Is he here? I dart my gaze around the inside of the car, scanning one face after another, and then I look out the windows, tossing glances over both shoulders.

But I don't see Hunter inside the truck, and there aren't any cars following us.

How did he see the exchange?

I draw in air through my nose, hovering my thumb over my screen for a moment before I type.

But instead of asking *Can I see you?* like I've asked before, I text *Where are you?*

Where the hell is he? Why is he texting me now? After all this time?

The *Read* receipt appears, but he doesn't reply.

Of course. I have half a mind to block his number. He doesn't get to show up tonight. Now that I'm leaving.

Was Beck lying? Was Hunter in one of the St. Matthew's cars, watching the whole time?

"We haven't gotten a girl in the prisoner exchange in…" the guy in the passenger's seat muses, checking with Farrow. "In how long?"

"You know how long," Farrow Kelly replies, gripping the steering wheel with one hand and digging in his back pocket with the other.

He pulls out his phone, which I can hear buzzing.

The other one smiles back at me. "Oh, yeah," he coos. "That."

That.

The only other Pirate girl to get traded who, legend has it, died here.

I tear off the tape over my mouth.

They think they're going to be something that happens to me. I'm done with that.

"Farrow, right?" I ask, meeting the driver's eyes in the rearview mirror as he looks up from his phone. "I know you. Football star, team captain…" I pause and then say under my breath, "But that's not fair, since you were also captain your senior year…which…was…last…year."

A gleam hits his eyes, and I wonder if he blew off last semester just so he could play another season.

I turn to Coral Lapinski at my right, dropping my eyes to the necktie wrapped around her wrist over and over again like some kind of bracelet. "I watched you run last spring in the Regionals. One of the fastest miles in the state."

She's been offered scholarships, but I hear she has no interest in college, not even if it's free.

She keeps her eyes forward, not acknowledging me. Her long, blonde hair is flipped over to one side, blowing across her face in the gust coming through the crack in the window. Everything from the tops of her ears down is shaved off.

I face the guy in the front passenger seat, half of his grin turned toward me. "Calvin Calderon?" I say, but then I fall quiet for a second. "I honestly don't know much about you, except that I heard you think all dogs are boys and all cats are girls."

Farrow shakes with a laugh.

"How good do you want to know me?" Calvin asks over his shoulder.

I cock an eyebrow. "How *well*..." I correct him.

And last but not least, I look to my left, to the dark-haired girl with the three roses tattooed on her hand. Aro's told me about her. She's the youngest of four.

"Mace, right?" I ask. "You—"

"I don't give a shit what you think you know about me."

Her brown eyes loom over me like a storm cloud, and I flash my gaze to the hand, the three roses flexing as she balls her fist.

I turn away. "Understood."

"And you're the daughter of Jared Trent," Calvin calls out.

I stare at the back of his head. "It won't be what you remember."

Mace throws something in my lap, followed by a pen. "Sign it," she says.

I pick up the sheet of paper, my handcuffs jiggling as I squint at the words inside the dark car. "I can't read it."

Coral brings up the flashlight on her phone, hovering it over the document. I scan the list of conditions, realizing it's a permission slip for my enrollment at Weston High and my boarding here. "My parents are supposed to sign this."

"Will they?"

I meet Farrow's eyes in the rearview mirror. They probably would've signed it a year ago. They're mad at me a lot more these days.

31

Wrists still bound, I pick up the pen and scribble my dad's name and hand both back to Mace.

She only takes the pen. "Drop off the slip in the office tomorrow at school."

I fold it up and work it into my pocket.

"When am I getting my clothes?" I ask Farrow.

We're not heading in the direction of Shelburne Falls.

His phone lights up on the dash, and he swipes, then clicks out of the notification.

"I need things," I tell him when he doesn't reply. "My charger. My laptop and toothbrush. My pajamas."

Another notification rolls in for him. He ignores it. "We have everything you need," he finally says.

Calvin shoots him a look like Farrow's veered off plan, and I study them both. *What's going on?*

Farrow's phone lights up again. He plucks it out of the stand and throws it in a cup holder.

I tense. They don't have everything I need.

Like my underwear?

Farrow keeps going, though. Into town, up a road of broken concrete, and deep into the hills. Any remaining lights of Shelburne Falls on the other side of the river disappear.

I sigh. "So will I be able to get some sleep before the hazing starts?"

Farrow looks out his side window, flashing his Green Street tattoo in the rearview mirror—the word RIVER inked vertically, starting behind the earlobe and running down to nearly the base of his neck. A line strikes through the middle of the letters, from top to bottom.

Green Street is a gang, and I'm not sure if Farrow works for them yet, but that tattoo means he will. I don't see one on Calvin, and I don't want to turn my head to study Coral or Mace's necks, because they'll know I'm staring.

My cousin Hawke has the tattoo, but only because Aro, his girlfriend, is from here. She was Green Street property. If he wanted what was theirs, he had to get branded.

I look down at my phone again, still not seeing a response from Hunter.

The truck swerves, and I glance at Farrow, trying to type on his phone as he drives.

"Everything okay up there?" I ask him.

Someone is burning up his phone.

But he keeps typing. "Don't worry."

We wind through a neighborhood, left and then right, orange, red, and brown leaves kicking up under the tires and flying into the air. Abandoned storefronts and dark apartment buildings sit on both sides of the street, and I spot a small park, shrouded under a canopy of leaves. I can just make out a playset with a slide through a hole in the trees.

Farrow blows through a red light, cruising past a bar with one light outside the door and no windows, and I watch as he takes another left, not signaling.

"So, who am I staying with?" I ask them.

"I doubt any of our places will be up to your standards," Mace says.

"Try me."

"No Starbucks," Coral chimes in. "No little shopping districts. No city landscaping."

"No traffic laws either, it appears," I add, feeling Farrow speed way above the limit. "What do you all want out of this?"

They won't let me go home, not even to collect my belongings.

They won't tell me who I'm staying with.

"I won't run away screaming," I warn them.

Farrow slows, pulling up alongside the curb in front of a row of townhouses. "But we're certainly going to piss you off," he says.

A snort goes off somewhere in the truck, and then everyone pops open their doors and climbs out. Peering beyond the windows, I see others loitering in the street and on the sidewalk, music vibrating under the tires. I only hesitate a moment before I follow.

Groups of people sit in tiered positions on porch stairs, while others stand around burnt-out street lamps and cars that look like they haven't moved in a decade. An '80s, two-door green Dodge that looks like it weighs more than my house sits lopsided on two flat tires, a young guy with dark hair and a leather jacket, fisting a plastic cup, leans against it.

I slam the door to the truck, Farrow and his crew waiting for me. Turning, they lead me like we're on parade, everyone's eyes following me as I float past.

They still haven't told me where I'm sleeping. I cast my gaze around, seeing both sides of the street lined with the same style brownstone townhouses, but for whatever reason—either age, wear, or damage—they're close to looking black. They might've been impressive once.

Gazing ahead, I see this street disappear into the horizon, a few lights in Shelburne Falls glittering in the distance.

We're high. This neighborhood sits on a hill.

And these houses...they're not cheap. Or they weren't back in the day.

Something pulls at my memory.

What is this place? Most of the houses in Weston are one story, with clapboard siding and overrun lawns.

Here, wrought iron railings lead the way up stone staircases to rich, wooden doors and mostly dark windows, although the house to my right has a soft glow coming from the second floor.

"Oh, shit," someone gasps.

I look to see a guy with his head turned over his shoulder, gaping at me.

Mace stops me and unfastens my cuffs, taking them off as another young guy drifts past me. "It's going to be a long two weeks, baby," he taunts.

"Has she had her shots?" someone else jokes.

But then Farrow swipes something off the top of an old wooden barrel, handing me a drink. About two fingers of something cloudy white.

I don't even smell it. I hand it back.

Amused, Farrow swallows the contents in one gulp.

"Where are—" But my phone rings, cutting me off.

I look at the screen, hoping it's not my parents.

Kind of wanting it to be Kade. Kind of not.

But Aro's name stares back at me instead. I answer. "Hey."

"Dylan!" she shouts, but static suddenly fills my ear. "Don't go in—"

And then more static.

I look at the screen, seeing the call is still connected. "What?" I shout for her to repeat.

"Someone—" Again, her voice disappears.

Farrow Kelly starts to head deeper into the crowd, and I crane my neck, trying to keep tabs on him.

"Can I call you back?" I start to follow. "You're cutting out."

"Knock Hill—"

"Huh?" I cover my other ear to hear better.

"Dylan!" she shouts again.

"I can't hear you." I shake my head, losing sight of Farrow and pushing through people to catch up. "Text me, okay?"

I hang up, remembering as soon as I end the call that she's from Weston. Kade would've told her and Hawke by now that I got traded in the prisoner exchange. She sounded worried.

I hop up onto the sidewalk, stopping at Farrow's side as he pulls off his hat and tosses it through a back seat window of an old black Pontiac GTO. I withhold my shudder. *Pontiacs...*

"Where are the adults?" I ask.

I don't see anyone here over twenty.

He starts to walk away, glancing back at me. "You know, some people wanted your cousin in the prisoner exchange." He runs his fingers through his greasy blond hair as I follow. "They thought he'd be fun. Personally, I wanted Thomasin Dietrich." He takes a shot off another barrel tabletop, turning to face me. "I mean, she's practically a Rebel anyway, and in no time, she'll be an adult. She wants to be one of us."

"But she's not old enough."

He nods. "Yeah..." Almost like he's thinking out loud.

Thomasin Dietrich is Nate and Piper's kid, and she's a freshman. And she's a Pirate, but only reluctantly. If she weren't at the mercy of her address, she'd come to school here instead. I've seen her hanging out with the Rebels a lot over the past couple of years when she was—and still is—far too young to be out of the house, on her own, at any hour of the night.

This place is an escape for her. She suffocates in the Falls like I do, both, in part, due to our parents' history.

"But more than anything," Farrow continues, "I wanted a girl."

I tilt my head, seeing him grin. His eyes dance like something downright evil is playing behind them, which is even more eerie, because they're such an innocent shade of blue. Like cornflowers.

"It couldn't have worked out better," he boasts.

"Yeah, considering—" Calvin starts to say.

But Farrow interjects. "Shhh."

People drift by, their eyes taking me in, and he continues walking, passing an old Nova with the engine running. The six-liter pipes pump out exhaust in clouds, the car rumbling on the pavement as a young woman leans back against the fender with her shirt unbuttoned.

I don't watch where I'm walking. Just stare as the car vibrates against her body, making the slivers of her breasts I can see shake. She peels off the shirt, standing topless as everyone gazes at her, and some guy stalks up to her, pulling off his T-shirt. She dares him with her eyes, and everyone watches as he takes her ass in his hands and presses his naked chest to hers.

And they keep going.

I narrow my eyes, watching him unzip the back of her skirt and then start to unfasten his jeans, their eyes never leaving each other, and no one else's gaze faltering from them. Their bodies pulsate against each other, trembling with the car, and my feet move under me, taking them out of my line of sight.

What the f—?

"So why did you volunteer?" I hear Farrow ask.

But I still crane my neck, trying to see if the exhibitionists are taking *everything* off. "What are they doing?"

But my voice is barely a whisper.

"Was it ego?" he doesn't seem to hear me.

"Escape?" Calvin chimes in.

I turn my attention back to them, Farrow broaching further. "Entertainment, maybe? Is that why you volunteered?"

"We're soooo entertaining," Mace jeers, circling me.

A deep brown townhouse looms behind Farrow, a light glowing in both of the bottom-floor windows and one on the second. Tattered curtains hang over them, and I spot the house number on a black oval plaque with gold trim next to the large brown front door.

01.

I open my mouth, but I'm not sure what I wanted to say. Something scratches at a far corner of my brain.

House numbers beginning with zero are rare. I'm remembering something.

01…10. Zero-one. One-zero.

I glance at the houses on both sides of this one. 1313 to my left. 1323 to my right. 1333 next to that one…

I'm lost in thought when Farrow continues. "You came with us because you thought that who your father is would matter. You wanted a fresh audience, didn't you?"

The house behind Farrow is misnumbered. It doesn't fit in the sequence with the others on the street.

Zero-one.

And backwards, it reads, *One-zero.*

Zero-one.

One-zero.

Zero-one.

One-zero.

And then it hits me.

01 and 10. My face falls. *Their football numbers.*

I shoot my eyes up, taking in the house again. Three stories, a gable over the entryway, a small lantern on the right side of the grand door, and the shadow of the flame inside dancing against the dark house.

This is where she was last seen.

"Knock Hill," I whisper.

That's what Aro had said.

This neighborhood is Knock Hill, but while all of the houses lining both sides of the road are similar, there's only one that's infamous.

He brought me to *the* house.

"Well, it does matter who your father is," Farrow goes on.

"Good," I say, but my voice shakes a little now. "He doesn't take his anger out on who deserves it. He takes it out on whoever he can reach. Be careful."

I steel my jaw. I'm not running home.

My phone rings, buzzing in my hand, and I hold it up, but before I can see who's calling, Mace snatches it away.

"Hey." I reach to take it back, but she tosses it to Calvin, who glances at the screen and smirks.

"Aro Marquez," he says, handing it to Farrow.

He takes it. "She's too late."

"Where are the adults?" I ask.

"I'm an adult."

"Where am I staying?" I demand next. "What's going on?"

They stare at me, Mace and Calvin flanking their boy. Calvin tips his head toward Farrow. "He won't like this."

He?

But Farrow tells him, "He'll love it."

Who will love what? Jesus, fuck.

The door to the house opens, and Coral Lapinski appears, jogging down the steps with a couple of other girls.

"We good?" Farrow asks her.

She nods, sliding her hands into her jacket pockets and looking at me.

"Are you sure about this?" Calvin questions Farrow.

But Farrow ignores him, closing the distance between us and holding out his hand. "You need sleep. Come on."

I fold my arms over my chest. He drops his hand, turns, and leads the way up the stairs.

Everyone else stays put, as do I.

They'd be stupid to harm me, right?

But then again, are any of them smart? Prone to common sense?

They didn't know I was coming tonight, though. I don't think they had a chance to throw together a prank.

Or plan a murder.

Right now, most of the people I care about don't know where I am or what I'm doing, and I kind of like that, because I'm always the one chasing.

Chasing Kade's notice.

Chasing my dad and his approval.

Chasing Hunter.

If I completely disappear, maybe they'll wonder about me for once.

I start after Farrow, the others staying behind.

He opens the door to the house, a small light glowing in the foyer. I see a hardwood floor, the sheen worn away, and stairs leading up to the second floor. A gloomy lantern hangs over the top landing.

He holds the door open, and I step inside, hearing him close it behind me.

I cast my eyes in a long sweep over the area. What appears to be a living room sits to my right. There's a green velvet couch and a small end table, but nothing else. No TV that I can see.

I arch my neck though the entryway, seeing a refrigerator in the next space, but I can't see the whole kitchen from here.

There's a hallway ahead, more doorways, possibly to a dining room and bathroom. There's probably a back door, but I'm not sure about a yard. The houses are close together.

I don't see parents. No host family.

"About twenty years ago, there was a flood here," Farrow tells me. "You knew that, right?"

I shift, the gritty unvarnished floor grinding under my shoes.

"Yes," I mumble.

We climbed higher in elevation from the bridge to get to Knock Hill, but the river isn't the only thing that threatens to flood during heavy rains.

The waterfalls my town is named after empty into a pool that feeds a stream that overflows into a spillway when needed.

But that year, as I was told, the spillway didn't hold.

The highway was washed out, people literally had to stop their cars, get out, and run.

"Shelburne Falls had the infrastructure to keep the overflow at bay," he tells me. "We didn't, because our city budget went right into bad peoples' pockets. They got rich, driving this town into the ground."

It would be unrealistic to harbor a grudge against my town over weather that we couldn't control, but if I were them, I might be bitter. It's understandable. I'm just impressed he knows the City of Weston is to blame too.

The water filled this neighborhood like dirty water in a shallow teacup, and even though these houses sit six feet off the ground, relatively safe, the businesses downtown didn't survive. The owners, many of them Knock Hill residents, evacuated.

"And most of Weston never came back," he says.

Even after the water receded...

It was this week, twenty-two years ago, in fact. The same year the last girl from Shelburne Falls was a prisoner here.

She was in this house.

There were brothers.

Pranks, parties, the big game...

And rain. There was lots of rain.

But no one knows what happened in this house. I don't think people in Weston even know that their story started in the Falls, either.

In Carnival Tower.

It's an old speakeasy hidden away, between Rivertown—the bar and grill on High Street—and Frosted, my aunt Quinn's bake shop. Only a few of us know it's there, tucked away between the walls to unsuspecting people walking by on the sidewalk.

Our story tells of a Weston guy in love with a Falls girl, but she hated him. In his desperation, he killed himself, and his best friend—along with his crew—invaded a house one night while she was babysitting. Some say he intended to kill her. Get revenge. But the story says he seduced her instead, up against the floor-to-ceiling mirror that still hangs in Quinn's shop.

And some say the boy who reportedly killed himself over her watched his friend get revenge for him from the other side of the glass.

We discovered through old cell phones left in the tower that they weren't friends at all. They were brothers—twins—and maybe, just maybe, the one who loved her faked his death to plot revenge. Or maybe, he was the one pinning her up against the glass, finally getting what he wanted.

The story goes that they decided to prolong their payback. They let her live that night and invented the tradition of the prisoner exchange to get her across the river and into their house instead. This house.

"You want the place?" Farrow asks me.

I turn my head. "What?"

He approaches me, hands in his pockets. "You're going to have freedom here you've never known." The vein under the Green Street tattoo on his tan neck throbs. "No supervision. No curfews. And we'll get you keys to a bike."

My eyes widen.

"Yeah, I know all about you and your daddy not training you." He smirks, suddenly looking twelve instead of nineteen. "You're going to have a great time here, kid."

A bike? They're really lending one to me? Maybe this won't be so bad—

But then he grabs me, circling my waist with one arm and squeezing my neck with his other hand as he backs me into the wall.

I gasp, immediately planting my hands on his chest and shoving as hard as I can.

He just comes closer, biting out words in my face. "But you will stand with us through everything we do to Shelburne Falls over the next two weeks," he grits out. "And I promise..." He tightens his arm around me so hard I can't breathe. "Dylan Trent, you will sweat in this house."

I suck in a breath. *What?*

"Your virginity won't leave Weston."

I stare at him, and then he pinches my jaw, jerking my head to the side, so he can bite out in my ear, "I want your blood on our sheets."

What the fuck? Anger boils in my stomach. I shove him away, and he finally releases me, holding up his hands, chuckling.

"Oh, make no mistake. You're going to consent the fuck out of that, you'll want it so bad."

"I dare you," I spit back.

No one has ever tried to get me into bed, and I would do it if I wanted to, but I won't be some trophy. He can try.

And how the hell did he know I was still a virgin?

He chuckles. "The house is yours," he tells me. "School tomorrow. I'll pick you up at seven." He starts to leave, tossing a final thought over his shoulder. "If you're still here."

He opens the door, turning for just a moment to fling my phone back to me. I catch it, watching as he closes the door, and I rush up to lock it behind him.

Asshole.

I turn, crashing back against the door. What the hell? They have parents. The school is run by adults. Is no one worried about a liability issue? This is sanctioned by the school board and the parents. The teachers are expecting someone. Wouldn't the administration already have a host family ready?

I'll have to tell them where I'm living when I show up to the school tomorrow. They'll sort it out then.

I listen to the party outside, a couple of engines rumbling and fading away, and I drift my gaze around the foyer and up the stairs.

Wallpaper peels from the walls, dust coats the modest chandelier above my head, and the varnish is worn away on every step up to the second floor. There are no pictures on the walls or furniture in the entryway, and I push off, strolling into the living room.

I'm anxious to see if there's a bed upstairs, but I want to make sure the back door and windows are locked.

I should call Aro.

I should call my mom and have her pick me up.

At the very least, I know I'm safe at home. Maybe this isn't worth it.

Checking the living room, I secure one window, but the other latch won't slide. I lock eyes with some dude outside as he laughs and drinks with his friends. He flips me off, and I yank the curtains closed like it does any good, because they're sheer and full of holes, so he can still see me. I can practically feel his amusement as I spin around and head into the kitchen.

I open up the two-door fridge, the off-white color yellowed with age, with wood-grain accents on the handles popular way before my parents were born.

There's a plastic pitcher of something red on the top shelf, a loaf of bread half gone, and a small container of butter. I take it out and open it, seeing knife marks in the spread and toast crumbs. Mold grows around the edges of the container, and I put it back, grabbing the bread. Turning over the package in my hands, all I see is green inside. I throw it back in the fridge and close the door, taking another look around.

That food isn't recent, but it's not twenty years old, either.

The house, from what I've seen so far, isn't comfortable or very clean, but it doesn't look mistreated. Not like it's used by teenagers who just want to drink and practice their graffiti, or by squatters who hole up here day in and day out.

A table sits in the small room on the other side of the kitchen, an old Ethan Allen six-seater. Windows show trees behind the house, but I don't walk over to investigate further.

I check all the windows and the back door before heading through the kitchen, into the living room again, and toward the foyer.

I start up the stairs, dialing Aro back, but before I can send the call, the floor above me creaks.

I halt.

Gripping the railing with one hand and my phone with the other, I listen.

That sounded like a footstep.

I train my ears, waiting for it again, but nothing happens.

It's probably a prank.

I rock back and forth a little, because I don't want to stay, but the last thing I want to do is swallow my pride and run, either.

It's a prank. I take another step, a creak vibrating under my foot, and I sigh, continuing up. Houses creak. Maybe it was just the stairs.

Upstairs, the walls are just as empty, except for the five closed doors. If anyone is in the house, they're behind one of them.

Taking the handle of the door to my left, I open it to find a bathroom. I flip on the light.

There's a porcelain sink, built-in shelves and drawers for storage, and a bathtub shower with the curtain closed. I don't hesitate. I throw it open, sucking in a breath and thankful to find it empty.

I move to the next room, seeing a linen closet behind the door, but all it's stocked with is old two-by-fours with nails sticking out of them and a Dustbuster. Like, the first Dustbuster ever.

There's a bedroom to the right, empty except for a corner table and chair.

No dark, mysterious shadows loom behind the curtains. No bloodstains on the floor.

I close the door, moving to the next room which has a bed. Yay. And a dresser. And torn posters plastered on the walls, most of which I can't make out what they're advertising. Movies? Bands?

There's no bedding, not even a pillow, and I am not that brave. I'd rather sleep on the floor than on an unwashed mattress with an undocumented history.

Closing the door, I move to the last one, not sure what I'm going to do if it's a bust, as well.

But when I open the door, I'm hit with the scent of flowers. Something warms under my skin, making my hair rise, and I step in, unable to take it in fast enough.

It's a guy's room, but it certainly doesn't smell like Hawke's or my brother's. It smells like shampoo and my mom's perfume and Juliet's candles.

Unlike the others, this one is furnished with a full bed, black wooden dresser to match the headboard, and a nightstand on the wall next to the bed. A desk sits to my right, next to the closet door, with an old wooden chair that looks like it might've been part of the dining set downstairs. A bookshelf stands behind me, to my left, and there's a Chesterfield chair in the diagonal corner, next to the desk.

And ahead of me, there's a window. Leaves flutter outside, and I see brick through the branches. Must be the next house on the other side of the tree. *Hmm*. I have a tree outside my bedroom window at home. Except my room— my mom's old room—has French doors instead of a window.

Reaching over, I feel for a switch, but when I flip it, nothing happens. I flip it a few more times, with no success. A lamp sits on the bedside table, so I walk over and reach under the shade, turning the knob. Soft light fills the room, and I'm about to go to the window, but I spot the white sheets on the bed below. Peeling them back, I scan the fitted sheet, just making sure I don't see anything weird.

I lean down. It even smells good. I grunt my approval, pretty damn grateful. This must've been what Coral was doing in the house. Putting fresh sheets on the bed.

Which means they weren't expecting to keep anyone here before I jumped in the truck tonight. Otherwise, they would've had the room ready. Why the change of plans?

The walls are café au lait, but I can tell they're faded from age and probably from the sunlight that streams though the windows during the day. There are several dark patches where pictures used to hang.

Walking to the closet, I breathe deep, expecting anything. It's the last place I haven't checked.

But when I open the white door, there are only clothes. No hidden prankster. No monsters or Pirate girl killers.

The house is empty.

But I thin my eyes, noticing something. The clothes aren't men's.

Shoving hangers aside, I slide one after another, taking in the jeans, T-shirts, three classic Gap tees—which I think they stopped making years ago—two skirts, a few tanks, and one silk crop top. I pull out the jacket, running my fingers down the black wool and large orange S on the breast. It's a Pirate varsity jacket like mine, but this one has a number on the arm—eighty-two.

And it's the real deal. My school doesn't sell these anymore.

We have everything you need...

I shake my head, hanging the coat back in the closet. They certainly went to great lengths to keep up the pretense of an urban legend. Like I'm really supposed to think these are Winslet's clothes? The Pirate girl who supposedly died during Rivalry Week?

I start to close the door, but I hear bells and stop.

I freeze, listening to the one special ringtone that I haven't heard in a year.

The one especially for Hunter.

I release the door, my heart punching like a hammer every time I exhale.

He liked bells. Chimes.

I hold up my phone, seeing his name.

Swiping, I hold my phone to my ear.

"You should go home," he says.

I close my eyes.

I haven't heard his voice in a long time. It's quiet, parts of his words falling to whispers but always strong. Strolling to the window, I tip my chin a little higher as I stare into the dark night.

"How do you know where I am?" I ask.

Hunter is silent for a moment. And then finally, he repeats, "You should go home."

"Then come and get me."

I have no idea what's going on or how he knows I left Shelburne Falls, but if he's worried and wants me home, then he can come here and make me. He had his chance to answer the phone. Or any one of my texts.

"Where are you?" I ask. "You're not at Ciaran's anymore."

He was staying with his grandfather in the Chicago suburbs while he attended St. Matthew's. If he's not going to school there this year, then where is he?

"Are you home?" I press. "Maybe in Hawke's hideout doing your classes online?"

Lurking right under our noses...

Hawke discovered Carnival Tower, and since one of the entrances is in Frosted, we can access it easily. Especially since Frosted is only open in the summers right now with Quinn still attending college at Notre Dame, and we don't have to worry about her finding out and telling our parents.

She's our dads' sister, but we don't call her aunt. It feels weird. With only a few years on us, she's more of a cousin to us.

Maybe Hunter knows about it, and that's where he's been. I don't give a shit.

"Are you strong now?" I taunt. "Did you come back to face us finally?"

"You think I still have a chip on my shoulder after a year?" Hunter keeps his tone low. "I have my own life now. You're not that important."

Leaves sway in the light breeze, and I notice the music outside has long-since stopped. I only hear him in my ear.

It's good to know where I stand. As if his silence over the past several months wasn't enough of a hint.

"Neither are you," I tell him. "Either of you. So let me be."

I'm staying.

He's quiet for several moments, and I expect to hear the click of him hanging up, but before he does, he speaks one more time. "You're not alone in that house."

My stomach dips, and he ends the call.

What?

I train my ears, listening.

But the house is quiet. He's just trying to scare me off. If he really thought I was in danger, he'd haul me out of here. He may be angry for whatever reason, but he wouldn't let me be hurt.

Would he?

I hover my thumb over my phone screen, diving in and opening the app. I never looked in the year he's been gone, because I always thought I knew where he was, and it wasn't cool to be some kind of stalker.

But I click on Hunter's name, and a blue dot suddenly

appears, the location of the phone he just called me from right next to me.

I zoom in, again and again, and I stop breathing.

Raising my eyes, I gaze through the tree outside my window and into the dark room in the house directly across from me.

He's here.

He's in Weston.

PIRATES

CHAPTER THREE

Dylan

"You will sweat in this house..."

I open my eyes, drawing in a lungful of morning air. Warm breath still tickles my ear, my T-shirt clings to my body and the words drift up, up, up, and through the billowing curtains.

It sounded so real. I touch under my ear, my skin just slightly damp as the ceiling comes into view above me.

But I can't move. I don't want to. I close my eyes again, thoughts sailing in and floating out just as quickly.

It's morning...

There's light...

A breeze blows through the room...

Did I leave the window open last night?

The world tilts behind my eyes, and my heart flutters a little, feeling like I'm on a roller coaster. Just for a second.

Hunter's in Weston. That's how he knew I was traded here. He was on the docks or something, watching.

That's who was blowing up Farrow's phone last night in the truck. Hunter saw me taken as a hostage, and either he didn't like it, or he told Farrow where to house me. Or both. It didn't seem like this house was the plan until they found out it was me coming, and it definitely sounded like Hunter didn't want me here.

I feel a smile pull at the corners of my mouth, my eyes still closed.

You're not alone in that house.

What did he mean?

Will something happen to me?

Will they try to lock me in a trunk and push me over the side of the bridge, just like what everyone believes happened to the other Pirate girl who came here?

Will they feed me drinks and see what I do? Maybe post it online?

Will they get me to do something that gets me arrested? Will I have to run and hide in Carnival Tower?

I open my eyes, watching the shadows of the leaves on the tree outside dance across the ceiling.

Will I resist all of it or happily ask for more of some of it?

Will the nights be long? Will my bed always be this warm?

Will I scream?

Will they scare me?

You will sweat in this house...

My T-shirt grazes the sensitive flesh on my chest, and the points of my breasts harden. I close my eyes again and arch my back off the bed, drawing in another lungful of air and feeling the muscles in my body burn with the stretch.

My head swims, heat builds down low, and I press my arms close to my body, pushing my breasts together and feeling them chafe against my T-shirt.

54

You're not alone in that house.

I brush my fingertips across my stomach as I lay my back on the bed again and then glide my hand down under the sheet.

I am alone.

Sliding inside of my underwear, I just touch. Let my hand wander, trying to imagine if what I'm touching is something someone else might like to feel. Pressing my finger to the hard nub, I lift a knee and push up on the bed, thrusting my back against the mattress as my hair falls in my face. I gasp, feeling his body on mine.

I won't run. I was ready to grow up a long time ago.

Again. I rub myself and thrust again.

But just then...my phone rings, slicing through my ear, and I pop my eyes open. *Shit.*

I yank my hand off myself and sit up, but as soon as I do, I freeze.

Hunter sits in the corner chair.

Hunter...

I can't swallow. The vein in my neck throbs. He was sitting there...

He's been sitting there this whole time.

I fist the sheet, making sure I'm covered. *Oh, no.*

He sits there, his expression unreadable but entirely on me. His mother's green eyes gaze at me, unyielding, as he grips both arms of the cushioned chair.

I knew I didn't leave the window open last night.

I don't know how long I stare at him or how long my phone rings, but he eventually tips his chin at my nightstand, telling me to answer it.

It takes a second, but I look over, grabbing my phone off the charger they'd left for me. I notice a ton of notifications that must've come in overnight. Texts and missed calls that were delayed. I would've seen some of this before I went to sleep.

Mom shows on the screen. I clear my throat, answering, "Morning."

"Why haven't I been able to reach you?"

Her voice is too loud for this early. I wince, knowing Hunter can hear her too. "There was a lot of wind here last night, and I don't think I have Wi-Fi." I sit up completely and cross my legs, feeling his eyes on me. "I'm surprised you didn't send out a search party."

"Well, Mr. Kelly called," she tells me. "He let us know where you were and assured us that you were in good hands with his family."

I meet Hunter's eyes. "Mr. Kelly..." I muse, detecting a shred of mischief in his stare. Or a dare. Whatever it is, it's quickly gone.

"Yeah, I'm fine." The October wind breezes in, filling the room with the scent of leaves and chimney smoke from somewhere in the neighborhood. "I'll be at school during the day, so if my cell isn't working, they have a landline."

"Text when you wake up, and text when you go to sleep," she instructs.

"I know the drill."

"And send me a pic of your room."

"I have clean sheets," I point out.

"Send me a pic," she orders again in slow, enunciated words.

I love my mom. I'm never left wondering if she cares.

But I'm a little shocked she wasn't aware she was speaking to a teenager instead of a parent last night when *Mr*. Kelly called. It's not easy, getting something by her.

"Is Dad mad?" I ask.

"Your dad loves you to hell and back." She pauses, not really answering the question, but that's okay. "Don't worry," she says. "I think doing your own thing for a couple of weeks is exactly what he needs."

I snort. Not what I need. What *he* needs...

Yeah. Fair enough.

"Just no drinking, drugs, or unprotected sex," she goes on, "but if you do those things, just know I'm here if you need me, so call. I won't be mad."

"Please stop."

"I'd rather you were safe and sound..."

"Goodbye!" I snap. "Tell James to stay out of my room."

"Wait!"

I sigh, stopping.

"Your birthday is Thursday," she points out. "You mentioned maybe an outdoor movie night?"

Oh, that's right. I'd forgotten.

I hesitate. I want to do something, but I think I'd like to...not leave captivity between now and the big game. I need these two weeks.

"How about we do it when I get back?" I ask. "I don't need cake *on* my birthday. Any time, really, is fine."

She laughs at me. "Are you sure? It doesn't feel right."

"It's fine," I tell her. "I need this right now. But...I expect really good stuff when I get home."

"You got it."

"Talk later."

"Love you..." she sings as I hang up.

I toss my phone onto the bed and try to raise my eyes, but it takes a moment. I can feel the wetness between my legs, and embarrassment rises to my cheeks.

Finally, I look up, the air between us growing so thick it hurts to breathe. God, he's changed. I was too shocked to find him here at first to take inventory, but it's surreal to be in the same room with him—alone—after more than a year. He looks like a stranger.

And yet, I can't really say what's different. Blond hair like his dad mixed in with strands of his mom's light brown. Cropped close in the back, a little longer on top as it messily grazes his temples. Green eyes like grass, sun-kissed cheeks, and the collar of his gray T-shirt stretched out a little to show that his collarbone is just as tan as his neck. He's spent a lot of time outside without his shirt this past summer.

And while he and Kade are both the same age, Hunter seems older than him now. Maybe it's the clothes. He wears jeans and a collarless black leather jacket. Not the usual hoodie he used to wear, or that his brother still wears, because Kade loves being an athlete.

Or maybe it's the eyes. I don't like the way he's looking at me, and I used to. I fight the urge to shrink.

"If you're not leaving, then I want a few things understood," he says.

I tense.

"We're not family here. We're not friends." His tone is resolute. "Leave me alone and don't interfere."

My nostrils flare.

I'm just supposed to pretend like we're not in some class together, or not talk to him at lunch?

"You will not speak to Kade about me," he orders next. "Where I go, what I do, or who I talk to, is none of his business."

He doesn't trust me now?

"And you're on your own," he tells me. "I'm not going to hold your hand here."

I swallow hard, clenching my sheet in my hands as I watch him rise and head for my bedroom door.

I don't believe this. What the hell did I do? I...

But I stop.

No.

I don't care about this anymore. If they don't want to explain why they both pulled away from me, I'm not giving it my attention.

"I missed you," is all I say.

It's all I want him to know before we're never alone together again.

But he just stops at the door and laughs. Turning his mean eyes on me, he asks, "Why?"

I go still.

He doesn't give me time to reply. Swinging open the door, he's gone quickly, his footfalls fading down the stairs until I hear the front door slam shut.

It takes a moment to steady myself. I'll stay away from him. Fine. No problem.

He better not think I came here to be with him as a motive in the first place. I came here to be on my own anyway.

Checking the time, I see it's just after six. I whip off the sheet and climb out of bed, dialing Aro as I head into the bathroom. Before I start the shower, though, I check the shelf for clean towels.

There are two. Brilliant. I think I saw a washer and dryer just off the kitchen, in the mudroom by the back door. I'll have to go to school today in the same clothes I came in, but I can wash them tonight.

The line picks up. "Are you okay?" Aro says, almost sounding like an accusation.

"Yeah, why wouldn't I be?"

I hear her sigh, muttering, "Seriously..."

I reach into the shower, turning on the water and running my hand under the ice-cold spray. After a few moments, the water doesn't get warm, so I leave it running and walk back to the bedroom. I better have hot water.

"Why couldn't I get a call out last night?" I ask her.

"They probably put out a signal jammer."

I exhale a laugh, closing the window. "Christ. They're...a lot, aren't they?"

But she chastises me instead. "Dylan, you shouldn't have gone there."

"And I'm tired of everyone telling me what I should and shouldn't do," I reply. "Can you just be the one person I don't have to hear it from?"

"Listen to me—"

"I'm fine."

"Maybe today—""If they were going to hurt me, they would've done it last night," I retort.

"Dylan—"

But I just swing open the closet door. "I'm still in one piece. Not even a scratch."

"Because they have you for two weeks!" she finally yells into my ear. "They're not going to swallow you whole the first night."

I pause, falling silent. Jesus. She really does sound concerned.

Her breath rushes into the phone, and I'm not sure if I should panic, too, because she's hard to scare. If she's worried, then maybe I should be.

But I also kind of want to laugh, as well. "Shivers," I tease.

I take out a shirt from the closet and sniff it, seeing if it's fresh. The scent of oranges and linen fills my nose, and I hang it back up, sifting through the rest.

"If you're so worried about me," I say, "why didn't you come and get me last night?"

"Because Hawke and I were busy stopping Kade from coming to get you." She lowers her voice to a mutter. "He makes everything worse."

Something tightens in my chest. Kade wanted to come and get me? Why?

"What does he care if..."

But I trail off, realization hitting. He was happy to send me off to St. Matthew's for two weeks, but not to Weston.

When he learned Hunter is here.

He doesn't want us together. He never did. Not in the same room. Not in the same car. And certainly not alone. I used to think that he was jealous. Possessive. That someone liked me.

But when Hunter left, the distance between Kade and me only grew. I couldn't make sense out of it.

"If I go back," I say with a hard breath, "nothing changes."

Plain and simple. All those self-help gurus telling us to 'stay where we are if we don't know where we're going.' Blah, blah, blah. Nope. Standing still is based on the belief that what I want will just land in my lap. It won't. I have to keep moving.

"Are you on Knock Hill?" she asks.

"How'd you know?"

"Number zero-one?"

I stop shuffling hangers. Great. What is she going to tell me that I don't want to know?

She clears her throat. "If you hear creaks in the attic, it's a rocking chair tied to a tether," she tells me. "The other end is tied to the tree between the houses. And then when the wind blows, the chair rocks."

I race to the window, looking up and spotting the ratty old rope tied to a branch. The other end stretches for the house, disappearing through what I can only assume is the attic window.

I roll my eyes and back away. "Yeah, I heard the creaks. I was too smart for that."

I knew they were messing with me.

"If you hear any other noises," she says, "you should leave."

I laugh under my breath, pulling out a pair of whitewash jeans and a baby tee. "Are these supposed to be her clothes, too?" I muse, putting Aro on speaker and setting the phone down on the desk as I hold up the jeans to my body. "Good thing the '90s are back in style."

"Dylan," she interrupts. "Listen to me."

"I'm listening." *Damn.*

"I'm not much for stories, okay?" she goes on. "And I don't believe in ghosts. But it's the last place she slept. And it's the one house on Knock Hill no one stays in overnight."

"They don't seem scared of much."

"It's not fear," she replies. "It's respect. That house is taken."

My eyebrows dive for a moment, her words reminiscent of Hunter's warning.

I inhale a deep breath and square my shoulders. "Bring me some underwear after school, please?"

She's quiet for a minute, and I know she wants me to come home, but she knows I'll be angry at myself if I do.

I think the worst thing I have to fear in Weston is free-flowing alcohol. Maybe some misogyny.

Finally, she asks, "You want the fun ones?"

I smile, thinking about the "buy five, get the sixth free" sale on sexy panties we caught before school started this year. "Surprise me," I tell her and hang up.

No one will see them. I won't get a boyfriend while I'm here.

But my cheeks warm, picturing Hunter watching me when I didn't know he was in the room. Thank goodness I didn't go too far, but he had to know what I was doing underneath the covers. Why didn't he speak up?

I start to pull the sheet and comforter up the bed, but then I stop.

I'm not at home. I don't have to do anything I don't want to do. I drop the bedding, leaving it mussed, and take off for the bathroom, tying my hair up as I go.

The shower is surprisingly clean, despite the slightly yellowed grout between the tiles and the sheen on the fixtures gone. There's no mold. No hair. No sprays of blood or guts from murder victims.

And thankfully, the water is warm now.

I rinse off, avoiding the used bar of green and white marbled soap that rests on a ledge at the corner of the shower. Dried suds cake the bottom, and while it doesn't look like it's been used recently, it's been used since the last Pirate girl.

Hitting the knob, I turn off the shower and grab a towel. Drying off, I step out and head quickly back to the bedroom, pulling on my pair of jeans from last night. I only wore them for a few hours, but I skip the underwear, holding out for Aro to bring clean ones later today.

Donning my bra, I choose a dark gray "D.A.R.E. to keep kids off drugs" T-shirt from the closet and pull it on. I brush my hair, pull it up into a high ponytail, and slip my arms into my Pirate varsity jacket. I want them all to know that I have no intention of going unnoticed.

I slip my phone inside my jacket and yank open the desk drawers, scanning for school supplies. There's not much. A tattered green Mead notebook, a pen with no cap, two well-used pencils, wrappers from what looks like a roll of SweeTARTS, and an old flip phone. I take it and open it up, seeing it's dead. I toss it back in the drawer, feeling the residue it left on my fingertips as I rub them together. I hold my hand up to my nose and inhale the scent of fire and smoke. *Hmm.*

I snatch up the notebook, pen, and pencils and start to leave, but then I stop.

You're not alone in that house.

I hop up on the bed, peering up at the vent in the ceiling.

But I don't notice anything. No light streaming in from a window in the attic above or a glint from a camera lens. Stepping off, I inspect every corner, searching for hidden lenses in between books on the shelves and looking for peep holes in the walls.

There's nothing.

I commit the room to memory, taking note of how the charging cord hangs over the nightstand drawer, and how the closet door is closed, so I might be able to detect any changes if someone comes in while I'm at school.

I close the bedroom door and jog downstairs, but as soon as I step into the kitchen, I see it's full of men.

I halt.

Calvin Calderon and Farrow Kelly stand next to the stove, four others spread throughout the kitchen and dining room.

Did they come with Hunter? Were they here the whole time I was in the shower?

I think I recognize all of them, though. All Rebel players. T.C. Wills rests his elbow on the counter, his skin golden and taut over the muscles peeking out of his light gray T-shirt. Luca Tarquin and Anders LaForest sit at the small kitchen table, slouching a little with their long legs taking up all the space.

And I glance behind them, seeing Constin De La Cruz standing at the window. I do a quick inventory, seeing they all have the tattoo.

Except for Constin.

His Green Street mark is etched into his skin, the scar white and pebbled against his dark, tawny skin, because it was knifed into him.

And I believe that was entirely his idea. I immediately turn away from his ice blue eyes.

"Love the jacket," T.C. taunts.

Farrow steps over, holding out a black, disposable cup of coffee. "Are you ready for school?"

I take the cup, about to nod, but he speaks as they all rise.

"Tomorrow, you'll ride," he says, walking past me. "Today, you walk."

Out they all go, leaving the house and me behind.

"Prepare to be boarded, Pirate," Constin says.

It's raining.

Of course, it is.

I climb the soft incline up to the school, a cemetery covered in years of brown leaves sits to my right, and an old Victorian behind a chain-link fence with shutters over the windows to my left.

A stream of water runs down my nose and over my lip, the raindrops light but constant.

I walk. I don't run.

Lifting my chin, I head through the parking lot as cars race past, swinging into empty spots. Students loiter between old trucks and rusty sedans, a group of three guys jumping out of an ancient Bronco that reminds me of the one in my mom's pictures from high school. It's even white like hers was.

People turn to watch me as I pass on my way to the front doors, and I half-expect to get hit with a tomato or a bag of dog poop, but the worst that happens is the staring. Everyone's quiet.

Farrow stands at the top of the cement stairs, leaning on the ledge and surrounded again by Calvin, Luca, T.C., Anders, and Constin. The overhang of the roof high above shields them from the rain.

I try to breeze past, but they all turn, surrounding me as T.C. opens the door for us. Farrow pulls up to my right, and everyone else follows. I'm not sure if they think I'll run, or if they just want attention by making a spectacle, but I don't avoid any gazes this time. I lock eyes with a young woman hanging on her locker, and then her friend who leans against the wall, hugging her notebook and chewing gum. Then I slide my gaze to a guy sucking on a Tootsie Pop. He smiles, twirling his tongue around the candy.

I glance to Farrow, unfazed. "Is Hunter on the football team?"

"Why wouldn't he be?"

I spot a sign on the wall, directing me to the Front Office. It's the same way we're going, so I stay with them.

"Why don't you have him in tow like the rest of these guys?" I ask.

But he simply replies. "Hunter makes his own rules, wouldn't you say?"

"And you allow that?"

We stop in front of the office doors, and I see two receptionists through the windows.

"You don't really know him, do you?" Farrow asks instead.

I slide my hands into the pockets of my jacket, trying to make my glare feel more stern than angry. *I don't know him?* I've spent more time with him than anyone.

"You promised me keys," I tell Farrow, changing the subject.

The corner of his mouth quirks in a smile, because he can see he touched a nerve. Reaching into his pocket, he comes in close, staring down, and drops keys into the palm of my hand.

"And the bike?" I question.

His grin widens as he and his friends back away. "Later," he says, leaving me. "We'll find you at lunch."

They walk away, disappearing through a set of double doors on the other side of the hall and into a courtyard. I only see rain pummeling a picnic table before the doors close again.

Turning, I whip open the office door, turning my phone on silent before I step up to the desk.

"Morning," I tell the receptionist, taking in her jeans and T-shirt. A lanyard filled with keys sits around her neck. "I'm Dylan Trent. Your Shelburne Falls Exchange Student for the next two weeks."

She glances up, giving me a close-lipped smile as she pulls a pair of dirty sneakers from somewhere under the counter and holds them out. I look behind me to see a girl standing next to the chairs. She darts her eyes from the receptionist to me and then drops her gaze, quickly pushing her hair behind her ear as she grabs the shoes. The ankles of her jeans are soaked three-inches high, and her feet are red from the cold in her pink flipflops.

I flash my eyes back up to her and then quickly turn away.

She leaves.

"Codi!" the receptions calls after her.

I watch as the red-haired woman, whose ID card on her lanyard says Michelle Something, tosses the student a white ball that looks like rolled-up socks. I don't turn to watch the girl catch them.

The door opens, students' voices pour in from the hallway, and then it closes again, leaving us alone.

"Do you have the permission slip?" the lady asks me.

I pause, taking a minute to remember the form Farrow had me sign last night. I pat the back pocket of my jeans, feeling the folded paper I'd tucked away last night.

Digging it out, I unfold it and hand it to her, my heart skipping a beat, because my school knows what my parents' signatures look like. Almost as quickly as they know my cousin Hawke's mom's signature, because her signature is an autograph and people pay attention to that.

But...the receptionist only glances at it before setting it aside.

I relax.

"Now," she says, handing me one sheet after another, "as is customary, your assignments at your home school will be excused, but you are required to do your work here, except for anything due after your last day."

Sounds fair.

"Here's your schedule." She slides a paper over to me.

I don't think I've gotten a hard copy of my schedule in high school ever. But I suppose I won't have an account in whatever software system they use for their students to keep track of their records and grades digitally.

"Your locker assignment is at the top," she tells me.

I scan the schedule first, making sure everything is comparable to what I'm taking now. English 4, TASK which I assume is a study period. Intro to Economics instead of Pre-calculus—*sweet*. Government and the Constitution instead of Eastern World Heritage—which will be easy, because I took Government last year. And Forensic Science which I don't need, because I've already completed the minimum science requirement for graduation. I open my mouth to tell her, but I paused too long and she's talking again.

"You have a complimentary lunch allowance," she tells me. "When you go through the cafeteria, just tell them your name."

Which is nice for a school that can't even afford the arts.

She pushes another paper at me. "Can you please check this information? Make sure it's correct?"

I drop my eyes, reading over all of my personal details—address, phone number, emergency contact, parents, my allergy to shellfish...*Jesus*. "How did..."

But I stop speaking when she answers her phone. It makes sense to think Hunter gave them all of this info, but I don't think he did. Farrow Kelly called my mom last night. Maybe she told him.

The receptionist hangs up the phone, and I read her name tag as she makes her way back over to me. *Michelle Howard*.

"Did a student from St. Matthew's volunteer, Ms. Howard?"

She smiles, but her eyebrows pinch together sympathetically. "They usually don't."

Right. I told Kade they were stuck up.

It might be nice not to be the only hostage, but it's not like I would've had a friend in a St. Matthew's student, either.

"First bell rings in five minutes," she announces. "I wouldn't wander too far...alone."

The last comes out under her breath, amusement playing in her eyes but still a little serious too.

I push through the door and head into the hallway, students milling around. I look at the paper she gave me and then follow the numbers on the lockers.

Why did Hunter come here? There was logic in him transferring to St. Matthew's, even if I knew he only did it to get away from Shelburne Falls.

St. Matthew's is a superior school. It's a pipeline to Northwestern, Notre Dame, and the University of Chicago, any of which Hunter could easily get into. His grades were always exceptional.

But Weston is a wolf's den. Like literally, the Rebel symbol is a wolf. I've never met a person who went to school here who actually went on to college. It's simply a recruiting station for the Green Street gang.

These people can't challenge Hunter. Thank God Aro got out.

I spot my locker—number two-sixteen—and realize I don't have anything to put in it yet. I press my hand to the cold black steel and check the time on my phone.

My dad hasn't called or texted.

Of course, I haven't reached out to him, either, but he's the dad. My mom undoubtedly told him she spoke to me, and that I'm fine, but still.

Kade hasn't texted, either.

A guy drifts behind me slowly, and I hear laughter down the hall. The exaggerated feeling that everyone's attention is on me sits on the back of my neck.

Noticing a stairwell ahead, I dive through the doorway and escape down the steps.

I can leave whenever I want.

I have no friends here.

But no one wants me to be at home, either.

I'm here by choice. I can leave anytime.

Homemade posters decorate the walls as I descend to the ground floor, clever little slogans like, "Your town. Your field. Our Game." and "The only protection we bring to the Falls is a condom. Go hard, Rebels!" painted in blue and black block letters. I snort, unable to stop the laughter. That last one's pretty clever, but damn, I can't believe the principal allowed it. Ours wouldn't.

Jack-o'-lanterns and witches adorn advertisements for the homecoming dance, and a cork board hangs on the wall at the bottom of the stairs, pictures of St. Matthew's and Shelburne Falls players pinned with rusty nails.

Not thumbtacks.

Nails.

To their faces.

In the center of the board, it reads "Sniff, sniff, sniff. Smell the privilege."

I find Kade's picture, but only because of the number on his jersey. There's one nail in his face, several in his chest.

I keep walking. No one is down here, though. Any laughter, looks, or whispers fade away as I stroll down the hall and pass an art room, a few offices, and a kitchen with about eight stoves. But then I stop, peering through an open door, seeing classic cars in a high-ceilinged garage with their hoods up and racks of parts, tools, and motor oil along the walls.

I start to smile. *An auto shop.*

One of the large, red bay doors is raised, letting daylight spill in, and I see a '90s stereo with a dual tape deck and CD changer on the worktable against the far wall.

Paint splatters everything, and dirty work cloths lay over toolboxes, discarded car seats, and the old Army green metal desk in the corner.

I walk in, not seeing any teachers or students yet, and draw in the smells that are as home to me as my mom's perfume. Dank, dark, musky. Dirty oil and leather seats and... I inhale deep. *And tires.*

That smell feels like a blanket. My dad always smells like that.

I move for the Mustang, but a round of laughter goes off to my right, and I glance over. One guy, then another, passes in my line of sight in the adjoining room, both of them shirtless. Someone I can't see flips on music, and a cover of "Don't Fear the Reaper" starts blasting.

Hunter drifts by, and I step back, behind the door I just came through, shielding myself.

He lays down on a bench, his feet on the floor and one leg on each side, and reaches back to grab a bar. His chest rises and falls with every heavy breath as he pumps the weights up and down, and all of my muscles burn. I haven't seen him without a shirt in a long time. The curves and cuts of his arms are more pronounced, and his stomach flexes as he lifts the bar, the ridges in his abs deeper and more toned. I take hold of the door handle and arch my neck to the side, seeing the chain-link fence surrounding their small workout area in the center of the room. "The Cage," I murmur.

I've heard of it. My fingers curl, feeling myself clutch the chain-link.

Other machine sounds—a treadmill, for sure—hit my ears, but I can hardly see anything from here. It's where they keep the expensive equipment to lock it up.

Ringing blasts overhead, and I pop my head up. "Shit."

The bell.

I turn around, dash into the hallway, and jog back up the stairs. Being late to my first class is an entrance, and I don't want to make an entrance. I race into the hallway, looking at my schedule to see what room I should be in.

Two-oh-two.

Following the room numbers, I speed-walk through the school, a few students still lingering in the hallways. I yank open the door to the classroom and rush inside, all of the students stopping and looking up.

The teacher pauses at the whiteboard, and I do a double take at how his chest fills out his blue Oxford that's tucked into fitted khakis, and the brown leather belt around his waist. I think there are students in the Falls who'd love for him to be teaching over there instead. Even if he is my dad's age.

After just a moment, he offers a tight smile, brushes his thick, brown hair back over the top of his head, and walks to his desk, checking his laptop. "Dylan Trent, right?"

I glance at the students again, only seeing about twelve.

"Yes," I finally reply. "I'm sorry I'm late."

"Have a seat."

He holds out his hand, directing me to an empty one in front, next to Mace. I slide into the desk, taking out the notebook and pen I found this morning.

"I hear you volunteered," the teacher asks.

Mr. Bastien, I think the schedule listed his name as when I looked.

"Shouldn't I have?" I tease.

"As long as you plan on doing the work, I think you'll be fine."

Quiet chuckles go off around the room, and I don't think I will be fine, even if I do all the work.

The person behind me leans in, their whisper hitting my ear. "I like your jacket," he says.

People keep saying that.

I slide my fists in my pockets, holding it tight to my body.

The teacher moves around his desk, an uncapped marker still between his fingers, and a piece of paper in the other.

"The Weston-Shelburne Falls-St. Matthew's rivalry is actually a good example of what we've been talking about in class," he tells me. "The role of ideology in conflict. How belief systems, propaganda, religion, symbols, flags, colors... can organize *and* mobilize mass groups of people under the guise of pride."

"Guise?" I repeat.

As if loyalty is meaningless.

I shouldn't be offended. He's insulting his own students with that assessment too.

"Think about it," he goes on, half-sitting on the edge of his desk. "If you were born here, would you have any stake in being a Pirate?"

"No, you're right." I nod, taking the pen and grinding it between my fingers. "Most Christians are Christian because that's what they were raised to be. Most Americans are loyal to America because this is where they were born. I'm a Pirate because..."

"Because..." he presses.

I remain silent. I'm not the only student in this class. Someone else can participate.

"Because of your roots," a young woman replies off to my left, near the windows. "Your parents, your friends, your history..."

With the pen, I trace the figure eight that was already etched onto my notebook cover.

"You don't question it," she goes on, "because something to believe in gives you an identity. It feels good to stand for something. To wear a label and say 'this is who I am,' oblivious to the fact that you are only who you were ever taught to be."

I turn the eight that someone else drew from blue to black, burrowing into the cardboard cover deeper and deeper.

"How easy it was for them to shape you to drive what your daddy drives," she tells me, digging in, "and vote for your uncle's politics as soon as you turn eighteen."

"Isn't it the same here?" the teacher asks us. "The colors, the rivalry, the pranks?"

"So, what if it is?" the guy behind me replies. "At least we're aware of it."

I pinch the pen tightly.

"And it's fun," someone else adds. "It kills time."

The corner of my mouth lifts just slightly.

Mace looks to Mr. Bastien, chiming in, "You know my grandma would be pissed that you're calling religion propaganda."

She holds a Hydro Flask and hands it to the girl on her other side. I wonder if the teacher can smell the rum in it. I do.

Mr. Bastien gets up and goes back behind his desk. "Your grandmother can talk to me about that over spaghetti dinner this weekend."

"She invited you again?" Mace whines. "No..."

But Mr. Bastien moves on. "So, what do you think?" he asks the class. "Refer to the examples we discussed last week. Rosie the Riveter, Uncle Sam, Triumph of the Will...a lot of which was commanded with the task of grooming youth to think a certain way. To work for the state in some capacity."

"Yeah, a hundred years ago..." a guy argues.

"Social media then!" the teacher interjects.

"Oh, here we go..." another student grumbles.

"Like the radio, like the television..." Bastien lists off, "...the Internet connects the world, but it does it almost instantaneously, the massive amount of influence—"

They continue on, but their words and assumptions keep spinning in my head.

...drive what your daddy drives and vote for your uncle's politics...

As if they're better.

Why do people do that? Why do they think they're the only ones with deep thoughts or awareness, like the rest of us aren't really awake? No one is truly human until we know them, are they?

I suddenly interject, "It's not, actually."

Whatever conversation was still happening immediately dies, and I look up, meeting the teacher's gaze.

He stands behind his desk. "What's not what?" he asks, confused.

"It's not the same here." I clear my throat, answering his question from earlier. "It's not the same here as it is in the Falls. You're actually more loyal to being Rebels than we are to being Pirates."

"Damn straight," the guy behind me growls in a low voice.

I wet my lips, holding the teacher's eyes. "I enjoy being a Pirate. But when I go off to college, I'll enjoy being an Eagle or a Spartan or a Buccaneer for four years there, too. And next, maybe I'll be a New Yorker or a Jeep enthusiast or a Green Bay Packers fan." I don't blink. "You'll always be Rebels, because there is nothing else."

Time seems to stop as no one utters a breath or says a word. My heart beats faster. Bubbles pop under my skin, and a light sweat breaks out on my neck, but I don't bid the words back.

I know exactly what I said.

I knew before I said it.

There's something satisfying about...about being the one who ends a conversation.

I watch Mr. Bastien's gaze sharpen to a knife without shifting a hair. "Jared Trent," he says under his breath, looking back down at his paper. "The apple didn't fall far, did it?"

A very small smile I didn't know I was wearing fades away.

"Take out your copies of *Cockney Reds*," the teacher calls out and gives us his back as he continues writing on the board.

People shift around, ruffling papers, and I don't meet the eyes of those at my sides as I feel their glares.

The whisper hits my ear again, and this time I can almost feel his lips. "I *love* your jacket."

REBELS

CHAPTER FOUR

Hunter

Her hand was moving under the blanket...

I lay on the weight bench, pumping the bar high.

And then I bring it back down.

Up.

And then down.

Her hand...

She was touching herself. I should've spoken up. Cleared my throat or something. When that phone rang and stopped her, I was simultaneously relieved and pissed.

Jesus.

Farrow stands over me, spotting as I bench press, but he's staring down at me, and I can't look at his goddamn face right now. I raise the weights, drop it on the barbell rack, and sit up quickly, subtly pressing down my fucking hard-on.

She's still so much trouble. I could hear it over the phone with her last night. Devious, mischievous, destructive—still addictive.

Her body in those sheets. Under them…

"What are you doing?" Farrow asks. "You've only done six reps."

I grab my towel, rise to my feet, and head to the lat tower. Calvin works on the machine next to me, Luca, Anders, T.C., and Constin milling around the cage.

"Didn't get much sleep last night?" he taunts.

I adjust the pin to one-forty and sit, reaching up to grab the bar with both hands.

"If you're so worried about her in that house," he says, leaning on the machine next to me, "why didn't you just tell me to bring her home to stay with us last night? Ciaran would demand it, if he knew she was in Weston."

I pull the bar, pinching my shoulder blades together through each rep.

"I'm not worried." I breathe out. "I just had your fucking lab to type up. I stayed up late."

My grandfather would absolutely demand that I bring my cousin to his house next door. He knows how unsafe Knock Hill is, even when he is in town. Which he's not. He stays at his home near Chicago almost entirely now.

The house in Weston is one of many hideouts he had back when he made his money in really bad ways.

"I expected you to be more protective of her," Farrow says.

"Well, I'm not."

My muscles start to burn already, and I feel a trickle of sweat glide down my chest.

"Not even if I give her a bike?" he asks.

"She knows what she's doing."

He lowers his voice to sound silky smooth. "Not even if I keep her out late?"

I shrug. "I come and go as I like."

I breathe in.

And then out.

In.

Out.

Then, he leans in. "Not even if the whole team keeps her out late?"

I cock my eyebrow, throwing him a look. He's fucking determined to piss me off.

That's why he has a place in my grandfather's heart and lives in his house—with me—rent-free. My grandpa thinks I need people around who piss me off once in a while.

"You're her family," he points out.

"Yeah, not her boyfriend." I let the bar fly and stand up, grabbing my towel and wiping off the sweat. "I want my cousin to do exactly what she wants."

She always did anyway. I've never held influence over her.

I grab some chalk powder, rub it between my hands, and leap up to the bar, pulling my chin over it again and again.

"She's pretty," Farrow says behind me. "Not really sexy, but—"

"I disagree," Calvin pipes up. "Those tomboys are attractive as hell. When you got one underneath you, it's like you're discovering something completely new that's just for you. Something you weren't really seeing before."

I grip the bar tightly, the memory of the blanket moving with her hand running through my head.

"Her hair stuck to her wet skin," he coos. "The smoothness of every inch, that hot tongue…"

I pull my chin up once, twice, three more times, my jaw hard.

"Everything goes soft," he tells us.

I heard a little moan escape her this morning.

"And then you flip her over," T.C. shouts. "Yank her up onto her knees, and show her what the hell she was really built for."

A round of laughter goes off, and I release the bar, falling back to the floor. I jerk my head side to side, cracking my neck.

"Are we sure she's a virgin?" Calvin asks.

I don't know if he's asking me, but T.C. replies instead. "I hope she is."

"I hope she's not," Calvin retorts. "They're easier to get into bed if they've done it before."

I twist around, whipping my towel off the rack where I tossed it. Farrow watches me.

Constin passes by, taking a seat at the rower. "I don't like things easy."

I swipe my phone off the weight bench where I left it and head toward the treadmill. I leap up, starting to press buttons.

"She hangs around a lot of guys," Calvin adds. "At that track, her dad's shop... I mean, Noah Van der Berg lives in her fucking house, for Christ's sake, and the girls love him. I bet they'd love to see him in a towel as much as she probably has."

What the fuck? I turn my head, glaring at Calvin.

His face falls. "Sorry, Hunter."

They get back to work, and I kick up the speed, starting to jog.

I can't be thinking about this now. I can't be worrying about the guys around her. We should be concentrating on the upcoming game.

She's going to distract us, and I've waited for this. I've waited a *year* to meet my brother on the field and win. Our game against the Pirates is a week from Friday. That's what we should be concentrating on.

I blink long and hard.

I just need her to go home.

My phone lights up, and I look down, seeing Kade's name on the screen. My heart skips a beat, and I step off the belt, stopping the machine.

I avoid most calls from home. Simply because I don't want to be reminded of how much I miss them. My parents, my uncles and aunts, my sister…

I lose nothing if I avoid this one, too, but yeah, this is what I waited for, isn't it? It's Rivalry Week.

I swipe and hold the cell to my ear, hearing silence for a few moments.

"You never answer," he says finally.

"You never try very hard."

"Shouldn't you be in class?" he asks.

Amusement curls my lips. So that's why he called now? Because he thought I wouldn't be able to answer and then I'd have to call him back?

"Team workout first period," I say. "Shouldn't you be in class?"

"Probably."

I smile a little, despite myself. Kade always did whatever he wanted. I hated him for that.

But he never pretended to be sorry for it, either, and for that, I envied him.

"So, I had a fun idea," he tells me.

"Yeah?"

"Yeah," he says. "I was thinking you should get a haircut."

I stand there, listening. My hair isn't long, but it was never coiffed like his. Maybe I would've liked to comb it as a kid. Style it, even. But once he started getting on my case when we were eleven if I didn't look like an exact replica of him, I decided I'd never style it again. I comb it with my fingers.

"Get some decent friends, smile once in a while..." he taunts. "Borrow one of my T-shirts that smells like me... Maybe then she'll look at you."

I squeeze the phone, hearing him laugh under his breath.

Dylan doesn't matter. She's not a factor in what goes on between him and me. I should tell him that.

But he wants me to argue because it puts me on the defensive.

I spot Farrow out of the corner of my eye, watching me, and now I'm aware of the tightness in my muscles. My rigid spine. My flexed jaw.

I turn my head away, itching to say something back to Kade, but the seconds stretch. The moment becomes longer and further away until it's gone, and now he knows he won.

I yank the phone away from my ear and end the call.

I shake my head. *Fuck.*

I wrap my fist around the phone, hearing it crack in my hand. All I had to say was something. Some dumb, fucking quip that would've been fine if I'd just said it with confidence.

But no. I was brain dead, as usual, when it comes to him.

A shadow of him.

I disappear around him.

Turns out, after a year, he's still better.

Farrow is at my side. "Was that your brother?"

I jump off the treadmill. "Forget it."

I start to walk away, but he grabs my arm. "Did you fucking hang up on him?"

I push him off, but he clenches the back of my neck, and I growl as he pushes me to the ground. He comes down on my back, pressing me into the mat. I grit my teeth, breathing hard.

"Did he get the last fucking word?" Farrow yells at me.

I flip over, grabbing his head and attempt to lock it under my arm, but he throws himself over my shoulders and wraps an arm around my neck.

"Did he?" he growls as everyone stops their workout to watch us.

Twisting around, I rise, and so does he, but I pin him to the mat before he has a chance to get his feet under him. I straddle his back, growling in his ear. "Back off. We'll have the last word...when we win."

"And her?" he inquires. "You're mad at her, too?"

Screw this. I climb off him and stand up. He follows, brushing invisible dust from his chest.

Walking over to the barbell rack, he retrieves a cigarette and lights it.

"You're pissed at her too," Farrow points out. "Why?"

I just stare at him, breathing hard. I'm not pissed at her, other than that she's a distraction I don't need right now. She's preoccupying this team's attention.

Farrow moves toward me. "Does he love her?"

"Of course, he does," I say through my teeth. "She's his family."

"Does he *want* her?" he says like he's spelling it out for me.

They all know Dylan doesn't share any blood with Kade and me. We're family through marriage only.

"Does she want him?" he asks next.

I narrow my eyes.

He comes in, grabbing the back of my neck and bringing me in. "We'll see him at the game," he says. "You'll win, have the best fucking year of your life, and then go off to the University of Chicago and leave him and his circle of influence behind for good."

Fucking yes.

"But we have her now," he points out. "She can be first."

"I don't give a shit about her—"

"Because if we beat them on the field," he continues, "and he still gets to go home and have her at his beck and call, are you still going to feel like you won anything?"

I look at him, but my gaze falters.

"Oh, Jesus Christ." He rears back a little, eyes gleaming with realization. "I can't believe I actually called that shit." He has the decency to keep his voice low. "She's the reason for the rift between you and Kade," he says. "She's the reason for all of this."

No. My problems with Kade aren't Dylan's fault.

I never cared about her beyond the fact that she was a friend.

It never hurt when she wanted to be around him instead.

"Fuck," I murmur.

Farrow squeezes the back of my neck. "She needs to pay too," he tells me. "Your fun...starts now."

PIRATES

CHAPTER FIVE

Dylan

The apple didn't fall far, indeed. Not only did I make a vile comment to people I don't know in that classroom, I also don't feel badly about it yet.

It's weird. I knew it was wrong the second it came out, and I knew why. But even now, a few hours later, and on my way to face everyone at lunch, the guilt hasn't really set in.

I'm like my dad.

I'd always understood that he had problems in school. He spent years, not only forcing himself to hate my mother, but to actively—and unjustly—take it out on her. Treating her harshly, he'd told me, felt better than facing everything that was hurting him. His past, his parents, his lack of hope in the future, his jealousy over others' happiness...

And his fear that she was too good for him.

Fear.

We only ever do anything out of love or fear, and I certainly didn't say those things this morning out of love.

I don't want to be like my dad was when he was younger. Bitter.

I stop at my locker, lifting my notebook and the two books I'd been distributed—a copy of *Cockney Reds* and an economics book—but as soon as I open the steel door, a flutter of little papers spills out. I watch them float to the tile at my feet. Torn-up pieces of lined school paper with jagged serial killer penmanship.

I slip my belongings onto the shelf without looking and squat down, plucking a note off the ground to unfold it.

Hang the Pirate! it reads.

I laugh under my breath. I pick up another one and unfold it. Students probably slipped these through the vent.

We're coming for you tonight.

The period at the end instead of an exclamation point really drives home the finality of the statement. It's a fact, not a threat. I should be scared. Maybe I will be later.

Letting the notes fall, I swipe up another one. And then another.

You will never leave Weston.

Rich bitch.

Always Rebels.

Slut.

I drop each one, shaking my head as I pinch another one between my fingers, holding it open.

I'm going to kill you with my car.

My face falls a little. *Okay, that was...specific.*

I turn the paper over, seeing if there's a name on it, but no one signed their handiwork on any of these little treats. I know they're just trying to scare me, but that one was weird.

Slowly, I lift up another note.

I liked watching you this morning.

I narrow my eyes.

I study the words as my pulse kicks up a notch, and I read them again. *Watching you this morning...*

Remembering what I was doing in bed when the phone rang—what I was doing with Hunter sitting right there—I feel something crawl up my spine.

Even if Hunter registered what I was doing underneath the covers, he wouldn't write this note.

But it looks like a guy's writing. Blue ink, block letters, small. Jagged. Kind of like Kade and Hawke's penmanship.

I turn the paper over.

She used to touch herself in that bed too.
Will you do it for me again tonight?

I drop the note.

I stare at the pile of papers.

It could be a coincidence. Maybe? Everyone knew where I slept last night. They could just be taking a shot in the dark. Messing with me.

I scoop all of the notes in my hands, crumpling them in my fists, and toss them onto the floor of my locker. I don't want to keep them, but it's evidence if any of these threats turn out to be real.

A shake rolls through my body, and I slam the door shut. I'll do a better search of the house when I get back this afternoon.

I head to the cafeteria, noticing a Pirate skull and crossbones flag hanging upside down on the wall above some lockers.

I inhale a deep breath before I pull open the door. I don't have anyone to sit with, even if Hunter does have this lunch period. He made that clear this morning.

I can't hide out, though, either.

I walk in, my ears suddenly flooded with noise. Dozens of conversations go on to my left and right, the legs of tables and chairs meeting the floor as students sit or rise, and music plays somewhere, probably from someone's phone.

And then, just like that, it starts to quiet.

Conversations fade, movement slows, and all I hear is the MXMS song playing from a table near the windows.

I scan from one side to the other, spotting Farrow and his crew at a table far to my right. Hunter sits on top of it, his foot propped up on the chair. A young woman stands close, between his legs.

Who...

But I turn away, grabbing a tray as I try to hide the lump rising up my throat. Is he seeing someone?

Waiting in the lunch line, I take a hamburger in a paper sleeve, moving for the carrots. The chatter starts picking up again, whispers mostly.

"Keep your voice down!" someone shouts behind me. "She'll hear you!"

Laughter rolls across the cafeteria, and my back feels like it has a target on it. I exhale.

"Oh, don't point at her like that!" another voice booms.

"Hey, hey, hey, Baby Trent," a guy calls out.

Then others whistle.

I ignore it. I don't like it, but I do like that Hunter is hearing all of it. He can't escape my presence, whether he looks at me over the next two weeks or not.

I move down, taking an apple from the young woman on the other side.

I meet her eyes. "Thank you."

"I'm good at it," she says in a snide voice. "There's nothing else for me, right?"

I hold her gaze for a moment, aware too late of the person stepping up and hacking up some spit before he drops it right on top of my hamburger.

I freeze for a second.

I guess my little monologue this morning has spread through the school.

"Rebel-lious for life," the girl behind the counter taunts.

Farrow shows up at my side, laughing and pushing the guy away. He tosses my hamburger and grabs me another one. "Come on, guys," he says. "We gotta keep her strength up. Let her eat."

He puts an arm around me, but I shake him off as I follow him through the lunchroom.

"How was your morning?" he asks.

"Piece of cake."

"Your hair is blue."

It is?

Someone must've put something—or sprayed something—in my hair, although I don't know how that escaped my notice. I'll go to the bathroom and look later. Not now.

We stop, and I drop my tray on the round table next to Hunter's. All the guys that were in my kitchen this morning loiter around, and I recognize the girl from the office—Codi.

She sits to the right of Hunter, Mace and Coral in the chairs next to her. I sit on the table, facing Hunter, and stick my apple in my jacket pocket.

Picking up the new hamburger, I peel back the paper sleeve.

Hunter stares at me.

"Is it satisfying," I ask him, "seeing me with no allies and you with all of them?"

"Why do you think that would satisfy me?"

Farrow drifts between us, reaching around Codi to grab a football.

"It was never that you didn't have friends at home." I take a small bite and then lift my eyes, staring straight at my cousin. "You just let Kade take them all."

No one around is looking at us, but they're quiet. Listening.

"You'd socialize as little as possible," I say. "Skip lunch. You'd go listen to music in your car. Maybe kill time in the library."

He tilts his head back. "I miss the library," he muses. "Perfect place to be alone."

Something about his tone makes me pause.

The girl in front of him moves out of his way as if reading a signal, and my stare flits from her to him.

He glances at Farrow, I turn to Farrow, and then...

Farrow launches his football across the cafeteria, and I watch as Calvin is already running, leaping into the air to catch it. It sinks into his arms, and for some reason, he collapses onto a table of lunch trays that he could've easily missed, students screaming and food flying everywhere.

People cheer and howl, the entire lunchroom erupting in chaos.

Calvin slides into a girl's lap, covered in crap, and she cries out. "Get off me!"

I just stare, wide-eyed.

A teacher rushes into the fray. "Enough!" he barks.

But just as everyone's distracted, Mace is in front of me, hauling me off the table.

"What?" I gasp as she throws me over her shoulder, her shoulder bone in my stomach knocking the wind out of me.

"Stop!" I scream.

But I can barely hear my own voice over the disruption Calvin has going.

Mace carries me out of the lunchroom, and I twist and turn, catching sight of a half-dozen pair of shoes walking with us.

"Let me go!" I shout.

How the hell can she hold me? She doesn't have that much muscle on me.

They cart me down the hallway, to the right, and through a pair of double doors. I claw and scratch any wall I can reach, trying to grab door frames for leverage, but in less than twenty seconds, I'm standing upright again, my jacket is being peeled off, and my wrists are secured behind me. A long piece of rope is wrapped around my wrists, my spine pinned to a wooden beam that rises from the first floor to the second floor of the school library. I look up and around, noticing the lights are off, papers scattered around the floor, and chairs stacked on top of worktables. Old iMacs sit in various cubicles, and dust coats just about everything. Books still sit on shelves, but the place looks like it hasn't been used in a decade. Or two.

Mace holds my jacket, reaching into the pocket and pulling out my wallet. She takes my cash, flipping though it with her fingernail. "Not much," she tells everybody.

"Bitches like her get credit cards," Calvin says.

Codi stands behind everyone, quietly observing.

"Leave the cards," Farrow tells them as he takes my cell phone from Mace and tosses it to Hunter. "Shred the driver's license."

I dart my gaze to Mace. She slips my I.D. out of the wallet and pockets it with my cash.

"No!" I yell. Then, I shift my glare to Farrow. "You said I could ride."

"You can," he teases. "All you want. Just don't get pulled over." His eyes gleam. "Or you could be here for sixty days longer than you planned."

Everyone laughs, and they all turn to leave, Mace throwing my wallet back at me.

I pull against the bindings, watching them go and leaving me in the dark. Mace pulls on my jacket. I growl.

Hunter remains, stepping in front of me to slip my phone into my jeans pocket. How could he just stand there while I got robbed?

"What did you do for their loyalty?" I spit out.

"Go home."

I ignore him. "What have you been up to here? Hmm?"

He leans in, pulling the key Farrow gave me out of my pocket.

"Hunter..."

"Go home," he whispers. "Killer."

My heart flutters in my chest. *Killer.* People called me that when I was a kid because I was always racing. Skates, bicycles, dirt bikes, then my car, my motorcycle...

I never found it cute. I found it condescending to give a girl a pet name for doing what racers do. They go fast. It was like it was all so cute. Me trying to drive.

But he says it differently. It sounded like an endearment because it was proof that he remembered.

I lean in. "You can't make me leave."

Amusement dances behind his eyes, and he takes out his phone, hitting the screen with his thumb a few times.

He holds it to his ear, and I hear it ring as he stares at me.

"Hunter," the voice on the other end says.

Kade.

I go still, hearing his twin's voice.

"Why don't you come and get her?" Hunter asks him. "She doesn't belong here."

What?

"Zero-one Knock Hill," he tells his brother.

I start to shake my head but stop. I'm not ready to go home.

And despite the hardness in my heart, my eyes well with tears as I whisper, "You don't get to decide where I belong. Neither of you."

My chin trembles, and I lock my jaw to still it.

I roll my wrists inside the rope.

"I've got a better idea," Kade replies. "How about we fight for her? Whoever wins gets to take her."

Hunter plants his hand over my head, against the beam, boring down into me with his eyes. "Just like when we were ten?" he says to Kade. "You're still so sure of yourself."

"Yeah." Kade's tone is final. "I know I'm better. Just like when we were ten."

I'm able to slip my thumb inside the binding. I pull, working it farther and farther off my hand.

"And if I win, you're fine with her staying here?" Hunter asks him. "With me?"

"You won't win."

Kade doesn't want me home. If he did, he would've called.

If he did, he would've just come.

Hunter knows that. He wants to make sure I do too.

"Let's meet," he says. "Have it out. I'm fucking dying to see you, little brother."

"Soon," Hunter replies.

And then he pulls the phone away from his ear and hangs up. Tucking it into the pocket of his jacket, he leans in. "We're not ten anymore," he tells me. "The next time I fight him, it'll be for something more important."

I hold his gaze, clenching my teeth to stay hard.

He slips the key into my jeans pocket as I work free of the cloth.

"Red and white bike parked in the lot," he instructs, "near the fence, on the side of the football field. Don't—"

But just then, the rope slips from my arms, and I shove him away, running. I burst out of the library and into the hallway, flying past the cafeteria. Leaping high, I rip the Pirate Flag off the wall and dive down the stairwell, back to the auto shop. Rushing inside, I ignore the students working, and the teacher barking, "Hey!"

I search for anything, grabbing the first thing I see. Plucking a can of lacquer thinner off the shelf, I toss the flag over my shoulder and scurry back upstairs, some of the students following me as I race.

Charging outside and back down the front steps of the school, I hurry up to the flagpole, set down the lacquer, and clip the flag in through both metal rings as students come spilling out the doors.

"What are you doing, Dylan?" someone calls.

But I don't stop. Windows fly open as students poke their heads out, and I grab the rope, wrap my arms and legs around the pole and climb. People watch from below as I scale only as high as is out of their reach—seven or eight feet—and loop the rope around the pole, tying it off.

"Ohhh!" comes howls as the Pirate banner whips in the wind, high above for all to see.

More people rush out of the school and onto the lawn, toward me. Sliding back down, I swipe the can of lacquer thinner off the ground, uncap it, and squeeze hard. The fluid shoots out of the can, onto the pole, as Farrow and Calvin move toward me.

I smile, side-stepping swiftly around the flagpole, raising my arms and spraying the thinner as high as I can. I cover every inch.

Farrow reaches for me, and just then, I drop the can, hands up in the air.

He stands over me, and I stare at the ground, trying not to laugh.

"Get that flag off the fucking pole!" someone shouts from a window.

"What's going on?" a teacher shouts from somewhere.

And I watch as Calvin jumps onto the pole to try to lower the enemy flag, but immediately...he slides back down on the lacquer thinner.

Howls and shouts go off in constant succession, angry curses filling the air as one by one, people try to get up the pole to rip the flag off.

I fold my arms over my chest, laughing, and I almost take out my phone to video, but that'll just lose me my phone. Avoiding Farrow's eyes, I gaze up with love at the skull and crossbones waving in the Weston sky.

But just then, a flicker ignites to my left. I look over as Hunter steps up, holding a lighter to the pole. My heart thumps in my chest as the flame catches, spreading like the wind up the steel beam, following the trail of lacquer thinner higher and higher. The corner of the flag ignites, and I watch the Pirate banner go up in flames as everyone erupts into cheers.

In a moment, it's gone, Farrow and his friends laughing as Hunter lifts his eyes, looking at me.

Damn.

Motor oil isn't flammable. Just combustible. I should've used motor oil.

Near the fence...

I pull the key out of my pocket, trailing down the edge of the parking lot. A whistle goes off, filling the air, and I hear shouts from the football field, catching glimpses through the slits in the bleachers. Players run back and forth, sweating under the warm fall sun, and I step up to the fence, watching the light breeze blow through Hunter's hair.

Coach Dewitt stands over him, yelling as Hunter does push-ups with the sun beating down on his shoulders and back. I can't see the sweat curling up the ends of his hair above his neck or around his temples, but I know what he looks like when he's getting a workout.

At least they're not making *me* do push-ups for the flag incident. I'm surprised he's getting punished, though, but I guess starting a fire was going too far for the teachers.

It was so unlike Hunter. And yet, exactly like him to be so resourceful in a crunch. Still a straight-A student, I'll bet.

The palms of his hands press into the burnt grass of the field, and I can hear the rickety bleachers whining against the wind. Car engines kick up behind me as people leave school, and I take out my phone, holding it up and snapping a picture of the team at work on the field.

No prey, no pay, I type out the caption.

#underablackflagwesail

I tuck my phone away, already feeling it vibrate with notifications. Over my shoulder, I spot the bike Farrow left me. Red and white, late model Ninja. I shoot my eyebrows up, impressed, but then I immediately adjust my surprise because it's probably stolen.

I glance back once more at Hunter, seeing Farrow and the guys line up with him as he continues his push-ups.

One by one, they all drop to their hands and toes, taking his punishment alongside him, exercising in sync.

The Pirates never would've done that for him. For anyone.

Moving for the bike, I throw my leg over and stick in the key. I should inspect it—check the tires, look at the brakes, do a practice run around the lot to make sure they didn't sabotage it—but I just want to get out of here.

Taking the helmet off the handlebar, I slide it on, fasten it, and grab the bars. I start the bike, giving it some gas and feeling the machine pull underneath me. Rocking my wrist back and forth, I feel the wheels spin, and I turn, racing off, propping my feet up on the footrests.

I race through the parking lot, zooming around a car and hearing it honk at me as I peel out onto the street ahead. The bike whirs under my thighs, pulsing through the handlebars and up my arms, into my chest, and in less than three seconds, everything relaxes. I lean down, at one with my line of sight, and I flex my jaw to keep the smile at bay.

The house isn't far, and I want to do a spin to get a feel for the bike, just a basic lay of the land.

But I don't have my license.

I need to get online, request a replacement, and see if I can print off a copy to carry with me until it comes.

I turn onto Knock Hill, fly down the street like a dart, and slide into a parking spot at the curb. Turning off the bike, I climb off and remove my helmet, noticing my bedroom on the second floor. The curtains billow in the wind pouring through the open window on the side of the house. The overhead light is on too.

Did I leave the light on?

I look both ways, seeing a barber across the street sweeping the floor of his converted-garage shop. Down the road, a woman sits at the top of her steps on a lawn chair.

The cars look the same as the ones this morning. I don't recognize any of them.

Tightening my grip on my helmet, I stick my key between my fingers and head up the staircase to my front door. I twist the handle and push it open, angling my head to keep my ears peeled.

When I don't hear anything, I slip inside and quietly shut the door.

I move toward the kitchen, but then, the floor above me creaks. I stop and stare at the ceiling.

Another slow step whines across the floor upstairs.

Oh, shit.

The rocking chair? No, that's in the attic, on the third floor. The sounds are coming from my room directly above.

I hurry into the kitchen and grab a blue plastic broom just as footfalls descend closer to me. I face the living room and entryway again, rearing the broom back behind my head, but then the pantry door to my right suddenly opens, and an arm appears. I whip around and swing, but he shoots his hand out, catching the broom and glaring down at me.

"Whoa!" Hawke chides.

I expel the air in my lungs, gazing up at my cousin. His father's azure blue eyes regard me like I'm crazy.

"Hawke?" I growl. "What the hell?"

He yanks the broom out of my hands. "Give me that."

He reaches over, still dressed from his own school day in jeans and a brown Oxford, shirttails out. He sets the broom aside.

Of course, he's here. I should've known he'd show up to check on me. His college is close.

I pull open the door to the pantry—or to what I thought was a pantry. "There are stairs here?"

Lifting my eyes, I take in the narrow wooden spiral steps until they disappear around a curve above me.

"Yeah, they go up to the second floor."

I look over at him, annoyance setting in. "What were you doing?"

"Investigating."

I'm not shocked he's here. Like his dad, Hawke has a penchant for sticking his nose into his family's business. He wants to see all, hear all, and know all, and Hawke does not like surprises. He wants to be there if we need help, even before we ask for it.

"Did Aro tell you where I was?" I ask him. "Or are you tracking my phone too?"

The Trent men are all the same.

"I'm not tracking you," he retorts. "I mean, I could. Easily." He walks toward the living room. "When Aro and I pieced together the clues on those old cell phones and realized our Carnival Tower story in the Falls is related to Weston's urban legend of Rivalry Week—and that you were the first female student they've taken since Winslet—she knew where you'd be."

"Where is she?" I question. "She was bringing me stuff."

He picks up a duffel that I didn't see on the floor and tosses it at me. I smile, catching it. Yes. Clean clothes. *My* clean clothes.

"She packed it. I didn't look," he spits out. "Your dad needed her at the shop today."

I'm not sure that's true because my dad would've let her bring me things I needed. I don't think Hawke wants her here. Green Street wants her back.

He gestures to the counter. "Brought you some tacos too."

I suck in a breath, rushing to the brown bag and ripping it open. The scent immediately makes my mouth water. "Thanks," I groan a little, pulling out a tortilla chip. "I'm starving. There's no food here."

I stuff the chip into my mouth as he pulls open the refrigerator. "There's food now," he says.

I arch my neck, peering into the fridge. Bread, deli meat, juice, milk, a little produce… I walk to the pantry, opening the door. There's an unopened box of cereal, some microwave popcorn, canned soups….

"Did you put all this in here?" I ask him.

He shakes his head.

Hmm. Maybe Farrow and the guys brought it this morning before I came downstairs.

He picks up a cheese stick and tosses it back in. "It's not much, but it's only two weeks." He closes the door and faces me. "I could place an order on Instacart, but I don't think they deliver here."

"It's fine." I wave him off, pulling out the foil-wrapped tacos and opening them up. "I'll get to the store if I need anything."

I pick one of the three grilled chicken tacos up and take a bite, my stomach growling. "That's good," I sigh, grateful. "Thank you."

Seriously. Other than the bite of hamburger at lunch, I haven't eaten anything in eighteen hours. Mace took my apple when she took my coat.

I take another bite. "You shouldn't stay too long."

There's no telling how long the Rebels' football practice will last.

But he rushes to add, "No one saw me."

"Someone saw you," I fire back. "Did your *investigation* reveal anything?"

"Maybe." He looks around, and I can tell he'd like to have more time here. "There's no way in hell I'm taking a blacklight to this house, though. It'll give me nightmares."

I snort. "If you were that worried, you wouldn't let me stay."

"I'm still deciding."

Hawke's only slightly older than Kade, Hunter, and me, but he knows more, and we never forget it.

He takes something out of his back pocket. "Spare phone." He hands it to me. "Keep it charged. Keep it hidden. Keep it silent."

I take it, pressing the button to see the screen light up.

"You know the code if you're in danger," he tells me.

I nod. I text *2357* to him. He came up with it. Prime numbers. Don't ask me why.

Next, he pulls out a smartwatch and wraps it around my wrist. "This will give you a notification if I'm calling or texting it, but I only will if I have to," he explains. "Otherwise, I'll call your regular phone."

Great. Something else to keep charged. How does he expect me to do that with one cord?

"Where's your jacket?" he suddenly asks.

I take another bite. "Somewhere," I mumble over the food, avoiding his eyes.

"You got robbed."

I take another bite.

I hear him blow out a breath, reaching into his breast pocket, taking my hand, and slapping a wad of cash.

I widen my eyes, holding up the bills. "Wha—" I cough over the food, meeting his eyes. "Oh, I love being cousins with a doomsday prepper!"

"I'm not a doomsday prepper," he grumbles. "You just never know when you might have to go into hiding. Or suddenly leave the country."

I chuckle, slipping the money into my pocket.

"It's for necessities only," he states. "If you don't spend it, you give it back. And don't let them get it. Act like a Trent, for Christ's sake."

I toss him a salute and pick up the drink he brought, tasting lemonade through the straw.

"Come on. I want to show you something," he says.

I set down the taco and dust off my hands, pulling off the hoodie wrapped around his waist and slipping it on. He moves for the door I thought was a pantry and stands aside for me.

"Go first," he says.

I wouldn't if it were anyone else telling me, but I follow instructions and ascend the stairs. I climb, winding step after step, but I've only taken a few before Hawke orders, "Okay, now stop."

I turn, seeing him just below me. But instead of following me to the right, he runs his hand along the panel to the left— the wall—and pounds his fist. The board snaps back, and he slides it easily, revealing more staircase, leading farther down.

Light spills in from somewhere I can't see, but the stairwell is considerably more ragged. Stones are coated with cobwebs and a draft pours up from the basement. Why was it concealed?

"That's scary," I say more to myself.

He waves for me to follow, and he descends, spiraling around and around as I follow.

We come to the bottom, into a large room, but instead of boxes, old lamps, or an ancient wooden wardrobe, the room has a table and chairs, a fireplace big enough to sit in, and cabinets lining the walls with shelves holding old jars, dishes, and tins. A lone white plate lays discarded on the table, the late afternoon sun spilling through all the windows on the west side.

I gaze around, noticing two hallways, maybe another room down at the end of one. "It's like..."

"Another kitchen," Hawke tells me.

I spot the large basin sink, and a wood-burning stove, but there are no electric appliances. No fridge, no dishwasher. Judging from the grayed marble tiles that were once black and white, this room hasn't been used in more than a hundred years.

"I had no idea these houses were this old," I murmur.

"They were something back in the day," he offers. "This was probably the servants' quarters, and that was the servants' staircase."

He gestures to the stairwell we just came down.

"It gets better," he tells me.

Bidding me to follow, he moves across the kitchen, around the fireplace, to one of the hallways I saw. We stop, looking ahead to the door flapping in the breeze, the dry leaves of the walled-in back yard blowing just outside.

Ground-level entry. Unsecured door. No knob. *Great.*

I move toward it.

"Granted, it wouldn't be hard to get in the front door if they really wanted to get to you," Hawke says behind me.

"But someone using this entrance will use it when they don't want witnesses," I add, his concern heard even without him saying.

"Assume the worst," he repeats what he already trained me to know years ago.

I squat down and remove a shoelace from my sneaker. Slipping it through the hole for the doorknob, I pull the door closed as tightly as I can and secure the shoelace around a nail jutting from just inside the door.

I back up, satisfied it's shut, and turn, seeing Hawke look at me like I'm an idiot.

"Hunter is next door," I point out. "And this was all here long before me."

I walk past him, into the servants' kitchen, and toward the stairs.

"What makes you think I won't tell your parents that you're living here unsupervised," he goes on, "next door to one of Ciaran's safe houses?"

Safe houses?

Now it makes sense. Hunter's grandfather owning that house is why Hunter stays there. His parents probably believe Ciaran is there all the time.

Hawke goes on, "And sleeping in probably the same bed where the last Pirate slept before she was murdered?" We climb the steps. "This entire situation feels..."

We come back into the upstairs kitchen, and I hear him quietly grunt as he searches for a word.

"Rapey?" I offer.

"Yeah, rapey."

I turn to face him. "Because if you ruin this for me—when I will undoubtedly ruin it all on my own just fine—I will tell Hunter all about Carnival Tower." I smile. "And its location. He's family. He should know. It won't be my fault if he tells the Rebels."

"You brat." He pinches his eyebrows together. "You wouldn't."

I offer a contrite look. "I would hate myself a little, Hawke, but gosh, it would make tonight fun, wouldn't it?"

And I bat my eyelashes twice.

He arches a brow, tipping his chin up. "I guess you've kept all of my secrets."

"I've helped you and Aro hide from the *police*."

"Yeah, all right," he spits out.

"Stand by me, not in front of me."

"All right," he growls.

I grab the lemonade and take another drink, really damn grateful for my overbearing cousin. Thanks to him, I now have dinner, clothes, a spare phone, and money.

"How does Hunter look?" he asks.

I shrug. "Healthy." I'm not sure how to answer that. Hunter looks very healthy. "A little bigger," I tell him. "He got on the weights, it looks like."

"Well, at least you have him here." He breathes out, appearing to relax. "He'll keep an eye out for you."

I swallow the truth and simply say, "Yeah. Sure."

I don't have the energy, and he doesn't have the time for me to explain that Hunter won't be protecting me from shit.

I start to close the stairwell door, but Hawke stops me, peering back inside. "What's that?"

I open it again, following his gaze to the frame, just inside. Notches are carved into the wood in two distinct lines, the kind you see when parents record heights, along with children's ages. Four, five, six, and so on. Both of them, head-to-head, in sync.

At the top are names.

"Deacon." I trace the carvings with my fingers. "And Conor."

I reach up, touching the highest cuts, and then bring my hand over to Hawke. Just about his height the last time they were measured. Both of them.

I look up at my cousin. "Twins."

"Yeah," he whispers, lost in thought.

If this was the house, then...

"It was only twenty-two years ago." I tell him. "They *have* to be on the Internet somewhere."

He flexes his jaw. "On it."

Birth certificates, school records, social media pictures. No one is invisible. And now we have their names.

Engines rumble in the distance, motorcycles and at least one car. I look to Hawke. "Go."

He ruffles my hair and slips out the back door to his car, hopefully parked on another street.

REBELS

CHAPTER SIX

Hunter

I push the hoodie off my head, leaving my duffel bag in the car.

"Hunter!"

"I need a shower," I call out to Farrow behind me.

We all head to the barber shop every Monday, but I've seen them enough today.

He slams my car door just as I hear everyone's bike engines roar down the street. They skid to halts at the curb, and I step up onto the sidewalk, heading for the house.

"She's coming with me to Phelan's Throat!" Farrow yells.

"I don't give a shit."

I jog up the steps in my track pants and sneakers, unlocking the door with my keys, but the lock is already unsecured. I push it open and slip inside.

Farrow's shout hits my back. "You need someone to suck your dick, you know that?"

I hear their laughter behind me before I close the door and shut my eyes.

Prick. I may as well be home with Kade.

I've barely spoken to Kade in a year, and I've talked to him twice today.

I don't want to talk to him again before the game. Not when I'm so close. If we're ever going to get over this, it can wait until I beat him on the field. After that, I'll be happy to talk.

I doubt he really wants to, though. He called this morning to get in my head. He had Dylan, now he doesn't. He feels like he's losing control.

He hasn't changed one bit.

Coral Lapinksi breezes past, carrying a trash bag into the living room. "Hey."

I head for the stairs, glancing in and seeing Codi Gundry, Coral, and Arlet Rhodes sweeping, dusting, and picking up Farrow and the guys' pizza boxes.

"I told you, you guys don't have to do that," I grumble.

Arlet dumps an armful of beer cans in the bag that Coral holds open. "Farrow says we do."

I shake my head. "My mother would never pick up my dad's shit," I say. "And he married her. Farrow Kelly won't fall in love with you for this. Put it down."

"Who says he's the one we come over here to see?" Coral teases.

I arch my brow.

Arlet's eyes gleam. "You're cute."

"And nice," Coral adds. "Smart."

"And rich," Arlet chimes in again.

They both laugh.

"And," the latter continues, "There's two of you."

They laugh louder, and I turn away. That was pretty much the gist of it in Shelburne Falls too.

Codi can hang around all she wants, but I need to tell Farrow to keep those other girls out of here. He can clean up his own shit.

I climb the stairs, feeling my phone vibrate in my hoodie.

I reach into my pocket, hearing Arlet behind me. "At your service, Hunter Caruthers," she sing-songs.

Dad appears on the screen. I answer, "Hi."

"So, A.J. has collected every college brochure and mailer that arrives," he tells me without a greeting back. "She's saving them for you."

I smile a little as I open the door to my room. My little sister is hard for everyone to keep up with, and I wouldn't have her any other way.

"She inspects everything," he says, "reads it thoroughly, and has sorted them according to location, and then specialty. She's changed her major six times, Hunter."

I can't help it. I shake with a laugh I don't let him hear. A.J. is nine years old, and she won't leave for college for another nine, but that doesn't stop her from being proactive about her future. I'm sure all the college mail Kade and I are getting has spurred her imagination.

"I'm going to have to go through this with her again for real someday," my dad grumbles. "Would you give me a break here?"

I pull the phone away from my ear, slipping the hoodie over my head, taking the T-shirt with it. "Tell her I'm not going to college."

"You're not what?" he blurts out. "If you think you're just going to—"

"No, no. I'm going," I assure him, kicking off my shoes. "I said *tell* her I'm not. See how her head explodes."

A.J. is very goal oriented. As an adult, she'd be intimidating. As a kid, it's kind of creepy. I love it, though. Even if I do worry a little. When she gets old enough to start executing all of these grand plans, she's going to find that nothing will go how she wants. People come along and fuck you up.

My dad quiets for a moment, getting ready to be serious now. When he needs to talk to us, he tries to start off with something funny. I'm not sure if it's a Madoc Caruthers's thing or a politician thing, but he's good at easing into people's space. With me, he leads with my sister because he knows I adore her.

"I agreed to this," he tells me in a stern tone, "because you said it would settle things."

"It will."

My dad didn't want me to come here. He missed me when I left and went to St. Matthew's, but it's a good school, so he sucked it up. Weston doesn't send anyone to good colleges.

"Twelve days." His tone is clear and firm. "You will walk through our door, home to your mother, win or lose, in *twelve* days."

"I remember," I reply, but it sounds more like I'm re-agreeing to our terms.

"I love you," he says.

"You, too, Dad."

"Bye."

We hang up, and I toss my phone onto my bed.

I release a breath.

I'm lucky in the parent department. They weren't dumb enough to believe my grandpa when he said he'd be leaving his mansion in the Chicago suburbs and living here with me, but I'm not Kade. I don't make them worry about drinking, fighting, or petty crime.

And I don't sneak girls into my room.

I walk to my window, seeing Dylan walk past her bed and open her closet. She disappears inside.

I've only snuck one girl into my room.

"Take her!" Kade yells to me as he pulls his girlfriend's hand.

I glare at him across the hall as he shoves Gemma Ledger out of his room and toward mine. She pulls her sweatshirt on over her bra, the shirt cut halfway up her stomach and sliced at the neck to hang off her shoulder. She scurries into the hall in her white sweatpants and sneakers.

I hang out my door. "Kade, seriously."

I cast a worried glance down the hall, knowing our parents are on the move. We have a picnic for Memorial Day.

But he just spits back, "Oh, Dad'll be happy if he finds a girl in your room."

Gemma shifts on her feet. "Will someone get me out of here, please?"

Footfalls hit the stairs, a shadow climbs the wall, and Kade practically snarls at me, baring his teeth.

I slide back, opening my door. Gemma scurries inside, and I step back in place, watching my father reach the second-floor landing. He charges toward Kade. "Whose car is parked outside and has been there all night?"

"I don't know."

My brother shrugs, and if I didn't know for a fact that he was lying, I would still know. And so does our dad. Kade's certainty that our parents can't punish him for things they can't prove shines through in his arrogance.

Dad steps up to him. "Open the door."

"It's my room." Kade doesn't budge. "I don't invade your privacy."

"You trying to lose your phone too?" Dad growls. "Move."

Finally, Kade steps back, giving our dad space to enter. He goes in, and I watch him look around and dive into Kade's bathroom, searching for the girl who slept over last night.

I almost smile. It's kind of funny, my dad trying to catch his kid with a girl in the same room that we accidentally found out that our dad took our mom's virginity in when they were sixteen. Same age as we are now. I'm not going to remind my dad of that. He's not mad at me—yet.

Kade stands there, his chin up but his eyes down, relishing in the knowledge that our father will come up empty-handed.

Gemma stands behind my door, listening.

Dad comes back to Kade, his jaw hard as his chest rises and falls. "Are you really going to make me install cameras inside this house?" he asks Kade. "Is this what it's coming to?"

"Do whatever you want," Kade says. "You won't install them in the bathroom."

My brother breaks into laughter, and my dad yanks at his tie, loosening his collar already and it's only nine.

"And why are you always blaming me?" Kade blurts out. "Check Hunter's room."

He waves his hand in my direction. My face falls, and Dad looks at me.

I glare at Kade. Oh, you motherf—

Kade laughs quietly, his eyes gleaming with amusement.

But Dad turns back to Kade, half-rolling his eyes, because I don't have sleepovers.

More footsteps hit the staircase, and Kade swats our dad in the stomach. "Come on. We're going to be late. Let's get a move on."

Dad grabs the back of his son's neck, pulling him in. "I'm not raising your kids. Got it?"

Kade nods, finally looking contrite. "Yeah, yeah..."

Dylan appears at the top of the stairs, and Dad twists around, meeting her halfway. "Make sure they're downstairs in twenty," he instructs her.

She nods once, big and decisive, like he's her general, and she continues toward us while he disappears down the stairs.

I watch her eyes light up when she sees us, the blue so marine behind the brown hair framing her face and falling down her arms. She skips up to us, tan legs so full of energy in her blue shorts. I love the way her smiles start close-lipped but so big, making you notice how her eyes dance and the blush on her cheeks before she shows you her teeth and all you see is her perfect mouth.

My chest tightens.

"You're not going dressed like that, are you?" Kade asks her.

I jerk my head, glaring at him. "Shut up."

But it comes out breathless because my heart is beating too fast.

She looks at him, her smile fading, but she turns back to me, forcing another one. Close-lipped, and it won't go any further this time. I already know that.

She clears her throat. "Can I borrow your JV jersey today?" she asks me.

I start to nod, but just then, Gemma comes out and slips between the doorframe and me, stepping into the hallway.

Dylan's spine straightens, and she watches Gemma put a hand on my chest. "Thanks," the girl says.

Her voice is silky smooth, and I open my mouth to... what? I don't know. Tell her to get back in Kade's room? Or 'no more hiding in mine?' Anything to make it clear that I didn't fuck the girl last night who talks about Dylan behind her back and makes fun of her.

But before I figure it out, she's throwing Dylan a look and walking the opposite way my dad came, heading for the rear entrance through one of the guestrooms. It has an outdoor staircase she can get down from and make it to her car.

I lift my eyes, seeing the crease in Dylan's brow.

"Wear mine," Kade tells her. "I want you to."

He walks back into his room and opens a drawer, grabbing the jersey.

He returns, holding it out to her. "It got a lot more wear than Hunter's did, but it's clean."

I clench my teeth as she takes it, looking at him like he's her fucking hero. "Thanks." She walks back toward the stairs, not looking at me again. "See you guys downstairs."

I watch her go, my stomach sinking into the goddamn floor.

Kade's voice is light with humor. "You could've just told her."

It takes a second, but finally, I say, "So could you."

I retreat back into my room, slamming the door between us.

It wasn't Dylan's fault for believing I fucked a girl who treated her badly. For believing I'd been a disloyal friend.

It wasn't my fault she thought that, either.

It was Kade's. I shouldn't have had to explain myself, and even if I did, he still would've come out of it innocent.

Because as it happens, I would hate for her to think he'd been a disloyal friend, either. I didn't tell her because it wouldn't have made me feel better to make him look bad in her eyes.

I was so fucking stupid.

I gaze out the window as Dylan stands just inside her closet door, with her shirt off. She thinks she's shielded behind the closet door between us, but there's a mirror on the wall. Her hair is out of its ponytail, and I can almost feel it on my fingers as I run my hand up her skin. The cool strands caress my knuckles.

She turns, her breasts bare in the mirror.

I drop my eyes.

It's not the first time I've seen her. I accidentally walked into the bathroom at my house when she was cleaning up after we went swimming. The room was thick with shower steam. She still doesn't know the door had been opened at all.

Still doesn't know she's the only one I've ever seen like that.

When I think about touching someone, it's always the same body I see. Teardrop breasts. Full and firm. The skin looks so soft, with a tight waist, curving beautifully the farther down I let my eyes go. My fingertips hum, and so does my mouth, because God, I want to touch her with more than just my hands.

Slowly, I raise my eyes again, watching her stare at herself in the mirror. Her head tilts like she's studying her body or something. She doesn't know how many people would love the feel of her.

For a moment, I see myself standing behind her, both of us shirtless, and I'm about to touch her, but when I look up at us, into the mirror, it's him. It could be me, but she'll see Kade. Everyone does.

Even I do sometimes.

Grabbing my towel, I throw it over my shoulder, heading for the shower, but my phone vibrates on the bed.

I flip it over, seeing Ciaran's name.

In person, I call him Grandpa, but for some reason it felt weird to have him listed like that in my phone once I moved in with Farrow. He sees him as Ciaran Pierce—Irish Mobster.

I answer, holding the phone to my ear. "Everyone's calling to check on me today," I say. "I'm still alive."

My grandfather doesn't hesitate. "What's this about you not going to the barber for your weekly appointment?"

I throw down my towel. Farrow called him? Really?

"It's not an appointment," I retort. "It's some old guy shooting the shit in his garage all day who's good with a razor. I needed some time alone."

"So, Samson Fletcher has twenty dollars less in his pocket this week, because you're wallowing under your perpetual teenage black cloud of 'Life just sucks so badly?'"

I close my eyes.

Jesus Christ.

"I'll go." I exhale. "I'm going now."

"Good boy," he replies. "And spend some money at Breaker's for dinner. Hugo's kid just had another kid."

I snarl, shaking my head.

But I keep my damn mouth shut.

"Love you," he says.

"Mm-hmm."

And we hang up.

After showering, I pull on some jeans, a T-shirt, and a fresh hoodie, and leave the girls still cleaning our house as I head across the darkening street to Fletcher's Barber Shop.

The sun is setting, the leaves sounding like paper as they blow across the pavement.

As soon as I walk in, Farrow starts chuckling from his chair.

"Fuck you," I mumble.

That just makes him laugh more. Fletcher, a seventy-four-year-old Haitian who still wears the white barber's coat from back in the day, drags a straight-edge up Farrow's neck to his chin.

He lifts his gaze to me. "Haircut?"

"Do I ever want a haircut?"

I have things to do. I head past the guys sitting in the chairs along the windows and pull out a twenty. I drop it on the counter, in front of the mirror, and grab a pair of clippers to snip off a lock and call it a day.

But Farrow snaps at me, "Sit your ass down. This man works for a living."

I drop the clippers.

He'll tell Ciaran if I don't stay. It was worth a try.

Fletcher continues to shave Farrow as some Nat King Cole song plays, because that's all Samson Fletcher plays.

I gesture to the razor. "You're gonna sterilize that before you use it on me?"

"What's that supposed to mean?" Farrow mumbles.

"I know where you've been,"

"You don't know everywhere I've been."

"Is this a mom joke?" I chuckle, drifting to the wall of photos.

"I didn't say it was a joke."

Calvin and T.C. laugh along with him, and I stare up at old photos, some of them black and white, and some with the gradient color of the '70s and '80s.

The shop is filled with guys in all the pictures, some of them in uniforms for factory jobs, some of them in suits, and others with boys, getting their first haircuts. The pictures capture men of all ages sitting in the same spots T.C., Constin, Luca, Anders, and Calvin sit in now, and I notice the same street outside; but in the photos, it's lined with cars and pedestrians on their way home or off to work.

Mothers.

Families.

The town was busy back then.

I peer in closer, gazing at one from the '80s, judging by the texture of the image. A man who looks like Farrow stands there with long hair.

Blond hair down to his shoulders, hanging over his hard eyes as they neither welcome nor smile at the photographer.

His hard, *green* eyes.

Like my mom's. And mine.

Like Ciaran's.

It's my grandfather in the picture.

I glance at Farrow, reclined with eyes closed, and that stern Pierce set to his eyebrows.

I wonder if he knows.

"You want to take her a snack, Constin?" Farrow asks as Fletcher wipes down his face and applies an antiseptic.

I look over at Constin, seeing him stand at the window, staring across the street.

He's had his eyes on her all day.

"She's got to be hungry," Calvin chimes in. "We didn't leave her any food."

They didn't?

And then I didn't let her eat lunch.

Shit.

Farrow's seat pops back up, and he rises, rubbing the aftershave into his skin.

"Come on, son," Fletcher slaps the back of the red leather chair twice.

I walk over, taking a seat, and he immediately tilts me back, removing a hot towel from the warmer.

He fans it out, leaning over to put it on my face.

I jerk away. "I don't need all that."

"Yes, you do," he states clearly. He wraps the towel around my face, and I'm forced to close my eyes, the heat coursing straight down my arms, and it's fucking heavenly.

"Your generation—and your parents' generation—for that matter," he points out, "need to relearn that living is an art. To do things with care and pride, instead of speed, just for the sake of convenience. You understand?"

"I'm sure the old dudes in your time had their complaints about your generation, too," T.C. retorts.

"Yeah," Fletcher fires back. "They hated us, because we fought against segregation and Vietnam, you little shit."

I hear quiet laughter from my left, but I don't know whose.

Fletcher presses down on the towel, forcing the heat in to open up my pores or whatever the hell it does. I can't argue that it doesn't feel good, though. My nerves start to settle for the first time since they put her in that house yesterday.

"Doing one little thing with regard makes you feel better," Fletcher explains. "And if you feel better, your day will go better. How you do anything, is how you do everything."

"Amen," Farrow says.

Pulling off the towel, Fletcher dispenses some hot lather from his machine and works it between his hands.

He closes in with it, and I shut my eyes as he covers my jaw, cheeks, and neck with the warmth.

My head starts to float high, and I expel all the breath I was holding since she arrived. That actually feels really nice.

"Your whole world can go to shit," he goes on, "and

everything could be falling on your head all at once, but you can still make your bed and get a gentleman's shave."

"Hell yeah," Calvin calls out, and I hear a round of two beats as they all knock on something to show their agreement.

I know why my grandpa always liked it here. It was the people. Ciaran was old school long before he was old, and the citizens of Weston didn't like change. They didn't get vacations to the Caribbean, so if life's pleasures were smaller, then why not do them right? They do things like go for walks, play cards, and a big night for kids is going for a ninety-nine cent ice cream cone at the Village Drug Store.

I'd heard what Dylan had said in first period, and she was right. There was nothing else for them.

And that had made them a unit.

That's why I came to Weston. We're going to win.

I hear a small lid close, and then I feel Fletcher place his hand on my cheekbone, pulling the skin taut before he slides the sterilized razor up my face.

"What time was she in bed last night?" Farrow asks.

Constin replies, "Lights were definitely out by eleven."

Yeah, they were. I close my hands around the ends of the armrests. Constin was watching, too.

"We should've put cameras in there," he says.

"We had no time," Farrow retorts. "I didn't think we were getting a girl, and definitely not her."

"Someone could do it tonight," Constin points out. "We'll take her to eat, come back, get the bikes. We can keep her out of the house for hours."

"I'm not hearing this," Mr. Fletcher says as he moves across my jaw.

"I'll stay with her," Constin goes on. "I want to drive her to Breaker's too. I want her to get used to being alone with me."

I flex my jaw, Fletcher's razor slips, and I feel the slice in my skin.

I grunt, breathing hard, and Fletcher pats the wound with a towel. "Boy, keep still."

"You okay, Hunter?" Farrow calls out.

But his voice is amused. I lift my middle finger.

He chuckles.

"We're not gonna do some shit, right?" T.C. asks them. "To her, I mean? I'm not into that."

"We're not going to hurt her," Farrow tells him. "We're going to *groom* her."

My stomach coils.

"And then she'll be begging us to 'hurt' her between the sheets all night long," Constin coos.

I pull so hard on the armrests, I hear them whine under my fingers.

Fletcher clears his throat, and Constin pipes up again, "Relax, Mr. Fletcher. She's eighteen."

I push Fletcher's arm away and bolt out of the seat, kicking his tray into the air as I charge for Constin. He meets me head on, both of us chest to chest.

Farrow pushes me back, and I stumble as he steps between us. "Are you claiming her?" he asks me.

I shake my head, the challenge in his gaze clear.

"Are you claiming her?" he says slower, his voice deeper.

Air pours in and out of my lungs. "Yes," I whisper.

The corner of his mouth curls.

He's not sending her back. And she won't go home. I have no choice.

"Hey, where is she going?" Calvin asks.

Farrow doesn't look away from me.

"Whoa, what the hell?" Luca blurts out.

"She's going to the Falls!" Calvin shouts.

Farrow spins around, looking out the window with the rest of them. The bike races off down the street, and I stand there, still seething.

"You fucking gave her a bike!" Constin bitches at Farrow.

But Farrow's not listening. "Get her before she gets to the bridge!"

Everyone spills out of the barber shop and into the street, running for their bikes.

And for a second, I smile as I grab the towel Fletcher offers. I wipe the shaving cream off my face.

They're about to learn just like the men in my family learned years ago. Dylan Trent never goes according to anyone's plan.

PIRATES

CHAPTER SEVEN

Dylan

I rev the engine, damn near pressing my stomach into the tank as I fly down the road. The river flows to my left, and I pass the train bridge that I jumped from on Grudge Night two months ago and spot the other one upriver that I crossed last night when I was taken as a hostage.

I kick it into higher gear, my heart swelling painfully in my chest, but I can't stop grinning behind the helmet.

I love this. I'm thirty miles over the speed limit, but judging from the overgrowth spilling onto the street, I don't think this road is ever used. Much of this town isn't.

I squeeze the handlebars, the rumble of the bike coursing through my body. I wasn't able to print off a copy of my license, but I can't resist.

I need this.

The image of Farrow and the guys joining Hunter on the field and taking his punishment with him today keeps sitting in my head.

Kade would never have done that. No one in the Falls would've done that for Hunter.

I don't think he's ever coming back.

I race past the bridge, laying off the gas for a second. Maybe I should be tossing coins too. But I push the idea aside and speed ahead. I don't have any coins, and besides, you toss when you cross. I'm not leaving Weston yet.

Curving to the right, I zoom up into the hills instead, past dilapidated houses, one with a porch swing hanging lopsided from a broken chain and another with years of some teenager's stickers all over two of the upstairs windows.

All of the houses need fresh paint and new roofs, but there are lights inside and valid efforts with the occasional door wreath. One house has a lawn display full of homemade Halloween decorations. Skeletons wear Dad's old clothes, and foam gravestones line the lawn along the sidewalk.

Climbing the hill, I lean as far forward as I can as the incline grows steeper. The houses fade away and a forest surrounds me, a dense collection of trees to my left and right.

Glancing into one of my sideview mirrors, I see headlights far behind me. Several.

Motorcycles.

I go faster, the road old and the blacktop faded, but it's less broken than the flood-damaged streets downtown.

Reaching the top of the first hill, I screech to a halt and lift my visor, scanning the road ahead. A thick brush surrounds the path, weeds and years of fallen leaves coating the edges of the street. A *Road Closed* sign sits half on the pavement, moved aside to make way for people who don't care if it is safe or not.

I put my feet on the ground, turn off the bike, and slip off my helmet. Engines rumble behind me, closing in, and I gaze ahead, knowing that the deserted, flat road in front of me—like a dark tunnel under the cover of trees—

becomes one of the hardest to navigate once you go inside.

Rumor has it, anyway. I've never been.

Bikes stop behind me, one by one all going silent, and I look over my shoulder, seeing Constin, Calvin, and all the rest. Farrow charges straight for me.

"You thought I was running away?" I ask, a smile pulling at my mouth. "What were you going to do? Stop me?"

"Yes."

I face forward again. "I said I wanted to ride."

"You didn't say where." He stops at my side, planting his hands on my seat and handlebar. He gets in my face. "No one comes out here alone. You do it again—"

"You'll take my keys?"

I turn and face him, my nose nearly touching his.

His eyes sparkle as his blond hair blows on the breeze. "I'll take your clothes."

My mouth closes, my teeth locking together of their own accord. I don't falter otherwise, though, even though I know he's not lying.

"Someone needs to be here to hide your body when you crash."

He sounds like my father.

Just then, another bike enters the party, the helmeted driver rocking left and then right on his dirt bike, smooth as ice as he maneuvers through the other riders and halts just behind me.

Farrow rises up straight, eyeing the newcomer.

"I'm not alone," I finally reply to him. "Noah Van der Berg watches me."

Noah removes his helmet, his gear—pants, jersey, boots, armor—already dirty from a day of training with my father. But he smiles, not looking the least bit exhausted as the sweat makes hair stand in all directions and his sun-kissed skin shine.

I called him from the house and asked him to come because Farrow is right. Even I'm not reckless enough to be out here alone. At least not my first time.

Climbing off his bike, he does a survey of mine as he walks over. He grabs my helmet. "This isn't yours..."

But I don't have to answer. He knows the only brand my father uses, and this isn't it.

He shoves it back at Farrow, handing me his own instead.

I pull the chin strap out as Noah takes an earpiece and fits it into my ear. It's not something we normally use, but we're out here without my father's permission, and he doesn't want to lose contact with me if he loses sight of me.

Farrow glares at Noah. "We got her."

"So do I."

Noah busies himself with connecting the Bluetooth and his own earbud.

Farrow's lowers his voice. "You need to leave."

But Noah just taunts back, "You know it'll be more fun if I stay."

He doesn't look at Farrow, and I can feel the heat rolling off the latter.

"I need someone here I trust," I explain to Farrow.

"Did you walk it first?" Noah asks in a low voice.

I shake my head, and he meets my eyes, silently chiding me.

"Keep it under fifty the first time," he says. "I need to map it out."

And with that, he presses a GoPro camera to the Velcro on the front of my (his) helmet.

"Look for the connecting stretches," he instructs, "and throttle up."

I nod, pulling the helmet over my head and fastening the strap under my chin.

"Elbows up, mind your weight..." he continues as I reach inside the face shield and adjust my earpiece. "And talk to yourself." He grins at me. "No one can hear you."

"You will," I point out.

"And I'll understand."

Yeah. Normally, we wouldn't have contact, and I could talk, sing, shout—do whatever—to push myself and keep my head zoned in on the track. It's not something my dad did, but Noah does. He says when he thinks, he loses focus, and if he talks, he won't think. I feel like that's an indication of some deeper insight into his personality, but I can't think about that now.

But one day, I took his advice about the talking, and I've been doing it ever since.

Finally, he lifts his gaze, meeting Farrow's. "Anything to add?" he asks him.

"No," he replies, the twitch of a smile on his lips. "Fifty sounds fine."

I narrow my eyes just a hair. I don't like how he said that.

Soft laughter resonates behind us.

Noah climbs on his bike, reaching behind him to take the spare helmet he has secured there. Fitting it onto his head, he starts his bike and crawls up to my side. He nods once, and I do too. His thumb comes up, and my thumb comes up. And then he raises his right hand just a little, counting off.

Three.

Two.

I press the button on my GoPro.

And one.

We're off.

Noah lets me take the lead, and I rock side to side, swerving around the *Road Closed* sign before speeding ahead. Leaning into the wind, I scan the road, seeing cracks and potholes, and I curve quickly, avoiding them. My heart pumps hard because I don't know what's coming.

Coasting down the abandoned road, I dip and then hear the engine whir louder as the bike launches up a hill, the climb of Phelan's Throat beginning now.

I break fifty, pushing it a little harder to fifty-five. I glance behind me, Noah keeping up.

Trees create a cover around us, thick trunks fencing us in as the canopies shroud us from the sun. I kick it up to sixty.

"Come on, come on, come on," I repeat.

"Keep your eyes peeled," I hear him in my ear.

For what? A deer? That's about the only danger I'm anticipating right now.

The path takes a sharp curve left, and I slow just enough to brush the ground with my foot before zooming off again. A pothole races toward me, and I swerve just in time.

"We're not racing," he reminds me.

I ignore him because he's only saying it, so he can say that he said it, if I get hurt. Noah is like me. We don't go slowly.

Fast is the whole point.

We wind around bends, the road ahead opening up, and I lay on the gas, racing hard. I jerk the handlebars left and right, maneuvering around holes and pieces of broken road, feeling my heart leap into my throat, because the obstacles come so fast. I twist the bike right, almost spilling over, and I let out a laugh as the excitement rushes to my head. I drop my foot, catching myself, and then give it some more speed, barreling ahead.

I race, the wind flying at me, the cool air drifting up the gap in the helmet just above my neck, and I can smell the bark on the trees.

Faster.

But as the road whips by underneath me, climbing, climbing, climbing, something glints in the sunlight on the old pavement.

I keep glancing down, seeing it again.

And again.

Something copper-colored.

My face falls, déjà vu hitting me. *Pennies.*

There are pennies on the road.

I let off the gas, realizing too late when Noah flies by.

Oh, no.

"Noah, stop!" I shout, but I forgot about my visor. I slide it up. "Noah!" I scream again.

He revs up the hill, but then, his tires leave the ground, his bike soars through the air, and I gasp as he plummets back to the earth, his body leaving the bike just as he disappears.

"Noah!" I cry.

I ride to the top of the hill, keeping my speed low, because I have no idea what's on the other side. I stop, seeing Noah splayed on the downslope, his head lolling back and forth. His bike lays twenty yards farther, on its side. I drive down to him, parking my bike on the side of the road, and jump off. I run over, ripping off my helmet and dropping it to the ground.

He grunts, one knee bent as he pulls off his helmet and drops his head back to the ground.

"And that's…" He breathes heavy. "Why you walk the track first."

I do a once-over, inventorying the scuff marks on his elbows and underneath his shoulders. I don't see any blood, but he's going to have a hard time sitting tonight.

"Are you okay?" I ask.

But just as he starts to answer, bike engines roar, flying closer and closer until all of a sudden, one, two, three, four, five, and six come skidding over the hill. Noah turns his head with me, and it all happens in slow motion, Farrow and the guys skidding out and then leaning to the right, almost laying on their goddamn sides, but never quite touching the ground as they drift around the immediate turn that happens right over the hill.

One by one, they all tilt back upright, not one of them a seasoned racer like Noah Van der Berg, but not a single one of them falling, either.

And that's when I finally get the name. *Phelan's Throat.* It's what my dad keeps trying to pound into me. Racing isn't about speed.

It's science. You can't beat Phelan's Throat with guts. There's a method to letting it swallow you down.

They all slow to a stop and turn around, heading back up to us.

"Don't tell your dad about this," Noah whispers as if they can hear over their engines. "He'll tell mine."

I laugh a little. I've never met Jake Van der Berg, but Noah avoids him like I avoid homework.

In a moment, the guys are strolling up to us.

"You little shit," Noah says, glowering. "You could've warned us."

Farrow just smiles, looking smug. "Who am I to teach Noah Van der Berg and the daughter of Jared Trent anything?"

Striding up, he grabs me and hauls me away from my friend. "Hey!" I yelp.

"Like I said, we got it from here," he tells Noah. "Don't come without an invitation again."

And he wraps his arm around my waist, carrying me off.

He deposits me on the back of his bike, climbs in front of me, and starts the engine.

Farrow shoots off, leaving my bike behind, and I grab his waist on reflex, gazing back at Noah as we speed off.

The cool air nips at my face.

Farrow speeds way too fast back down to the river and over into the old fairgrounds. The bikes cruise down the dirt path toward a bonfire, and headlights appear ahead, people congregating in the empty field.

Everyone stops, and I yank my arms off Farrow's waist.

"If he's not home in one piece when I call..." I say.

He turns off the bike and climbs off. "As long as you remember, you're not a guest. You're a hostage." He looks down at me. "Don't ever go up to Phelan's Throat without us again. Don't go *anywhere* without us again."

I may as well be at home if I'm going to have a dad here too.

"And don't speak to anyone here tonight," he commands. "Understood? If I see you talking..."

"Then what?"

The others leave their bikes, and I swing my leg off.

"You know what," Farrow says. "Aren't you ever interested in seeing what happens when you actually do what you're told for a change?"

I lift my chin.

He leans in when I don't answer, and I spot Hunter to my right, far behind Farrow's shoulder. He sits on the hood of his car, part of the circle of vehicles around the bonfire. People walk and dance, the fire glimmers in his eyes as he watches me and lifts a drink to his lips.

"Come on, virgin," Farrow murmurs. "Try a change of pace."

He takes my hand and leads me toward the party, Hunter's eyes still on us as I take my hand back.

We stop in a crowd of people, the heat of the bonfire surrounding me but not quite hitting my face. Farrow and Calvin stand in front of me, looming several inches over my line of sight as music plays and whistles go off.

Something is happening by the bonfire, but I can't see over the guys to tell what.

"Whoo!" T.C. howls, but I don't know at what.

Followed by someone behind me. "Hell yeah!"

I try to peer around everyone, but a drink appears over my shoulder, something brown with ice. I glance up at Constin, the flesh of his Green Street scar raised and bumpy. It must've hurt.

"It's not roofied," he says, still holding it out to me.

Farrow stands next to me, taking a drink out of a beer that's now magically in his hand. "You're surrounded by six guys who all have sixty pounds of muscle on you," he points out. "We wouldn't need you drugged to get what we want."

"And you only belong to one of us, anyway," Calvin adds. "He'll see you soon. I doubt he wants to waste any of his twelve nights left with you."

What? Who?

Farrow chuckles as the crowd cheers, but no one says more.

I take the drink without thinking. I want to ask what they mean. Who do I belong to?

But it's probably no one. It's clearly a threat, and I'm not going to grace it with my attention. They just want to mess with my head.

I sniff the drink, smelling rum and Coke. And I actually don't think they'd use drugs to get me into bed, but I have no doubt they'd use them to make me act stupid on video. My parents taught me early. Cameras are everywhere, and people are shitty.

"Besides," Calvin says in a low voice. "There's prettier stuff here anyway. Ever hear of fucking lipstick?"

I take a sip of the drink. "I'm sorry you're not attracted to me. That sucks."

Someone breathes out a laugh, and Farrow tips back his beer, downing the rest of the bottle. He hands it off to Calvin and then walks to the bonfire, and I'm finally able to see what's happening.

A naked girl is pressed against a car, a dark-haired guy in black pants grinding against her.

They're doing that thing I saw last night.

The couple is different, though.

I can't tell if she's completely naked, but I spot naked arms, shoulders, and a sliver of bare skin. Way below her hips.

How old is she?

Hunter takes a sip of his drink, his feet propped up on the bumper of his car as the people around him catcall and whistle. He lifts his eyes, watching the show, and I watch him.

Not the show. Him.

He sits there as Farrow pulls off his shirt, taps the other guy on the shoulder, and waits for him to step away, as if he's being relieved of duty. Moving in, Farrow wraps his body around hers, both of them moving slowly into each other, Hunter's eyes on them the whole time.

I can't see her face clearly, but her head falls back, her breath fanning the hair in her face. Hunter watches his friend hold her, and I almost can't breathe.

He likes it.

I don't know why it surprises me. He's not a priest, and I'm always shocked when I realize that. When it hits me that he's going to be alone with girls. He already has been, I'm sure.

He's just very private about everything. Not like Kade, who wants everyone to know he just got laid.

I head over to Hunter, leaving Farrow's crew behind as I traipse across the cold grass. Hunter meets my eyes, seeing me approach, but turns back to the show as he takes another drink.

I stop next to his car, but I face the bonfire, watching Farrow not-quite fuck the girl.

"So," I mumble. "Pennies?"

"What?"

I draw in a deep breath. "You put the pennies on the road."

I turn my head, looking at him. It was a signal we used—he, Kade, and me—when we were little, before we had phones. It was a way to alert the others of danger. Like to sneak in the back door to avoid our parents if we were late. To tell the others not to come in at all if we were in trouble for mischief. Hell, sometimes we even dropped a penny to signal the others to get us out of a boring conversation.

I don't know when he did it, but he knew I'd be up there eventually.

He starts to take another drink. "I don't know what you're talking about."

"You're such a fucking liar."

His eyes dart to me, and I look to Farrow again, then the other guys. They told me not to talk to anyone. Not sure if Hunter counts.

I wet my lips, covering my mouth with my cup. "You should've warned me," I whisper.

"I warned you to go home, didn't I?"

I shake my head. On the one hand, I'm grateful. I should've walked the track. I didn't, and I know better. If I hadn't seen the pennies, I might've not been able to avoid injury as skillfully as Noah.

But what if I hadn't seen the pennies?

I guess I didn't expect Hunter to be in Weston anyway, so I should be grateful for any kind of warning.

Still, though. He should've come and stopped me. I would've done that for him.

"You know," I say, watching Farrow and the girl. "Farrow and his friends crashed a party at your parents' house on Grudge Night a couple of months ago. One of them was in a mask. Only one. He handcuffed Kade and me together."

I didn't even question it at the time. Why was only one of them in a mask? Now it makes sense. That was just before school started. Hunter was with the Rebels by then.

"Maybe he wanted Kade to know what it was like to sleep next to someone who loved him." He meets my gaze. "For a change."

My eye twitches a little. *Someone who loves him...*

Should I tell him where I really slept that night?

I turn my attention back to the show.

"What are they doing?" I ask, changing the subject.

Farrow takes her head in his hand, their lips almost touching as he pants with her.

"Teasing each other," Hunter explains. "Trying to come without hands or mouths. It's just a game they play."

The engine rumbles against her body that I see now is completely naked, making them both tremble. Their hands roam, his chest pressed against hers, but they don't kiss and they don't finger. Just grind, the car helping with the vibration.

Finally, she leans back a little, exposing her body for him as howls go off loud and deep through the crowd. The tremble of the car makes her breasts shake, and he holds her hips, dry-fucking her.

"Why are they doing it in front of everyone?" I ask.

"Because it's exciting." He answers without hesitation. "To be watched and to watch."

"You like to watch this?"

He's quiet, and when I look over, he's watching me. "Something like that."

His green eyes study me, but then he clears his throat, turning back to the crowd.

"People don't explain themselves here, Dylan." He chews the inside of his lip for a moment. "It's like they don't do things, because they feel good. They do them, because they know they're doomed."

As if everyone doesn't know that. Do we?

He continues. "The storm that destroyed this town more than twenty years ago taught them that almost everything is out of our control, and time is all we really have. We have a limited supply of it, and we can't buy more of it. Today is the best day of Farrow's life, Dylan."

I don't look to Farrow, though. I stare at Hunter.

"If he wakes up tomorrow," his voice falls to a whisper, "It'll be the best day of his life again."

My heart pounds in my chest, and I barely breathe. Hunter's lips continue to move, and I think I hear what he's telling me, but I don't process it as I just stare at him.

I let my eyes roam over his hair. It falls in every direction, the blond looking a little darker—maybe wet—as it hangs over his temples and forehead, nearly in his eyes. Arched eyebrows, straight nose, strong lips... His cheekbones are sharper, making his face look oval, until he flexes his jaw, and then he goes from looking like a...

Like a Roman senator to a Roman soldier.

I love how he watches them. I love how he looks at the world. I remember sitting in his car, out at the lake, in the rain, talking. That's all we needed. Us, a view, and a couple of sodas.

I blink, turning back to the bonfire. Farrow's thrusts grow slower, deeper, more intense, and her moans get louder. Sweat glistens on his back. She's coming.

My voice is smaller than I like. "Do you think you'd like to be watched like this?"

I wait for him to respond, and I almost don't think he will when he finally says. "I would never do something like this."

"Yeah, you would."

I feel his eyes on me, and I meet them. "People are capable of almost anything, given the right circumstances or motivation," I say.

"Would you do this?"

I almost smile. Not because my answer embarrasses me, but because I haven't had a conversation this stimulating with a guy in a long time.

I missed Hunter.

"Given the right circumstances or motivation..." I finally reply.

I don't look at him again as I leave and head back the way I came. I can't go back to the house because I don't have the bike. They left it up on Phelan's Throat, probably as my punishment for running off.

But I don't want to watch Farrow ejac in his jeans, either, even though her cries carry on behind me like she's going for an Oscar.

I head back to the bikes, somewhere quiet to call Aro and tell her how the Pirates' hostage did today. First, I shoot a text to Noah, making sure he's okay.

I'm cool, he says. *Hit me up next time. I'll be there.*

I grin. Noah won't wait for any invitations from Farrow Kelly.

I start to call Aro, but I look up and see Thomasin Dietrich. Everyone calls her Tommy, for short. A guy with shoulder-length dark hair holds her up against a tree and kisses her hard.

I slow my steps, all at once taking notice of his hands all over her, in places they shouldn't be. She kisses him back, her hair completely white, the blue tips recently touched up, but her hands are pressed to his chest, like she's deciding if she wants to push him away.

So far, she's not.

My phone rings, and she opens her eyes, hearing it and meeting my eyes over his shoulder as his tongue burrows in her mouth.

I look down, seeing Kade's name on my screen.

But just then, that pedophile kissing Tommy starts to slide a hand up her shirt. I don't know if he's older than me, but he's definitely not as young as her.

146

She gives me the finger, and I ignore Kade's call, charging toward her.

She pushes him away, bracing for me, but instead, I grab his shoulder and jam a knee right between his legs. He growls, and I glare at him. "She's fourteen years old. What's your name?"

His eyes water, and he holds his crotch, and even though he doesn't answer, he doesn't look surprised. He knows who she is. Everyone knows who she is. He heaves breath after breath, and barrels around me, stumbling away from both of us.

Tommy balls her fists, fury in her blue eyes.

"What's his name?" I ask.

"Screw you."

And she whips around, running away.

I would laugh because she's a Pirate Girl. We're tough.

But she's not tough because she was raised to be. She's tough because she's bitter, and it's the direct result of how she has to come here to feel any acceptance when she doesn't back home.

The phone rings again, and I see Kade's name.

He's going to tell me to come home. He's not going to be nice.

Inhaling a deep breath, I swipe the screen and hold the phone to my ear. "Hey."

"You want a ride home?"

I smile a little. "No, I'm okay."

He sounds soft. Normally, he wouldn't ask. He'd just tell me what he's going to do.

"I'll come and get you right now," he says.

I wander in slow steps. "I'm okay."

My voice is raspy, and I swallow the lump.

"You're mad at me."

I shake my head, looking up and around. Hunter still sits on his car, but his eyes are completely on me now. He's watching me.

"Not everything is about you," I tell Kade.

"Why?" he retorts. "You love him more?"

Love him more? What is he talking about?

"Not everything is about you," I whisper.

"Yeah, it is." His tone is resolute. "You left because I ignored you."

I pinch my brows together, facing the fire. But I can't look up from the ground.

"It's all about me," he growls. "You never fucking noticed Hunter when I was around."

"That's not true."

"He didn't even exist when I was around, did he?"

I shake my head.

"You wanted to be where I was," he goes on and tears fill my eyes. Is that what Hunter thinks? "Always where I was. All you saw was me."

I...

That's not true.

Shoes appear, then legs, and I look up, seeing Hunter standing in front of me.

"You know why?" Kade asks as I stare up at his brother. "Because you and I are alike, Dylan. We race into trouble, and I wouldn't have you any other way. He would put a leash on you. He always tried to control you. To calm you down and restrain you."

Hunter holds my eyes, unblinking.

"It's our senior year," Kade tells me. "I need you here, Dylan. You know he bores you."

Hunter takes the phone out of my hand, looks at the screen, and swipes, hanging up on his twin.

He slides it into the pocket of my hoodie and then takes my hand, threading his fingers through mine. "Let's go."

REBELS

CHAPTER EIGHT

Hunter

She steals glances at me as I drive.

I knew she was talking to Kade on the phone. From fifty yards away, I recognized the body language. The bowed head, the frown, the limited movement of her lips, because he was dominating the conversation, as usual.

"I thought you said I was going to be on my own here," she says next to me.

Yeah, I remember what I said.

I don't know why I thought I'd be able to ignore her presence. It's all I'm aware of since she arrived. I shouldn't give a shit if she talks to Kade while she's here. I want her to miss home and leave Weston.

But it pissed me off.

She's not home.

She's here. He can talk to her later.

The cool wind sweeps through the car as "Keep the Streets Empty for Me" plays on the stereo, and I hear her unclick her seatbelt. Looking over, I watch her shift in my passenger seat and lay her head back over the open window. Closing her eyes and with her face toward the sky, she lays there, letting her hair whip in the wind as we fly down the highway.

Locks of her hair dance over her eyelids and mouth. My chest tightens.

I turn my eyes back to the road, swallowing hard. "Dylan, sit up."

My car is old. It doesn't set off an alert when someone isn't wearing their seatbelt, and she's taking full advantage of it.

"Dylan," I bark again, glancing at her. "Come on, it's dangerous."

"I know."

Her soft voice sounds so innocent, and I shake my head. Of course, she knows. Living on the edge is *fun,* and putting yourself in unnecessary danger is worth a thrill.

But...I don't slow down the car, either.

I keep my foot pressed on the gas, flitting my gaze to her every once in a while and seeing a smile spread over her closed mouth.

In a few minutes, we're pulling into Breaker's, some '70s rock song playing over the speakers as vehicles enter and exit. Farrow and the team will be at the party for a while, taking advantage of the keg before they head here for food. We'll be gone by then.

Servers coast around the parking lot in roller skates, and Dylan sits up, smiling wider as she watches them. She loves anything with wheels.

I slide into a bay and park, the menu with a speaker in the center lit up in bright colors outside my window. I reach out, pressing the blue button for service.

I meet her gaze. "You hungry?"

She nods.

The speaker crackles, and then I hear, "Hi. May I take your order?"

I turn to Dylan again, double-checking. "Bacon?"

Again, she nods.

I lean out the window just a bit. "May I get two number ones?" I call out. "Both with bacon. One with onion rings and a Coke. The other with fries and a strawberry shake."

"Anything else?"

I glance at Dylan. She shakes her head, smiling a little as déjà vu hits me, and probably her too. It's our fast-food order. When we were little and both wanted fries *and* onion rings and both wanted milkshakes, but they're not good enough for washing down food, so we needed a soda too. Our parents would never let us get that much food, so we each put in an order and shared it.

"No, that'll be it," I tell the cashier.

"Nineteen eighty-two," she says.

"Thanks."

I reach over, avoiding Dylan's knee as I open the glove box and retrieve my wallet.

"I have money," she says, starting to dig in her back pocket.

But I shove the box closed and sit back up, not looking at her. "My parents' money or your parents' money, it doesn't matter."

She's quiet for a second and then finally pulls her hand out of her pocket.

I slip out cash, and she opens her door. "I'll be back."

I toss my wallet back into the glove compartment, darting my eyes up just in time to see her pull her hair up into a high ponytail. Her hoodie rides up as she raises her arms just enough for two of my classmates, Marius Kent and

Daniel Kocur, to turn their eyes on her bare stomach and naked hips as they lean against the exterior of the restaurant. She fastens her hair and grabs the doorknob to the women's restroom, the guys watching her as she goes.

I slam the glove compartment shut. If people look at her like that here, they must in the Falls too. When I lived there, not many guys were vocal about their interest, simply because they were intimidated. Either by her or Jared. Everyone's scared of Dylan's dad.

Except me.

And Kade.

We know him.

But she'll be off to college next year, and she'll meet a lot of guys who have no idea who her dad is.

Climbing out of the car, I walk around to the front, leaving the battery running and my music playing. Leaning back on the hood, I unlock my phone.

I want to call Kade. I tried not to think about it at the time or why I had them handcuffed together on Grudge Night. There were both there, together, and I was in a mask. It was a spur-of-the-moment decision.

But I didn't consider why I did it until she asked me tonight.

How long were they trapped together? Did they share a bed?

I need to stop giving a shit. If I'm ever going to have a life where he doesn't matter, I have to give her up too. And Hawke and Quinn and...

A.J.

I lower my eyes, the weight on my heart getting heavier at the thought of my little sister. I'm not sure if she'll ever see her brothers in a room together again.

She will see us together in a stadium, though.

Sarah Powers rolls up on her skates, holding a carrier with two drinks in one hand and a brown bag in another.

"Hey, Hunter," she says, handing me the bag. "You ready for the game?"

I set the food on the car and take the drinks, handing her the cash. "Getting there," I tell her. "Keep the change."

She smiles, spinning around and passing Dylan as she skates away.

I hand Dylan her milkshake. "Do you need to hit a grocery store?" I ask. "They didn't leave you any food at the house."

I pull the burgers, fries, and rings out of the bag. We both rest against the car, unwrapping our sandwiches.

"Well, someone did," she tells me. "I came home from school and the fridge was stocked."

She turns the burger left to right, cocking her head, before she finds the perfect place to attack. She takes a bite, her lips pursing together as she chews.

I take a bite too.

Someone put food in her fridge? If it were one of the guys, they would've said so at the barber shop earlier. It was probably Hawke. Or his girlfriend that Dylan talked about in her texts. She's from Weston, I heard.

Dylan jerks her chin at the server, Sarah. "Does she have a boyfriend?"

I glance at Sarah as she takes an order from the window and rolls to a car five spots down from us. Her T-shirt is tied above her belly button, and her pink leggings show all of her curves.

"I don't know," I tell her, looking down.

"Where did you find this song?"

"I don't remember."

She's trying to start a conversation, and I guess I asked for it, but I don't want to talk like things haven't changed.

I stick the straw in my drink, but she takes my Coke before I can and sips it.

She hands it to me, and I drink while she uncaps her milkshake and dips a fry in. "What colleges are you applying to?" she asks.

"I haven't decided."

"Are you going to Weston's homecoming dance?"

"I haven't thought about it."

She eats. I eat. And we drink the soda while she dips her fries in the ice cream.

She inspects her burger for where her next bite will happen. "Do you want to know what he said to me?" she asks.

I stop mid-chew and clench my teeth for a split-second. *He*. Kade.

I hear her swallow, and then she takes another drink of my Coke before continuing, "I loved growing up with you two, you know?"

Yeah, I know. She followed him, I followed her...

"I loved growing up with Hawke and Quinn, too, but mostly you and Kade," she goes on. "We were the same age. Same teachers, same milestones."

Dylan was born a couple of months after us, so we started school together. Got our licenses around the same time.

"Everyone idolized him," she says. "Kade, I mean."

I flip the top of the wrapper back over the burger, covering it, no longer hungry.

"He was always the first one to choose a direction." She smiles softly, musing. "The first one to charge ahead, so before anyone even had a chance to decide what they wanted you do, they were just following him."

She dips a fry in her milkshake, and I feel his shadow descend like it always hovered at home.

"He'll always be dominating conversations, the one everyone gravitates toward," she continues, "because of that confidence. It's not that he always says the right thing, but you just listen to whoever's talking."

I don't need to be reminded of the power he has over people.

"He never has any problems." She just keeps dipping her fry, lost in thought. "He doesn't tolerate problems, and having his approval or attention makes you feel worth more."

I swallow my last bite, crumpling the rest of my burger into a ball inside the tin foil.

"Knowing Kade is knowing he'll always be the center of attention in any room." she says. "And if you want to be in the fun, you better stay close or you'll be alone."

Yeah. Sounds about right. Everyone surrounds him.

"And you know what people liked about me?" I ask her. "That I looked like him."

She chews and swallows, dusting off the crumb that fell on her sleeve. "He doesn't feel like you, though."

My eyebrows pinch together. *Feel like me?*

What do I feel like?

She stops eating, just stands there as if she realized how that sounded.

It's good to know that she sees through his mystique a little. She's never asked why I left. She's only ever asked why I left *her*.

Taking her fries, I dump them back into the bag, and then I take my onion rings and do the same. She watches as I fist the bag closed and shake, mixing up the contents.

Opening it back up, I pluck out a handful of onion rings and fries, dipping one into her shake as we share the Coke.

We eat and drink, music playing and people pulling in and out of the parking lot, and I want to take out my phone and reply to one of the many texts she's sent me over the past year that I never answered, and I want to do it with her sitting right here, because I want to see her smile.

But I don't want her thinking we're friends. We can never be friends again.

"Don't race Phelan's Throat, okay?" I warn.

She doesn't look at me as she pulls an onion ring out of the bag and a tiny laugh escapes her.

"I didn't have my lucky charm today," she says. "That's why I had bad luck."

I look away before I roll my eyes. She always races with the same necklace her dad raced with. A piece of clay with her mother's childhood thumbprint.

"And you don't look like Kade," she tells me, swallowing down her food. "You look like your mom. A little more than he does."

My heart kicks up speed, and I take a big bite of an onion ring to hide my smile.

I inhale a deep breath, close my eyes, and lock my fingers behind my head. I tense every muscle in my body as I lay in bed.

I didn't sleep for shit last night.

I couldn't stop staring at her mouth at Breaker's. I know she saw it. Every time she chewed, swallowed, spoke...

My cock stretches against my sleep pants, straining to stand.

My abs tighten harder still, and my biceps brush my ears as I try to get everything to burn, so I'll be too tired to think about her today.

She told me I looked more like my mom, who still has that mildly aggravated, 'your-idea-of-fun-isn't-my-idea-of-fun, I'm judging you' glint in her eyes that she had in all the photos I've seen of her as a teenager. I don't look like that.

And yet, I like that Dylan thinks I do. My mom's cool. I love my dad, but he thrives off bullshit that I find intolerable. Suits, politics, compromising, and never being able to say exactly what you mean. I know it has to be done by someone, but I'm glad it's not me.

Light fills the room on the other side of my eyelids, and I focus on a face—any face but hers. Coral's blonde hair and her eyes that amplify her smile. Mace's curves. Arlet washing Farrow's car weeks ago in a bikini that I couldn't help rolling my eyes at, because it's ridiculous how he coerces women into being his maids, but I also did a double-take at the view too. She likes me. She's been sending me signals the size of Mack trucks.

But all I see is me last night, tearing Dylan's phone out of her hand at the bonfire and almost crushing it in my fist, because I'm sick of how he troubles her. Her spine straightened like a steel rod, and she barely looked like she was breathing.

Not nervous.

Tense.

Maybe I want her to feel me like that with me.

And maybe she will, now that he's not here to interfere like he always did.

"No, I don't want to get in," Dylan cries.
But she's totally smiling too.

Kade grabs at her ankles, water sloshing around his waist as she leaps around the pool deck, just out of his reach. Stoli and Dirk have Danielle Hardy and Gemma Ledger on their shoulders, the girls trying to push each other off and into the water. Dylan wants to get in the pool, but she and Ledger aren't okay. Kade doesn't give a shit.

She pops a grape into her mouth from the handful she holds as she slides out of his reach again.

"Kade, leave her alone," I say.

But he captures her ankle with one hand and then snags the hem of her shorts with the other and yanks her in.

"Ah!" she screams.

She crashes into the water, and Kade and the guys howl with laughter. I swim, one stroke carrying me over as she pops up, hair draped over her face and her grapes gone.

She heaves breath after breath, rising to her feet and hugging herself as her teeth chatter. "It's cold."

She shivers, and I grip the back of her neck, pushing her hair out of her face with my other hand.

I meet her eyes, and she smiles up at me, her chest shaking with laughter.

Everyone blurs behind her.

Her blue eyes under dark lashes gaze up at me, and I feel her thighs press into mine as I become aware that she's wet. Her clothes stick to her, and I blink, my gaze dropping to her white T-shirt plastered to her stomach, her belly button visible just underneath.

She takes a step closer, coming in to get warm. She trembles against my body, and everything starts throbbing. Heat rushes down low, and my chest caves, feeling her hips in my hands even though I'm not touching her there. I want to. I want to hold her close so badly.

Her smile suddenly falls, and I know she feels me. I rip my hand off her hair and back away. "Dylan, Jesus Christ..."

I say it like she did something wrong, and her brow pinches together.

I chuckle a little to shake it off, about to tell her she can have my towel on the deck chair, but Kade sinks beneath the water, through her legs, and rises back up with Dylan on his shoulders.

He spins her away from me, taking her to the others.

But she holds my eyes over her shoulder as she goes.

I wish they hadn't been there. I wouldn't have pushed her away.

Maybe I would've. I don't know. It wasn't the first time I'd gotten hard, but I think she noticed, and it freaked me out because I didn't want it to freak her out.

I just couldn't help it. Kade had started having sex a couple of months earlier, and it's not like I took that as my cue to start doing it, too; but it gave me permission to want it, at least. And he seemed to know, because he never let us be alone together for very long from then on out.

I told myself a hundred times it had nothing to do with Dylan. She was a girl, and I trusted her completely. My thoughts about her weren't a choice. They were simply a lack of options. I thought that whenever I left home, I'd find that there were others who made me feel good too.

I reach down and fist myself over my pants, too fucking hard.

"It's dangerous," she whispers against my mouth.
In my head, we're somewhere dark. Hidden. Soft.
A bed.

I thrust into her, desperate to remove my jeans, her underwear. "I know."

I bite her lip. She whimpers, pants. I grip her cotton panties, throbbing.

I squeeze myself, groaning at the daydream. There are others out there who will make me feel just as good. She could be anyone.

I close my eyes, trying to imagine another face. Another body.

"Fuck," I moan as I dive into her mouth. "Are you sure?"

"It's dangerous here," she tells me in between kisses.

"I know." My chest presses into her breasts. "But I want your first time to be in a bed."

I draw in a deep breath, feeling her body underneath mine. She wants to have sex, and I don't trust anyone else to touch her right.

"Are you sure?" I ask again, clenching her underwear in my fist.

She arches her back, holds me between her thighs, and digs her nails into my arms. "Don't stop, Hunter."

I grunt, swelling painfully and feeling her in my arms, but then...a clamor hits the wall on the left side of my bed.

"Fuck!" a girl cries out from the other room. "Yeah, yeah, yeah... Oh!"

I open my eyes, sighing, and my hard-on already ebbing away. *Seriously?*

"Ah! Yeah!"

Farrow's headboard hits the other side of the wall, faster and harder, over and over again, and I remove my hand from my cock before running it through my hair.

"Oh!" she moans at the top of her lungs.

I punch the wall with the side of my fist, her laughter following quickly after. "Sorry!" she shouts. I don't recognize the voice. It could be anyone.

But they don't shut up. His bed rocks against the wall, and I whip off my blanket, rising out of bed.

I walk to the window, the tree outside spilling leaves in the wind, but I don't have time to appreciate the colors or to even check the temperature this morning when I see Constin walking up the steps of the house next door.

What the hell is he doing?

He was no doubt with Farrow yesterday when she was escorted into the school on her first day, but I don't want him around her alone.

I crane my neck, trying to see if he goes in, but I can't tell. I can't see the door from here.

But he disappears from my sight, and he doesn't come back. There was no one else with him.

Hurrying to my closet, I yank a T-shirt off the hanger, pull it on, and then push down my lounge pants and pull on some jeans. Slipping into a hoodie, I don't bother to deal with my hair before I put on some socks and shoes and bolt out of my bedroom.

There's not one good fucking reason for Constin to be there alone with her.

I race out of the house and slam the door, damn near leaping down the steps.

He's not standing at her door.

And he's not on the street.

He's inside.

I launch up her porch stairs, twist the door handle, finding it unlocked. I swallow the bitching I'm going to do at her later and step inside.

A dish clangs in the kitchen, and I charge through the living room, gaping at them both standing next to the sink.

What the fuck?

Dylan's eyes meet mine, and Constin turns, following her gaze.

She stands there in a tank top and blue-and-white-checkered boxer shorts. Boxer shorts? Are those hers?

My heavy breathing is the only sound. "What are you doing?" I finally ask.

I don't know if I'm talking to her or him, but I'm looking at her. She's barely dressed.

Her expression is soft, a gentle smile pulling at the corners of her mouth. "He's giving me a ride to school."

Constin grins.

I take a step. "Get out."

This time I'm looking at him. I don't know him as well as Farrow knows him, but I know enough, and he treats everyone like shit. He's not taking her anywhere alone.

"Go," I bark.

Dylan moves around him, addressing me. "Are you kidding me?"

But this isn't her decision.

"Out!" I growl at Constin.

He swaggers past me, throwing me a look, and I know I probably can't make him leave, but he's not going to be left alone with her like he planned now.

He walks out the front door, and Dylan throws out her arms. "Why do men suddenly think women didn't survive at all before their arrival into their lives?"

I close the distance between us. "He just walked into your house?"

"He could've come in any time while we were both asleep last night!"

"And that's probably true!" I shout. "It doesn't seem like you know how to lock a door!"

He could get past a lock if he really wanted to, but that's not the point.

"Go get dressed!" I yell down at her.

She scowls back up at me. "I need a shower!"

She marches past me and stomps up the stairs, and I glare at her back as she goes.

She disappears into her bedroom, and I cross my arms over my chest, standing in the foyer below. When she comes out again, she's wrapped in a towel, and I watch her cross the hallway and throw me a glower as she kicks open the door to the bathroom.

I stand guard the entire time.

She pouts all the way to school. She glares at me in Forensics. Ignores me in the hallway. Snarls on her way to P.E.

Every time I look at her, she looks away, and I struggle not to laugh, because it reminds me of when we were kids. The little spats we'd get into that always bummed me out because I hated her being mad at me. Now I realize if she's mad, she cares. I can still piss her off. Good to know.

"You want to go to the homecoming dance?" someone asks during lunch.

I turn back to the lunch table, seeing Arlet in Farrow's abandoned seat, except she sits on the table with her shoes propped up in his chair.

"You didn't ask anyone else." She peels an orange, her red hair swept over to one side of her head. "I'd like to go with you."

I glance over at Dylan, sitting at a long rectangular table to my left. She's alone, acting like she's preoccupied with her phone and that I can't see her periodically looking up to watch me.

"You don't need to babysit your cousin that night," Arlet tells me.

A couple sits at the end of Dylan's table, the girl dressed in a makeshift Pirates cheerleading uniform as she bounces on top of her boyfriend.

I narrow my eyes, hearing him chant, "pirate girl, aw yeah, pirate girl" as the young woman laughs.

"She'll be back in the Falls by then anyway," Arlet goes on. "To her own homecoming."

Another guy comes up, pawing the cheerleader's breasts while she moans, as if Pirate Girls love to be sexually harassed.

I start to stand, forgetting Arlet, but then a guy is behind Dylan, emptying a bottle of water into her lap. She flies up from her seat and shoves him in the chest, and I throw my chair back, running over.

The whole room erupts into cheers and chants as Dylan attacks and the dude grabs her by the collar. I'm there, pushing him away from her as the teachers rush in.

I wrap my arms around my cousin's thighs, picking her up and feeling the water on her jeans seep through my hoodie. "I got her," I tell Mr. Green before he has a chance to say anything.

I carry her back to my table.

"Let me go," she grits through her teeth.

The excitement dies down, and I pull my chair back in, sitting and plopping her down in my lap.

"Let me go!" she shouts this time.

I pull my tray in and secure my arms around her waist. "Eat," I tell her.

I'm not letting her go to retrieve her own tray.

But she glares. "I'm not hungry."

"If you don't eat," I tease. "I'm not giving you your surprise."

My table goes quiet, Calvin, Mace, Arlet, Farrow, and Constin all listening. Dylan stares at me but keeps her mouth shut.

I quirk a smile. "We're going to sneak into the Falls tonight and get your good luck charm."

Laughter and snorts go off around the table. "Really?" Calvin asks me.

But Dylan frowns a little, looking guilty. "We'll have to sneak really well," she warns.

I cock my head.

She grabs my apple and lifts it to her mouth. "I left it at your house."

The table erupts in squeals, someone pounding on the table in excitement.

PIRATES

CHAPTER NINE

Dylan

I think I made a mistake.

I grip both handlebars, revving the engine. "It can just be you and me," I tell Hunter. "Not everyone has to come."

He tosses gear into the trunk of his car, Farrow and Constin running down the steps of Hunter's brownstone, and all of them ready to make a full-blown invasion.

"It's Rivalry Week," he says, as if that explains it.

I clench my teeth and pull my helmet off the back of my bike. Or the bike Farrow gave me. Thankfully, he retrieved it from Phelan's Throat.

When Hunter said '*we're* going to sneak...' I thought he meant him and me. Us, together. I thought we'd be alone for a little while.

But he's determined not to chance running into Kade without backup.

Sure, they'll fight. And they'll probably fight a dozen more times about what, I'm not sure, but eventually, the yelling will stop, and they'll talk. I just know that nothing will change if they don't *see* each other.

Mace and Coral climb on bikes, Mace riding her own. Arlet lingers on the other side of Hunter's car.

"Shouldn't we wait until like ten or something?" I press. "People will still be out on the streets."

"It's Rivalry Week," he says again.

He doesn't think Kade will be home. It's only after seven, and after dinner, Kade often heads back out with friends, or whoever he's dating.

Hunter will be able to slip into the house with me, grab the necklace, and get out before anyone's the wiser. But just in case, he's bringing the whole motley crew and hey, they may snap some pictures or video to post online and brag that they snuck into the Shelburne Falls mayor's house, with me helping them do it.

Arlet flashes a look to me and then approaches Hunter. "I'll ride with you," she tells him.

He slams the trunk shut and nods, not looking at her. She was the one close to him in the lunchroom on Monday. Are they together?

She hops in the car, and he moves toward the driver's side. He looks over the hood at me, but I speak up before he can tell me what to do. "I'll meet you there," I say.

He tips his chin at me, and everyone takes off, Hunter climbing into his car. I see him adjust the rearview mirror as I pull on my helmet.

He shoots off down the street, after his friends, and I grab hold of my handlebars, flipping up the kickstand.

But as soon as he rounds the corner, racing off out of sight, I kill the engine and pull off my helmet. Taking out my phone, I dial Kade.

"You okay?" he asks.

"They're heading to your house."

He's quiet for a moment, and I hear music and a dozen conversations going on in the background. Sounds like he's at Rivertown.

"They..." he murmurs. "Is Hunter with them?"

"Yeah."

"Good."

He hangs up, and I tuck my phone away again, slipping on my helmet. That probably wasn't the nicest thing to do, but Hunter's plan had a predictable outcome. Now it doesn't.

And the Rebels are forgetting... I'm still a Pirate.

Squeezing the handles, I speed off, my engine reverberating through Knock Hill before descending down into the mill district. I turn onto River Road, speeding past fishermen and crumbling boathouses. When I curve left, onto the same bridge I crossed Sunday night, I hesitate only a moment before I dig in my pocket for a coin and flip it over the side, down to the sunken car. *Pay to pass.*

I wonder if anyone ever dives down to rob her ghost. There has to be a couple of hundred dollars down there, considering I never see anyone pay in pennies. As if the more you pay, the more good grace you'll buy. It doesn't make sense, though. To give a pirate girl that much reverence. I wonder how the tradition started at all.

Exiting the bridge, I turn left, and run parallel to the river again, keeping my speed down since I don't have my license on me.

Plus, I want to keep the Rebels far enough ahead so that they've turned right off High Street, toward the Caruthers' house, before they see me head in the opposite direction. My necklace was never at Hunter and Kade's house. I simply wanted to get them together, but since Hunter decided to bring everyone, he can walk into the ambush I have no doubt Kade will have waiting.

Making my way into town, I slow a little, on the lookout for my parents' cars. I pass Rivertown, not seeing Kade's truck or any of his friends, which means they've bolted to his house already to head off Hunter.

I race by the unremarkable expanse of red brick between Rivertown and Frosted, Quinn's bakery, only me and a handful of other people knowing the old speakeasy that hides between the two businesses. Quinn doesn't know yet. Rivertown's owner doesn't know. Hunter doesn't know.

Reaching the *Stop* sign, I see no sight of the Rebels and swing left, kicking it up a gear, and then another. I quickly cut a sharp right into the empty school parking lot.

The moon gleams white off the second-story windows, and I race around the stadium, skidding to a halt in front of the same door that Aro and I broke into on Sunday night.

Parking, I hop off the bike and dig in my pocket for a pick set. *Please, please, please...* Reaching the door, I slide the pieces in, find the lever, and hold my breath as I nudge it. I twist the handle, the door opens, and I smile at how proud Aro would be.

Slipping the tools back into my pocket, I whip open the door and step inside with a little spin, closing it behind me. I jog down the hall, opening the flashlight on my phone and pushing into the locker room. I move toward Aro's and my locker, dialing in the combination and opening the black steel door. I flash my light on the green ribbon and grab the necklace with a fossil of my mom's childhood thumbprint that no one ever actually wears. I stuff it into my jeans pocket and slam the locker door, running back the way I came in.

I grip the locker room door handle and yank.

But it doesn't open.

My heart skips.

I pull harder. "What the fuck?" I whisper.

I tug again and again, the locker room door I just came in through is now locked.

I press my ear to the door, hearing the squeak of someone's shoes against the floor on the other side.

"Hey!" I call out. "Hello!"

Is a janitor still here? Maybe they're just closing up.

I grab the handle with both hands, growling as I try to wrench the door free. "Please..."

My phone starts ringing with notifications. Then a buzz.

"Hello?" I yell as I pound my fist against the door. "Let me out!"

A low, distant howl echoes followed by laughter from a separate voice.

"Who's there?" I cry out. "What's going on?"

My phone goes off, one beep after another, and I pull it out, scrolling through.

I tap on a pic of me running through the school just minutes ago, and while it's blurry, it's unmistakable. The caption reads *B&E*.

Breaking and Entering. It's posted from an account I don't recognize. The location: Shelburne Falls High School.

I expel all my breath, closing my eyes for a moment. "Shit."

Whirling around, I flee to the other end of the locker room, bolt through the door to the gym, and run across the basketball court.

I barrel through the door, into the school hallway, and past the display cases with all the alumni shit, memories, and throwback lockers.

But I notice a blue line spray-painted down the glass case. I slow, letting my gaze trail farther down, seeing that it continues across the office doors and over the walls.

My stomach sinks. My phone continues to buzz and beep.

"Oh, no." I stop, taking in the blue swirls and the Xs sprayed over all the players' pictures on the bulletin board. "No, no, no…"

They followed me.

They didn't go to Hunter's house.

Laughter echoes from down one of the side hallways as red and blue lights flash in my peripheral. I whip around, seeing two cop cars race across the parking lot and hear a door slam shut far off to my left.

"Shit," I mouth, closing my eyes.

I run, hearing engines—one of them definitely Hunter's car—start up and peel away. Chasing after them, I crash through the back door, seeing the police cars cruising alongside the football field.

Toward me.

Bile crawls up my throat. I'm going to be grounded for life.

Dammit. I scurry to my bike and climb on, speeding away. Their sirens scream into the air when they see me making my escape. I don't know what the hell I'm doing, but I'm not ready to surrender.

I dart out of the parking lot, spotting the security camera on the lamp post above.

And I just gave it a nice, full view of my goddamn face. *Awesome.*

I jerk away, coasting left and racing back onto High Street. But then I make a sharp right and then another immediate left, speeding into the alleyway behind Frosted.

I hide the bike between two dumpsters and pull out my keys, letting myself in the back door of Quinn's shop. I hide inside, safe in the darkness.

This is going to be too much for my parents. They'll force me to come home.

I run my fingers through my hair, gripping tightly right before I reel my foot back to kick one of her metal kitchen cabinets. But I stop short. I don't want to dent it. I've done enough damage tonight.

Drifting into the front customer area, I take out my phone and scroll pictures of me, texts, comments...

Ur over!!!!

We'll get her when she comes back.

Loyal to whoever shows her attention...

A laugh escapes me that kind of sounds like a little bit of a sob. "Seriously?"

Is that what people think? That I traded sides and actually vandalized my own school? That I'm so desperate to belong?

My eyes fill with tears, but I don't let them fall. I'm not quite there yet. I squeeze my phone in my fist, pacing back and forth, but then Farrow bursts through the doors from the kitchen, followed by his entourage.

I throw my phone at him and charge, leaping up and losing my mind as I throw pathetic punches. He slams me down on one of the round tables for customers, prying my arms and legs off of him. I roll off the table, landing on my feet and glaring at all of them, including Hunter who leans against the wall behind the counter. His arms are folded over his chest, his eyes amused.

"Vandalizing schools now?" I growl.

"What did you think they were going to do to my house when you tried to lure everyone there instead?"

I wasn't trying to lure everyone there. I was trying to lure *him* there. Bringing the Rebels was his idea.

His eyes sharpen. "Was Kade waiting for us?"

"A lot was waiting, I'm sure," I retort.

Sure. I warned Kade they were coming, which I wouldn't have done if it were just Hunter coming. That's Hunter's fault.

And it's mine that I underestimated him.

"How am I supposed to keep the cops from arresting me?" I ask.

"It's Rivalry Week," he says yet again. "They expect this."

One of my eyebrows shoots up. He got arrested right along with Kade, Hawke, and me when we half-buried someone's car on Weston's football field more than a year ago. It was property damage. Same as this. Our parents got us out of it. They might not again.

Finally, he shrugs. "I'll call my dad. You'll be fine."

"She won't be fine." Farrow looks at me when he says it, though. "The Pirates will never trust her again. Not completely."

I glare at all of them—T.C., Anders, Luca, Calvin, Constin, Farrow, and Hunter. "I have ten days to turn this around. I can still make your life hell before I leave."

"You're never leaving."

But it's not Farrow who says it. Or Hunter.

"They don't want you," Constin tells me. "We do."

I stare at him, everyone else falling silent. I'm never leaving? So what, if I try, they'll kill me and keep my body in Weston forever like Winslet?

"You don't want me," I tell them. "You want a Pirate. You don't give a shit about me. You don't even know me—"

The alarm goes off and everyone jumps.

But I don't. "I forgot to disengage the alarm," I say. "Hunter knows the code."

He hoods his eyes and pushes off the wall, everyone following him into the kitchen to cut the alarm before the cops show up.

I back up quickly, while everyone is out of sight, and spin around, feeling behind the frame of the mirror for the latch. I press it, the mirror clicking open, and I slip inside, smoothly closing the secret entrance to the old, hidden speakeasy. I stand on the other side of the glass, hearing the alarm go silent as I tap out a text to Kade.

Frosted.

One by one, everyone slips back through the kitchen door, into the bakery, and Calvin whirls around, looking for me.

"Where'd she go?" he shouts. He runs to the front door of the store, yanking on it, but it's locked.

Hunter steps back into the shop, his eyes slowly drifting around for me.

I stand there, watching them look right over me, only a thin piece of glass between us.

Quinn almost had the mirror removed when she bought the place. What a weird thing to have in a bakery anyway. Especially a mirror rising from nearly floor to ceiling—same size as a door.

But Hawke, after realizing what was here, stopped her before she looked too closely. And before a contractor could try to pry it off.

Then, when she wanted the old wallpaper peeled away, Hawke volunteered himself for the job. He repaired the drywall, primed, and painted. She never concerned herself with it again.

He'll tell her, of course, but Quinn is a rule-follower. He wants me to be eighteen, and a legal adult, before I get up to whatever trouble she thinks I might get up to in here. Otherwise, she might tell our parents about our hideout.

I'm not sure when Hawke planned on telling Hunter, but as Hunter's eyes stop on the mirror and he steps closer and closer to me, looking like he's barely breathing, I'm a little worried Hawke might not need to.

I might not be able to watch Kade show up, after all.

Behind him, his friends look behind the counter and under the tables as Calvin twists the deadbolt and peers outside. Hunter remains still, his frame filling the mirror.

I watch his eyes glide around the perimeter. Placing his fingertips against the glass, he presses, but it doesn't give way.

He knows, though. It's only a matter of time before—

Just then, my phone rings in my hand, and I suck in a breath as Hunter's eyes widen. Kade's name appears on my screen just as Hunter's gaze sharpens, knowing I'm here. I don't know if the others have caught on yet, but I don't wait to find out.

I rush through Carnival Tower, down the steps, into the great room with a kitchen and common area, and climb the spiral staircase to the roof. Lifting the hatch, I slip through and let it slam shut.

God, I'm in so much trouble. Hawke's going to kill me if the Rebels suspect there's a hideout there.

Racing across the roof, I leap down the fire escape and jump to the ground, scurrying back into the alleyway again. Heart punching through my chest, I climb back on my bike and start the engine.

"She's outside!" I hear someone shout from inside the bakery.

I ride away, fast down High Street, back toward Weston. A group of guys outside Rivertown look up at me, and I check my rearview mirror, seeing them scurry into their brand-new Mazda 3, but there are already two other pairs of headlights on me.

One of them is probably Hunter.

Go, I growl inwardly. I accelerate, whipping down the highway and then left onto Frontage Road, heading for the bridge. Should I be going to Weston? They just framed me for vandalism.

But I don't think I can stay in the Falls, either. Which— it just occurs to me—was probably their whole plan. I don't want to go home yet.

I cut right, kicking into a high gear and flying across the bridge. Horns honk behind me, and I feel them on my ass. I can hear their engines gaining closer and closer, and I hit a pothole, skidding off the bridge. I gasp, putting my foot out and dragging it on the ground to keep the bike upright.

My phone vibrates with notifications, and I know I hear two cars slam into each other behind me. I race off, the rumble of a truck right on my tail, and I whimper, but at the same time, I want to laugh. My stomach somersaults a thousand times a minute, and if I live through this, it'll be the most fun I ever had.

If I don't, it'll be the stupidest thing I've ever done.

A horn belts out a piercing screech, and shouts fill the air as people lean out their windows. "You can't hide!"

A car races up to my side and closes in. I scream, swerve, and plummet into another pothole, my phone slipping out of my pocket and falling onto the river bank as I bounce over the shoulder of the road. I fly into the air as water gleams below and suck in a breath as I crash into the river.

I sink beneath the surface, squeezing my eyes shut, and shoving off my helmet. My bike plummets, and I kick and push with my arms, but something tugs at my jacket, stopping me. I look down and start screaming, my imagination going wild, and I'm sure that it's Winslet's ghost. I grab where my clothing is caught, but it's just the handlebar. I get dragged down with my bike, struggling to free myself, and then something else crashes through the water, and I see Hunter.

He yanks the hoodie over my head and lets it go. It follows the bike to the muddy depths below, and I swim for the surface, gasping for breath.

I blink away the water in my eyes, Hunter at my side, and look to the empty riverbank.

Everyone who just tried to kill me is gone.

I ball my fists over and over again, shivering under the hot water as it soaks my icy clothes.

Congrats, Dylan. Everyone hates you now.

As if they didn't already.

For my family, I'm something to handle. For Kade, someone to tolerate. To the Pirates, I'm a girl taking up too much space. And to the Rebels, I'm a toy. Maybe even Aro's only kind to me because of Hawke.

I peel off my flannel and drop it on the shower floor, hearing it slosh like a wet mop. My teeth chatter and locks of wet hair hang in my eyes as I hug myself over my tank top and jeans.

All the Rebels are no doubt congratulating themselves. They're probably down in the street, watching the front door in hopes of seeing me run out and back to the Falls.

I squeeze my fists again so tight my nails dig into my palms.

I'm alone here. I'm alone at home.

The shower curtain whips open and I dart my eyes up, seeing Hunter glaring down at me.

"I don't want you here," I tell him.

But he steps into the stall anyway, wearing fresh, dry jeans as he squats down in front of me, getting wet again. "I'm the reason you didn't drown tonight."

"You're the reason for all of this," I try to shout at him, but my throat is thick with tears.

He's supposed to be on my side. Not Pirates or Rebels. *My* side. What the hell did I ever do to him? He cut me off. He'll barely speak to me now.

Steam billows around us and everything blurs in my view. Does he have any idea how hard it's been at home? What made him think I wouldn't miss him? This is *all* his fault.

"You were my *best* friend," I say, tearing up. "Did you know that?"

I search his green eyes. They never used to look like his twin brother's, though. Hunter's were always a little bigger, as if he were either perpetually in wonder of something or waiting for something.

Now, they're angry. They're always formidable.

"I don't have very many friends," I tell him, in case he gives a shit. "They talk about me behind my back at school. They're nice to my face, but they think I'm a joke."

He narrows his eyes.

"Did you know that?" I ask.

He says nothing.

I swallow through the needles in my throat. People all but pat me on the head and think my entire personality is some phase that I'll grow out of.

"And you keep looking at me like you hate me," I whisper, my cheeks burning under his scowl. "I didn't do anything wrong."

I care about him. I care what he thinks. He's not just anybody. He's a part of me. Our fathers are only stepbrothers, but that never mattered.

"Why do you hate me?" I ask. "I needed you. There were so many times when I was dying to tell you things."

"Tell Kade."

"I wanted to tell you!" I shout.

Why is he trying to insert me into his and Kade's bullshit? We're not a package deal. This is about him and me. No one else.

I know him best.

Or I did.

He was good.

Creative. Generous.

Why is he different now?

"I love you," I tell him.

He sucks in a short, shallow breath.

The shower spills over his shoulders, down his chest, and the steam wets his hair. His gaze doesn't falter, though.

"There's no one like you." I smile a little as I soften my voice. "You're always reading five books at a time. You buy Christmas presents for other people's pets. You never eat bread crust. Like even if it's a hamburger bun, you'll invent a crust that isn't there..."

Like, seriously. He leaves a crescent of bread. Even on a hot dog bun.

"You tell me everything I missed when I come back from the bathroom at a movie theater," I point out.

My brother hates it when I do that.

"And you hate it as much as I do," I add, "when people eat while talking on TikTok videos, and then they make you wait while they take more bites and chew. It's so obnoxious, right?"

Amusement rises in his eyes.

"I can hear your smiles when you talk," I say. "I love that all of my baseball caps were once yours, and I love that you look for me." I pause. "Or you used to."

Maybe I didn't realize all of this when he was around—or realize how much I'd miss him—but I always knew I loved him. He and Kade were never one person. It wasn't both or nothing. They were always distinguishable from each other. I need Hunter.

"It seems I'm always chasing something." I shake my head, thinking about home and school. "Other cars on the track. My parents with their busy schedules. School..." I meet his eyes. "I used to wake up as a kid and you'd be asleep next to me. You'd just show up at some point through the night. I never felt unwanted. You looked for me when you walked into a room." I lower my voice. "Me."

My parents love me, but they don't count. I've been homesick for him since he left.

I stare at his face, seeing the slight way his right eye zones in on me more than the left, because he doesn't want to stay mad, but he's trying hard to.

His stern jaw that looks more angular than it did when we were twelve.

His eyebrows and how they got a little darker. His bottom lip and how it's fuller than I remember. I gaze at it.

I used to know everything about him. Now, it's like I've missed so much.

He's kissed girls. I know he has.

They look at him at school. A lot.

I should know about girlfriends, right? Those are things he should be telling me because we're close. Or we used to be.

I should know who and when and how far he's gone. I should know everything about him.

I clench my jaw. Girls at that roller skating restaurant looked at him like I wasn't standing right there. I mean, it's not like they need my permission or anything, but I just...

I...

It's like...

It's just...

I...

I just don't like it.

The words crawl up my throat, but I'm almost too scared to think them, let alone say them. *He's mine.*

I grind my teeth together.

He has a tan left over from summer that still makes his neck and chest look golden, the veins in his hands and arms course just underneath the skin. His muscles are bigger now because he spent the summer getting ready to face Kade on the field this season.

His fingers are still the same, though—long, like an artist's.

It makes them good at holding a football too, I guess.

"We've slept in the same bed a hundred times and taken baths together," I laugh under my breath. "I've spent more of my waking hours with you than anyone. You're in all of my history, Hunter."

"History..." he murmurs. "Yes."

He says it as if I meant something bad by it.

My heart starts to ache, but he rises, looking down at me. "Things have changed, Dylan. We can't be friends anymore."

"Why?" I leap to my feet. "Nothing has changed."

"Everything has changed!" he snaps. "We're not kids anymore. When are you going to grow up?"

I recoil like I'm being hammered into the dirt. I'm not grown up? He's the one who ran away.

I drop my eyes, seeing his jeans, soaked again, and his bare feet on the tile. Why does anything have to change?

I stare at his waist as water spills off his belt that hangs open. The top button of his jeans is open too. I force down the lump in my throat.

I was sixteen the last time I had my arms around his waist. What changed in only a couple of years?

"You want everything to be how it used to be?" he asks. "You think we can still play? Like we used to? Really?"

"Can't we?"

I still like to climb trees.

"Aren't we too old?" he asks.

I shake my head. "We can still race bikes. It's just motorcycles now. Right?"

A faint smile crosses his lips.

"Explore caves?" he presses. "Roller blade? Dive for swim rings? Hide and seek?"

"Build a fort?" I say, starting to smile. "Water balloons?"

See? He's getting the hang of it again. I'll remind him of how fun we were together.

But then he takes a step toward me and reaches out, placing one hand on the shower wall and the other on the shower rod, his chest splayed in front of me. My heart thuds hard in my chest.

"Take a bath?" he adds.

My chest caves. *Take a bath…*

Like we used to.

I hold Hunter's eyes, his steady, hard gaze unblinking, and I barely notice the music pumping from the first floor of the house.

He's testing me. Trying to get me to fold. Trying to make me angry. To make me cry or pout or run.

The pulse in my neck throbs, but I don't get mad.

I don't run.

The skin of my nipples tightens under my tank top.

And I watch as he pulls the curtain closed, shielding us both inside.

REBELS

CHAPTER TEN

Hunter

Her lips tremble. "People are here. Downstairs."

"Yeah." I release the curtain, not taking my eyes off of her. "They're partying. And in the street." I lower my voice. "No one will come in here, though."

A lump moves down her throat, and I drop my eyes to the pink bra strap laying over her arm, having fallen off her shoulder.

"I just..." She flexes her jaw. "I want things to go back to how they were."

"And I told you they can't." I step closer. "If you didn't think so, too, you'd be naked and washing already."

We've grown up. Everything is different. I've always loved her, but now...

Her gaze flits to me and then down, and I can see her chest rising with big breaths. I should just let her off the hook. I knew she would fold. I didn't actually want to trick her into a shower together, but...

She crosses her arms at her waist, grabs the hem of her tank top, and lifts it over her head. Raising her eyes to me, she tilts up her defiant little chin and drops the shirt to the floor. A gleam brightens her eyes.

It takes everything not to smile back because my heart is swimming and my body is stirring at everything I see, even as I keep my eyes pinned to her face. The pink of the lace—like bubblegum. The golden skin of her stomach and her chest, and her breasts held in cups with flowery trim. Nothing like I thought Dylan would wear.

A lock of hair snakes over her collarbone, down her pretty skin, and I finally lower my eyes, watching it curl over her breast, the flesh underneath looking soft and full.

"You next," she says.

I meet her eyes again. "My shirt's already off."

I let a small smile out now, and to her credit, she doesn't fight me. As she unfastens her jeans, I feel my groin ache with heat, watching her push her pants down her thighs, and then shimmy a little until they drop to the shower floor.

I almost groan, but I close my mouth and force my breathing to slow as she steps out of them, shoving them to the side with her foot. Her black underwear looks like the bottom half of a string bikini, connected just below her hips on both sides with a thin strap. In my head, I hear it rip in my hand.

It takes a moment, but when she just stands there, I remember it's finally my turn. I pull open my fly and drop my pants, almost wishing I weren't wearing briefs. I feel more vulnerable than if I'd just gone for broke and shocked the hell out of her by wearing absolutely nothing underneath. I don't look down to see what she sees. I know I'm hard. I can feel it trying to grow through the fabric.

"Have you ever seen a naked girl before?" she asks me. "I mean, other than the ones who play against the cars with Farrow and the other guys?"

"Yeah."

Her eyes falter. "Who?"

I tip my head back, wetting my hair. "The first one or the last one?"

Her big eyes narrow, and she frowns. I keep my smile contained.

She's the only one I've ever seen naked, other than Weston's public displays.

She reaches behind her back, unclasping her bra.

I tilt my head back up, my arms weak as I smooth my hair back over the top of my head and watch her.

"You don't have a girlfriend right now, do you?" she asks me as she works the hooks.

I watch the straps on her shoulder, waiting for them to go lax. Do I have a girlfriend? *No.* I shake my head.

The pink bra loosens, and she peels it off, her breasts spilling out for me. I suck in a breath, and the bra disappears. I don't know where.

"No one's ever seen me naked," she whispers.

Jesus, she's beautiful. Pink nipples already hard, the curves of her flesh perfect, and I'm dying to touch her. I want to feel her in my hands.

Dylan stands there, steam billowing around her wet skin, and she starts to raise her arms but then lowers them again, resisting the instinct to cover herself.

I've seen her naked before, but this is the first time she's aware of it.

And she's giving it to *me*.

I lower my eyes, suddenly guilty. This was all a game. A bluff. She shouldn't have given this to me.

But she never runs when she should. Dylan is childish and defiant and frustrating, but she's pure. What you see is what you get, and she just wants us all to be happy. Nothing she does ever comes from a bad intention. She would give you the clothes on her back.

I shouldn't be fucking with her right now.

But I don't want to leave.

"Can you turn around?" I ask her.

She does, and I push the rest of my clothes off, stepping up to her and stopping within an inch. She slips her panties down her legs, and after our clothes are forgotten and the water runs hot around us, I look down at her ass and my dick throbbing for her.

"Sorry I don't have any bath toys," I joke.

"I do."

It's just a murmur, but I hear it, and it takes a moment to process what she means. I exhale a laugh. "Seriously?"

She has a vibrator?

"Seriously," she says. "It's waterproof. Aro and I bought them online one night on a high of rum."

She reaches over to the dish and grabs a new bar of soap. I take it from her, wetting her washcloth and soaping it up. I hand both to her over her shoulder, tempted to wash her myself.

"I haven't even opened it." She continues facing away from me, rubbing the cloth over her breasts slowly. I stare down over her shoulder, watching her.

"I was so nervous when it came in the mail," she whispers. "I thought the box might read *Giant Vibrating Penis* on the side."

I chuckle, despite the ache in my groin. Her dad would not handle that well. I grab the soap from her and start running it over my chest.

"I haven't had a chance to try it out with no one in the house yet." Her soapy fingers massage her breasts before gliding down to her stomach. "I just hid it in my hope chest."

"Your hope chest..."

I remember that. A huge treasure trunk that sits at the foot of her bed and holds her dreams. Traditionally, girls back in the day put things in there to start a home with their husbands when they got married. Linens, china, family photos.

Dylan, daughter of Tatum Brandt, was never taught to do that. She used it to hold her secrets. Pictures of her celebrity crushes, a Mercedes hood ornament she ripped off the car of the doctor who stole her mom's promotion at the hospital when Dylan was thirteen, and her bloody bandages sealed in a Ziploc bag from skinning her arm in her first motorcycle accident that her parents never found out about.

She also kept pictures of places she wanted to go, notes she and her friends passed in class, and the ashes of Madman, her parents' beloved dog. Their honorary "first born."

I don't know what she keeps in there now. I mean, other than a sex toy.

"Aro says an orgasm from a vibrator is ten times better than one from my fingers," she tells me. "I'm hoping that's true."

The soap pops right out of my fist and falls to the floor. *Jesus, Dylan.* My heart tries to beat a hole out of my chest. *What the hell?*

Images of her in her room at home—in her bed that I've crashed in a hundred times—sweep through my head, and I feel like I'm sweating. I draw in a deep breath, but I can't breathe in here.

"Can I turn around now?" she asks.

She starts to twist, but I close the distance between us, pressing my chest into her back and stopping her.

Unfortunately, it's not just my chest pressing into her, though. She freezes.

I tremble. *Shit*. I didn't want her to see it, but she definitely fucking feels it.

"Are you...hard?" she asks softly.

"Yeah."

She moves just a hair, like she's about to turn, but she doesn't. I grab the shampoo and squeeze some on top of her head and then on mine.

"Don't read anything into it," I tell her. "I'm eighteen. It's hard all the time."

The corner of her mouth reveals a smile. "Can I see it?"

I don't reply. Instead, I pull her back with me a few steps, using the shower to lather up her hair. I rub her scalp with both hands.

No one's ever seen me. I don't know if I want mine to be the first one that she sees, either.

"Do you remember that week of snow days we had, like four years ago?" she asks me, her head moving as I scrub. "It was in February, I think?"

"I remember." We had four days off from school in a row. Trees were down, some homes in the rural areas were out of power.

"I hated it," she gripes. "The extra time off school only meant we'd have to make up the days, which would cut into our summer vacation, but..." She pauses. "More than that, I was sick of the snow. It was bitter cold. Everything was wet all the time. The world sounded dead because no one was outside."

I sink my fingers into her locks, vaguely remembering how bored she got that year. I couldn't care less about being outside. She and Kade both needed to feel the wind. Not me.

"It was gray everywhere," she continues. "Gray smoke from the chimneys. Gray snow from greasy cars and tires. I wanted to swim. Ride our bikes. Smell my dad's grill in the neighborhood."

I tug her backward a little, guiding her head back and rinsing her hair. I watch the suds cascade over her ass and down her thighs.

I lower my mouth to her hair, closing my eyes. *Fuck.*

"So you told me," she goes on, unaware of how turned on I am. "You told me 'to make it beautiful.'"

I said what?

She continues, "You said there was a way to find beauty in almost anything. To think about things I like and apply them to how I see. To frame it in a way I find alluring."

Huh, I did say that, didn't I?

"You pointed out that I loved nighttime and the tree outside my bedroom window and how it made noises in a breeze," she says, "and you reminded me that I liked to sneak around and loved to see new things."

Yeah, by the time we were fourteen, I knew everything about Dylan.

I run my hands down her hair, smoothing out the remaining soap.

"And then you snuck me out of the house that night." Her voice sounds like she's smiling. "Took me to Blackhawk Lake, and we shared sips of your dad's Jägermeister, while we laid in the snow. We listened to the winter wind sweep through the bare, black branches that stretched up into the night sky. I heard the creaking sound of the wood that I never noticed in the summer, because I only hear the leaves rustling or the birds singing." She drops her head, slowly rubbing the soap off her hands. "But when they're gone in the winter, you can hear the icicles. See the way they shimmer in the moonlight and how scary the quiet is."

I don't remember telling her any of that. Guess the Jäger was a good idea, after all.

"Or you said to just smile to change my perspective," she adds. "You said if you smile, something is already more beautiful because you're looking at something with kind eyes."

Definitely sounds like something weird I would've said when I was that age.

"I started to understand that's why you had your headphones on so much back then. Music makes things beautiful too."

I slow my hands on her hair. My dad was always on my case for shutting out the world with those headphones.

But...

"You've been practicing making something beautiful in your head for a long time, haven't you?" she asks me. "And it worked, until it didn't anymore."

A lump seizes my throat.

She's right.

I don't think I even realized what I was doing back then until she said it just now, but the headphones helped me love the world around me. It set my mood. I needed them a lot.

Eventually, though, they weren't enough. I had to leave.

She turns her face a little. "Can I turn around now?"

I'm still hard.

"Your eyes will be kind," she says in almost a whisper, and I realize she's nervous about me seeing her too.

I clasp her upper arm, nudging her around to face me.

Our eyes meet, but not for long. Her gaze trails down my chest, and the closer she gets, the harder I become.

She licks her lips and inhales deep as she takes me in, and in the inches between our bodies, I soak her up. I take my time because she's letting me.

Droplets of water dot her breasts, making it look like sweat, and I know the curve of her waist would fit my hand perfectly. I lower my gaze to her flat tummy and the thin strip of hair between her legs.

I frown.

It doesn't grow like that. She's getting waxed. Why?

My mom has been very vocal that she only endures that hardship for my dad's sake.

I relax, though. She says no one has ever seen her naked, so I know it's not for a boyfriend.

"Do you ever rub one out?"

I shoot my eyes back up to hers, processing her question.

Rub one out? Do I ever masturbate? Is she kidding?

I arch a brow, and she chuckles, rolling her eyes at herself. "I mean, how *often* do you rub one out?"

I laugh, rubbing my jaw. "A...a lot," I finally reply. "You?"

Her cheeks get rosy, and she looks away shyly. "A lot."

My chest swells with a hundred fucking emotions. I can't believe we're talking about this.

She turns to the wall, propping her foot up on the ledge and grabbing her razor, running it up her leg. I can't take my eyes off the curve of her ass, her toned thigh, the water spilling down her body. She sees me looking, her gaze falling to my dick again. She opens her mouth, looks at me, closes it, and then opens it again. "Can I...?"

But she doesn't finish her question.

"What?" I press.

She shakes her head, looking away again. "Nothing."

What was she going to ask? If she could touch it?

I skim her body with my eyes again. She let me wash her hair. Maybe she'll let me watch her touch herself.

"What?" she asks.

I look up, realizing she's staring at me. I need to get out of here. I grab the towel over the rod and open the curtain. "Nothing."

I wrap the towel around my waist and step out.

She finishes and shuts off the shower, following me out. "Are you going to do it tonight?" she asks.

"What?"

She doesn't reply, and I look at her, waiting. Something mischievous lights in her eyes, and she glances to my dick again, now covered with the towel.

"Don't flatter yourself," I tell her, grabbing the only other towel off the shelf and handing it to her.

I want to masturbate. Badly. But I won't tell her that.

She smiles, happy enough to shoot her shot.

"Did you get the necklace?" I ask.

She nods, wrapping the towel around her body.

"Lock your doors, understand?" I pinch her chin, forcing her to pay attention. "There are eyes everywhere on this street, keeping an eye out for your safety, but that doesn't mean your old friends won't try to come for you."

Farrow will try to stop them, but not if he's passed out. She needs to lock up and be alert.

I take my phone off the sink counter and turn to open the door, but she speaks up. "I could sleep at your house," she says.

I look over my shoulder at her, heat pooling in my stomach. She's not safer in my house.

I narrow my eyes. "You stay here."

She shrugs, and I open the door, shuffling her through.

"There were some men's joggers in the closet when I got here. If you want them," she offers.

"Yeah." I follow her into the hallway, toward her room. I'd rather not walk outside in a towel.

But I only take three steps when I crash into her.

"Dylan, what are you doing?"

She's stopped in the hallway, and I follow her gaze to the first floor below.

Farrow, Calvin, and Constin stand in the foyer with beers, surrounded by other students talking and laughing as music plays. But nearly everyone's attention is on us as Calvin holds up his phone, filming.

"Goddammit," I growl.

I push Dylan across the hall and into her room, and then I swing back around the banister and charge.

"Delete it," I snap.

People scurry out of the way, girls squealing, some giggling as Calvin hurriedly types. "Just a minute..." he sings.

I back him into the wall, and he finishes posting, throwing up his hands in surrender.

"Give me the damn phone." I grab it out of his hand and press the *Power* button, but there's a code to unlock. I glare at him, slamming the phone back in his chest. "That's great. Thanks a lot."

At least one person has screenshot it by now, I'm sure.

In two seconds, my phone starts buzzing, and Farrow laughs. "Is it Kade?"

I look down, seeing Hawke's name. *Nope. Worse.* He's already seen the picture—a pic of Dylan and me, coming out of a bathroom half-naked together—and if he doesn't rip out every follicle of hair on my head, her dad will.

"Go!" I shout. "Everyone out!"

Farrow chuckles, leaning on his friends as everyone piles out into the street.

"Yeah, glad y'all are having fun!" I fire back, slamming the door behind them.

They just laugh louder.

My phone keeps ringing.

I hold the wheel with one hand, swiping the screen and ignoring my uncle Jax's second call with the other.

Hawke's called and texted, my mom's called, and I've gotten a slew of texts from Pirates. Nothing from Kade.

And nothing from Jared.

Perfect. It means he's still asleep and missing the action.

I shouldn't have been dumb enough to shower with her while people were in the house. It should've just been us.

Next time, it will be.

But I don't know if I could take it again. I need more. I need to see her with my hands. God, she's beautiful.

I cruise down Fall Away Lane, porch lights and lamp posts lit up to boast the beautiful orange, red, and yellow leaves on all of the trees. Lawns of green, with flower beds and small vegetable gardens, pepper the air with the scent of herbs and perfume, and a light stream of water coasts down the pristine gutter, emptying into the sewer.

There are parts of the Falls that aren't so clean, and parts that are wealthier, but while I loved my house growing up, I was always a little jealous of Dylan's neighborhood. Not just because these homes look like houses do on sitcoms, but also because you have friends who live next door. Or a few houses away, maybe. You have everything you need. Trees to climb. Streets to ride bikes.

And this was a perfect neighborhood for trick-or-treating in the fall and block parties in the summer.

Dylan grew up with people everywhere around her.

At my house, I'd just had Kade.

Which was great, until it wasn't.

I pull up to the curb on the other side of Dylan's house and shut off the engine. Gazing out my driver's side window, I take in the dark Trent house, except for the lanterns lit up on both sides of the front door, and a dim light coming through the living room window. It's the small light above the stove, streaming out all the way from the kitchen.

Jared's old Mustang Boss 302 sits in the driveway. It's not his only car, but it's still his favorite. He likes it to stay visible.

Checking down the street both ways, I climb out of the car and jog across the lane. I leap up onto the sidewalk and veer right, to the side of the house, avoiding the front door. Picking up the pace, I run hard toward the tree between Dylan's house and Hawke's, scaling the trunk in two giant leaps and hopping up onto the first thick branch. I crawl up another ten feet, glancing at Hawke's dark bedroom window. He's a first year at Clarke University and lives in the dorms.

But he's close if Dylan needs him.

I step in the opposite direction, toward the French doors of Dylan's bedroom, holding the branch above my head for support. We've been navigating this tree for almost our entire lives. Limbs have been trimmed, generations of squirrels have lived, it's survived storms, even a tornado when we were five, and nearly being cut down in a tantrum between Dylan's parents who grew up with this tree between their bedrooms too.

But every year, the leaves abound and not a branch breaks. I half-think Jared and Jax kept ownership of the houses just to keep the tree.

I open Dylan's French doors, always unlocked, and jump over the railing, landing inside. I cringe, hearing my heavy footfall echo through the house. I pause, listening.

After a few seconds and not seeing the hall light pop on from under her bedroom door, I lean over and pull open her hope chest.

I smile, still seeing a stack of magazines, but instead of celebrity crushes, they're motorcycle periodicals now. I lift them up, finding a box of trinkets underneath: Euro coins from when her mom took her to France, a few keys that even she probably doesn't remember what they go to, and a nearly full bottle of perfume.

There's a snow globe that I know she used to have sitting on her desk, and I see books and more books, and I lift the stack, seeing a paperback cover with a couple caught in a passionate embrace hiding underneath.

I lift a coffee table book of Route 66 and finally find what I'm looking for. My throat tightens as I pick up the clear package with the pink plastic vibrator inside. The shaft is long with an extra piece protruding at the base about half the length. Everything all at once starts happening to my body, and I know why I came here when I couldn't sleep after showering with her tonight. I want her to use this, and I want the first time to be in Weston. In that house.

I want her to have a lot of fun this weekend.

I start to close the hope chest, but I see a glint of silver and stop. Reaching down, I pluck out a steel ring with another chained to it. I hold up the handcuffs, recognizing the ones she mentioned at the bonfire Monday night. The ones I put on her and Kade several weeks ago when Farrow and the guys crashed Kade's party on Grudge Night.

She kept them.

And I still have the key.

I take them and the sex toy and quietly close the chest.

Holding everything in one hand, I climb back out through the French doors and close them behind me.

Twisting around, I suddenly spot a light and a girl in Hawke's window.

"So, you're Hunter," the brunette says.

She leans down a little, hands propped on the window above her head as she peers at me from Hawke's old room. I glance in, seeing soft grays and a furry pillow on the bed now.

"Aro Marquez," I say, realizing I still have a plastic, pink dick in my hand.

She looks like she's holding back a laugh.

I forgot that Hawke's girlfriend now lives with his parents—along with her younger brother and sister—while she finishes high school. Dylan texted me about her weeks ago.

"How's Mace?" she asks me.

"Scary."

Her smile widens. "Still?"

I nod once.

"And Codi?"

I start to make my way for the tree trunk to scale back down.

"Not great, but everyone's got her back," I tell her.

"Good."

It's nice of her to ask after Codi. The kid doesn't have much security, but everyone shows up for her.

I pause and look over at her. "How'd you know I wasn't Kade?"

She just holds my eyes, mischief playing in hers. "It's rechargeable." She jerks her chin at the vibrator in my hand. "In case you want to get it juiced up ahead of time."

Noted.

I drop down to the ground and run back to the car, tossing the toy and handcuffs onto the passenger seat.

Speeding away, I stop at the end of the lane and turn right, but when High Street comes up, I don't take the turn back toward Weston.

I pass it by, continuing down the road until it becomes a highway, the old familiar route amping me up with something between excitement and dread.

I cruise past my favorite pine tree with a base of branches that spreads out wider than my parents' living room, and see the trail where cross country skiers will be traveling in a couple of months. I speed into the quiet neighborhood of homes far bigger than Dylan's or Hawke's, and even though I was jealous of their neighborhoods and the close-knit surroundings, my home never felt any less cozy. And for a long time, it was just as happy.

I see the lanterns flickering at the end of my parents' driveway and pull over to the side of the road, turning off the car.

I get out and gaze across the street at the house my dad grew up in and his kids grew up in. A light dims and brightens again on the second floor, A.J. probably watching TV, while more rooms glow downstairs.

Kade's truck is parked in the driveway. It was ours, but it was always his. My parents are probably home, but they tuck their cars away in the garage.

Taking out my phone, I dial my brother.

It rings three times, and I think he might avoid me, but then the line picks up.

He doesn't say anything.

Neither do I. For a moment.

When I do, my voice is calm. "Sorry we missed you tonight," I tell him.

"That's okay." His tone is steady. Sincere. "You were busy."

I wait. Kade is almost always cocky. Full of words and a tone that leaves no room for mistake that he's on top.

Now, he sounds like he did when we were younger. When we used to make tents with our blankets in the basement and work on our superhero gadgets, just the two of us.

We were nine. But it was great.

"You need to talk to Dad to make sure Dylan doesn't get into trouble for what your friends did in the school tonight."

"No need," I reply. "Farrow took care of it."

"Green Street."

"Yeah."

Rumor is that a Shelburne Falls cop is the true leader of Weston's gang, and Farrow has his ear. The police will chalk it up to Rivalry Week shenanigans.

But the Pirates are coming. Kade won't warn me. He won't goad me. He'll just come.

I hate to admit it, because the football game is more important, but I want him to. I want to see him.

Just then, a figure appears in his bedroom window, and I don't know if he knows I'm outside, but I doubt he can see me in the dark.

"You know," he says. "I can't see you doing it in the shower."

I blink, looking down for a moment. For a few minutes, I'd forgotten about the picture Calvin posted.

"I'm actually impressed," he tells me. "I always thought you'd arrange a fancy hotel room and give them flowers and shit before a monotonous two-minute missionary fuck on starched sheets."

Watching his dark form standing in the window, I breathe in the night air. Slow. And steady.

"She's pretty, isn't she?"

His voice turns taunting.

"It's easy to forget when she starts talking," he teases, "but she always comes when she's called. That's what I love about Dylan."

I bite down, hard.

"Thanks for those handcuffs, by the way." I almost hear him grin. "That was a fun night."

He's lying.

But she kept the handcuffs.

"Don't believe me?" he taunts. "Ask her if she slept in her own bed that night. See what she says."

I squeeze the phone in my fist.

"Ask her," he tells me again.

PIRATES

CHAPTER ELEVEN

Dylan

I pop my eyes open, my heart skipping a beat.

I stare at my bedroom ceiling, frozen.

I swear I heard furniture moving up there.

Wiping the sleep from my eyes, I glance to the window and see the tree outside dancing wildly in the wind. Branches swing and leaves flutter, a few orange ones flying off into the air.

The floor above creaks, and I draw in a short, quick breath. And then I hear it again and again.

Back. And forth.

Back. And forth.

The chair rocks over and over, and I exhale. But the chills on my spine don't go away. That wasn't the sound I heard that woke me up. It was like something being pulled across the floor. It only lasted two seconds, but it was a heavy sound. Different.

My phone rings, and I glance, seeing my mom calling. I grab it, noticing a ton of notifications, as well.

I open a text from Aro.

Happy Birthday! Wanna bet I can get to Weston tonight?

I suck in a breath and smile. It's Thursday. It's my birthday. For real, how did I forget?

Which is why my mom is calling. I send her to voicemail and tap out a text.

Got to get to school! HB to me! Talk soon. Love you!

She replies, *Happy Birthday! One of your presents is on your debit card. Enjoy.*

Yay, money. *Thank you. Talk soon.*

After school, she insists. *We miss you. Have a great day! Remember, you can go to prison now, so watch it.*

I snort. Sitting up in bed, I set my phone down, and I'm about to get up, but I hesitate, listening to the ceiling for another minute.

The tree sways, and the only sound I hear coming from the attic is the chair.

I know no one's up there. If there was danger, it would've happened last night while I was vulnerable.

But I slept peacefully.

Semi-peacefully.

A smile pulls at my mouth, and I can't stop it, no matter how hard I try. My cheeks warm.

I know what I really want for my birthday.

I want to feel him. He was so hard, too much for me not to stare at Tuesday night, and every time I tried to touch myself afterward, I just keep seeing him. Wanting to know what it feels like to have him inside me.

I bury my face in my hands, my insides ready to implode. *Hunter.*

I fantasized about Hunter last night and the night before.

He didn't talk to me much yesterday. He had practice before and after school, and was AWOL at lunch. I was worried he was feeling weird about what we did and didn't want to face me, but then he shoved a guy into the lockers who was messing with me before fifth period, and then he grabbed my hand and walked me to class. I don't normally go for that "saving a damsel-in-distress" type of thing; but God, it was hot.

I know what his body looks like now. His whole body.

Any time I've masturbated, it's been to faceless fantasies. Maybe we're in a car or he's snuck into my room in the middle of the night, but I never knew who it was. I've seen the hair or the clothes, but never the face.

Now, though, it's Hunter on top of me. His mouth in my neck. His body under the sheets.

I was worried he'd be able to read it all over my face when we saw each other, but I couldn't stop picturing him.

He said he was hard all the time—not to read anything into it.

But last night wasn't the first time he was hard around me.

I've noticed it before.

"No, no, no!" I squeal, steering my PS5 controller into his space like I steer a car.

Hunter ducks away, laughing and trying to keep his car on the track and eyes on the TV screen through my invading arms and body as I bounce next to him.

"I'm not letting you win this time!" he shouts.

"Let me win?" I growl, scowling at the screen as we race side by side. "Let me win?"

YONAKA plays on the speakers in the Caruthers's basement, and our parents are outside, relaxing with margaritas after the barbecue Madoc and Fallon threw today for Kade and Hunter's fifteenth birthday. I love summers. My dad would never admit it to his face, but he loves everything my uncle Madoc grills.

Hunter elbows me as I push into him, and I elbow him back. He cruises over a hill, and we both bob up and down, moving our whole bodies as if that helps our game.

He cruises around a bend, and I follow, steering my controller in a wide circle, standing up, and falling on Hunter.

He cries out, I laugh, both of us trying to keep control as I lay half on his body. My shorts and shirt ride up, and I dig my bare foot into the area rug on the floor, resisting as he tries to push me off.

I pass his car and gasp, smiling wide as I shift and nudge on top of him, trying to win.

But something presses into my stomach.

Hunter's car slows, mine nearly goes off the track, and I look up at him.

He stares at the screen, jaw clenched.

I shift a little, a grunt escapes him, and I let my mouth fall open, realizing what the hard ridge thickening against my tummy is. Oh my God.

I start to look down, but he shoves me off. "Your winning streak is overrrrr."

It takes a minute to remember to breathe, but eventually, I let out a laugh, sinking back into the game. "Nothing is over," I say.

I elbow him, he elbows me, and I speed over the last hump, raising my controller in the air, about to claim my win.

We fall together, chuckling, but the next thing I know someone is grabbing me.

In a moment, I'm in a lap on the other side of the couch from Hunter. Kade puts his hands over mine on the controller, holding me tightly between his arms.

The warmth of his bare chest hits my back.

"Come on," he tells me, starting the game again. "Let's do this, my queen."

I sit there, letting his fingers work, the room suddenly quiet. Hunter stares at the screen, racing us but differently now. His shoulders are tight and his knuckles white.

"Where's Lake?" He jerks the controller, speeding past Kade. "Or River or Ocean or whatever this one's name is?"

"Sent her home," Kade replies, still holding me in his lap. "I'd rather hang out with Dylan."

The hair on my arms rises. Kade is like this sometimes. He's not usually affectionate or playful like Hunter is, but when he does show this side of himself, it's like he's jealous.

Is he jealous?

After a few moments, Hunter tosses his controller toward me. It lands on the couch. "Here, you can both play," he says to me, not looking at either of us.

Then he leaves the basement.

There were lots of instances like that, now that I think about it. It seemed, for years, like Kade just wanted me to go away. Later, I chalked it up to boys against girls and kids' stuff, and I tried not to be hurt by it, but when we grew up, things changed. He started showing me more attention. Wanting me around. Including me. Even insisting I sit next to him at a movie or in the car.

And that's about the time his and Hunter's relationship deteriorated to the point where everyone could feel how thick the air was whenever they were in a room together. All the energy shifted, and I just wanted to be with them. I didn't—and still don't—understand what was wrong.

Sometimes I felt things for Hunter—like longing—but he never brought it up, and I was too embarrassed to think about it. Kade would touch me, hold me, and serve me lots of attention, and then other times, he would ignore me.

I've missed them both.

I throw off my covers and head into the hallway, looking left to right, and only hesitating a moment before I walk to the attic door. Opening it, I lift my eyes up the staircase, lit by the gray morning light coming in through the windows up there.

I don't hear the rocking chair now.

I ponder going up, but almost immediately, I slam the door shut again, shaking off the chills.

The ghosts are leaving me alone. I'll leave them alone.

I grab a pile of clothes and carry them downstairs to the washer. Dumping everything in, I find some powder on the shelf above and scatter it in the machine, starting the cycle.

The washer vibrates against my thighs as it starts, and I remember Weston's obsession with exhibitionism. Reaching over, I turn on the empty dryer and move in front of it, slowly resting my hips against the machine.

The tremors shake through me, the ancient dryer rocking more than it probably should. But I tingle between my legs, and it's not entirely unpleasant. I turn one of my legs out, pressing myself a little harder into it, and I close my eyes, letting it quake through my sleep shorts. My clit throbs, and I break out in a sudden smile.

My phone rings upstairs, and I jump, opening my eyes. *Shit.*

I turn off the dryer and run back upstairs. I race into my room and grab my phone, seeing it's my dad.

I answer it. "Dad?"

"Can you tell me why I woke up to a half-naked photo of you online this morning?" he snaps.

The smile I didn't know I was wearing falls. *Photo...* Calvin grabbed a pic of Hunter and me the night before last coming out of the shower.

And my dad's just seeing it now. I'm guessing my uncles and Hawke worked very hard to hide it from him this long.

I blow out a breath and grab the towel I left at the bottom of the bed. "Because someone took an unauthorized picture of me coming out of the shower in my house?" I explain, making no effort to disguise the sarcasm from my tone. "Dad, you know where I am. These people are going to mess with me."

"That's not what I'm talking about!"

His growl is like a needle in my ear. I flinch.

"You need to calm down." I hear my mom in the background.

But my dad doesn't seem to hear anything she's saying. "You were in a towel, and Hunter was in a towel!"

"Right now, babe," my mom warns.

"You sit tight," his voice pulls away from the phone slightly, like he's covering the speaker. "I'm not happy with you, either. Who are these people she's staying with that just let this go on under their roof?"

"Do you expect them to do it in the car like we always did?"

I press my lips together to stifle my laugh.

"I can still hear you when you cover my ears," James says loudly, to Mom, I assume.

I head to the shower. "Nobody's doing anything," I assure him.

But my dad just gripes, "Goddammit," and I hear a door slam shut.

He probably went into his den for privacy.

He hasn't said happy birthday. He's definitely not concerned with the other pictures of me breaking into the school.

"What do you want from me?" I ask.

"I want you to find a new hobby." His reply comes quickly. "I'm glad you're ambitious and excited, but you don't know the world yet. Trust that I do, and there are a dozen other things you'll love just as much, if you open your mind."

I drop my eyes, clenching my teeth. He just doesn't get it. I'm in love with motorcycles. I'm in love with racing.

"And I want you to behave," he continues. "There's nothing to prove. I don't know why you act like there is."

I shake my head. He says that to me? Right now? At the same time he's trying to make me feel like I'll never be able to have what I really want? There's everything to prove.

"Won't you ask me what I want from you?" I press.

He says nothing. Because of course, he's perfect. Everyone else is wrong.

"I want to feel like I don't always have to lie to you," I tell him, but a sob lodges in my throat, making it almost a whisper. "I'm not bad, you know?"

Tears fill my eyes.

I'm pretty great, and he shouldn't forget it. I'm not letting him make me forget that, either.

He doesn't say anything, and I simply tell him, "I have to go to school."

I hang up, but I doubt he wanted the conversation to continue anyway. He won't apologize or admit he's wrong, and he's not ready to surrender. Let him process for a while.

I start the shower, scrolling through texts, TikTok, Instagram, and Snapchat, seeing the picture of Hunter and me everywhere. Pirates are talking shit, and the Rebels aren't helping.

I power off my phone. "Great."

I strip down, even though I had a shower last night.

Standing in front of the mirror, steam fills the bathroom, and I gaze at myself in the mirror.

Someone is always going to misunderstand me. Everything I do will be a problem to someone.

All I can do is what I must. "You're going to be someone's villain," I say into the mirror. "So be their fucking villain."

I turn off the shower, get dressed, and grab all the money Hawke gave me.

I walk briskly through the school parking lot, gazing around haphazardly at the sparse number of cars. I'm about forty-five minutes early—on purpose—but there are usually a few more people here by now. Track and band have morning practice, but there's no one around. No sounds. The place is nearly empty.

I jog up the steps and dive into the school. Following the same route that I took when I explored on Monday, I hurry down the hall, to the stairs, and descend to the lower level. I run into the auto shop and spin around, looking for a crowbar. Spotting one on a rack, I snatch it and leave, glancing through the door to my left and spot the empty cage. The guys aren't working out this morning. *Hmm.*

I leap back up the steps, all the rushing keeping me warm during the chilly morning.

I slip into the women's locker room, my school bag knocking against my thigh as I trail down a row of lockers. Stopping at eighty-one, I plant my hand on the steel of Mace's locker—black, like ours. A combination padlock secures it.

A shower runs down the hall to my left, but I look around, not seeing or hearing anyone else.

I don't waste time. Jamming the straight end of the crowbar through the loop of the lock, I throw all of my weight and muscle into it, yanking and prying, until the locker door pops open. But not because I broke the lock. The whole damn latch busted. *Whoops.*

It falls to the ground, and I drop the crowbar, grabbing my jacket hanging inside.

I give it a shake, holding it up and seeing that it's entirely unharmed. She made a very good show of putting it in her locker yesterday.

Slipping it on, I catch sight of pictures taped to the inside of the door. One of her flanked by two guys dressed in military fatigues. Another of a woman with a baby in one arm and a cigarette in the other hand. She stands on a porch, in the midst of people in lawn chairs around her. The woman doesn't look much older than Mace is now.

I close the door, best I can, and leave the rest. There's no way to hide what I've done. I won't try.

I start to leave but notice Codi coming out of the shower, wrapping a towel around her body. I quickly jump down another aisle before she sees me.

I leave the locker room, suspicion climbing up my skin.

She could have sports before school, but something tells me this is the only place she has to shower.

I've never heard her speak, but everyone seems to care about her a lot.

The hallways are still empty except for a janitor installing a tarp over the broken window to my left. I turn and start to pass my first class, but I see Mr. Bastien holding a packet of stapled papers and reading from it as he writes on the whiteboard.

I was going to head back outside for a bit, but I stop in the doorway, noticing the empty classroom.

"I thought the clocks didn't fall back for another couple of weeks." I joke. "Am I early?"

He turns his head. "It's Ditch Day."

He says that as if I should know what he's talking about. "Ditch Day?"

He twists around, tossing his papers on his desk. "It's a Rivalry Week thing. Most of the school ditches," he tells me. Then he smiles to himself. "Nobody told you, did they?"

I arch a brow and walk in, taking a seat at my desk. "But the teachers still come?"

"In case students show up." He leans down, working his mouse and looking at his laptop. "It's still technically a school day, and we are their care while their parents work, after all."

I take in his jeans and a tan and blue plaid button-down. His sleeves are rolled up. His forearms are tan and thick, like he didn't always have a desk job.

"You went to high school here?" I ask.

He was insulted by my comments on Monday. At first, I assumed he was defensive of his students, but I don't think many people are willing to move into Weston. Most are just stuck staying.

He nods. "About twenty-five years ago."

Before the storm. The flooding. Her.

He was here when the town thrived.

I remove my bag and set it on the floor. "Was the rivalry the same back then?"

He scoffs. "No. Not everyone had a cell phone. There weren't cameras everywhere. No Internet in every house to spread news like a fire, and no social media to wrangle a posse." He looks at me, and I can see the happiness as he remembers. "You didn't go to jail for anything, and the only consequence was someone dying. It was *a lot* worse."

Sounds exciting.

"Did you do anything you'd go to jail for if someone had caught it on camera?" I inquire.

He shoots me a look, and I'm shocked to hear him say, "Yes. You?"

I look away, biting back my smile. "Fair enough."

I've done a lot I could've gotten arrested for, if not for my dad and my uncles.

I peer up at him. "You knew my father."

"I knew of him," he says. "Saw him race a few times when the Loop was young."

He comes around the front of his desk and sits on the edge.

"What did you think of him?" I ask.

"Initial impression, I thought he was a little shit." He smiles, combing his brown hair back over the top of his head. "I thought, here was this kid who comes and goes as he likes and answers to no one. No one's on his back, making demands. Why the chip on his shoulder? Why's he always pissed off?"

"Pretty much."

Mr. Bastien locks eyes with me, his smile softening. "And now, I think, here was this *kid*, answering to no one," he pauses for a moment before continuing. "No one on his back, caring where the hell he was or what he was doing."

I fall silent. I know my dad's history, but I guess I know my grandma as she is now, and it's hard to picture anything different. He was on his own a lot, wasn't he?

"Your parents were around?" I ask Bastien.

"No." He shakes his head. "I still couldn't come and go as I liked, though. Siblings."

"Did you know the people who lived in the house where I'm staying?"

He holds my gaze. "What have you heard?"

"Nothing." I shrug. "Just that the only Pirate girl to trade to Weston twenty-two years ago stayed there. She never made it back home. Drowned in the car you can still see on the bottom of the river when the water level is low. But we don't have a record of any student deaths that year. Or the year before or the year after."

He folds his arms across his chest. "But I'll bet she doesn't show up to any of the class reunions, does she?"

Does she? I didn't think of that. I'll have to ask Hawke.

Bastien seems to believe the story, though.

"I don't know anyone who was in school with her," I admit, "and happenings back then are hard to track online."

He exhales a laugh. "Winslet MacCreary," he tells me. "I was a few years ahead of her in school. Our version is that she was dead before she was put in the car that went over the bridge."

That would be a blessing. What a terrible way to die otherwise.

"Her body was washed away," he explains. "Her parents probably held out hope for a while, which is why there was no memorial before the end of the school year or mention in the yearbook or school paper."

"What does your version say happened to her here?"

He draws in a breath, bowing his head for a moment.

"Twin brothers." He meets my eyes again. "One in love with her to the point of madness, and when she refused him, he stood on the bridge, with rocks in his pockets, and swallowed the key to the handcuffs around his wrists."

Wow.

"Just before he jumped," Bastien adds.

A shiver courses down my spine. *That's* a terrible way to die.

"He waited for a stormy night," he goes on. "When the water would be high, the current strong, and the visibility zero. It took eight days for his body to wash up about ten miles downriver."

"So, it was found?"

"His grave is in the town cemetery." He nods. "Conor Doran."

Conor. It is his house I'm staying in then.

"His twin, in the vein of revenge," Bastien retells the story, "secured himself as her host for the prisoner exchange. After that, it's anyone's guess. Some say he hurt her. Others say he took everything she didn't give his brother. Some say he was the one she was in love with all along, and when he still hated her, she knew everything his twin felt and took her own life too."

Deacon. The story in the Falls is that it was a guy and his best friend, but Hawke realized several weeks back that they were twins. I need to tell Hawke about the grave. If Conor is really dead, then we know it was Deacon who lived with her in that house. And no one else.

Mr. Bastien continues, "Maybe he put her body in the

car and pushed her over the edge of the bridge, as was her due, her soul to rest with his twin forever."

"But they never found *her* body..." I say, just to see if their version of that matches ours.

He nods. "A few of us like to think she survived and escaped them. And they're continuously on the hunt for her."

He smiles a little, and I almost do too. I'd like to think that. It's a little convenient and real-life stories never leave much mystery. Or hope.

But as long as there's no body, it's possible.

The room goes quiet, and we're still alone. No one has shown up for class.

I sigh. "I'm going to ditch."

He smiles, pushing off the desk and walking back around it. "Be safe."

Picking up my bag, I walk for the door, but something he said keeps picking at the corner of my brain.

I stop and turn toward him. "You said 'them.'"

He looks up at me.

"You said 'a few of us like to think she escaped *them*.'" I tell him.

If Conor is really dead, and it's just Deacon, then who else...

"The Rebels," he finally replies.

Ah. Okay.

"See you tomorrow," I say.

I walk out, heading down the hallway and back out the front entrance, my mind wandering through all the pieces of this story.

I'm not paying attention when Farrow Kelly takes my collar in one hand and shoves me up against the wall of the school.

"You left without us this morning," he scolds, glaring down at me. "I told you not to go anywhere without us."

I don't listen. Everyone knows that.

Not to mention, his crew, or at least some of them, tried to kill me last night. Or maybe they just wanted to scare me, but either way, I don't believe my safety is all that important to him.

Pulling out the wad of cash Hawke gave me, I hold it up between him and me. He smirks, grabbing it out of my hand. "Is this a payment for the bike sitting at the bottom of the river?" he asks as he flips through the bills.

"You mean, the stolen one?"

I don't owe him for a bike he didn't pay for.

"I need you to get me some party supplies," I tell him.

He narrows his blue eyes. "Like drugs?"

Idiot.

"Girls," I tell him, grinning. "Lots and lots of girls."

REBELS

CHAPTER TWELVE

Hunter

"**S**houlders squared!" Coach Dewitt shouts.

I scramble backward and stop, dig in with my right foot, rear my arm back, and launch the football down the field.

"Again!"

T.C. snaps the football. I catch it.

"Laces up!" Dewitt shouts.

I quickly spin the ball as I scurry backward, my pinkie and ring finger on the laces as I throw the ball toward the end zone.

But it skids off the grass way before that, the spin putting it into a dive that's too fast.

"You're not listening." The coach charges up to me, grabbing a ball out of the basket as he approaches me. "Elbow forward..." He holds the ball, demonstrating. "Rotate your wrist, and then elbow extended. You keep doing it like that, you're going to throw out your shoulder, and you're going to be in a world of pain."

"I'm defense," I tell him. "I've been defense. Why are you bringing me in to QB?"

Farrow's the quarterback. Why am I stepping in for him this game?

Dewitt drops the ball, sporadic rain dotting his light blue T-shirt. "What was that tone?"

He narrows his eyes, and I close my mouth, collecting myself.

It's Ditch Day, but he called us in for a mini-workout when, really, it's just me he wanted. I've played offense before, but I've been a tackle here since I joined the team. That means I have opportunities to sack my brother—the Shelburne Falls quarterback—since his ego often demands that he rush for yardage out of the pocket instead of letting someone else run the ball.

I jerk my head, hearing my neck crack. Kade's taunt from the other night still sits in my head. I tried not to take it out on Dylan, which is why I mostly stayed away from her yesterday. It's none of my business where she slept that night.

I just need to concentrate on the game, and it's not going well. I think about him too much, and her all the time. Her body, her smile, how she must feel to hold... Does he know?

The coach closes the distance between us, looking at me sternly. "We don't give a shit who your dad is here?"

I know. I know I can't talk to him like Kade talked to our coach in the Falls, and I've never smarted off to a coach before.

But... "If I'm offense," I explain, "I won't be on the field at the same time as my brother. It's the only reason I joined this team."

Well, not the only reason, but it was a non-negotiable, for sure.

"He knows I've been playing defense," I point out. "If I suddenly switch, he's going to think I'm afraid to face him."

"And I think you bringing your baggage onto the field is bad for our chances," Dewitt replies.

I cast my gaze to the side, seeing the guys fooling around by the benches. Calvin stands shirtless, sweat dripping from his hair as he speaks animatedly, probably telling a story. Everyone else loiters around, listening and laughing.

Dewitt sends T.C. back to the team, leaving us alone as he faces me again. "Do you think any of us care about you and Kade Caruthers settling a score?" he asks. "I'm old, kid. I've seen thousands come and go." He looks over his shoulder, continuing. "Constin will be serving twenty to life in five years. I'll bet you a million dollars on that."

I find Constin in the group, tattoos already covering his arms and half of his chest. His dad died in prison, and he works for Green Street to help pay the bills.

"Luca will have three baby mamas in seven years," the coach adds. "Calvin will be dead in three. Probably from an overdose. And a couple of them will be shot." He looks at me again. "Probably by Farrow, because you know he's not going anywhere good."

All the air tries to leave my lungs, but I keep my composure. I glance at the guys again, no idea where Farrow is. He walked off a while ago.

Dewitt is right. Farrow works for Green Street, just like Constin, but Farrow is being groomed for more. Constin reports to him. More than a few people do. Does my grandfather know that?

"This is the last year they'll ever truly be free," the coach tells me. "This game may be the highlight of their lives."

But not mine. He knows I have everything in front of me, and I'll leave this place in the dust once I graduate.

I gaze over the faces of my team as they smile and joke around. In ten years, most of them will have a life no one will want.

"Go on!" Coach yells at them. "Get out of here!"

"Yeah!" they howl.

I start after them, but Dewitt stops me with two fingers in my chest.

"You run," he orders me. "Three miles. Then you can go."

He nudges me back, and I look at everyone gathering up their gear and making their way out to enjoy their day off.

Withholding my sigh, because I know I deserve this, I pivot and jog for the track that circles the football field. Stepping onto the broken, faded clay, I start the first of twelve laps, trying to be quick about it, but I eventually settle into an easy pace, indulging in the quiet and the light sprinkle of rain.

Dewitt is right. I have tunnel vision. I want to win, but I'm using them, and I used to be better than this. Making everything about me makes me no better than Kade, and I like it here. I like these people.

I was a good kid. I liked doing science experiments and research just for the hell of it. Because I was curious.

I read and collected, explored and tried new things, and now...

Now I'm him.

He never used to be this way, either. Cocky and arrogant and smug. He was always bolder than me, but he liked me.

What good is winning the game if he changes me?

I don't know how many laps I've done, but I spot Dylan and Farrow leaving on his bike and pick up my pace. She wears her jacket—the same one Mace stole a few days ago—

and she and Farrow rush off, looking like they're in a hurry. It's her birthday today. I should say something.

I race a couple of more laps for good measure and gather my stuff from my gym locker, not bothering to change.

Heading into the parking lot, I see Constin hanging with a few others.

"Give me your bike and take my car," I tell him, holding out my keys.

He stares at my hand, sucking a drag off a cigarette. He's not one to be told things, especially when I came down on him the other morning for being in Dylan's house.

But he digs out his keys, tossing them to me, because my car is worth a lot more than his bike. I hand him my set and take his helmet before climbing on his motorcycle.

I head home.

I'll shower, change clothes... Maybe run into the Falls to see my parents. The Pirates have school today, so Kade won't be around town.

But the first thing I check for when I pull up in front of my grandfather's brownstone is Farrow's bike. I run inside Dylan's house, finding the door unlocked and no sign of her.

It takes about two seconds for me to realize where he took her.

Jumping back on the bike, I coast down the hill, toward the docks, and turn onto River Road. I don't have a motorcycle license or a lot of experience, so I cruise slowly, the bike rocking ever so slightly as I navigate the bumpy roads and swerve around potholes.

I'm glad Dylan can't see me now, but to my satisfaction, Kade isn't a whole lot better on a bike. He has one, but he prefers his truck. It fits his crew.

I stop at the sign, just before the hill, and lift my visor before I take out my phone. Holding it up, I zoom in on the track snaking through the trees higher and higher, spotting Dylan and Farrow zooming in and out of view.

She's on another bike. Goddammit. Did he take her to Green Street to get one? I'm going to kill him.

She's there again, in my lens, but then I lose sight of her as she curves with the street. I hold my breath as she slides around the Throat, disappearing.

And then...she's there, and I exhale as she finishes her turn and speeds away.

I watch them ride Phelan's Throat a few times, both of them disappearing for spells where Farrow is probably giving her pointers, each time she gets smoother and faster.

Then, I watch him nudge his bike into the trees, off the track, and she follows.

I zoom in on my camera, trying to catch a glimpse, but they don't come back. They're not riding. What are they doing?

"Hey, Hunter."

I drop my arms, startled. Turning, I see Coral's car cruise up to the *Stop* sign, the old Corvair packed with girls. Arlet hangs out the passenger side window. "What are you doing today?" she asks.

No idea.

I think I should welcome a distraction, though. I tuck away my phone. "At your service," I offer.

She smiles wide and jumps out of the car. "This is supposed to be girls only, but I could use a ride."

She hops on behind me, and I remove my helmet, handing it to her.

"Where are we going?" I ask.

"Phelan's Throat," she replies, pulling on the helmet. "Let's get Farrow and that Pirate first." And then to the girls in the car. "Meet you in the Falls!"

The Falls?

They drive off, and Arlet wraps her arms around me before I kick off. Keeping my speed down, I grip the handlebars tightly, doing everything to not let her know that I've never ridden with someone else.

But after a minute, I push it faster. She leans when I lean, doesn't fight the distribution of weight. Not bad. She knows how to ride with someone.

We climb the hill, coming up on the halfway mark to the top, and I see Dylan and Farrow off to the right, in the trees. He sits behind her on her bike, holding her hips, and something coils in my gut.

We stop, and Farrow looks over at me. Dylan holds her handlebars, a soft smile appearing when she sees me.

"Hunter," Farrow says.

He climbs off Dylan's bike, and my hands ache before I realize I'm squeezing the handlebars. "You gave her another bike?"

He arches an eyebrow like he doesn't explain himself.

I look to Dylan. "Where's your helmet?"

She reaches down on her other side, picking it up off the ground.

She smiles wider, but I don't return it. Her gaze flashes to the girl behind me, and her expression falters.

"Your friend was about to give me a sex lesson," she blurts out.

A what?

Farrow tells Dylan, "Well, no one else is giving you one."

But he looks at me when he says it.

"Navigating the throat is about rhythm," he says. "Moving with the machine, controlling it and knowing when not to." He pulls his hoodie back on over his sleeveless white

233

T-shirt. "Look at Arlet." He jerks his chin toward us. "Look at her body on his."

I go still. Their eyes take us in, and I feel Arlet's arms tighten around me as I become hyperaware of her weight on my back.

"She's positioned in a way that she could lay her head down and go to sleep," he points. "She's completely in his care. Her thighs hugging, not holding, and there is a difference, Dylan."

Arlet's legs, bare in shorts, even though it's only in the sixties today, press against mine, and I watch Dylan's eyes trail along our bodies.

Farrow's gaze rises a little. "Her breasts are pressed into his back, her pussy into his body."

I blink long and hard. Arlet lets out a quiet laugh.

And now that's all I feel—how warm I am between her legs—and I don't like it. It feels like I'm tied up. Or constricted.

"He moves, she moves, he leans, she leans," he goes on. "He rides the bike, she rides him."

My gaze lowers to Dylan's thighs in tight black jeans. Images of the other night and what she looks like underneath flash in my mind.

He stands opposite of her and grabs her handlebars, pinning her with a hard look. "This bike is your fucking boyfriend. Throw your thighs around it and let it move."

Dylan looks at him, unfazed.

"Everything ready?" Farrow looks to Arlet.

"They'll be there when we arrive," she tells them.

I don't know what they're talking about, but I assume we're going wherever Coral went.

Dylan pulls on her helmet, eyeing the girl behind me. "You'd be safer riding with me," she tells Arlet as she fastens the strap under her chin. "What is this, your second time on a bike, Hunter?"

"You want to ride with Dylan?" I ask Arlet over my shoulder.

She hugs me tighter. "No, I'm good here."

I ask Farrow, "So where are we going?"

But it's Dylan who answers. "Helm's Field."

She starts her new bike and flies off, the three of us following.

Back to the Falls.

What is she up to now? And what did Arlet mean about 'girls only?'

Cruising into my hometown, I see the shops on High Street just waking up. People arrive to work, unlocking offices, and vendors move their sidewalk displays out from their stores. We pass Frosted, and I take in the expanse of bare brick wall between my aunt's bakery and Rivertown, the bar and grill next door. She was hiding in the walls the other night.

And I doubt she's the only one who knows about it. It feels weird if Hawke, Kade, Dylan, and Quinn are in on something I'm not.

But I guess it's fair. I left. My choice.

It's only after nine in the morning, but everyone will be at school by now. It's a short trip through town, and I follow Farrow and Dylan around the back of Helm's Field, the football stadium, just before we reach the parking lot. Coasting alongside the wooded area to our right, we come around the other side of the field and park, the school's two stories rising just over the other side of the field and the track that surrounds it.

Coral's car is already there, along with another one carrying a small flatbed trailer. Canisters of fireworks sit on top.

"We should wait for the end of the day," Coral tells Dylan. "Then they can chase after us."

"This isn't supposed to be fun for them." Dylan unwraps each cylinder, exposing the fuses. "Let them simmer for the rest of the day in class. It'll give us time to get ready."

"Us?" Mace repeats, grabbing her and taking a long look at the jacket Dylan's wearing. "Who do you think you are now?"

"Who am I?" Dylan asks her. "I'm a girl. Sick of boy shit. This rivalry isn't just between the teams, is it?"

I hold back my smile. All the Pirates and Rebels should be allowed to have fun.

"Today, we play together," Dylan tells her. "In ten days, when I'm back on the other side, you can try to kill me again."

Mace hoods her eyes, clearing her throat. "We weren't trying to kill you the other night. That was mostly the Pirates. Farrow scratched up his own truck trying to run one of them off the road before they ran you off."

She narrows her eyes. "He did?"

She looks impressed. She won't be when he tries to send her the bill for all these damages.

Arlet climbs off to help them with the fireworks, but I rev the bike, starting to inch away. I don't need to be here for this.

"Wait," Dylan tells me. "I need you."

For what?

But she turns to Mace. "Give me ten minutes. If I'm not out by then, go ahead and light it."

Dylan charges over and pulls my arm.

But I resist. "What are we doing?"

"Hurry," she says. "We have to go now, before the next bell rings."

She pulls me, and I relent, turning off the bike, pressing down the kickstand, and throwing my leg over, following.

She scales the fence, and I climb over as well.

"What are you doing?" I bark, walking across the field with her.

"Just look casual."

I look around, spotting a girls' P.E. class running the track around us, and I glance over my shoulder, making sure the Rebels are hidden under the trees.

Dylan opens the door, and I follow her inside my old school.

The smell hits me immediately. Fresh paint, perfume, and the leather from jackets, handbags, and car interiors. The scent I grew up with.

Weston High smells like damp wood and school hamburgers.

We walk, our shoes squeaking against the clean floor, and Dylan heads toward the front of the school, hands in her pockets. Everyone is in class, but we pass a couple of people here and there. They look at her, meet my eyes, and then move on. The lockers are new. Orange against black walls.

I prefer the Rebel colors.

Dylan halts in front of the display cases—right next to the front office—and starts to slide open a glass door.

"What are you doing?" I ask again in a low voice.

"Help me."

She starts to pry what looks like one of our old yellow lockers out of the case.

"No," I reply. "Why are we—"

"Hunter!" She stops, glaring at me.

The urgency in her eyes makes me shut up.

"It's Piper Burke's old locker," she whispers.

I drop my eyes, taking in the rusted edges, chipped paint, and the number 1622 etched into the plate on the front.

I lock eyes with her. "Why's it in here?"

"They were saving a few to display when they bought new ones," she admits quickly. "Kade made sure this was one of them." She pauses, pursing her lips. "Thomasin started high school this year."

Piper's kid. Fathered by Nate Dietrich. Both of whom put Dylan's parents through hell when they were our age.

And sure, Kade cares about that. He cares for any reason to exact revenge on anyone, even if it has nothing at all to do with him. Even if it's through their fourteen-year-old child, or through Dylan who has to have the past rubbed in her face every time she passes this fucking case.

My brother...

"Move," I tell her, stepping in.

I grab hold of the locker, lifting it into my arms.

She hovers behind me. "I can help."

"Out of my way, baby."

I freeze, feeling her eyes on me at my side. I didn't mean that.

I heave the locker onto my shoulder, and she shuts the glass case behind me. We move through the school, ignoring the stares of the two people we pass, and exit through the back, Dylan holds the door open for me. Crossing the football field, we hear chatter, finally catching the notice of the P.E. class, but we don't stop.

Farrow stands on the other side of the fence, and I lift the locker over. He takes the end, and I slowly lower it into his arms. Dylan and I hop the fence.

Farrow and I carry the locker as I jerk my chin at Coral. "Trunk."

Quickly pulling out her keys, she unlocks the trunk of her Corvair and Farrow and I set the locker inside, closing the lid. I'm not sure what Dylan wants to do with it, but I have a few ideas.

Dylan cups her hands around her mouth. "Go for it," she calls out to Mace.

Mace pulls out a utility lighter and lights fucking everything.

I yank Dylan back.

"Codi," I snap. "Coral. All of you get back."

An ember from one could make others explode before their fuse even runs out.

A rocket shoots up, into the sky, whistling in a high-pitched screech, and the class running the track lets out shouts and gasps. We watch as, one by one, fireworks fly off the trailer into the air. They pop, fizz, and crackle as they light up the blue sky with sparks of blue and white. Rebel colors.

A couple of adults spill out the door to the school, seeing us across the field as students hang out the windows, pointing. Some laugh, some take pictures and video, and some shout "Fuck the Rebels."

And some shoot out their middle fingers.

"Ahoy, Pirates!" Mace bellows through a megaphone with Property of WHS printed on the side. "Have a good day at school! We'll see you tonight. If you can find us!"

Coral takes a shot from a pint bottle of Smirnoff, passing it around to everyone else, while Dylan opens a pack of M&Ms and pours some into Codi's palm.

Farrow chuckles, watching the show. They all do.

I move toward Constin's bike, leaving.

"What's wrong?" Dylan asks, and I see her approach out of the corner of

my eye.

I shake my head. "Nothing. I have things to do."

She takes my arm, turning me to face her.

Her blue eyes sparkle. "I wouldn't have been able to carry that by myself. And wasn't it fun? Stealing something with me?"

"You needed me because I look like Kade," I tell her. "In case we ran into people, right?"

They wouldn't have batted an eyelash at her walking around the school with him.

Her smile falls, and I climb on the bike, starting the engine. Arlet can catch a ride with Coral.

"Hunter..." she says.

But I act like I can't hear her as I rev the engine and pull on my helmet.

Finally, she turns and rejoins the Rebels, and I spot Aro Marquez approaching the fence. She's dressed in a pair of Shelburne Falls shorts and T-shirt, the rest of her P.E. class drifting back to the building.

"So, if you took those handcuffs from Dylan's room, then you must have the key, right?" she asks me. "I should've figured that out a long time ago." She smiles. "It was you on Grudge Night. In the mask."

I push off the kickstand.

"Why did you do that?" she asks, clutching the fence. "Lock them up together?"

"Just a prank."

She looks off toward Dylan, musing. "I think Dylan enjoyed it. She kept the cuffs, after all."

I think they both enjoyed it. Kade's words from the night before haunt me. *Thanks for those handcuffs, by the way...*

"I know something about self-sabotage," Aro says. "You're sure it's coming anyway, so you just want to get the pain over with. Then you don't have to lose."

I tighten the strap, my jaw clenching.

"Then you don't have to fail," she goes on, her eyes boring into me. "You don't have to contend with not getting what you want, and you finally have a reason for the anger you feel. It's easier to believe the lie that things happened exactly as you intended all along."

I wasn't trying to push Dylan and Kade together. It wasn't self-sabotage.

"It was just a prank," I say again and then tease, "maybe I'll throw them on you and Hawke next."

"You'll have to do better than that." She laughs. "I've known how to pick locks since I was nine."

Interesting. I'm sure there's a story there, but it'll have to wait.

I start to go but then stop, something occurring to me.

"So, *you* got Dylan out of those cuffs?"

She wasn't trapped all night, then?

"I was a little distracted, but yeah..." Aro nods. "She was free within an hour."

Right.

"And she still crashed with Kade that night." I point out. "You see, it wasn't self-sabotage. It was as it should be. She was always going to be right where she wanted to be."

I give the bike some gas.

"Dylan slept in your room that night," Aro tells me.

I stop. I turn my head. "What?"

Aro drops her hands from the fence, backing away. "She always sleeps in your bed when a party or family gathering runs late. In the time I've known her anyway," she adds. "She thinks you might sneak in to get something and she can see you."

She leaves, following her class back into the building, and I sit there, the bike rumbling underneath me.

He lied to me.

Well, not exactly. He said to ask her if she slept in her own bed that night, to which he was right. She didn't.

He's still playing with me, and still so good at it.

But more importantly... I lift my gaze, watching Dylan discreetly slip some folded-up bills into Codi's hoodie pocket as she stands right next to her and doesn't notice. She sleeps in my room. Not his.

PIRATES

CHAPTER THIRTEEN

Dylan

I skid around the Loop, taking the last left before blowing through the finish line. I grip the steering wheel, shifting back into fourth, then fifth, and feeling the car quake underneath me as my tail fans out with the next turn.

I haven't raced the Loop in a car in over a year. I think it was the last time my dad helped me with anything. He would love it if I raced cars. It's a little safer, especially when my name is traditionally male, and no one can see me inside. Many assume I'll be a guy until I climb out and take off my helmet. Maybe I'd *invite* less scrutiny and less aggression on the track, hidden that way. And hey, I can still ride motorcycles as a—insert air quotes—hobby.

And then there's Hunter and whatever bullshit he's on again.

I'm going to turn off the volume tonight. I'm turning it all off—everyone else's voices—and enjoying my birthday.

The track is still empty—the Pirates just getting out of school—and I race around the last bend, waving at the guys in the tower who work here every day, getting ready for the evening races. I should get out of here before anyone shows up.

I drop the Mustang—one of many my dad has—back in the rear parking lot of his shop and climb on the new bike Farrow gave me. It's not new, but it's new to me, and I'm to understand that if I put this one in the river too, he'll put me there with it.

Running back home, I spot my dad's car in front of the curb and make a short right, into Monika Swenson's carport two houses down. She's a nurse at the hospital where Mom works. Hopefully she'll be there for a little while longer.

I climb out and jog down to my house, keeping my eyes peeled for my parents. I just need in my room for a minute.

Jumping up into the tree between mine and Hawke's houses, I scale it until I reach my bedroom. I lean over the thigh-high fence and open my French doors, leaping into my room.

Laptop. Maybe some makeup. I go through the list in my head as I grab things.

Hesitating at my underwear drawer, I pluck out another pair of cute ones. Just in case. I don't know if I'll be in another situation where someone is watching me undress in a shower, but there's nothing wrong with being ready for it.

Tossing the stuff on the bed, I grab my backpack and stuff everything inside, taking a body spray and a pair of earrings that Juliet bought me too.

I stop, remembering. *Razors*. I need replacement cartridges. At least one. I tiptoe to my door and peek into the hallway, spotting my little brother coming up the stairs. He has a Polar seltzer in one hand and a bag of Fritos in the other. He stuffs his face inside, grabbing chips with his mouth.

When he reaches the top, I grab him, whip him around, and he starts to shout, but I plant a hand over his mouth.

"Where's the mark?" I growl in his ear.

"Mum muh muh mum."

I remove my hand.

"In the kitchen," he whispers with his mouth full of chips.

"Is he armed?" I ask.

"Always."

We listen for our father below. A cabinet closes, then the door off the kitchen into the garage.

"I've exceeded my energy consumption," I tell James.

"Energy conversion power recharge?" he suggests.

"Negative. My suit's in the cleaners."

"What are we going to do?" he cries.

"Radioactive spiders?"

"Too dangerous," he gripes. "You remember what happened last time."

"Hammer?"

"It's mine," my kid brother Thor snarls.

Just then, my dad passes through the foyer below, heading into the living room.

"Oh, he stalks." I back up, taking my kid brother deeper into the hallway with me. "He might get me this time."

"We need Bruce," he presses.

"Banner or Wayne?"

And then both of us say in sync, "Banner."

I release him, and he turns, smiling.

I ruffle his blond hair, exactly the color of our mom's. "Make the call," I tell him.

He throws me a salute. "Happy birthday," he says before diving into his bedroom, probably to play a video game.

The one consolation in this family is that my dad finds about as much common ground with my brother as he does with me anymore. He does love us, though. And we know that.

Walking cautiously, I grab a new razor cartridge from the bathroom and sink back into my room, about to grab my vibrator and get out of here, but a gorgeous blonde is sitting on the end of my bed. I close my door, squealing as quietly as I can.

"Oh my God," I whisper, running and throwing my arms around Quinn.

"Hey." She squeezes me tightly, rocking me side to side.

My dad's little sister just started her second year at Notre Dame. I thought I wouldn't see her until the holidays.

"What are you doing home?" I ask, pressing my finger to my lips so she knows to be quiet.

"It's fall break," she says. "I have a long weekend. I was coming over to meet you on your way home from school, but I saw you sneaking into your bedroom, so I did the same."

"Yeah, I didn't want to run into your brother."

"You mean, your father?"

"Whatever." I roll my eyes. "I'm the Weston prisoner for Rivalry Week, so I've been over there the past few days, but it's Ditch Day, so I snuck home to get some things."

Her brown eyes widen. "You're the hostage? First girl since—"

"*Only* girl other than you know who," I correct her.

I take in her hair, a few inches longer and parted in the middle. Different than it was this past summer. Her skin glows, the tiny mole on her cheek beautiful against her flushed cheeks.

"Well, you look unharmed," she finally says, surveying me up and down.

I nod, putting the rest of my things in my backpack. "It's kind of peaceful there, if you can believe it."

"Are you heading back now?"

I nod, wiggling my eyebrows. "And you're coming with me. It's my day."

"Mm-hmm," she says. "I know."

She pulls a box off the bed that I didn't see sitting there.

She hands me a birthday present, and I flip the lid off the box, removing a red leather jacket with silver buckles and zippers. I hold it up, looking at the little thing. "Wow."

"It's a motorcycle jacket."

I laugh, dropping the box and holding the jacket by the shoulders. The leather is really thin, and I'm not sure I'll even be able to get it zipped up.

"Not sure this will protect me from anything," I tease. "It looks like it might not fit."

"It'll fit." She plants her hands on her waist. "No pressure to wear it. I just thought I'd take a chance."

"Thank you."

I give her a hug and fold it, sticking it in my backpack.

"We should get out of here," I tell her.

I start to move, but she pulls me back and forces me to sit down at my desk. I look at her through the mirror in front of us as she stands behind me.

"He won't say shit to you with me here," she tells me, pulling out my ponytail.

She must see the look on my face, because everyone who's met my father knows that my mother is the only person he watches his mouth around, and barely even then.

"Okay, he'll say *less* with me here," she jokes.

Yeah, yeah.

"Let's get this hair sorted."

And she picks up the hairbrush on my desk and starts working.

⚡

"So where are we going?" I ask.

"You'll see."

Coral stuffs her hands in her pockets, leading the way down the steps of 01 Knock Hill. Quinn follows her, and I close my door.

A car door slams shut, and I look up, seeing Aro heading toward us.

"You came?" I chirp, bouncing down the steps.

"How could I not?" she tells me.

"I'm guessing Hawke doesn't know, otherwise you'd be tied up right now."

"I'll tell him." She whips out her phone, moves in beside me, and holds up her camera for a selfie of us. "Smile." And she snaps the pic.

I laugh, knowing Hawke won't want to find out she's here in an Instagram post.

She starts typing. "Location: Roller Dome," she says.

"Roller Dome?" I retort, looking at Coral.

She shrugs. After the trip into the Falls today, Farrow said they were throwing me a party. I was skeptical until Mace chimed in that I could bring friends. Roller skating wasn't what I had in mind, though. I thought that place shut down, actually.

I stick my phone in the back pocket of my jean shorts, tempted to button up my flannel against the chill, but we won't be outside long.

"Hawke's going to be mad at you," I tell Aro.

"I love him that way."

I snort.

Aro finally notices the woman next to me. "Who are you?"

She pinches her eyebrows together, her tone accusing, and I have to stifle my amusement because she'll scare Quinn. She scares almost everyone when they first meet her.

"Uh, hi," Quinn stammers. "I'm Quinn." She offers her hand to Aro. "Caruthers."

Aro takes her hand. "Aro. Nice to meet you."

We start for the cars. "Heard a lot about you," Quinn tells her.

"Yeah. *Love* your shop, by the way."

Quinn cocks her head, confused, but Aro just keeps walking. I shake my head. Since the bakery is only open during the summers when Quinn isn't at school, she's probably wondering when she missed seeing Aro in as a customer. I think it's time to tell her that Hawke and Aro—and a few more of us—use her bakery when we get hungry while hanging out in the secret clubhouse buried in her walls.

A motorbike pulls up, and Farrow lifts his visor, tipping his chin in greeting. "Aro."

"Piss off," she replies and heads to her car.

His deep laugh rumbles to my right. "Take the blonde," he calls out to whoever is listening. "I've got Dylan."

Quinn meets my eyes, and I gesture for her to go with Aro. "Meet you there."

She nods, jogging around the Mustang to the passenger's side, and within a few seconds, Aro peels away.

I climb on behind Farrow.

"So you wanted girls, right?" he asks over his shoulder.

"What do you mean?"

I thought I paid for the girls' prank earlier with the fireworks and stealing the locker.

But he just tells me, "You'll see." And he flips his visor back down.

We speed the short distance to the edge of town, down to the mill district, through the warehouses and decaying office buildings, and under the streetlights bobbing overhead in the wind. I hold him tightly, shivering a little in the cold.

We pull off the highway, cruise down a short, broken road lined with trees and overrun by weeds. They fill the air with the same scent I smell when we go to the pumpkin patch in the Falls. Hay and cornstalks, but with a little something sweet that's dulled by the chill in the air.

The trees end, dozens of cars surround us, and I look ahead at an old cinderblock building painted in blue and purple. The colors are weathered, parts dusty and blocks chipped, revealing the gray concrete underneath. But the neon sign shines bright, the only letters not lit are the double LLs in Roller, so it reads Ro er Dome, which reads as Roar Dome in my head, which has its own poetry.

Music thunders against the walls from inside.

Grabbing my hand, Farrow walks me in, bypassing the ticket counter and opening one of the heavy steel doors. He pulls me through, and all at once, a thousand moving parts flash in front of my eyes.

A disco ball twirls above the center of the rink. Spotlights of blue, pink, and green sweep up, down, and around as people on skates and rollerblades coast around the oval track, or through the tables on their way to the bathroom or concession stand. Fifty pairs of wheels hit the floor, and the scent of cheap slices of pizza fill the air.

I spot Aro and Quinn already getting their skates, and I lock my gaze on one woman rolling around the bend of the rink. She pulls her shirt over her head and tosses it over the wall, skating in her bra.

I go still. Searching the room, I don't see any kids in here. Like little kids. It's all teenagers. Young adults. Some of them look a little older, though. Some of the women especially. Short skirts. Revealing shorts. Lingerie tops.

I look at Farrow, wide-eyed. "Where did you find these people?"

"Strip club."

Holy shit. I knew all that money didn't go to fireworks. When I said I wanted girls, he just went for it, didn't he?

"I feel overdressed," I mumble.

"Oh, they're about to not be dressed at all."

My face falls. "Farrow."

He just laughs and pulls me along. He lifts me under my arms and plops me down on the high counter, and I stare down at him as he removes my sneakers.

An older man in a faded, blue polo approaches, racks of skates rising behind him, but he doesn't have a chance to speak before Farrow orders, "Size eight."

The guy nods once and shoots off, searching for my size.

I lean back on my hands a little, looking down at Farrow Kelly on one knee at my feet. I could make a joke.

But I won't. He's the only Rebel who's been consistently kind to me today, and that includes Hunter.

I sit still, keeping my eyes lowered and trying not to look for him as Farrow turns in my sneakers and takes the skates that appear on the counter.

Is Hunter here?

I feel him.

But I feel like they're all watching me, and maybe my senses are just hyperaware.

I bend my knee, slipping my foot into the skate that sits on Farrow's thigh, and he gets busy, lacing me up.

Unable to stop myself, I look up and scan the room. Aro and Quinn step onto the rink. Mace, Coral, Arlet, and a few others talk closely at a table, Mace's eyes darting up to me.

No Hunter.

Pulling up my camera, I snap a picture of Farrow putting on my skates. I type up my post.

A Pirate's Life for Me.

But then I delete the caption and just say *Ditch Day B-day.*

I don't post the location. It won't be hard for the Pirates to figure it out.

Farrow puts on my other skate. "Will the Pirates come?"

I shrug. "I don't care."

"They'd be stupid to."

Yes, but the Pirates have let enough slide this week. Maybe they were waiting until after their game against St. Matthew's tomorrow night. I don't know, but...

"I think they'll engage in some way," I warn him.

He finishes lacing me up and gives my skate a little slap. "Good."

I look down at him, and he looks up at me, and I don't know what it is about him, but he always feels familiar. He has a bad reputation, and I don't know if he's just playing the long game with me, but so far, he hasn't lived up to it. I'm happy about that.

"Why do you care about this rivalry?" I ask him, staying on the counter. "What do you get out of all of this?"

"Practice."

"For what?"

He falls silent but holds my gaze.

I grin. "Come on, what do you want to be when you grow up?"

"A last resort."

A smile taunts the corner of his mouth, and I laugh quietly.

I like that. A last resort is scary. It's the path no one wants to take, but it is a path you can count on when everything else has failed you.

Hunter always gave weird answers to that question too.

"I can see why you and Hunter get along," I muse but then add. "You can't hurt Kade, though, okay?"

This rivalry is fun, but it almost always turns bad. And if the legend is true, at least one person has died because of it. I eye the tattoo on Farrow's neck, and he wouldn't have gotten that without earning it.

"I won't kill him," he retorts, his tone nonchalant. "I might make him cry a little, but...I would *never* hurt him."

I'm glad to hear it, but he worded that strangely.

He sighs and rises to his feet. "Quinn is fucking hot." He looks over his shoulder, toward the rink. "You think she'll sit on me?"

I burst out in a laugh. *Idiot.*

Jumping off the counter, I roll away, wobbly and throwing out my arms to keep my balance.

Grabbing onto the wall next to the entrance to the rink, I lean in, hanging on.

"Come on!" Quinn calls with Aro at her side.

I yell after them. "I actually haven't skated since I was ten!"

"You're good on wheels." Quinn assures me.

They both circle around, coming back to me against the traffic. Taking my hand, Quinn pulls me, and I clutch both of their arms as I skate onto the rink.

I push off with my toe stopper, finding my balance, and soon let go before we've even circled once.

"Who paid for all this?" Aro asks.

"I think Hawke did."

She looks at me, her eyes wide. "Uh-oh."

I know. He's going to be pissed, and I'll deserve it. Luckily, I can pay him back, but of course, I'll get the "it's the principle of the matter" talk.

It'll be worth it, though. I'm already having fun.

"Farrow is looking at her," Aro tells me.

I glance at Farrow, seeing him hang back at the counter, watching us. Watching Quinn.

And then I spot someone else leaning on the other side of the rink wall with his back to us, drinking a beer. His eyes are turned on Quinn too.

"Noah Van der Berg is also watching her," I say.

I throw Noah a wave, wondering how he ended up here. He tips his chin at me and then turns back around. I follow his gaze, suddenly seeing one long dare stretching like a rope between his eyes and Farrow's.

"That's a lot of blond in one bed," Aro teases.

And I throw my head back, laughing. Farrow, Quinn, and Noah...yeah, a lot of blond.

"Who are you guys talking about?" Quinn gripes.

"You've been gone too long," I coo. "There are new men on the scene."

"And I'm still as disinterested as I ever was."

I circle around in front of them, seeing if I remember how to skate backward. I wobble but manage to stay upright.

"Her heart is taken," I inform Aro.

"Shush," Quinn growls a little.

But I don't. "Have you heard anything from him?" I ask Quinn.

"From who?" Aro asks.

"Lucas Morrow," I tell her, throwing Quinn a glance. "Another blond."

Quinn is twenty. Lucas must be more than thirty by now. But she knew him when he was a teenager and she was a kid, and she followed him everywhere.

Quinn just cocks an eyebrow at me. "I'm not ten anymore. I left crushes behind."

"Have you gone out with anyone at school?"

"Have you?" She smiles, challenging me.

Hunter showering with me comes to the front of my mind, and I know I'm blushing as images of his body flood my head.

Quinn gasps, seeing my face. "Tell me."

"There's nothing to tell."

Nothing I can tell her anyway. She's his family, too, and I doubt she wants to hear the details any more than I want to hear about all the places Aro and Hawke have done it.

God, I wanted to touch Hunter, though. I almost asked if I could watch him touch himself that night. I can't believe I almost said the words. They nearly popped out, and I don't know why he would think that was going too far after we'd already gotten naked together, but I stopped myself before I asked.

"*Will* there be anything to tell?" she inquires.

Butterflies swarm as we fly faster and faster around the rink.

"Is he nice?" she asks about my mystery guy.

I think about it. He used to be nice. I always felt good and safe with Hunter.

Now...

"He makes me mad all the time," I reply. "And excited all the time."

"Sounds about right," Aro chimes in.

Quinn touches my arm, but we don't slow down. "You'll be careful?"

I want to laugh, because if anyone asks me what I want to be when I grow up, the answer is, above all else, 'not-careful,'

"I'll be myself." I meet her eyes. "And I'm prepared that nothing will ever be easy because of it."

That's all I can do.

"Let's go," I say, jetting off faster.

People surround us, the dancers go wild, and the air fills with heat that blankets my skin. A brunette unzips her leather jacket, revealing a black lace bra underneath, and two women whirl around us, skating backward, one in a bikini.

It must be '70s night because Olivia Newton-John comes on, and I just realized that every song has been old.

Aro shoots me a look, and I shrug. "Let's just go with it."

We laugh, and I'm a little baffled we all know the words. The chorus kicks off, we bob our heads, dancing as we roll, and I let my shirt slip down my arms. I don't drop it, though. My hair flies behind me, sweat coats my neck, and we all tip our heads back, belting out the lyrics.

But when I open my eyes, I see a black T-shirt lingering in the background of my line of sight. I almost freeze as we cruise past, and then he's gone, and I can't see him.

Swallowing my heart back down my throat, I keep going, but he's all I feel now. Rolling my head back and forth, I sing with Quinn and Aro, my hair tickling the parts of my back that are bare in my tank top and feeling his eyes on my every move.

I tip my head back, running my fingers through my hair, and when I bring it level again, I lock eyes with him.

Hunter stands just inside the steel doors, leaning slightly on the frame with his hands in his pockets, and my lungs empty at just the sight of him.

I think if he asked me for a sleepover, I'd go right now.

His hair sits messily across both sides of his head, never coiffed like Kade, because he's like his mom and doesn't like attention. If he didn't look so much like Madoc, I'd wonder if he'd gotten any of his dad's genes.

My stomach sinks, nerves setting in. He's so unpredictable anymore, and I'm scared he'll leave. *Why am I afraid? Let him go.*

I pull Aro and Quinn's arms, smiling again, but just then, everything goes dark.

Screams slide through the air, and I halt in my skates, trying to avoid a collision. Big mistake. Someone crashes into my back, and before I know it, we're all on the floor. Grunts and cries go off, others yelling, and I can't help but laugh. I dig in my pocket for my phone to bring up the flashlight, but fingers clutch my arms, hauling me off the ground.

"Ow," I say. It feels like more than one person grabbing me.

"They're here!" a voice growls. "We have to hide!"

That's not Quinn or Aro's voice.

They grab my hand, and I stumble in my skates, looking around me. I can't see anything.

"What?" I blurt out, struggling to keep up as I slide my phone back into my pocket. "Who?"

"The Pirates!"

They rush me outside, and I call out behind me. "Aro! Quinn!"

I'm shoved against a car, my wrists pinned behind my back, and I fight as I try to blow the hair from my eyes.

"Guys, what the hell?" I bark.

In seconds, my wrists are tied behind my back, tape is over my mouth, and a blindfold covers my eyes.

Is this a game? It has to be.

They shove me in a car, my legs getting pushed out of the way as someone sits down next to me and starts tying my laces together. I pull against the bindings behind my back, but I'm not going to give them the satisfaction of having a tantrum. They're probably filming this.

Plus, I'm still wearing my skates. I won't get far if I try to escape.

The car takes off, music blasting so loud it hurts my ears, and I work myself into a sitting position. Who has me? Rebels? Pirates?

We drive for a minute, then two, as the wind sweeps through an open window, blowing my hair.

But when the song breaks, I hear something.

Tapping.

I listen.

It's the person next to me. They're texting.

Then an alert goes off on a phone up front. A short pause. And then the phone of the person next to me dings again.

They're texting each other.

And playing loud music so I can't recognize any sounds? Voices?

Fear grips me now. Why are they disguising everything possible for me to detect my location or abductors?

I strain to breathe.

Winslet comes to mind, and I quietly struggle against my restraints again. Am I coming back from this?

The air turns wetter, thicker, and in a minute, I feel drops of rain on my arm from the open window. I try to spread my lips and pry off the tape, but it stings too much, and I stop.

The air smells of dirt as the car swerves and then makes a sharp left. I brush my hand against my phone in my back pocket. Should I take it out?

No. I won't be able to see what I'm doing, and I'll risk them seeing the light from the screen. They may not care that I have it, but I can't risk them taking it.

But a thought occurs to me. What if they're dumping me straight into the river? I should try to call for help now, right? No time to waste.

Before I can decide, the car skids to a halt and everyone is exiting the vehicle. I'm pulled out, my feet rolling underneath me in my skates, and I have to grab on to whoever has me in order to stand up again.

"Help me," they whisper to someone.

Another pair of arms take me, but when they force me to move forward, I start fighting. More hands grab me, and soon I'm off my feet altogether, being carried into the brush. I hear them shuffle through fallen leaves and tall grass.

Crows caw, and I suddenly smell metal and rust. Like a junkyard.

Oh, no. A car. Just like her.

I flail, growling behind the tape, "Ah!"

I hear the creak of heavy hinges, and I'm shoved onto my back, landing against broken leather. The tears in the seat pinch the skin of my back, and I kick, my foot landing against something hard.

"Fuck!" they grunt, but I can't tell who it is. A woman, I think, but her voice is too low to recognize.

"Lock her inside," someone else says.

I squirm. No!

They slam the door shut, and I kick it with my skates again and again before I stop and try to rub my face against the seat. I need to get this blindfold off.

"And throw away the key," I hear someone say.

Laughter fades away, and I sit up, rubbing my head against the seat back. The whole time, though, I'm waiting for it. I breathe hard, sure that it's coming. The emergency brake to be released and the car to be pushed. That freefall feeling as I plummet into the river.

The blindfold slips free, and I shake my head, throwing it off. I blink, twisting my head back and forth, taking in my surroundings.

It takes a few seconds to blink away the blur, but I see trees. A forest.

I exhale. I'm not at the river.

And they're gone. I jerk my head around, checking for people.

No one is here, at least that I can see yet, and I'm the only one in the car.

It's an old one, too, sitting in a sea of old cars, all jam-packed together in the middle of the woods. What the hell is this? Trees sit on both sides, although I can spot the road to my right that we must've come in on.

Why are all of these vehicles abandoned here?

One of my windows is cracked, a light rain flying in, and I look over the front seat, taking in the four-door Pontiac Grand Prix. The dark red interior is all leather, and I spot the CD player and dated knobs and shifter. Gross carpet covers the floors, and the lining on the roof is peeling. This thing is from the '90s. I look around, not seeing a single car from this century. The moon peeks through the clouds, and there must be fifty more cars stretched out in front of me and fifty more behind me.

Where the hell am I?

Fog crawls in from each side, and I spot movement far ahead. At least, I think I do. I quickly dart back down, hiding.

"Dylan!" a guy sings. "Are you here?"

Dirk? Kade's friend.

Inching up, I peek over the seat, seeing three figures moving through the fog. They carry flashlights, peering in cars and pounding on roofs.

"Come out, come out!" he chants. "We've missed you."

I duck back down. His tone isn't inviting.

They know I'm here, but they don't know where. Which means it was the Rebels who delivered me. The left me here for the Pirates.

Was Farrow in on this?

I need to get out of here, but I won't make it far in skates.

I dig my phone out of my back pocket, contorting my shoulders as much as possible and looking behind me as best I can to see the screen. Pressing *Power*, I hit the *Phone* icon, about to dial Hunter.

Would he even care, though? He'd come for me, if he's not in on it, too, but I hold back.

Hawke is too far away, and I'd rather not call my parents.

Kade would kill for a chance to rescue me from Weston, though.

I call him, but the phone barely rings once before I hear a tolling pierce the air outside.

I go still.

The other end of my call rings, quickly followed by one mimicking it outside again. I stop breathing.

He's here. That's his phone out there.

"Shit." I end the call.

Fuck.

I don't think he'd hurt me, but he's not here to help.

"Did you think it was smart to gamble on their loyalty?" someone shouts, and it sounds like Stoli. "That's the thing about this ghost town, Dylan. They're loyal to nothing but getting paid."

Tears pool in my eyes, and if I weren't so scared, I might let them fall. I thought the girls and I had fun today, but no one really fucking likes me, do they? I'll walk into Weston High School tomorrow as alone as when I came, and no one misses me in the Falls. Except maybe Aro.

"We don't want you back," Dirk calls out. "But we are owed payback."

I shiver, my shirt still hanging down my arms, bunched up at the bindings around my wrists.

The door on my left clicks, and I lift my head, looking over.

It opens gently, and a form appears, crouched down as he turns his baseball cap backward and starts to climb in.

I blink in the darkness, through my tears. "Kade?"

He stops as I turn onto my back to try to see better.

"Is that you?" I ask.

He crawls to me, softly shutting the door behind him.

He comes down on top of me, planting a hand over my mouth.

REBELS

CHAPTER FOURTEEN

Hunter

"**Y**eah," I reply. "It's me."

I don't know what I'm doing, but the words just come out.

That's who she thinks of. The first person she saw when I opened the door. Kade.

To be fair, we're built the same now, and I rarely wear a cap. He wears one often.

But he wears body spray, and we carry ourselves differently. Does she really not know it's me?

I sink my body into hers, trying to ignore how good she feels underneath.

"Be quiet, Dyl," I add for extra measure. She hated it when Kade called her that when we were kids, and maybe I want her to keep thinking I'm him.

Maybe I'm afraid she'll be disappointed, finding out I'm not, or maybe I'm tempted to see what she's like with him when no one else is around.

I move down her body, working to untie her laces. "How've you been?" I ask, trying to mimic Kade's husky but relaxed tone.

She shifts, her arms pinned between her back and the seat. "Oh, you know...nothing is ever my fault."

I smile. "Whatever takes the focus off me with our parents, right?"

She laughs, that easy camaraderie they always had like a truck on my chest.

"Shhh," I warn, retying her laces properly. She won't be able to run in skates if we need to, but there are too many things in this junkyard that could hurt her feet. Skates are better than nothing.

I check out the windows. One figure moves ahead, shining his flashlight into cars.

I take out my knife and turn her over just enough to slice the zip tie around her wrists.

She exhales hard, rubbing her wrists. "What took you so long?"

I sheath my knife. *What took him so long...*

As if he can always be counted on to come and save her.

I slide the knife back into my pocket. "Were you waiting for me?"

"I'm not sure that's the right word," she teases, "but I always expect you."

I come back down on her again, and she doesn't resist. Not one bit.

Her breathing stutters, and she shivers.

"Cold?" I ask.

But I don't wait. Pushing up just a little, I hold my hat to my head and pull off my T-shirt. I cover her with it, noticing the hard points of her nipples through her tank top.

"Thanks," she says.

She huddles in close, warming her fingers against my stomach.

She's fucking freezing. Her hands are like icicles.

She lingers there, slowly grazing the backs of her hands and then her palms over my skin.

Whistles shoot off through the night air. "You can run!" Stoli shouts.

Followed by Dirk, "We're always up for that!"

I shake my head. They don't go anywhere without Kade. He sanctioned this? What the fuck?

But she still thinks he's made of gold.

"Hunter really doesn't give a shit, does he?" I look down at her, our lips inches apart. "Where the hell is he?"

But I don't think she's looking at me. Her lids are down but not closed. I can see her blink. She's staring down at her hands on my stomach. "Always closer than I think," she murmurs.

Her fingers grow lighter, touching me more than warming herself now, and she moves her thighs out from underneath me, letting my body settle in.

Heat pools low in my stomach as my groin presses into hers. "Miss me?" I whisper.

She nods. "But I'm not going home."

"If you're not careful, they won't want you back."

"Will you?"

My cock twitches.

Until I remember that she thinks she's talking to my brother.

"You're mine to protect," I tell her. "And to punish."

Her nose brushes mine, and I swear I feel her roll her hips into mine as she pulls my T-shirt off her body.

"I need your protection right now," she says, sounding so innocent.

"Dylan..."

I ache everywhere as I wrap my arm around the top of her head, hungry to feel every inch of her.

She grips my hips, and I don't know if it's her or me, but we're pressing into each other hard. She's going to feel it.

"It's just pretend," she whispers, her voice so small. "When they find me, they won't stop you from whatever you're doing. They'll leave. Just pretend."

She caresses my stomach, and I groan, taking her mouth.

An electric current sweeps through my lips, trailing along my jaw, and I just can't stop. I deepen the kiss, needing more. Her soft mouth, the taste, the feel of her between my teeth... For a second, I just take it. I don't give a shit who she thinks I am.

I sink into Dylan's mouth, her tongue dipping in to touch mine again and again, and I feel her moan reverberate through her.

Oh God, I want this. Just her and me, alone in rooms. I want her in my arms, smiling at me. She's the place I feel most alive.

Her whimpers hit my ear, but they don't belong to me. They're not *because* of me.

I rip myself away. "We can't."

She drags her fingers up my stomach, grazing my jaw with her lips. "Should've thought about that before you paid the Rebels to kidnap me and tie me up, Kade," she says. "My dad won't like that."

I shoot up, wrapping a hand around her throat and dipping my forehead into hers. "You threatening me?"

She gasps, grabbing my wrist with both hands, but I see the smile peek out on her face. She doesn't fight me.

"We're getting close!" they shout outside. "Aren't we?"

But I look down, seeing her bare stomach in her little shirt. I run my hand down her chest and slip a finger under her hem, pausing to see if she resists. When she doesn't, I move my finger back and forth, inching the shirt up and over her breasts.

My cock strains against my jeans as I take in the outline of her. I need more light. Fuck, I need to touch her.

"Look what I got in my family," I taunt. "It would be so easy. Our parents wouldn't think twice about us being alone together anytime we want."

She pulls me by the back of my neck, trying to get me down. "They're coming. I hear them."

I want to come down on her. I want her skin against mine. "I can't."

"It's just pretend."

"I can't."

I've gone too far already. She's going to hate me for what I've already done, and Kade will never let me forget this.

"It's just pretend," she begs again.

I feel myself between her legs, and she lifts a knee, her skate banging against the seat. I groan, knowing the only thing keeping me from being inside of her is our clothes.

"Dylan..." I plead. "Please."

She rolls her hips, her breasts flashing in the moonlight, and fuck...

I drop down, opening my mouth, but...

I stop, hovering over her nipple by just a hair.

I lift my hand, about to cup her at last, but I pull back before I do. Sweat covers my forehead, and she drops her hands again, caressing my stomach. *I can't. We can't.* I want to, but she wants him. I can't do this.

Her breathing slows, and her body calms.

"You know, it's funny..." She glides her nails up and down my stomach. "Kade is so ticklish," she says.

I open my eyes, just realizing they were closed.

"You don't grow up with someone and not know that," she tells me. "I could never touch him like this without it being torture for him."

Her fingertips trickle over my skin, and I go still, a chill sweeping through the car.

"Hunter isn't ticklish at all," she points out. "Not here anyway." She rubs her thumbs over my abs.

I growl and push up, but she catches me, circling my waist with her arms. "Why did you do that?" she asks me, looking up into my face with a crack in her voice.

She knew? She knew the whole time? I think back to when she started touching me there. She must've realized then.

"Why?" she demands.

"I don't know."

"Yes, you do."

I try to pry her arms off me. "Let go."

"Look at me."

It's the sadness in her voice. It stops my heart.

Looking down, I can just see her eyes. "I couldn't kiss you there," I say, tugging down her shirt to cover her breasts. "Not when you were giving your permission to Kade."

"And I would've let you, knowing you weren't him."

My lungs empty.

Her hold on me loosens, but I don't try to escape anymore.

"Your fingers are thinner," she whispers, a smile in her voice. "The hair peeking out of your hat hangs over your ears. And Kade has that triple triangle tattoo, same as your mom's, on the left side of his torso."

"He does?"

She nods. "She took him to get it on you guys' last birthday."

And I wasn't there. Mom and Dad wanted to come and see me, but I had football clinics. They dropped off presents, and I took a raincheck for dinner and cake. Which I also eventually canceled.

I should've been there. My mom should've had that experience with both of her sons. I would've loved to get that tattoo.

Dylan shakes her head. "You fooled me for a minute, but only because it's dark."

I can't help but laugh a little. I don't know why I thought she wouldn't know me. Kade and I are identical, but everyone can tell us apart. Even before puberty struck, and we developed very different personalities and style, it wasn't hard for people who loved us to pick up on body language and expressions. Dylan's known me her whole life.

And she let Hunter kiss her.

I caress her face, dropping my forehead to hers. "I—"

But then...the door behind me whips open, and I'm yanked out of the car. Stoli slams the door shut, and then his hands shove me in the chest so I fall back against it.

I look up, seeing Kade step in front of me.

I freeze, equal parts dread and longing hitting me at once. I haven't looked him in the eye in months.

"It's so nice to finally see you," he jeers.

I rise up, and he pushes me back again.

"Kade!" Dylan snaps, still in the car behind me. I hear her trying to open the door, but my weight is against it.

Kade lifts my arms and slaps my chin to the side, inspecting me. "No cuts, no bruises. They're treating you pretty good. You must be cooperating."

Pretty well. Not 'pretty good,' I used to correct him. I'm going to let it go this time.

"I like it here," I straighten my spine and look at him eye to eye. "No one gives a shit about my car. Or my dad. Wanna trade places?"

"Is there a Starbucks?"

I chuckle. Kade never apologized for his comforts. I really loved that about him. If anyone ever gave him shit about his preppy clothes, corporate coffee, or fitness tracker, he would simply say 'who should I be instead? You? How much does that pay?'

He always knew that no one who's coming after you is doing better than you.

And I think I finally understand.

"Think about it," I tell him. "You could take my place for a day. I'm due for a visit anyway. I miss A.J."

And my parents, everyone.

But he just grins. "That's Hunter." He looks at Stoli and Dirk standing just behind him. "Can't breathe on my hill, so he suffocates on his own."

They smirk, and I feel the car bounce a little behind me. Dylan is climbing up to the front seat.

"You're right." I swipe my baseball hat off the ground, having lost it at some point when they grabbed me from the car. "Leaving the Falls didn't help a lot. I still think about you too much, and why you were such a godawful prick to me for so long." His eyebrows dig deeper, and I fit the hat on my head, the bill at the back. "But the thing I just realized is that you're obviously thinking about me, too, aren't you?"

His jaw flexes.

"Does he talk about me?" I ask his friends, glancing between them. "He bitches a lot, I'll bet."

My brother's eyes darken, and for once, he's quiet. "And you know what else I found out?" I say, hearing Dylan roll down the window of the old car. "She didn't sleep in her own bed that night. You were right about that." I step in. "But she's never slept in yours."

"Hunter..." Dylan says.

"She sleeps in mine," I go on, dropping my voice to lower than a whisper. "But you knew that."

"What's going on?" Dylan steps out of the car and looks between us.

"Do you want her?" I ask him.

"Stop it," she tells me.

But I don't. "You always acted like you did."

Every time I was alone with her, he inserted himself. He talked down to me in front of her. Made fun of me.

"And you always acted like I was shit," I say. "So, I left. And for what? What the fuck do you want?"

Dylan stands a little taller next to us in her skates. "What are you guys doing? What is this?"

I look over at her, hurt watering her eyes.

"There was so much you didn't see," I murmur.

It's not her fault. As Hunter, I want her so badly. I always have.

As her family and her friend, I would tell her to get the hell away from both of us and meet new people.

"This is Hunter, Dylan," Kade chimes in. "Still trying to be more than me. You're never really alone with him. I'm always in the room."

Tears fill her eyes, and I drop mine, knowing there's a world of insults I could sling back at him right now, but nothing he said was a lie, either. I just wasted a fucking year being mad at the wrong people. None of this is his fault, either. It's mine, because I wasn't tougher.

Dylan pushes me away from the car and opens the back door, climbing in for her shirt. But before she crawls back out, Farrow and the guys are on the other side. He opens the back door and leans down.

"Come here," he tells her.

He doesn't wait, though. He grabs her and sweeps her into his arms. Tears are already streaming down her face.

"What do you think you're doing?" Kade barks.

Farrow just shoots him a look. "Not tonight."

He carries Dylan off. "Let's get you fucking drunk, huh? You deserve it."

Constin, Calvin, and the guys trail them, and in a second, they're gone. Except for one. He stands there, staring at Kade, defiant. Almost like a warning. It takes a moment, but I recognize him from stuff I've seen online. Noah Van der Berg, Jared's new protégé.

Kade's eyes dart between him and me, and he must figure he'd rather not have Noah seeing or hearing more, because he leaves, charging away with his friends.

I turn slowly, unable to fill my lungs with air as I reach into the car and get my shirt too.

"Look, I know I don't know you, but I do know brothers," Noah says to me over the roof of the car.

I pull on my shirt, avoiding his gaze.

"And I have one who hid behind bravado like Kade a lot," he tells me. "Hid being the key word there."

I slam the car door and meet his eyes. "So?"

"What you're seeing and hearing from him..." He holds my gaze. "I guarantee you, is to hide a problem that has nothing to do with a girl."

So, what does that mean?

He used Dylan as a way to hurt me? Why?

I never hurt him. He has a charmed life. Two amazing parents. Lots of friends. What problems does Kade have?

Noah leaves, and I'm left standing there in the middle of all the cars drowning in fog.

All of these vehicles were on the road when the dam collapsed during the storm twenty-two years ago. The traffic was bad, because of evacuations, and people literally had to climb out and run. When the water receded, they moved the cars off the road and meant to junk them later, but never did. So many people never came back. The town forgot.

All of the homes had families once, but most of the owners of these cars have moved on, their lives completely different than the last time they sat in them.

Shit can change really quickly. One second, you have a life, and the next, everything you own is gone.

For the past year, I've operated under the assumption that Kade and I would come back from this. Once I showed him that I was just as strong on the field, he would respect me.

What if that never happens?

And what if, in the process, I hurt Dylan, the best friend I've ever had?

I drive home as fast as I can, finding Knock Hill covered with cars.

People gather in the street, and every light in my grandfather's house is on.

I park and walk up the steps, my heart hammering at the idea of seeing her inside. He said he was getting her drunk tonight.

Opening the front door, I enter the house, my ears filled with the music pounding out of the speakers that Farrow has positioned all over the living room. I step into the foyer, gazing around at Calvin, Mace, Arlet, Luca, and Coral at the dining room table on my left.

None of them are drinking. Or smiling.

But excited chatter and laughter goes off to my right, and I glance at Farrow sitting in the high-back chair, the guys and several other students at our school hanging around.

"Hi, Hunter," some girl chirps.

I ignore her, fixing my gaze on Farrow.

"I wasn't in on it," he says.

"I know."

It was Mace and the rest of them sitting at the table right now. Farrow has them in timeout.

"Where is she?" I ask him.

"Just went to take a shower." He jerks his chin in the direction of her house next door. "I gave her a bottle."

I go up to my room, close the door, and stand there for about three seconds before I snatch her vibrator out of my desk drawer.

It's still her birthday.

I pull the charging cord off and wrap it in a hand towel, heading back downstairs and out the front door before anyone can stop me. Slipping through the Rebels partying on the sidewalk, I walk into her house and close the door behind me. Once upstairs, I approach the white door and knock.

It opens with a quick jerk, but not all the way. Dylan looks up at me through a sliver of space, still dressed and her lips red from our kiss.

"I have your bath toy," I tell her.

PIRATES

CHAPTER FIFTEEN

Dylan

I stare down at the pink toy peeking out from the hand towel in Hunter's hand. He went into my room?

I pierce him with my stare, embarrassment warming my cheeks.

"Let me in," he says.

I shake my head. "You sound like Kade. I'll bet he doesn't ask girls nicely, either."

I'm sick of this. I'm officially sick of them. Both of them pulling at me and pulling at me, like I'm a toy neither of them have played with for years and didn't want until the other one did. I don't matter. It's whoever wins who matters, right?

I start to shut the door, but he inserts his foot before I can close it.

"Dylan," he says, his voice strained. "Let me in."

His tone is softer, his eyes pained.

He doesn't wait, though. He forces the door open, and

I back up, past the sink on my left and the shower on my right, slamming into the wall.

Keeping his eyes on me, he sets the vibrator on the counter, unwraps it from the hand towel, and starts the water, steam quickly billowing from the faucet.

My gaze darts between him and the vibrator. "What are you doing?"

"I owe you a birthday present."

He runs the vibrator under the scalding hot water, and maybe he's warming it, but he's definitely sanitizing it. Is he...?

My mouth falls open. "And what are you giving me?"

He turns off the water and uses the towel to dry off the shaft. Then he closes the distance between us. "A really good memory."

The collar of my flannel chafes my neck. I buttoned it up on the way home, so much colder on the back of the bike than it had been earlier. My heart races. I eye the bottle of tequila Farrow gave me on the sink. I knew I should've drunk some.

Hunter touches his forehead to mine, slipping a finger inside my collar. "Take it off," he whispers.

"When you sound like you."

Hunter used to be gentle. Kind.

Tender.

I look at him, his eyes cast downward as he tugs my collar, finally pulling and pulling, harder and harder, until...

The top button flies off, bouncing against the shower curtain, onto the floor.

I growl under my breath, grabbing his arm with both hands before he can yank off another one. In one quick movement, though, he releases my collar, cradles my head with one hand and wraps his other arm around my waist. He buries his face in my neck.

And he just stays there.

I freeze, our chests in sync as we breathe hard, my eyelids growing heavy at the rush of his hot breath against in my skin. "Dylan..." he murmurs.

I close my eyes, sinking into his embrace. *Vulnerable.* Hunter used to be vulnerable too. It feels like him now.

Keeping his mouth on my neck, he pulls at my shirt, and I don't even think as I help him, holding the other side, so the buttons pop off easily, one after the other.

He hovers his mouth over mine, both of us unable to stand still as we graze our lips over each other's cheeks and jaws, about to kiss but don't.

"Still think we can play together?" he pants.

I press my body into his, but keep my hands on the wall behind me as I whisper, "I want to be your favorite toy."

I drop my shirt to the floor and unbutton my shorts, slipping my hand all the way inside. Leaning back on the wall, I move my fingers, feeling the warmth and wetness as I rub my clit.

He stares at my hand. "Slower."

I move in small circles, around and around, feeling the hard nub underneath as I grow wetter.

"Please, slower," he breathes out, my body on fire under my skin and my clothes chafing every inch.

He slides my shorts down with my underwear, and I pause, about to cover myself.

My stomach flips, and I don't know what I'm ready for, but I know Hunter will stop if I want him to. I can stop anytime.

Holding my eyes, he lifts my shirt over my head, and I remove my hand for just a moment. He plants his forearm on the wall next to my head as I go back to rocking my clit back and forth. I hook my other hand over his bicep, holding on as tingles fill my stomach and harden my nipples.

A light layer of sweat shines on his neck, and I smile a little, knowing he likes it.

He reaches behind him and takes my vibrator, pressing a button. It buzzes to life, and goosebumps climb my arms with the realization. He charged it.

He takes my hand off my body and places the vibrating toy in my palm. Flutters crawl up my arm as I hold it.

"Do it," he tells me softly. "Play."

Looking down, I guide the vibrator between my legs, press it to my clit and feel a single, hard jerk rock through my entire body.

I gasp and then smile. He starts to, as well. I touch it to myself again, massaging my clit. I moan and close my eyes.

"Dylan," he whispers, holding my face as I start to roll my hips.

"Ah," I moan. I open my mouth, coaxing his. I want to feel his tongue.

I want to feel his body. I want him to touch me. I want...

I push down my shorts and underwear all the way, moving to the sink. I place the vibrator on the towel, just over the edge, and look at him over my shoulder.

"Behind me. Come here."

His eyebrows are pinched, desperate, and he doesn't ask why. He moves in, taking my hips, and I lift my right leg, setting my knee on the counter. Leaning on my hands, I rub my clit over the toy, staring at him through the mirror in front of us. He wraps a hand around the front of my throat, burying his mouth in my neck and watching my body move in our reflection. Waving my hips in and out, I feel the orgasm already starting to build. I slam the mirror with one hand, going faster and harder and grinding myself over the vibrator.

"Dylan, my God," he growls, gripping the back of my hair. "God, don't stop."

I tip my head back, onto his shoulder. "I want to watch you too."

"I'll come," he warns. "Will that be okay?"

I break out in a smile. That's Hunter.

I nod.

"On you?" he broaches.

A shiver courses down my spine. I nod harder. Hell yes. I want him to love this. I want to feel him.

He pulls off his shirt, rips open his jeans, and holds my eyes in the mirror as he licks his palm. I suck in a breath, excited. He wraps an arm around my waist and presses his mouth and nose into my hair as he rubs his cock. I see his arm moving in up and down motions in our reflection, but I feel it too.

I moan with him pumping it behind me, and I roll and roll over the vibrator, giving him something good to look at.

And before I know it, it's like I'm fucking him. My ass hits his hips and his flesh, and he's so hard. God, I want it deeper. I want him to slide inside of me.

Heat grows low in my belly, lightning building between my thighs, and it's like I'm climbing and I'm almost at the top. I roll my head, sweat cooling the pores on my back. "Hunter, I'm ready," I whimper.

He jerks me back into him again and again, and then pushes me harder down on the vibrator. "Fucking come, Dylan."

I pump my hips, my orgasm cresting, and then it explodes, cascading through my entire body. A wave of pleasure crashes down on me, and my eyelids flutter. "Ahh," I cry. "Ah, ah, ah..."

"Fuck," he growls, jerking harder. His fist in my hair tightens, and he grabs my breast, something hot spilling onto me two or three times. "Ah, fuck."

I shudder, my orgasm coursing through me, and in a moment, he slows, his hand finally stopping and his grip in my hair loosening.

He lowers his mouth to my hair, whispering, "Happy birthday."

I try my best to hold back my smile as I feel his cum trickling down my left side. I wish I could see it.

Reaching back, I touch it and bring my hand back around, looking at him glisten on my finger. I hesitate for a sec and then put it in my mouth.

"Dylan," he groans.

But I wrap my lips around my finger, sucking him all the way off. It's warm. A little salty. It's certainly not bad, though. Would he like how I taste?

I turn off the vibrator and avoid his eyes as I put my leg back down. I'm not used to his mood swings, and he might regret what we just did.

The room cools, the air clears, and I wait for him to leave. To walk out. To get pissy.

He doesn't, though. He turns on the shower and then comes back to me, washing off my vibrator. He dries it and then wipes himself off me with the hand towel before picking up a hair tie from the counter and pulling my hair into a ponytail.

I let myself smile a little as we climb into the shower. He shuts the curtain, grabbing the soap, and I stand under the spray, getting my body wet.

"Have you..." I swallow. "Have you ever done anything like that?"

"No."

He wets his hands, lathering them with soap. I move, letting him under the water.

"And the other women you said you've seen naked?" I ask.

He doesn't reply, just comes in and washes me with his bare hands.

I point. "There's a washcloth."

But he just gives me a look, a smile playing over his mouth. He washes my arms and kneels down to clean my legs. Soaping up his hands again, he spins me around, bringing my back into his chest, and runs his fingers across my stomach before cupping my breasts. I lose the air in my lungs as he glides them up my back, down over my ass, and then hugs me to his body as he slides his hands down between my legs. Slipping inside, he cleans all of me.

"I want to take the vibrator home with me," he says.

To his house?

"Why?" I blurt out.

Him washing me is getting me worked up again. I'm going to need it.

"Because I want to be a part of when you use it."

I blink long and hard, thankful he can't see. While I like the sound of that, I'm confused. Are we, like, friends doing a little exploring together, or does he want me? What if this is more for me, and it's not the same for him?

My voice is smaller than I'd like when I admit, "I wanted to use it when I wake up in the morning."

"You know that already?"

He sounds like he wants to laugh.

"I'm most relaxed then," I explain. "I think about sex more in the morning."

But in one fell swoop, he removes his hands from me and rinses off under the shower.

He steps out, leaving me behind, and I stand there, still soapy and just as confused. "Hunter..."

"It'll be under my pillow," he says. "House will be unlocked."

He grabs a towel, dries off, and pulls on his clothes again.

Is he leaving? Seriously? "Hunter, please."

I want the vibrator tonight, actually.

"You know where it'll be." He grins. "Get some sleep. School tomorrow."

REBELS

CHAPTER SIXTEEN

Hunter

The next morning, I'm walking out of my bathroom in my sleep pants, rubbing the towel over my wet hair. Alone.

I thought for sure she'd come last night.

I thought she'd sneak into my bedroom a half an hour later, unable to sleep, because she was too worked up.

But no. She just went to bed after all that and didn't need more. Unlike me. It took me *for-fucking-ever* to finally drift off, especially because I just wanted to get to sleep, so I could wake up to her climbing over my body to get at her vibrator underneath my pillow.

I'm not saying I'm mad. Just...frustrated. I guess the vibrator wasn't better than her fingers because I woke up twenty minutes ago alone.

Or maybe she's feeling weird about it after-the-fact. I've baked cookies with her. Taken swimming lessons with her. Shared giant pretzels at the fair with her. Maybe I shouldn't have come on her. That was probably going too far.

It was like a frenzy, though. God, she was hot. And I still love the way we play. No matter how it changes.

"You okay?" someone asks.

I pop my head up, my heart skipping a beat. I stare at Hawke standing right in front of me on the second-floor landing of my grandfather's brownstone.

"Dude, what the hell?" I blurt out, dropping my arm. "You scared me."

I realize my eyebrows are pinched, and I probably looked in pain when I came out of the bathroom because I'm dying with my need for Dylan.

I drop the expression, heat stifling me as if he could tell what I was just thinking. Dylan's his *actual* cousin, and Hawke is like Jax. They know things, and you don't know how they know them.

Why is he here?

"How'd you get in?" I ask, looking downstairs for Rebels, but I don't see Farrow or anyone.

"Secret entrance," he tells me. "Dylan's house next door has one too."

Secret entrance? I head down the stairs, forcing him to follow me. "How do you know that? I don't even know that."

He doesn't reply, and I walk into the dining room, tossing my towel on the table.

I look around. "Where is it?" I ask.

He just gives me a half smile. "Ask Dylan," he tells me. "If she wants you to know, she can tell you."

"Well, now I really want to know," I bark. "I don't need a team of Pirates invading my house in the middle of the night."

"If I tell you, you'll seal it, and Dylan might need to get in for her safety."

Huh?

"Or get out for her safety," he adds.

I arch a brow.

But he's right. I will seal it. I don't want my brother or his crew finding out and slipping in. Hawke will tell me once Rivalry Week is over.

"So, what's up?" I ask as I walk to the window and pull aside the curtain. Hopefully he knows to hide his car.

But all I see is Constin leaning on his bike in front of Dylan's house.

"I understand you were in Frosted the other night?" Hawke announces, browsing the books stuffed in the old curio cabinet meant for fancy china.

"You mean when Dylan disappeared through a wall?"

"Through the mirror," he corrects. "Please keep that to yourself, okay?"

"You thought I would share that with the Rebels?"

I would never put Quinn's business, or my family's safety, at risk. And I certainly wouldn't tell anyone, no matter how much I trusted them, before talking to Dylan about it.

I release the curtain and turn toward him. "So only our family knows about it then?"

"Some Pirates do."

"But not me?"

"Man, we would've told you," he retorts, "but it's not exactly the kind of thing you call to divulge over the phone to someone you've barely seen in a year."

Or to someone playing football for a rival school. "Fine," I also admit, "And maybe, I would tell Farrow eventually."

"No, fuck, please don't do that."

With the way his face scrunches up in disgust, I can tell he doesn't think much of Farrow Kelly. I laugh quietly, because Farrow's never going to be far away, I don't think, and Hawke will have to contend with him more than he yet realizes. I glance at the Green Street tattoo on Hawke's neck, which I learned he only has so they would let him have Aro without any more grief. "We'll revisit this discussion another time," I say.

He pulls a book off my shelf, holding up *Algorithms to Live By*. "Can I borrow this?"

"Sure."

It's his dad's anyway.

"So, what is it?" I ask. "Behind the mirror."

"Rooms." He flips through the book. "It's better to see it rather than try to explain it. But it's related to the story of the house next door."

I wonder how much of that story is true. Everyone made a big deal about Dylan staying there, enough to keep me up most of her first night here to watch the house, but it's been almost a week and no ghosts.

Every story starts somewhere, though, and the idea of secret rooms between Rivertown and Quinn's shop is intriguing.

"Fill me in after the game then," I tell him.

I need to concentrate right now.

"You look good," he says, stepping closer. "I've missed you."

"Yeah, I've missed you too. I like Aro."

A smile spreads across this face, his azure-blue eyes filled with something I've never seen in them before.

He's in love.

"What about you?" He tips his chin at me. "What the hell was going on in that picture of you and Dylan in your towels?"

I'm about to tell him I'm not talking about it, but something hits the floor above. We both look up.

That's my room.

He fixes a knowing look on his face. "Maybe your parents need to know about you needing just as much adult supervision as Kade?"

I pick up my towel and ball it up. "Don't blackmail me." I shoot the towel into his chest like a basketball. "My grandfather will fit you with a pair of cement galoshes."

I walk off, toward the stairs.

He shouts behind me, "Please, Ciaran is practically my grandfather too. He loves my dad. More than he likes yours!"

I almost laugh as I climb the steps. That's probably true. My mom's dad is constantly in one argument or another with my father. But I think Ciaran knows my mom couldn't have gotten a better husband. No one could have.

I open the door to my room and see Dylan frozen, mid-crawl on my bed. She's dressed in a T-shirt and sleep shorts as she reaches under my pillow.

I close the door and rush over, grabbing her vibrator before she can reach it. "No, nuh-uh." I hold it away from her. "We have to go to school now. You should've been here earlier."

She hops off the bed, looking at me with her puppy dog eyes. "Please, I just need thirty seconds."

She shoots out her arm to take it, but I hold it high over my head as she claws for my arm. I try not to laugh, but I can't stop the slight grin on my face. How the hell did she get in here? Did she use the secret entrance, too, because that tree between our houses isn't like the one at her house in the Falls. She'll kill herself trying to scale it.

She grabs onto my neck, leaping up to snatch the vibrator out of my hand, and I'm about to give in, because it doesn't matter anymore that I got little sleep, wishing she was here all night. She definitely liked what we did and wants more.

She bats my hand, and the vibrator goes flying onto the bed. She scrambles, and so do I, but my long arms reach the toy first. I take it, she fights me, and I crash back on the bed, slipping it inside my pants. She sits there on her knees as I smile and slide my arm underneath my head. "No," I tell her. "You can't have it."

But fire lights in her eyes, and I almost stop breathing, reading her thoughts a split-second before she moves.

She throws a leg over my body and climbs on, rolling her hips over both dicks inside my pants.

"Oh, fuck." I suck in a breath, grabbing her waist in both hands as she throws off her shirt.

"Turn it on," she pants.

"Dylan..." I groan, reaching inside and feeling for the button. I press it, shivers rocking through the device and against my groin. My heart about stops. *Oh my God*.

Her lips hover over mine as she dry-fucks the cock in pants, her hot breath filled with moans and whimpers as I let my hands roam inside the back of her shorts.

I pull them down a little, hungry to feel her skin, but she takes the hint and rolls off me, slipping out of the rest of her clothes, and then climbs back on top. All in two seconds.

Sitting up, she rocks back and forth, her breasts too much to take. I arch up and take one in my mouth, sucking on it as she lets her head fall back, crying out.

My eyes go wide. *Shit*.

I almost put my hand over her mouth, because I'm about to come, too, and I can't think about anything else. I yank her hips into me again and again. "You're driving me insane, Dylan." I glide my tongue up her long neck, feeling her nails digging into my shoulders. "Come on, fuck me."

"Hunter," she whimpers and pulls me up close. Wrapping her arms around my neck, she hugs me, fucking me faster. "Hunter, I—"

But three knocks hit the door. "Hey, where do you keep the coffee?"

She startles, looking down at me, and I try to answer, but my throat is dry. "Fuck," I whisper.

"Is that Hawke?" she pants.

But then her faces pinches in pain, and she moans. I clasp my hand over her mouth.

"Hunter," Hawke barks.

"I'm getting dressed!" I growl, dropping back to the bed so she can grind harder. "It's on top of the fridge."

She crashes down on me, her chest to mine as she pumps her hips.

I grip her ass in both hands. "You almost there?"

"Yeah."

The headboard bangs against the wall, and my mouth falls open, knowing the whole house can hear that. But then her lips meet mine, and I forgot what I was going to say.

"He's going to hear," she whispers.

"I can't care about that right now." I hold her face, kissing, nibbling, and biting. "Come on. Ride me. Come on."

Sweat breaks out on my forehead, a blaze flooding my stomach down low, and I jerk as she thrusts. I bury my nose and mouth behind her ear, inhaling her scent as I squeeze my eyes shut.

Oh, fuck. "Ugh," I moan, the muscles inside me contracting, building, climbing, and then...pleasure floods my body, exploding with a wave of heat and her face blurs in front of me.

Her whimpers get louder and faster, and I feel every muscle in her body tense before she shudders and shakes in my arms.

And then she relaxes.

Her chest caves, and I gently cup a breast in one hand and a hip in the other. God, I wish I was inside of her.

Her breathing calms, her body melting into mine, and I pull out the vibrator, shutting it off. She shifts on top of me, and I wince, feeling the mess in my pants.

"Do you think he heard?" she asks.

I hold her head to my chest. "I'll just tell him I was doing what I was told. Taking care of you," I say.

She flashes me a smirk and climbs off, pulling the sheet up over her as she slips back into her shorts. I pick up her shirt, handing it to her. Pulling it on quickly, she sits up and leans on one arm, looking down at me.

I wait for her to say whatever it looks like she wants to say, but instead, she gazes around, taking in my room.

It's not like my bedroom at home. Or the one I have at my grandfather's house. I came here with one goal and didn't invest in staying. No maps on the walls or terrariums on the dressers. No stacks of books on the floor or the model Zeppelin I built with my dad and Kade when I was seven. Just a desk, dresser, bed, chair, and closet. Sparse. Clean.

She scoots off the bed and rises to her feet. "Do you remember when you put all those bird feeders in your yard to study which food they preferred?"

Yeah. But I don't answer out loud, just watch her as she inspects the receipts I dug out of my pocket and put on my dresser, along with the medical tape for football injuries.

She goes on, "And then you threw some small, leftover cuts of beef out there, and it attracted the wolves?" She smiles, glancing at me. "Your dad was so mad, but he was trying to hold it back because he didn't want to dissuade your creative curiosity or something?"

I sit up, swinging my legs over the bed. I need another shower.

"Or that time you ran out to see the tornado?" she asks. "Or the CDs and mixtapes you used to make for me?"

I rub the back of my neck before tilting it hard to crack it. "Are you..." I clear my throat. "Are you feeling guilty about what we just did?" I ask her.

"No."

"Then why..."

I fall silent, not wanting to ask why she's bringing up the past, because she's just going to ask why I never do. I don't like to think about back then. I always felt bad. I was either enduring Kade or following her, and being myself never got me what I longed for. We just had a very good morning. Why does she want me to remember anything before now?

Maybe she just wants her friend back? Maybe she's only here, naked on top of me a minute ago, because she misses how we used to be, and that's all she really wants.

I'm not sure I can remember a time when all I wanted from her was friendship. I've always wanted more.

Standing up, I pull out fresh clothes to take into the bathroom with me.

"Constin was parked in front of your house," I tell her. "Any idea what he wanted?"

"He knocked on the door and asked me to homecoming."

I dart my gaze to hers. "And what did you say?"

"I said maybe."

"You said what?"

I scowl, but I don't mean to. She licks her lips, wide-eyed and looking so sweet as she gives a half-hearted shrug. "Well, nobody else has asked m–"

I descend on her mouth, kissing her hard. Everyone else doesn't matter. I'm always her date.

I give her bottom lip a little bite before pulling back. "I'll get rid of Hawke," I tell her, now that that's settled. "You go get dressed. I'll take you to school."

She nods, smiling, and leaves through my door instead of the window. I almost follow her to see this secret entrance, but as soon as I move, I flinch again, feeling my wet pants.

Shower first.

The school day passes quicker than I expected. From the moment she leaves to get ready for class and I step into the shower, I can't stop thinking about a playlist and what I would put on it for her. Dylan loves everything. She could dance to polka if her mood suited.

And then I think about all the CDs I burned for her or mixtapes I made her, because the cars her dad loved still had tape decks and CD changers.

I liked making those lists for her, but I made them because I wanted to be important to her. To give her something Kade never would, as if it would make her love me.

I don't want to sink back into doing things for the wrong reasons.

So, I don't do anything.

I don't make her a playlist over the course of the day because it would feel like surrender.

Just like I don't tell my brother how much I miss him.

And I keep my mouth shut around her at lunch, and how I'm starting to dread that her time here is halfway up. I don't want to be away from her when she goes home.

I should tell them both all of that, because while being myself never got me what I wanted, I'm not happy being whoever I've been trying to be the past year, either.

By eight p.m., I cruise into the Falls, Dylan already at Helm's Field with Farrow and everyone else. I pull up to where their cars are parked, same place as when we came to set off the fireworks, on the other side of the fence.

We could've sat in the Visitor's section to watch the Pirates and Knights, both teams we hate, battle it out, but that would mean buying tickets, and no one here is giving their money to Shelburne Falls. At least until it's our turn to play next week. We'll be coming back here. Unfortunately, our field lacks all the amenities, like sufficient seating, concessions, and groundskeepers.

Farrow, Constin, and Calvin lean on the hood of Farrow's car smoking and passing around a Thermos of something that's probably not coffee, while others loiter around, various vehicles and motorcycles littering the area.

Circling the front of the car, I avoid the field, seeing players running in their uniforms out of the corner of my eye, and hearing the tackles, the whistles, and the cheers. The game should be over soon, but I don't check the scoreboard.

Instead, I watch Dylan.

She walks over to me dressed in a crewneck pullover sweater with thick stripes, half tucked in to tight, ripped jeans. A brown leather belt with notches all the way to the buckle is wrapped tightly around her waist, and all I can think about are the images of everywhere my hands roamed this morning.

I sit on the hood of my car, leaning back against the windshield, and I meet her eyes as she stops next to my car. "Our parents are probably here," I tell her.

Even Jared and Tate and Jax and Juliet always showed up to support us. My dad is probably standing on the sidelines with Kade's coach. I wonder which side he'll stand on next Friday.

"You're allowed to go say hi," I tell Dylan, smiling a little. "If you want."

The prisoner exchange isn't all that serious. I'm sure her parents would like to see her.

But she's quiet for a moment. "It's okay," she says. "The space is actually nice."

"For your dad or you?"

She gives me a look. "What do you know?"

I face the field again, finally glancing at the scoreboard. "Just what my dad fills me in on during our weekly chats." And then I paraphrase for her. "'Jared won't let you race, and sometimes he has trouble using his emotion words.'" She snorts, and I keep going. "'And you're just biding your time until you graduate, and he no longer has a say in what you do.'"

She shakes her head, but amusement is written all over her face. "Pretty much."

I get it, though—enjoying the space. No talking at least means no fighting.

But the truth is, we've had it pretty good. Loving, two-parent households, and none of us are on drugs. There are hills to climb once in a while, but I've never felt like I was on my own, and I don't think Dylan has ever felt like that, either.

"What do you think about it?" she asks. "My dad not wanting me to race motorbikes."

I draw in a breath and meet her eyes. "I think your dad loves you and he's scared for you." I drop my eyes to her mouth, feeling my heart quicken. "And...you're just as stubborn as he is, and you're going to be really glad when he takes his place in your corner eventually."

She looks away, her chin trembling a little.

"He'll come around, Dylan."

"Do you think so?"

I nod. "Yeah."

The expression on her face relaxes, and she opens my driver's side door, stepping on the hinge and stepping onto the hood behind me. She slides down the glass, and I rise up a little, letting her in as she fits me between her legs and wraps her arms around my stomach.

She hugs me. "Thank you."

I lean back into her, and we watch the game in silence.

I guess I don't have any room to give advice or to tell her that everything will work out when I didn't trust that at all. I just left.

I shouldn't have. I have just as much right to be in that house as Kade does.

"Do you want him to win or lose?" she asks me softly.

I swallow hard as I watch Kade get into position and turn his head in my direction, knowing I'm here.

I want to win.

Which means he'd have to lose.

That's not what I want. I don't want him unhappy.

"I always want him to win," I tell her.

We watch as the fourth quarter moves on, and the Pirates lead forty-nine to thirty-eight with one minute left in the game. The Knights have the ball with first and ten, and even if they make a touchdown, it's unlikely they'll make two, even if the offense can get on the field again before time runs out. I watch Kade throw, a Knight sacking him, but I don't watch the score or listen to the announcers.

And I only know the Pirates won when Dylan shoots her fists into the air, cheering.

"Whoo, whoo, whoo!"

Farrow and the rest of the Rebels scowl in our direction, but I just chuckle, pulling her arms back down. "I think that's sufficient."

"I would cheer for the Rebels if they were on the field too."

Yeah, it's a bye week for us. No game till next Friday.

Half the stadium cheers, players congratulating each other on the field, and people start to leave the stands, heading for their cars.

My brother will talk to our parents outside, shower, and go out with friends. Rivertown and High Street will be swarming with activity. They'll all be looking for him.

"Is it okay if you catch a ride with Farrow?" I ask her. "I have something I need to do."

She holds my eyes for a moment, and I can tell she's suspicious. But then she just says, "Okay."

I hop off the hood, and she slides off, stepping toward Farrow and only releasing my hand when she has to.

They all leave, but I stand there for a while longer, waiting for the traffic to dissipate. Maybe Kade will come back out. After his shower, alone. Without his friends.

He doesn't.

Everyone leaves, the stadium nearly empty, and the long stream of taillights slowly disappear down the road.

When the night is quiet again, I get in my car and drive home. Past High Street and the party on the sidewalks, and down the dark highway to the mansions on the northwest end.

One of the garage doors is open—the one my father uses—and I see my grandpa's Audi, his driver sitting inside, tapping away on his phone.

I park and walk up to the front door, turning the knob. It opens, and I step inside, smelling food instantly.

Portraits and paintings decorate the walls, all the same ones I remember from the last time I was here. The black and white one of Kade and me covered in mud when we were five after playing in the rain sits on the foyer table. His arm is around me, both of us with our silly grins, having lost our first teeth.

I stroll past the staircase, hearing talking and laughter in the kitchen as my grandfather, mom, dad, and A.J. come into view.

I lean in the doorway arch. "Hi."

Everyone pops their heads up, A.J. gasping. "Hunter!"

She races toward me, and I barely have time to catch her before she crashes into my stomach. My mom and dad smile, my dad shrugging out of his jacket.

I tug my little sister's ponytail, seeing that she's dressed in my old Pirate jersey, probably because she was just at the game. "Hey, Captain," I say, gesturing to the family. "Everyone's still alive, I see. Good job."

She's the one in charge. We've all known it since her birth.

She takes my hand and pulls me toward the kitchen island. "You have so much college mail."

"Everyone wants me, huh?"

I look at the stack of envelopes she digs out of a cupboard underneath.

"Or your tuition money," she tells me.

Everyone laughs, my dad snorting.

My grandpa simply tips his chin at me. He sees me pretty regularly.

My mom hugs me tightly. "Please tell me you're staying."

I pull back, looking down at her. "A couple of hours."

She drops her eyes, hesitating before she turns away and gets busy filling a bowl with something savory.

I hover over her, seeing beef stew. "Ooh, smells good." I reach for the bowl. "Gimme."

But I see her lips tremble.

"Please don't," I whisper, looking into her eyes and the tears she's holding back. "I'll be home soon. Just let me finish what I started, okay? I promise."

"Don't forget you have us, okay?"

Her jaw flexes, and I can tell she's trying to control herself. My mom has never been much of a crier. Most of the time she never had a reason to be.

"I won't," I tell her.

I smile and take a spoon as she hands me the bowl, and I head to the island to sit next to my grandpa.

"You eating enough?" Dad asks. "Not fast food, right?"

"No, we're cooking."

"We?" Mom inquires.

I glace at A.J. sorting my mail, checking off boxes on a spreadsheet she has pinned to her clipboard.

"Um, Farrow," I finally spit out. "Farrow Kelly. He's a senior, too, but a year older. Grandpa installed him in the house as a chaperone, I'm pretty sure."

I glance at Ciaran, but he just eats.

"Have I met him?" Mom asks.

I fill the spoon with stew. "You should," I say, throwing my double meaning out there for my grandfather to pick up.

He simply clears his throat and holds out his bowl to my mom. "May I have some more, please?"

He flashes me a scowl, and I spoon in another mouthful.

"So...senator?" I look to my dad. "That's going to make me get a haircut, isn't it?"

I thought being mayor of Shelburne Falls would be enough, but I spotted an article online mentioning him for next year's election. To be fair, he has discussed it with me. I just hoped he wasn't serious.

"If I have to wear pantsuits," my mom chimes in, "you're at least getting a trim."

"Are you kidding?" Dad teases. "The only reason I'm in politics is to see your ass in pantsuits." He puts an arm around my grandfather. "Your daughter has the nicest..."

"Shut up, ya gobshite," Ciaran growls.

I break down mid-bite, shaking with laughter with everyone else.

A.J. giggles, repeating the curse. "Gobshite."

"Greeeat." Mom gives Grandpa a dirty look. "Thanks a lot."

She turns off the stove and then pushes a cutting board filled with sliced French bread toward me. This is how we often ate as a family. The dining room sits through the doorway to my right, but we only used it on special occasions and holidays. Every other time, we ate at the small table to my left, or here at the island, some days just shoveling in food while standing next to the stove.

I loved it.

We were busy, one parent or the other always rushing off to take one of us to a music lesson or sports practice, and they had full-time careers on top of that. There was no pressure to uphold the façade of always having everything under control, and it meant that the older we got, the more freedom we had, because what we really wanted most after a certain point was privacy. I didn't want to tell them about my day every evening over dinner, feeling pressured to lie and say I was "fine" when I didn't want to tell them the truth either. I didn't want forced conversation and questions because being involved is what they thought made a healthy family. When my friends were lying to their parents, mine were the only thing that was easy for me.

After cleaning my bowl and stacking my dishes in the dishwasher, I walk upstairs. Opening the door to my room, I head to the closet and pull out my suit, still sealed inside the garment bag the tailor delivered it to us in. Kade has several. Dad loves suits and always made sure we had one to wear for impromptu occasions, but I haven't worn this one yet.

I open it up, checking the size of the jacket and pants.

And I hang it back up.

I was fitted for it a year and a half ago. It won't fit me now. It's not like Dylan will care what I wear to a school dance anyway.

But I will.

I turn my head, gazing at my bed and seeing that the navy-blue comforter rests at the bottom in a zigzag fold, the tan coverlet pulled up over the pillows at the head.

I don't make my bed like that. Neither do my parents or the house cleaners they bring in to help. I know they have my sheets washed every few weeks, in case I show up.

I step over to my bed and pick up one of my pillows, pressing my nose into the case. I close my eyes, smelling her shampoo, clean and crisp, like green apples and amber. She must've slept here not long before the prisoner exchange.

I guess I could take a suit from Kade's closet. It's tempting.

But I won't. I set the pillow back down on the bed and go to search for something else nice in my closet. But just then, my dad passes by the doorway and stops.

"Hey," he says. "Come see the GTO."

I close my closet door, and then my bedroom one behind me, glancing at Kade's room across the hall as I pass. His door is open, three tall green lockers anchored to the wall next to his bathroom. Those weren't there when I left.

I head back downstairs with my dad. "You know, if you keep modifying that car, it's going to be unsellable."

"I'll never sell it." He stops just before the door to the garage and slips into his leather shoes. He pushes up the sleeves of his pullover, a blue Oxford underneath. "One of my grandkids will get it, since none of my children have taste or style."

Sure. No one can tell my dad he's wrong about anything, especially clothes or cars.

We head out, stepping into the garage, and walk past my mom's Infiniti, as well as her old motorbike that she just could never get rid of. The rest of the garage is filled with something for every occasion. A truck, an SUV, a Jeep Wrangler, a McLaren convertible, and a Tesla for everyday use, because it's important to be seen as an environmentally conscious politician.

We stop at his silver GTO, the first car he ever owned in high school. He lifts the hood and grabs a wrench, leaning down to remove the engine cover. "Speaking of grandkids…" His eyes rise up to me.

It takes me a minute to realize what he's getting at. The picture of Dylan and me coming out of the bathroom in towels.

"Nothing happened."

"*Something* happened."

I lean down under the hood on the opposite side of the car. "I don't want to talk about this."

Nothing happened that night to warrant concern. I mean, lots has happened since then, but he wasn't asking about last night. Or this morning.

I just want to keep her to myself for now.

Dad twists the bolts, keeping his eyes on the task at hand. "Kade is very sexually active," he says in a calm tone. "I've never been ignorant of anything either of you do."

He was no angel as a teenager, either, so he doesn't delude himself when the vodka in his bottle is watered down, or Kade claims the condoms in the dryer that he forgot to remove from his pocket belong to a friend.

He continues, "But even though I worry about his level of disconnect in relationships, I worry just as much about you, because you connect hard." He meets my eyes. "To everything you love, you always have."

My body tenses.

"If she hurts you," he says softly, "whether she means to or not, you did nothing wrong."

Pain squeezes my throat, and I stand up straight, trying to look anywhere but at him.

"You deserve her," he says.

I clench my teeth to keep my chin still, because he knows that no matter how tough I talk inside my head, or how many times she smiles at me, I still think I fade in comparison to my brother.

"You deserve her," he repeats.

"Deserve who?" someone asks.

I startle, looking over at my uncle Jared walking into the garage. Quinn stands outside, wrapping A.J. in a bear hug. I forgot she was back for the weekend.

I blink away the water in my eyes as Dad clears his throat. "And uh, remember," he tells me, "women need to primed before intercourse."

I jerk my eyes to Dylan's father and then to mine. *What*?

"You know, get her body ready," he goes on. "A little foreplay. Sounds like you're figuring it out anyway. Good job."

I dart my eyes to Jared again, the pinch between his brow deepening.

"And don't forget to bring a towel into the bedroom beforehand, either," my dad says, "because then you have to leave to go get it, and that's a hassle. Women like men who bring their own towels."

Jared turns his head slowly toward me, his scowl darkening, because he's no doubt seen the picture of his daughter and me coming out of the bathroom too.

"And get in that habit quickly." My dad won't fucking shut up. "Because after our first time, we're doing it *all* the time. Like frickin' rabbits."

Oh my God.

"Would you like some condoms to take back to Weston with you?" he asks.

I blink long and hard, feeling Jared's glare, and I get the hell out of there. Walking back to the door, I dive inside, hearing tools drop to the floor, a scuffle, and my dad's laughter. "Dude, you're wrinkling me." I slam the door shut.

Son of a bitch. Seriously.

Maybe I really should stay in Weston. His jokes are going to get me killed here.

Steering toward the kitchen, I see my mom sitting at the island, working on her laptop. Her reading glasses catch the light of the chandelier, and her hair lays over one side of her head as she looks down, taking notes.

"Take some food with you?" she asks, already knowing I'm here.

She looks up and gestures to the two glass Pyrex dishes with lids stacked on the counter.

"That's actually great." I inch in. "Thank you."

She nods and goes back to jotting down whatever she's researching.

"And thank you for trusting me to be on my own over there," I say.

"I think that's what your brother needs." She keeps writing. "Some time to build life skills, like cleaning his own bathroom, washing his own sheets, cooking some meals..."

I know she's trying turn my absence into something positive, but I know she wouldn't choose for me to learn anything by being separated from her.

"What should I have done better with you?" she asks, finally looking up again.

I give a half-hearted shrug, not because I don't know, but because it's not her fault.

Parents are parents. Human like everyone else. They project their own dreams and hopes, standards and expectations, because it's innate to worry that we'll never figure it out on our own. We're all screwed up by our parents to some extent, but there was never a time when I didn't know how lucky I was. Never.

I lean my elbows down on the island. "How about a haircut?"

She smiles and reaches over, digging scissors out of the drawer.

PIRATES

CHAPTER SEVENTEEN

Dylan

At least Hunter didn't keep backup with him in the Falls. When he said he had something to do, I worried it was because he wanted to see Kade. I hope he does. I'm just glad he seemed to go wherever he was going alone because the Rebels would only encourage a fight.

But Hunter went his own way, and the rest of us stopped at Breaker's for cheeseburgers on the way home. They're getting drunk in the street now, but I need a shower.

Just in case the night isn't over yet. I smile to myself, my mind working overtime with the possibilities.

I close the front door, hearing a phone ring upstairs.

But I have my phone. I pull it out of my jeans. Why do I hear ringing...?

Then I remember the burner Hawke gave me. Right. I bolt up the stairs, into the bedroom, and yank open the bedside drawer, pulling the second phone off from the charger.

I swipe the screen. "Hey."

"Hey," Hawke replies. "I got your text. Sorry, I had a ton of classwork."

"Why are you calling this phone?"

"Because your other one was going to voicemail. Is it dead?"

Is it? I press the *Power* button, seeing it is, in fact, dead. I plug it into the charger.

"So, what's up?" I ask, remembering I texted him a rundown of the story Bastien told me yesterday.

"I've looked into the names." I hear a shuffle and a bunch of chatter in the background. He's probably at his dorm. "Conor Doran declared dead twenty-two years ago. Supposedly buried at Esplanade Street Cemetery. Check it out, okay?"

"What do you want me to do?" I walk to my window, gazing over at Hunter's dark bedroom. "Dig him up?"

"Just confirm the gravesite and take a picture for me."

"Anybody could be buried in that grave," I fire back.

"You watch too much TV."

Oh, whatever. He knows Murphy's Law as well as I do. Anything that can happen, will happen, and a gravestone for Conor Doran proves nothing.

"I'm checking Winslet," he says, "seeing if she's on any radars after that year."

"And—"

"And I'm on Deacon," he assures me. "Deacon Doran. So far, nothing. No social media, no credit history, no transfer paperwork for colleges... Just a birth certificate."

"No death certificate, though?"

He pauses, but only for a moment. "No."

So, he's hiding. Probably because he killed a girl two decades ago and is trying not to get caught.

But it's too easy. If it were that simple, why would there be any mystery at all? Why the varying versions? Why the confusion about what exactly happened?

We need to start piecing together what she did when she was here. She attended classes, met new people, probably endured a few pranks like I have...

And then I stop in my tracks, thinking.

Like I have...

"If Winslet's experience mirrors my own at all, being a hostage here, then the Rebels weren't the only ones targeting her," I point out.

"Meaning?"

I pace the room. "Is there any proof it was the Rebels at all?"

"You mean other than the creepy text conversations we uncovered?"

I roll my eyes, but at myself. *That's true.* The Doran boys, judging from those cell phones Hawke found in Carnival Tower, had a nefarious plan.

But still, that's not proof they actually went through with anything.

"The Pirates aren't happy with me being here," I point out. "What if it was them? What if Shelburne Falls killed her?"

He's quiet, and I can almost picture his eyes shooting up to the ceiling as I hear the quiet sigh, because I just made his pursual of this legend a lot more complicated.

"I'll let you know what I find," he finally says.

"Love ya," I tell him, my tone apologetic.

"Bye."

We hang up, and I check the time. It's just after ten.

I glance over at Hunter's bedroom window again, still not seeing any lights on.

I'm not sneaking into his room for my vibrator. I'd rather use it with him.

But I'm not tired yet, either.

Sweeping my hair up into a ponytail, I pull off my sweater and slip into a black T-shirt, grabbing my jacket on the way back out of the house.

I step onto the porch, seeing Constin and Luca pull up in front of Hunter's and grab a duffel bag out of the trunk. They carry it over to Farrow who stands just outside his and Hunter's front door. He looks inside and nods, taking it from them. They glance at me, and I look away, suddenly feeling like I saw something I wasn't supposed to see.

Farrow works for Green Street. I keep forgetting that.

He wouldn't keep illegal things in the house, would he? With Hunter there?

I spot Coral's car across the street and spy a group of girls in the barber shop. It's late for it to be open, but I don't think that guy keeps regular business hours. Fletcher's sign, the letters that still light up anyway, is on all the time.

I jog across the street.

Entering the shop, I see Coral in the chair, one foot propped up on the counter as the elderly dude shaves the back of her head. Everything above her ears is parted and wrapped in two buns, one on the left side and one on the right, the bottom half not quite bald as he etches a butterfly into the back of her scalp. She drinks from a tumbler filled with ice and something pink.

Mace sits in the chair along the storefront window, and I almost don't notice Tommy Dietrich leaning against the opposite wall by the old Coke machine.

She stares at me.

No one says hi.

I approach Coral. "How much have you had to drink?"

She looks up at me, and I drop my eyes to her tumbler.

"Why, you want some?" she asks, chewing gum.

"No, I need you to drive." I pull on my jacket, buttoning it up. "I'd like to get rid of what's in your trunk."

I'm not really concerned I'll get in trouble for stealing the locker. Anyone would understand why I got rid of it, but I don't want it getting put back. I need to make sure no one will ever find it.

"You have any money?" Coral asks me.

I refrain from mentioning the fireworks and party I— well, Hawke—paid for. I simply say, "No."

"Then how do you expect to pay me for my time?"

I open my mouth to question how valuably she spends her time otherwise, but I decide to play nice. "What would you like?"

A throat clears behind me, and I turn to lock eyes with Mace. She holds out her hand, and I literally bite my tongue, no confusion at all about what she wants.

I rip open the buttons and remove my jacket. Taking three steps, I hold it out to her. "On one condition," I say.

She grabs for it, and I pull it back. "If the Pirates win," I tell her. "You give it back."

She rises and snatches it out of my hand. "I'll take that bet."

The man, who I assume is Mr. Fletcher, takes a brush and dusts the hair off Coral's neck. She hops up, stuffing cash in his hand before taking her keys out of her pants. "Where are we going?" she asks me.

But I pluck her keys away from her instead. "I'm driving. You're toasted."

"No one drives my car."

But I'm already heading out of the barber shop.

"Let her drive your car," Mace mumbles.

I hold the door open for them and lock eyes with Tommy who still leans against the wall. "You coming?" I ask her. "I think you're going to want to be in on this."

I don't wait. Walking to the car, I slide into the driver's seat and hear the doors slam shut before I start the engine. As I shift it into *Drive*, one of the back doors opens again, and I see Tommy through the rearview mirror, climbing in.

I press the gas and pull out into the street.

I barely have to think about it before the only place to bury it that makes sense occurs to me. I drive to the bridge.

I suppose they all didn't need to come with me. I only need one person's help to lift the locker. But I'm sure Coral wasn't letting me take her car anywhere without her.

Still, though. I'm glad they're here.

I pull onto the bridge, cross to the halfway point, and swerve as far to the left as I can, parking. They follow me out of the car as I walk to the rear and unlock the trunk. Opening it up, I see the yellow locker laying amidst a bunch of other stuff. A blanket, a cooler, a kite, and a shovel. I shake my head. I'll process that later.

I start to lift the locker, Mace grabbing the other side.

"So, what's the story with this thing?" she asks me.

We carry it around the front of the car. "Just some family history bullshit that needs to die."

I throw a glance to Tommy as she leans on the fender. Her expression is blank, but she doesn't argue.

We lift it over the side of the bridge, Coral coming to my other side as I look down into the dark water. The wind blows, creating a ripple on the river, but I almost think I see the dark form of the car below.

But then, it's gone.

I grip the locker, hesitating as I turn my gaze on Thomasin, waiting for her to protest. It's her mom's old locker, after all.

She doesn't even blink.

"Ready?" I ask Mace, tilting it.

"Are you sure it's empty?" she questions.

But it's already gone.

Plummeting into the river, the steel box slowly fills with water and sinks as we all hang our heads over the side to watch it join the other ghosts at the bottom. There's nothing inside. We would've heard it shift while carrying it.

The girls drift off, and I hear chatter and laughter behind me, only me and Tommy remaining at the edge. She stands several feet away, déjà vu hitting me, because the last time we stood on a bridge together—the train bridge down the road two months ago—we were all jumping off from it.

"Kade will be gone at the end of the year," I say, still staring at the water. "And A.J. and James won't come in until after you graduate."

She'll have Shelburne Falls High to herself, without any Trents or Caruthers for three years.

"Things will get better," I tell her.

Although, I doubt A.J. or James would take issue with her the way Kade has. He's her burden, more so than I think he lets us know, because he knows we don't like his behavior toward her. Still though, it'll be nice for her not to hear our names in the hallway, even if sometimes, I wish we were closer in age. Being in the same schools for longer growing up, I might've been able to shield her more from him.

The sky, thick with clouds, hangs low, charging the air with the scent of rain. Locks of hair whip across my face, and I tilt my head back, closing my eyes.

"Drink?" I hear Coral offer, nudging my arm.

Hell yeah. But not yet.

"Tomorrow," I tell her, opening my eyes. "Storm's coming."

I think there'll be a party.

I look over the edge again, remember what the teacher said about how Conor waited for a stormy night. Maybe hoping his body would be lost to the current.

"Water's rising." I smile to myself.

I should stay away from the river tomorrow, in case they try to get rid of me for good.

I head for the car again.

Coral starts to speak as she follows me, "Hey, so, uh... we're sorry, okay?"

Sorry?

"For what?" I glance over my shoulder, opening the driver's side door. "Trying to get me arrested? Kidnapping me? Running me off the road?"

"Again, that wasn't us," Mace chimes in. "It was the Pirates."

"It was kind of us," Coral adds. "I mean, we were chasing her too."

Mace rolls her eyes at her friend because she's not helping. I laugh under my breath.

"Sorry for scaring you," Coral finally states.

"Farrow's making you guys apologize?"

"Yes," Mace replies quickly.

I laugh again.

"But..." Coral points her tumbler at me. "The roller skating was fun and the fireworks."

"And you always seem up for anything," Mace allows. "And you're not afraid of fun costing a price. I like that."

"And thanks for being kind to Codi," Coral adds.

I look around, realizing she's not here. Neither is Arlet.

"You don't need to give her money, though," Mace points out. "We're taking care of her."

I'm not sure how they knew about that. I only slipped a couple of twenties into her hoodie pocket, but I guess it wasn't my place to take care of one of theirs. At least not yet.

We climb into the car, and I start the engine.

"What do you guys normally do on Saturday nights?" I ask, thinking about tomorrow.

I catch Mace's smile through the rearview mirror. "You'll see."

"I'm not sure y'all can shock me." I swing the car around, making a U-turn. "Farrow said I wouldn't leave this town a virgin, and I'm halfway home."

"Oh, that's a challenge," Mace announces.

"Sounded like it," Coral adds.

Tommy stares out the window, her face so pale with her white hair up in a ponytail.

Mace rolls down the driver's side window, hanging her head in the wind. "We can do better."

"So much better," Coral echoes. "You're not going to finish the *weekend* a virgin."

My stomach dips, but I keep my expression calm. "And if I do?"

"Then we'll tattoo the Jolly Roger on our asses," Mace coos.

I burst out laughing, Coral groaning. "Oh, you did not just commit us to that," she whines.

I shake my head, but then I worry about what lengths they'll go to in order to make sure they don't have to get that tattoo. I'm not in the habit of accepting drinks I didn't make myself, but I'll be extra careful this weekend. For sure.

The whole way home other questions occur to me, like how will they know if I do it or not, and does oral count? And right away, an image of Hunter's head between my legs flashes in my mind, and I roll down my window, too, for cool air.

Taking the car back to the barbershop, I hop out and toss Mace the keys, not Coral.

"Tomorrow," they remind me.

"I'll bring the tequila."

They probably won't be in bed for hours, but now, I'm tired. At least that's what I tell myself, because Hunter's car still isn't in front of his house.

Closing my front door, I flip on the light and head up to my bedroom, pulling my phone off the charger and putting the one Hawke gave me back on. I restart my phone, tossing it on the bed, because I'm not anxious for a call or a text.

We're just playing around.

He's in a weird place, and I'm misreading what we're doing. Just like I misread any signals I thought I was getting from Kade.

I need to stop thinking about him and just go to sleep.

I tug the rubber band out of my hair and start for the door to go get some water, but I hear a notification go off and charge back for my bed.

I'll do a sweep of any messages. Get it over with and then get to sleep.

The notification is for Quinn's Instagram, though. There's nothing else. No missed calls or texts, a mixture of disappointment and relief washing over me, because no news is good news, I guess?

But he knows it's getting late. Wouldn't he like to see me? Or at least say goodnight?

I click to see what she posted, and a picture of Hunter appears, his head bowed as Fallon cuts his hair. I break into a smile, seeing A.J. posing next to him and making a goofy face.

He went home. That's good. I check the time stamp, seeing the picture was posted almost two hours ago.

That's really good. He must still be there.

I'm a little sad, though. His hair wasn't long, but I loved it. It was always sexy-messy, and I liked feeling it between my fingers.

He'll have to grow it back. I laugh to myself, tossing the phone back on the bed, but as soon as I look up and out my window, my heart stops.

My stomach clenches and needles prick my skin.

His room is dark, but I see her red hair, her naked back...

I narrow my gaze, stepping closer to my window, watching her hips roll on top of his bed and trying to make sense out of what's going on.

It's got to be Farrow.

Or one of the other guys.

They're using Hunter's bed.

But then he comes up, jerks Arlet's hips into him, and rolls them both over, his hair shorter now and his profile unmistakable.

A lump lodges in my throat, and I can't swallow.

It can't be him. He wouldn't do that.

REBELS

CHAPTER EIGHTEEN

Hunter

I stuff the washing machine with all my muddy gear from practice this afternoon, thankful that the pants are black, as well as the jersey. The only color on the uniforms are a few royal blue stripes around the collar and sleeves with some white trim. Easy to hide the mud stains. Dewitt had us on the schedule for practice, rain or shine, and it stormed all last night. The field was a mess, and more rain is on the way.

Not that we would've played well anyway, with half the team hungover from last night.

I throw in a Tide POD and start the cycle, heading back up to my room to get dressed. I glance out my window, seeing no sign of Dylan in her room.

But a distant thunder rolls across the sky, leaves fluttering against the wind as the charged air makes the hair on my arms rise.

I haven't seen her all day.

She was asleep when I got in last night—I snuck in and checked on her when she didn't answer her phone, just to make sure she was safe—and she hasn't replied to texts today, other than to say she was at the library.

Dylan doesn't go to the library. She's not a terrible student, but if she can't research it from her phone, then the assignment is too big of an investment.

She was no doubt up on Phelan's Throat, practicing.

I pick my dirty sheets up off the floor and dump them in the hallway to take down and wash later. My room smelled weird when I got home last night, and not a single one of my teammates, including Farrow, came clean about having sex in my fucking bed while I was at my parents. I don't think he would. He has his own room, but someone did. My bed was a mess, and Dylan wouldn't have left it like that if she just came in to use her vibrator.

Plus, I know what her body smells like, and that wasn't it. I tore off my sheets and grabbed the spare set in my closet.

Reaching into my desk drawer, I pull her toy off the charger, re-clean it under scalding hot water in the bathroom, and dry it off, putting it back underneath my pillow. I almost smile, thinking what a kick Kade would get out of finding out that I sleep with a dick under my head. If he didn't hate me, he'd find it hilarious.

I'm glad I didn't see him last night. I stayed late, pressing my luck, but he was still out when I said goodbye to my parents. I'm happy the night ended on a good note. My mom and dad deserved that.

Slipping on a hoodie, I leave the house, lock the door, and jog to my car. Farrow is probably already at the Rebel Revel, a pop-up party whenever there's a flood warning in effect. Of course, we won't stay at home tonight like we're supposed to. Danger is too exciting for some people. Especially Dylan.

I cruise the streets, driving past Breaker's, up to Phelan's Throat, and then the library, but I don't find Dylan or the new bike Farrow gave her parked anywhere. Maybe she's already at the school.

Leaves fly off trees and float through the air, and I drive down the empty main street, between abandoned mills and warehouses and the broken signs of long-lost businesses. The red stoplight blinks and bobs on the cable above as I cruise under it and make my way back up toward Knock Hill.

My phone rings, I grab it out of my hoodie, hoping it's Dylan.

But I look at the screen, seeing *Jared* instead. My chest caves a little. My uncle doesn't ever call with anything positive.

I answer it, though. "Hi."

"Dylan's not answering her phone," he says right away. "Have you seen her recently?"

I'm about to say yes, but that's not true. I haven't laid eyes on her since last night.

"Just a text earlier today, saying she was doing homework at the library," I tell him.

"A library?" he repeats. "Dylan?"

Right?

"Everything okay?" I ask.

It doesn't seem weird that he hasn't spoken to her. I know they're in the middle of an argument. But I would think her mom has spoken to her.

But he just replies, "Everything's fine. I just need to...to talk to her. Have her call me?"

"Sure."

"If I don't hear from her in an hour, I'm coming over."

If he comes over, he's going to see she's completely unsupervised by an adult.

I take a sharp right, heading immediately to the school. "Will do."

I wait for him to end the call, but he doesn't.

"How... How is she?" he stammers.

I know it's hard for him to ask. To appear vulnerable.

Jared's not like my dad, who wears his heart on his sleeve. Jared gave hugs, but not like the ones in my house. My dad is never the first one to pull away.

"She's good," I tell him.

At least she was last night.

"Tell her to call me."

"Okay," I reply. "Bye."

"Bye."

Lightning flashes across the sky, rolls of thunder following, and an electric current courses under my skin. Maybe it's the weather. Maybe it's the anticipation of whatever the night will bring. I don't care what happens, I just want her to myself for a little while. In a week, she'll be packing up what little she has to head back to the Falls.

Speeding through the school lot, I find a pool of cars and motorcycles already here.

I pull over and park, hopping out and running for the building. Security cameras perch on the corner of the brick edifice, as well as more on light poles, half of which have burnt-out bulbs. None of the cameras work, though. Which is why the Rebels often get away with sneaking in. Teachers don't realize anyone was here until they find beer cans all over the locker room.

Heading to the gym, I shake the leaves and whatever else has flown into my hair, the music pumping all the way down the hall. I yank open the doors, strobe lights swerving up and down, lighting an area and then casting it in darkness again. There are no other lights as people dance, and I look over at a couple making out against the wall to my right. I can just make out his hand up her skirt, inside her panties, fingering her.

I draw in a breath, my heart beating faster. I scan the crowd. Where's Dylan?

Arlet sticks out her long, bare leg, posing as she sweeps her hair up into a ponytail, making a big show in her strapless cocktail dress and heels. Mace sits on the bleachers, her arm hanging over Coral's shoulder who sits one level down, between her legs, as they pass a Hydro Flask between them.

I find Farrow sitting on a chair, far off in the corner, swallowing giant gulps of Coke and then holding the can out to his side, letting Calvin slip in some whiskey.

A large group dances in the middle of the floor, the clouds blotting out any moonlight that might shine through the glass dome above.

I head over to Farrow. "Hey."

"What's up?" he says, shaking his can at me. "You want some?"

"Later." I search the gym. "Have you seen—?"

But then I stop, watching Dylan walk through the doors I just came through.

She enters the dark gym, a backpack hanging off one shoulder, dressed in tight jeans and an even tighter, red leather jacket. The blue and pink lights glint off her buckles and zippers, and my gaze falls to her neck, visible with her hair pulled up.

Then, they drop to the three inches of bare stomach between her jeans and jacket, and my body warms even as relief hits me, seeing she's here and safe. She smiles, and I follow her gaze to the girls on the bleachers. She walks over to them, handing Coral the backpack.

Coral looks inside, smiles, and then uncaps her flask, trying to keep the liquor inside the bag as she pours more into her bottle.

Lightning strikes the sky, thunder cracks, and everyone howls, something that feels like wind swirling through the room. "Whoo!" they howl.

I move, trying to catch Dylan's eyes. A lock of hair hangs over her face, but even from here I can see the ease in her gorgeous face.

"You look pretty," I whisper, but I know she can't hear me.

Someone puts a small plastic cup in her hand, a shot of something gold inside.

I drift over and stop in front of her, her eyes still cast down at her cup. I ignore the girls on the bleachers to my right.

I lean in, so she can hear me. "You look pretty."

Beautiful.

She raises her eyes, giving me a small smile.

"Are you okay?"

She nods. "Yeah."

She holds the cup to her mouth and tips her head back, swallowing the alcohol in one gulp.

"Your dad wants you to call," I tell her.

"I will."

She hands the cup back to Coral, and I think she's getting another one.

"Space those out, okay?"

"I'm not having anymore." She shakes her head. "I'm not staying."

She starts to move, and I take a step. "What? Where are you going?"

"Everywhere." She grins at me. "Have fun tonight."

What?

She walks away, and Arlet grabs me. "Come on. Dance."

But I barely hear her as she pulls me onto the floor. Dylan disappears through the doors, and I'm fucking confused, because if she's mad at me, she'd let me know. If she's not, then what's the problem? Everyone's here. Dylan isn't a one-girl party. She likes people. Why is she leaving?

No sooner than I get on the dance floor, when commotion bursts through the gym doors, the entire room going silent except for the music.

"We're here for our traitors!" Stoli announces, flanked by Pirates.

He stands there with at least ten other guys, the light behind them blinding me to the point I can't make everyone out. Is Kade here?

They run in, the music seems to get louder—or maybe it's the screams—and I hear footfalls descend the bleachers.

People run and shout, angry but also excited by it.

I catch Farrow by the arm. "No weapons!"

"No promises!"

He rushes off, and I run my hand through my hair. "Jesus Christ."

"Get them out!" someone shouts over the DJ's microphone.

They came in right after Dylan left. *Was she in on this?*

Phones are out, snapping pics and videoing, and I'm not in the mood for this.

Students escape into locker rooms, others falling in the rush as the strobe lights cut out, and the music only gets louder.

"Call the cops!" someone shouts.

"Like they'll come," another says.

I run to the exit, passing Coral. "Where did Dylan go?"

"She mentioned riding in the rain," she shouts over the commotion.

Dammit.

I run out into the parking lot, thunder rumbling across the sky and wind whipping through my hair. "Dylan, where are you?" I whisper to myself.

Hopping in my car, I cruise the streets, keeping my eyes peeled. Leaves and trash blow across the roads, trees bending with the force, and the rain is going to start any moment. She shouldn't ride in this. She shouldn't ride with even a shot of alcohol in her. I shouldn't have let her go.

I swing past Knock Hill, the lane deserted, everyone inside, and then I climb up to Phelan's Throat. She knows better, but that doesn't mean she'll listen to her head.

I gas it uphill, making a slow right over the curve, exhaling when I don't see any trace of her or her bike.

Heading down past the docks, I sweep the mill district, spotting something in the road. I hit the brakes, hearing my tires skid across the pavement.

I shift into *Park* and open my car door. Putting one foot out, I stand up and gaze down at Dylan, laying in the middle of the street. In the intersection.

You've got to be kidding me.

I would be concerned that she was hurt, but her bike is parked at the curb, and her arms are splayed straight out, her legs crossed at the ankles, and she has a peaceful look on her face as her hair flies across her cheeks.

I look around, not a soul in sight. No cars. "What are you doing?" I call out to her.

She doesn't open her eyes, and I walk, stopping when I'm standing over her. My body hums, my eyes drawn to the sliver of bare waist below her jacket.

"Did you know the Pirates were going to crash the flood party?"

I don't even really care. She's so fucking stunning right now. Dangerous and silly and alive.

She blinks, looking up at me. "The Pirates are there?" she asks.

And I know she had no idea.

"What are you doing?" I press again.

A little smile pulls at her lips. "All the streets are empty," she tells me. "I always wanted to try this."

And despite the frustration I seem to always have these days—the worry, the aggravation, and the confusion—I want nothing more than for this moment to last all night. God, she's amazing.

Reaching down, I lift her up to her feet, because she can't stay in the street, no matter how much I want her to be happy.

She dusts off her clothes. "I don't need protection, Hunter."

I know. It won't stop me from wanting to be near her, though.

She looks down, and I don't like the look on her face.

Something's going on with her today. What happened? Why hasn't she sought me out?

"It's time for me to go home," she says calmly.

Home.

The Falls?

What does that mean?

She says it with finality, like she's done and found whatever she was looking for *or* made her peace with not finding it, and she's ready for this to be over.

What happened?

"Dylan—"

But I don't have a chance to ask her. Kade's black truck skids to a halt next to us, and I spin around in time to see Dirk and Stoli rush out, grab Dylan, and haul her into the back seat.

"We're taking her back!" Stoli shouts, slamming the door and hanging out the window, laughing.

There are two other guys in the truck, but I don't know if any of them are Kade.

They speed off, and I watch.

But not for long.

Reaching into my pocket for the only thing I have, I clutch my phone, rear back my hand, and launch it like a fucking football right into the driver's sideview mirror. It shatters the glass, he slams on the brakes, and I dig in my heels, charging up to the goddamn truck and yanking the back door open.

"You prick!" Dirk bellows, jumping out.

But my eyes are only on Dylan as she sits in the back, wide-eyed. I grab her legs and pull her to me, lifting her into my arms.

Dirk clutches my shoulder, but just then, Farrow and the boys pull up.

I walk away from all of it.

"So nice of you to make this easy," Farrow taunts them, and a fight ensues behind me.

But I just keep going. All I see is her.

I guide her legs around my waist, holding her tightly.

"He had you all to himself for a year," I tell her, looking up into her storm blue eyes. "You're mine for another week."

I pull the handcuffs out of my drawer, slam it shut, and lean over my bed, throwing her down onto it. I catch the back of her head before it hits anything and then grip her wrist, fitting a cuff around it.

I don't know what happened now, or where her mood is coming from, but I'm keeping her.

"Hunter!" she yells, pulling against the restraint.

I loop the small chain around a bar in my headboard, snatching up her other wrist and clicking the second cuff on it.

She growls, tugging at the bindings. "A few days ago, you were telling me to leave," she spits out.

And you should've listened. You're not crossing that bridge tonight.

Not for eight more nights.

I ball my hands into fists, hot blood rushing through my body as I stare down at her naked tummy, her jacket rising with her arms above her head.

She breathes hard, but her expression softens as she tries to reason. "Hunter..."

Twisting her wrists inside the cuffs, I see her skin start to redden.

"I would think you'd have your hands full enough without me here," she tells me. "Why is it that you're both allowed to have a life and I'm not? Why can't I be alone with a guy like Constin when you had a girl in your bed all night?"

I thin my eyes to slits. "What?"

What the hell is she talking about?

"Last night," she says, gesturing to the window. "I saw you in here with her."

With who?

I glance at my window, seeing hers beyond the tree branches.

"It was you, right? Not Kade?"

Kade...

I turn my gaze back on her, remember how I'd had to change the sheets, because someone fucked in my bed.

Kade.

"You're so different," she says, tears thickening her voice. "You used to want to be in love before you did that." She frowns. "So different."

"You're the same." My tone is flat. "Still so easy for him to manipulate."

Her gaze falters, and she falls quiet as I back away and fall into the cushioned chair next to my window.

You could've told her.

So could you.

No wonder I didn't run into him last night. He was all the way over here.

And the funny thing is, I'm not really mad at him. It hurts, but what Kade can do, he will do. There's almost an art to it.

But I'm fucking pissed that she believed it so easily. Is she jealous? At all? I want her to be.

And to make it worse, she knows me. I thought she knew me.

"Hunter, it hurts."

She struggles in her bindings, and I sit back in the chair, waiting for my head to get in the game and force my legs to move. To go to her and help her. The seconds tick by.

She stops fighting the handcuffs and looks to me. "What did you do with her?"

I lock my jaw so tight my teeth ache.

"How did you do it?" she presses. "What does she do that you like?"

"Why?"

"So, I'll know what other men will like."

I cock an eyebrow. Not 'boys' or 'guys.'

She said 'men.'

She will meet lots of men after she leaves Shelburne Falls. Men who are dicks. And immature. And unworthy.

But some will be strong. And confident. And driven. And know how to make love to her.

"Maybe I want to know what Kade likes," she taunts.

"Anything naked."

She's just trying to piss me off. She's good at invoking this new sensation inside of me, like I want to kill something.

She rolls her hips, accentuating her stomach, her ass, with her beautiful eyes. "You've seen me naked," she says so softly. "Will he like me?"

My nails dig into my palms.

"What else does he like?" She wets her lips.

Bending her knees up, her feet on the bed, she spreads her legs just a little and arches her back. My cock twitches, almost feeling my fingers digging into her hip as I bury myself between her thighs.

"Dylan..." I say, almost sounding like a warning.

"You both can't keep me locked up forever," she tells me. "Guys will fuck me at college."

I launch up, out of my chair, and swipe everything off my desk, like I don't even have control of it. I'm out of my mind.

I stalk over to her, leaning down. I squeeze her jaw, brushing my thumb over her perfect mouth. "You're not there yet," I growl.

There's still plenty of time to fuck her up.

And I want to right now. God, I want her naked in this bed so badly.

But I also want to punch a wall.

Pulling the key out of my pocket, I free her from the cuffs and toss them down on the bed. "Are you jealous?" I ask. "Tell me you're jealous."

She's hurt. Is it because she doesn't want me fucking around with anyone while I'm messing around with her, or is it because she's falling in love with me?

I lean down, in her face. "Say my name."

I want to make sure she knows who the fuck I am.

Her eyes search mine. "Hunter."

Just a little murmur, but her mouth looks so soft and supple. My body stirs, blood rushing low in my stomach.

"Say it again."

"Hunter."

I open my mouth, wanting to eat her little whisper. "Are you jealous?" I ask. "Say you're jealous."

I wait for her to answer. For her to come up. To touch me, ask me why I slept with someone else, tell me she's hurt, that she loves me, and that I'm hers... I want to hear all of it.

She doesn't.

"You can go now." She reaches underneath my pillow for her toy. "I fuck myself just fine."

PIRATES

CHAPTER NINETEEN

Dylan

Hunter leaves the room, slamming the door behind him. I clutch the vibrator beneath my head, under the pillow, feeling tears spring to my eyes. I let the toy go and roll over, burying my sobs in one of his pillows.

I want to be his. We weren't just playing around. It wasn't like that for me. I don't want anyone else to touch me.

I felt his eyes on me the moment I walked into the Revel tonight. *You look pretty.*

My skin was on fire. Simple words, something he would've said when we were kids with his big eyes and kind voice.

I feel every word like I feel every touch. I feel every look like I feel his mouth.

I don't want to be the little girl he grew up with. I want him to touch me and take me somewhere quiet and kiss me and ...

I shake with my tears.

Did I misread everything? Again?

The way he gripped my hair in my bathroom. His breath in my ear. His eyes and how it feels like he's fighting himself to not look at me all the time.

The way he asked if he could do what he did to me on the sink counter the other night.

I imagined everything I thought he was feeling. I wanted to hear the desire or desperation or some shit in his voice, so I did. I imagined he was mine.

I inhale, realizing he was on these sheets with someone else last night, and start to pull back.

They smell good, though. Freshly washed. Was he trying to hide what he did?

A door downstairs whips shut again and again, and in a minute, I hear laughter and music pump through the house. Footfalls grow closer, ascending the stairs, and then another door, perhaps across the hall, closes.

Farrow and his friends are back. Taking my phone out of my pocket, I start to dial Kade to make sure he's okay. I don't care who won the fight after Hunter grabbed me out of his truck, but I want to make sure he's safe.

But I just check Snapchat instead, seeing a picture of his hand posted ten minutes ago with the dashboard of his truck in the background. His knuckles are skinned.

I shake my head. He's fine. Letting the whole world know he got into a fight, which is just so cool.

I need to get out of here, and I don't want Hunter to see. I'm going to bed, and tomorrow, I'm training.

Before I can stand, though, my phone rings. I see Quinn's name on the screen.

I answer, pausing a moment before I hold it to my ear. "Hey," I say, trying to make my voice sound normal. "What are you up to?"

"You looked so good in that jacket," she sing-songs.

How did...

I sigh, wiping away my tears. Someone must've posted a pic of me. I look down, trying to pull the jacket over my stomach.

"It's tight."

"It's perfect, I'd say."

I can't help but laugh a little, her voice easing the pain.

I rise from the bed, almost grabbing my vibrator, but I don't want to risk the whole damn school downstairs seeing it. I'll have to come back for it another time. "What are you doing tonight?" I ask her.

"Hanging with my parents." I hear her chew something. "I spent the day at the bakery. Taking some inventory, making some treats to leave my mom."

"Heading back tomorrow?"

"Yeah," she replies. "I'll be back for the holidays, though."

And I barely saw her while she was here.

"Sorry I got...kidnapped on you," I tell her, not exactly forlorn at the time, considering the night ended amazingly, but now I'm pissed about it. She, Aro, and I were having fun at the rink.

But she says, "It's okay. It's been a good visit. My dad was happy to see Hunter last night. He actually smiled. Hunter, I mean."

I nod, because I don't know what else to do. "He went to your place too?" I ask. "After his Mom and Dad's?"

"No, I was hanging with Jared. We drove to Madoc's and ended up staying a while when Jax and Juliet showed up." I can hear the smile in her voice. "Hunter and A.J. played hide and seek outside for like two hours, and then we all joined in, but it sort of fizzled out when Jax started making out with Juliet and forgot to seek the rest of us."

I smile, picturing them all hiding behind rocks and in trees for half an hour.

"We were all up until midnight," she continues. "It was like old times, except for you and Kade not being there."

Midnight?

He was in the Falls until midnight?

"Kade wasn't there either?" I ask her.

"I didn't see him at all," she tells me. "He went out after the game."

I wander to the window, watching the rain drizzle down the glass and lightning flash across the sky. The rope up to my attic sways in the wind.

"Yeah," I murmur.

And all at once, everything I already knew and shouldn't have denied floods in.

I knew better.

And yes, I believed it so easily. Because it hurt. It made me sick to think of him not with me.

"We'll catch up tomorrow," I say. "I gotta go, okay?"

"'Night," she chirps.

I hang up and slip my phone into my back pocket, gazing out the window.

He's so stubborn. He'll let me believe the worst of him, just like the time Gemma Ledger came out of his bedroom when we were sixteen.

Of course, I found out later that he was hiding her for Kade, but I didn't understand why he would let himself be misunderstood like that.

Crossing the room, I peek my head out the door, seeing Mace coming out of the bathroom. She sticks her tongue out at me on her way back downstairs. I smile a little because she likes me. If she didn't, she'd ignore me.

Music thumps below, howls and loud chatter filling the rooms, and I head down, seeing Hunter, Constin, and Farrow around a small table. Hunter rolls dice, then Farrow scoops them up to take his turn. Others stand or sit, filling the living room to the left and the dining room to the right. Hunter's car keys sit on the table next to him, a scattering of cash piled in the center.

I stop at his side. "I want to go for a ride."

I feel the others' eyes on me, but Hunter just tosses more bills into the pile, rolling again. My bike is still down in the mill district, but I don't really want to go for a ride on that. I want to get out of here for a little while with him.

He doesn't look at me. "It's raining."

Farrow sees Hunter's roll, chuckles, and snatches up all the cash.

"I'm bored," I tell Hunter.

"Get upstairs," he says. "Go to sleep."

"I'm bored."

His jaw flexes, and I wish everyone would go away. I want him to myself.

"Then hide," Farrow suggests.

He looks at me, amused, and then stands up, announcing, "All the girls hide."

A round of silence, followed by gasps of excitement follow.

"Just the girls?" some guy asks.

A glint of mischief touches Farrow's eyes because how old-fashioned to assume men don't enjoy being prey once in a while too.

"Fuck it," Farrow says. "Whoever wants to be found by me."

Squeals and shuffling go off as everyone scrambles, and I lean down, waiting until Hunter looks me in the eyes,

347

distracted, before I slip his keys off the table and hide them in my fist.

"Bet you won't be the first to find me," I say softly.

Backing away, I avoid the stairs, taking the hallway leading to the kitchen. He doesn't want to play, but there are lots of guys here who will.

He won't like that.

"One, two…" Farrow starts counting. "Three…"

Twisting around, I dash into the kitchen, out of view, and step through the thin stairwell door. Codi sits at the kitchen table, sketching. She looks up at me and then back down.

I close myself into the spiral staircase and press the wall to my left, watching the panel slide right.

The stairs are wooden, unlike the stone ones in my house. I jog down, closing the panel again, and descend into the basement. I noticed yesterday morning when I rushed through here to sneak into his bedroom, taking the spiral staircase all the way up to the second floor, that this area of the house was renovated while the one in mine wasn't. It makes sense if this was a house Ciaran used, while the one next door was left to rot.

Walking briskly, I push through the basement door and into the backyard that's encased by a wall, whereas mine is surrounded by a rusty chain-link fence. Rain pours down on me, immediately plastering my flyaways to my face.

Holding the keys in my hand, I leave through the wooden door to my left, sneaking under the windows of his house, and beneath the tree next to mine.

His car is parked where he left it when he dragged me out, threw me over his shoulder, and carried me up to his room.

He should've just taken me for a ride, like I wanted. Now, I have to leave his Camaro downtown because I'm going to get my bike.

Fitting the key into the lock, I twist it and pull open the door, but a hand shoots out and slams it shut again.

My heart skips a beat as I look down at slender fingers, tanned with the veins coursing just underneath the skin. Water pours over his hand, and I can see our reflection in the window with light coming from the porch.

He covers my back, his chin resting at the side of my head.

"I'm going to get my bike," I say calmly. "You'll have to stop me."

"You think I can't?"

"I think you can't."

And I watch him watch me in the window as I pull down the zipper of the tight little jacket Quinn gave me, revealing I have nothing on underneath. No shirt. No bra. I don't smile, and I don't smirk.

My heart is trying to beat out of my chest.

The curves of my breasts peek out, and he exhales hard, pressing me into the wet glass. "Dylan," he pants. "We're on the street. Stop."

"I can't."

His hand circles the front of my neck, and he bows his forehead into my hair, breathing in my ear.

"Would you even know if I were Kade or Hunter right now?" he asks in a dark voice. "Because you seem to get us confused a lot."

"I know you're Hunter." I press my body back into his. "You feel like him."

"And what does he feel like?"

The heat of his body covers my back, and I suck in a breath, turn my head, and kiss the corner of his mouth. "Like I'm going to let him have his fun," I say. "No toys this time."

I nudge him with my nose and grab his lip with my teeth, his hand tightening just a little on my throat as he groans.

"Get in the car," he orders in my ear.

And I couldn't say no if I tried. He opens the door, and I clutch my jacket shut as I scramble inside.

He climbs in, shutting the door and combing his wet hair over the back of his head. "Keys," he growls.

I tighten my fist around them, watching annoyance light up behind his eyes when I don't do what I'm told.

"You fucking Trents love to pick a fight, don't you?" he spits out.

Yeah, screw you. I unlock the passenger side door and grab the handle, but in less than a second, he's on his knees, punching the lock back down, and yanking me by the backs of my legs until I'm on my back. Hovering over me, he holds my wrist, and I fight back as he pries his keys out of my fist.

I shoot up, but he shoves me back down, his eyes not on mine anymore. He gazes at my breasts, my jacket having fallen open, and the hard points of my nipples aimed straight up at him.

"And just like a Caruthers, you don't know how to finish one," I taunt.

He smiles, challenge accepted. Taking his seat, he starts the car and shifts into *Drive*. I push myself up, but he pushes me back down and fists the waist of my jeans, keeping me on my back.

He speeds out of Knock Hill, and I grunt, trying to get his hand off me. I almost start kicking, but I don't want him crashing.

I thrash a little, his eyes turning to me every once in a while, watching my breasts bob back and forth with the struggle.

We travel uphill, into the forest, before he pulls over, parking under the trees. He kills the engine, the headlights going dark, and rain spills down all of the windows.

I watch him rise up onto a knee, pull the back of his T-shirt over his head, and hover over me. He starts to unfasten his belt with one hand, and my heart leaps into my throat. I dart up, yanking his hands away from his jeans, gasping when he tugs my jacket off my shoulders.

"In the car?" I breathe out. "You mean Caruthers don't do it on thousand-thread-count sateen sheets? Isn't your skin too precious for leather?"

I shove his body off and flip over, reaching for the door, but he pulls my jacket off the rest of the way and comes down on my back, pinning me to the seat.

"My father never took issue with your dad's pissy attitude," he whispers in my ear, pinning one hand on the armrest and slipping the other underneath me to cup my breast. "You know why? Because he knew he'd have the last laugh. He knew one of his boys would be having a lot of fun with you one day."

He thrusts into my ass, our jeans between us, but I can still feel him. I close my eyes, feeling myself grow wetter.

My phone vibrates in my back pocket, followed by a ring, and I reach for it, but he gets it first.

"Kade," he says. "You want me to answer it?"

"What—"

"I think he'd come and save you if you asked," he tells me.

But instead, Hunter rolls down the window, and I look up just in time to see my phone fly out the window.

"What the fuck?" I snap, fighting hard now.

It's raining, goddammit! I texted my dad, telling him I'd call tomorrow. He's going to ask why I'm calling from a weird number when I use the phone Hawke gave me.

I grip the door, trying to pull myself out from underneath him as he rolls the window back up. Rain spatters my arms.

He releases me, and I spin around, backing up to my door and covering my breasts with my arms as I scowl.

One knee is under him, the other foot on the floor, and I gaze up his long and lean torso, my eyes finally falling to where his jeans hang.

"I've waited a long time for this," he tells me.

For what?

But he's already opening his door and climbing out. Without another word, he reaches in and grabs my ankles, hauling me out of the front seat and into his arms. Rain falls on my skin, hitting my eyelashes as he looks up at me, and before I know it, he's slamming the front door shut and opening another one, lying me down in his back seat.

I rest my arms at my side, loving his eyes all over me. "I'm so mad at you sometimes."

He starts to climb in, rain from his hair dripping on my chest. "How mad?" he asks. "Hmm?"

Diving down, he catches one of my nipples between his teeth, biting. I gasp and then whimper.

"That mad?" he asks me.

Then he sucks off the water, taking as much of me as he can into his mouth.

My eyelids flutter, tingles flowing under my skin.

I arch my back, giving him more of it. "More."

"This mad?" he continues, licking and kissing.

Unbuttoning my jeans, he pulls them down over my ass, finding I'm not wearing underwear, just like I wasn't wearing a bra. He stares down at me, between my legs, and I wait for him to start to unfasten his belt. Unbutton his jeans.

But instead, he clutches my thigh, runs his thumb up my pussy, opening me before he comes down and covers my clit with his mouth. I shudder, the wet warmth of his tongue sending a shockwave through me. "Please, Hunter, don't do that."

He stops immediately, his mouth hovering over me, and I can feel his heavy breaths as I clutch his shoulders.

"Do I..." I don't know how to ask. "Is it...do I taste okay?"

He drops his head, his wet hair grazing between my legs. "I don't want to stop," he begs. "Please don't stop me again."

I nod, and he yanks off the rest of my clothes, lifting my knees and spreading my legs wide. I start to cover myself a little, shy, but he's already coming back in to taste. I groan, holding his head and rolling my hips into his mouth as he sucks, licks, and dips his tongue inside me.

I shudder. "Ah..."

"Fuck," he whispers, dragging the tip of his tongue up both sides of my clit before sucking on it so softly.

I moan, rocking my hips. His hand comes up, holding my breast as I fuck his mouth, and I thread my fingers through his hair, feeling the orgasm start to rise. He licks me again and again, then sucks, and I hear him groan.

My orgasm climbs, but I don't want to come like this.

Part of his body is still out in the rain, and I claw at his back, feeling his cold skin. I sit up, forcing him to rise, and start unfastening his belt. "Close the door," I tell him, looking up into his eyes. "I want you inside me."

I open his jeans, but he grabs my wrists. "Are you sure?" he asks.

And I smile, because, as always, he protects me.

I dip my tongue out and lick his stomach before nibbling it with my teeth. "Why do you think I pick fights with you in the first place, Caruthers?"

He pushes me back down on the seat, pressing his body into mine and covering my mouth with his. I wrap my arms around his neck, tasting myself on his lips. I moan, the kisses getting harder and faster, and firecrackers go off underneath my skin as his mouth travels down my neck. He keeps going, over my breasts, down my stomach, and then he bites the curve where my thigh meets my hip.

"Hunter," I moan.

"Are you still on birth control?" he breathes out.

I nod. Since I was fifteen. Our whole family knows everything about each other. My mom told me it was to regulate my period, but I'm pretty sure all parents give out that excuse.

He stares down at me. "Can I not wear a condom?" he asks. "I want to..." He swallows. "I want to feel it my first time."

His first time...

We're each other's firsts.

I gaze into his eyes, whispering, "You can come inside me."

I want him to.

He swoops in again, kissing me, and all I taste is him. Hunter's scent I've known my whole life, his skin and toothpaste and the musk of his bodywash.

He reaches in and pulls himself out, the head of his flesh crowning my entrance. I hold my breath.

"What did you say about a Caruthers not finishing a fight?" he mocks.

I blink. *What?*

"Yeah, that's what I thought you said," he coos, smiling over my lips.

354

"Shut up," I pant.

He pushes inside me, and I wince. "Hunter," I whimper. "I'm nerv..."

But he's already thrusting again.

And then again.

I breathe shallow, feeling myself stretch as he sinks inside me, his hips rolling into me again and again. I hold his body, feeling him gasping, too, and after a couple more times it doesn't hurt anymore.

I press my forehead into his chest, squeezing my thighs around him, stunned for a minute.

He takes my face and tilts my head back, looking down into my eyes. "Are you okay?"

I relax my legs a little, spreading them wider. "Don't stop." And I kiss his lips, lying back down and letting him look at me while I move underneath him.

In less than a minute, his mouth is on mine again, our pace picking up as he grips my ass, burrowing deep inside me.

His cock hits, making my whole body shudder, and I moan against his mouth. "Keep doing that," I plead. "Right there. Yeah."

Planting a hand on the door, he lifts up to watch me as he pumps. "You feel so good. Tighter than my fucking hand."

I bite my bottom lip to keep from smiling. I like hearing that.

Sliding in and out, I roll my hips in rhythm with him, looking down to watch him slide in and out. I pull him in harder and faster into me, my orgasm building again, teasing and rising.

I whimper over and over again. "Come inside me," I beg against his mouth.

"Say it again."

I thread his lips with mine. "Come inside me."

He groans.

I mouth. "Come inside me."

"Oh, Dylan."

He props himself up, and I arch my back, taking what he can't hold back anymore. He thrusts hard, and I wrap my legs around him, holding him as he goes deeper and deeper. My eyes roll back a little as my orgasm breaks free, washing over me, and I come, shivering underneath him.

His dark blond hair is messy and beautiful and hanging in his eyes as he groans over my lips. "Fuck, Dylan."

He thrusts once hard, and then again, and then...once more, spilling his cum inside me. His lungs empty, he drops his forehead to mine. I hold him, running my thumbs over his cheeks and feeling rain or sweat, I don't know, but I do know I loved everything that just happened.

After a minute, he raises his body, sliding out of me a little, and that's

when he stops and flinches.

"What?" I ask.

He just blinks and then shakes his head. "I don't have a towel."

And then he laughs, more to himself, and I feel like I missed something.

Sinking back in, he moves down, circling my head with his arms.

I smile, but I try to hide it.

"What?" he asks this time.

I shrug. "I was your first too."

He chose me like I chose him, but thinking back on all the years, I wonder how much of it was ever a choice. I wonder now, how I didn't see this coming.

"Well, the night is still young." He brushes my nose with his. "Wanna be my second and third, as well?"

I wrap my legs around him again and bury my smile in his neck.

REBELS

CHAPTER TWENTY

Hunter

The rain patters the roof of the quiet house, and I'm so tired but too comfortable to want to fall asleep and miss any of this.

She's in my arms.

Her leg is draped over my body, her head on my shoulder, and I pull the sheet up over her back.

I almost told her I loved her so many times in the car tonight. And after we got back, went to bed, and made love again.

I'm glad I didn't say it. At least not yet. I want to keep this for just a little while longer before I possibly find out it's moving too fast for her.

"Will you come home?" she asks, just above a whisper.

I run my fingers up and down her arm. "Will you stay?"

I can't see her smile in the dark, but I hear her little laugh. There's no way her parents will let her stay once they find out she's unsupervised.

And I promised mine I'd be home next weekend. Win or lose.

It was always a promise I knew I might break, but it won't be for the reason I thought. When I told my parents I'd return, it was to make a deal. If they let me do this, I'd finish it and come home.

Now, it feels wrong.

I like my team. I like the teachers. I don't want to use them. Falls High doesn't want me back.

I have to get back in that house with Kade, though. Or I might be running from him forever.

"What's he been like with you?" I ask her.

She knows who I mean.

Has he been kind? Protected her? Stood up for her?

But she just says, "I don't want to talk about him right now."

She slides up a little, and I turn my head, feeling her breath on my mouth.

She whispers, "How long have you wanted to kiss me?"

I chuckle. "Uh...for as long as I can remember, I guess."

I don't remember a time when I wasn't drawn to her. As a kid, she was a ball of energy, and it didn't fade in the least as she grew up. She wanted to be the reason people smiled, and never the reason they cried.

"There was always a charge in the air when I was in the same room with you," I murmur, memories of all the longing hitting me hard. "I knew you didn't feel it, too, I just..."

"Left," she interjects. "You left."

It wasn't because of her. Maybe I wanted to see what would happen between them with me out of the way. Maybe my pride and ego constantly shriveled under his shadow.

What I do know for sure, though, is that I was sick of thinking about it. Wanting things I didn't know how to get, and worried that I'd always be worthless to everyone just because I meant nothing to him.

I was fucking sick of the talk, talk, talk, fucking talk in my head, and I had to go.

"Kade's like my dad," she tells me.

I look down, seeing her eyelashes fan in the faint light.

"Like all our dads." Her voice is so soft. "They dominate every crowd they're in, and when you wish you could be like that, it makes their attention feel like some gift." She threads her fingers up the back of my neck and into my hair. "He tugged at me. And then pushed me away. Tugged again. And then ignored me. By the time I was fifteen, I would go from feeling important one minute to just being one of the guys the next. I was a kid, Hunter. I still am in a lot of ways. There are so many feelings, I don't know what to do with them sometimes."

So many feelings. That's exactly what it was like. I just needed to not see him every day.

"But then we started to grow up," she says, and I hear her voice thicken with excitement. "And you grew your hair a little longer one summer and tanned really well and always seemed to be without a shirt or shoes."

I smile, listening to her and thinking back to what I might've been doing when she started looking at me.

"Looking like you just walked in from the beach in your shorts or jeans," she goes on. "And you started to get quieter and brooding, and I got a little sad when you stopped sneaking into my bed at night."

I tighten my arm around her, my other hand finding her thigh over my stomach. I grip it gently.

"When we reached a certain age, it felt like I should wait for an invitation," I admit.

"And what if I'm shy?" She lifts her head up, propping her elbow up underneath her. "What if I'm as shy as you and we fumble over our own insecurities and never do this again?"

Never again...

Her breasts press into me, the warmth between her legs touching my thigh but coursing through my whole body.

"What if I don't want to be the one chasing someone," she asks, "and you bury the things you want inside of you like you always do, and we go to colleges far away from each other and I meet someone else?"

I curl my fingers into her skin.

"And this time next year he's kissing me?" she continues. "And holding me?"

Images flood my brain, every muscle in my body turning to steel.

"And what if I love him?" she asks me.

I exhale hard, flipping her onto her back and rolling with her, settling between her legs. Staring down into her eyes, I guide my cock inside of her, thrusting deep.

She whimpers, tilting her head back as I slide inside again.

And again.

"I'm the one who does this to you," I whisper.

The idea of her falling in love...

Of her wanting anyone else...

"You were never anyone else's but mine," I tell her.

Throwing me over, she straddles me, and I grip her hips, watching her beautiful body ride mine.

And I was never anyone else's, either.

"Can we get pancakes?" she pleads, skipping down the stairs in front of me. "I'm so hungry I could eat my shoes."

We stroll into the foyer, and I pull her hips back into me, nuzzling her hair. "Yes, food," I tell her. "Lots of food."

It's after eight in the morning, and Sunday or not, I never sleep in. I couldn't move her, though. She fell asleep in my arms, and that's how we stayed until she woke up. I drifted in and out, but mostly, I just held her.

I thought about sewing, the clarinet lessons I took when I was eleven, and the statistics behind junk mail. Like it still exists. Are people really opening it? They need to stop.

I thought about anything boring just so I didn't get hard again with her naked body curled up into mine. The cute and soft little sounds she makes were impossible to ignore.

All I wanted to do was think about her. We should never have done it without a condom. I know what she feels like without one now and putting that between us won't feel the same.

"You'll have to pay for breakfast," she tells me, taking my hand. "I think my debit card is somewhere under your back seat."

I laugh, taking her face and kissing her, about to tell her I'll find it, but something catches my eye, and I stop, mid-kiss. Looking behind her, into the living room, I see everyone sprawled out with posters and paint.

Farrow looks away, scratching under his nose to hide his smile, while everyone else stares at us silently.

I pull away, and Dylan turns, following my gaze. I scan the room, making sure there are no phones out, taking pictures.

"What's all this?" Dylan asks, stepping closer to the massive piece of white butcher paper on the floor. Letters are painted in blue, but I can't read what it says with the girls sprawled over it. T.C., Anders, and Luca blow up blue and white balloons.

"The parade," Farrow announces. "In the Falls, remember?"

"Right." Dylan nods.

We both forgot.

"Can I help?" she asks.

But Farrow tells us, "Go eat." And then to me, "We'll meet you on High Street at eleven."

He tosses me my jersey that was in the wash.

I guide Dylan toward the door, hearing Coral's words as she paints inside the lines of a block letter. "Looks like we don't have to get those tattoos."

All the girls laugh, Dylan biting out, "Shut up."

They laugh harder, and I have no idea what's going on, but I don't really care.

I push Dylan out the door, taking out my keys as we jog down the steps.

I should've remembered the parade. We have another week of practices before the game, and they need me focused. Farrow wanted me to have her, but I can't get distracted.

We slide into our seats, and I start the engine. Tomorrow, I'll get back on track. Morning workout, after-school practice. The right food and plenty of sleep. I need to stay off her.

"Is something wrong?" she asks.

I look at her, sweat already breaking out on the back of my neck at the sight of my baseball cap over her hair, messy because of me. Fuck, all I want to do is drive out to the lake and only look at and talk to her for the rest of the day.

I clear my throat. "Yeah, you're not wearing your seatbelt."

I reach over and pull the belt across her lap and chest, strapping her in.

She kisses my cheek, and the tingle spreads down to my neck.

Heat rises to my face, and I turn away before she sees me blush.

I take her to eat at this old streetcar diner off the highway, out near the lake, and despite having a million questions for her, we don't speak much. She takes two bites of her pancakes, pushing the rest off on me, as usual, because she just wanted a taste before enjoying her usual two eggs sunny-side up, with bacon, toast, and hashbrowns.

I want to know what schools she's applying to for next year. If she wants to get a season lift pass for snowboarding with me this winter. If she's planning any trips for winter or spring break.

Instead, I just ask her to come closer, and she does, slipping her hands underneath the table and leaning her shoulders in as I slide the single strand of hair away from her eye. Her blue and white flannel is buttoned up to her neck, the bruise I left from sucking on her there last night peeking out.

"Will you come over for dinner next week when I'm home?" she asks. "Just you?"

My heart swells painfully, because I don't want her to go, but hell yes, I'll come to her house for dinner. Even if Jared will know with one look what's going on and will kill me before I even take my first bite.

"Depends," I tease. "Which side of the field are you sitting on this Friday?"

She breaks into a smile, filling her mouth with food, so she doesn't have to answer.

I won't be mad, either way. But if she sits on the Pirate side, I'll have some fun making her pay for that.

We finish eating and head into the Falls, certain streets on the parade route blocked off and families already in their lawn chairs along the sidewalks. Kids run around in peewee jerseys, and parents in school sweatshirts, showing their pride. Weston is even here, teachers, parents, and Mr. Fletcher, all arriving to support the team.

I find a place to park behind Quinn's shop, and Dylan and I head to the street, my chest tightening when we reach for each other at the time same. She takes my hand, I take hers.

Walking onto First Avenue, perpendicular to High Street, I look up and down the long line of floats, cars, marching bands, and cheerleaders. The Pirates are ahead, and Dylan and I walk toward the rear, finding Farrow and the guys.

He stands on a float decorated with wolves of papier-mâché, blue streamers and balloons attached everywhere.

"Aren't you afraid they'll throw milkshakes on you like last year?" Dylan calls up to him.

He lifts his eyebrows and walks over to the edge, lifting the lid on a cooler.

A dozen water guns lay inside, filled with something red.

"Paint?" I ask.

"Hot sauce."

Dylan scoffs, throwing me a look. But Farrow won't give a shit that it's illegal.

I pull off my sweatshirt, leaving the dark gray Under Armour shirt on before I pull my jersey over it. I push up my undershirt sleeves.

Dylan pops up on her tiptoes and kisses my cheek again. "Have fun."

"Oh, no," Farrows says before she can walk away. "The hostages are in the parade."

Her face falls, and she looks at me. I just shake my head. "You don't have to."

She shrugs. "I'm no chicken."

She hops up onto the float, while Farrow takes the throne, surrounded by the team, and instructs Dylan to sit at his feet. She rolls her eyes and plants her ass on the step between his legs.

"Hunter," someone calls.

I turn, seeing a man approach me. He wears a yellow Clarke University T-shirt with a turtleneck underneath. His graying beard is tidy over his black skin, and he holds out his hand for me to shake.

"Hunter Caruthers?" he asks again.

I take his hand, shaking it. "Yes."

"Good." He laughs, letting my hand go. "You two look a lot alike."

Yep. I've heard.

"Early admission letters will be going out first of November," he informs me, "but I saw you standing here and thought it best not to waste a second."

I dig in my eyebrows, not sure I understand.

"We'd hate to lose you to the University of Chicago." His grin widens, and he shakes my hand again. "Congratulations," he says. "I very much hope you choose to join us next fall."

I glance at his T-shirt again. "I'm sorry?"

"Clarke," he states as if I know what he means. "We were very impressed at your interview, and I must say, your admissions essay was incredible. Both yours and Kade's. A couple of the best we've ever read."

My interview? Admissions essay? Clarke is a university on the outskirts of Shelburne Falls. Hawke attends that school, and it's a great university, but I didn't apply there. My top choice is the University of Chicago, an hour away.

They interviewed me?

But almost immediately, realization hits.

Kade...

The pavement tilts under me. *No.*

"We should talk about maybe publishing it in the school magazine next fall," he says. "It will be an honor to have you both in attendance there."

He shakes my hand again, and I think I say, "Thank you."

But it's like someone else is saying the words because I can't think. The man leaves. I didn't even get his name. Obviously, he thinks we've already met.

Taking out my phone, I log into my application account for the University of Chicago, seeing the list of items needed to process my application—General Information, Transcripts, Essay, Recommendations...

And then I see, in red block letters, *Application Withdrawn.*

I drop my hand, my eyes burning. He called and had my application withdrawn.

I'm going to fucking kill him.

"Good morning, everyone!" my dad announces over a loudspeaker. "Thank you for being here on this beautiful Sunday, probably the last of the warm days this year..."

I rake my hand through my hair, feeling the sweat on my forehead. He had my application withdrawn for the only school I've wanted to go to since I learned it was one of the top research universities in the world.

He thinks I'm staying here with him after I fucking graduate? *He thinks this won't end?*

"And we have two undefeated teams facing off this Friday," Dad calls out to a round of cheers. "Please welcome the Shelburne Falls Marching Band leading our amazing Pirates' team and cheer squad!"

The band kicks up the Pirate fight song, and the line starts moving, turning onto High Street. Batons and flags fly into the air, the majorettes leading the team.

I glare at the ground. *I'll make it end.*

"There's the anger," a voice says next to me. "I was worried there when you came downstairs this morning looking like you were in love."

I grind my teeth together as Farrow, having climbed off the float, turns to face me.

"Now that you've fucked her, it's time to face him."

"Leave Dylan out of this," I say.

Weston's band and cheerleaders march out, the drums setting the pace while pom poms shake in my peripheral.

"I'll try," is all he says.

He jumps back on the float, and I walk, barely seeing anyone else as I zone in on the Pirates ahead.

"And please welcome a team that always demands our very best," Dad shouts, "the Weston High School Rebels!"

Boos fill the crowd, but the cheers and claps from Weston are louder, noisemakers and chants drowning out the assholes.

Groups of Rebels sing in sync, making everyone around me laugh.

I don't, though. I glance back at Dylan. She gives me a smile.

And I turn back around.

We walk, and I pick up pace, leaving my team behind. The march goes on, the crowd on the sidewalks waving banners and taking pictures as I make my way through the cheerleaders, around the car carrying the coach and the administration.

"Hunter," Dewitt calls, seeing me go.

I keep walking. Around the Pirate float. Through the Pirate football team. To the front of the pack where my brother walks.

I fall in next to him, keeping pace.

"Do you remember the time at the lake when you got me to jump off the dock?" I ask, raising my voice so he can hear me over all the music. "You'd done it a dozen times already, and I was scared."

He stares ahead, and I see Stoli on his other side, keeping an eye on us.

"You waded in the water for five minutes," I tell him, "encouraging me until I dove in?"

That was a good day, and the older we got, the less I remembered from being that young. But I always remembered that. He was in my corner, wanting me to succeed.

"Five years later..." I turn my head, staring ahead with him. "We were twelve, swimming in the same spot, and you got all of our friends to rush from the lake and leave me behind by myself." I swallow the lump in my throat. "*Your* friends," I correct myself. "All of you hid from me the rest of the day, and I went and read in the back of Dad's car, alone."

It hurt to feel like I was on the outside. Unwanted.

What hurt more was that they planned it. He told them to do it.

"I used to think 'I love him, but I don't think I like him much,'" I say. "Now, I just fucking hate you."

And I don't care that tears fill my eyes or that I see my father on a podium to my left, watching us.

"If you ever impersonate me again," I growl under my breath, "I'll beat the shit out of you."

"Do it now."

And I fucking do.

I can't contain it. Fisting his shirt, I slam my fist across his jaw and barely see him hit the ground before I'm on top of him.

"Oh, hell no!" someone shouts.

"Fight!"

Screams and shouting go off in the crowd, curses coming from the team. I straddle my brother and hit him again, my knuckles knocking the back of his hand as he shields himself.

He doesn't stay down for long, though. His friends try to catch my arms, but Kade wraps one of his around my waist and hauls me off. Rearing his fist back, he punches me across the face, and I barrel into him, planting my shoulder in his stomach.

We crash back to the pavement, my hands scraping against the hard ground.

"You boys stop it!" a woman cries.

Someone calls out over the loudspeaker, "Break it up, break it up!"

And then Dylan is there, her arms around me. "Stop." She comes in between us. "Please stop."

I rise to my feet, Kade doing the same as more fights start around us, Rebels and Pirates never needing an excuse to join in on the fun.

"He needs to stop!" I tell her. "Aren't you pissed? He made you think it was me with another girl in my bed? Don't you have anything to say to him?"

He deserves this, and she needs to understand why.

But she just looks at me, her misty eyes hiding under my cap. I see her trembling lips, though.

"Dylan doesn't want to be mad at anybody," Kade says. "You never really did see her, did you? She always had my back."

"And I had her in a way you never will," I spit back.

Silence seems to fall around us, people still moving and fighting, the parade massacred.

But I don't hear any of it, and the words have left my mouth and I can't get them back.

All I feel are Dylan's eyes.

I blink. *No*. I didn't just say that. She's not a competition. I didn't beat Kade at anything by getting her into bed.

But that's how it just sounded.

I look at her in time to see a tear spill down her cheek. She starts to back up, and I grab her to take her into my arms, but she shoves me away and runs.

She runs away, so fast, disappearing into the crowd.

PIRATES

CHAPTER TWENTY-ONE

Dylan

I went to the only place I wanted to be. Not to the Loop. Not to a friend or to Aro or to Quinn.

Home.

I climb up the tree between my house and Hawke's, not really trying to hide, but thankful for the cover.

And for the view.

The street where I learned to ride a bike. A street that looks amazing covered in fall leaves in a neighborhood that smells great on a summer night filled with grass, grills, and bug spray.

I can barely look up, though. Tears drip onto my hands as I play with the button on my shirt.

I thought maybe I loved him.

I don't.

I misjudged my connection to him as something more than it was, and maybe it was necessary to get here. We needed to scratch the itch in order to get past it, otherwise we'd always wonder.

It hurts, though.

Other girls I've talked to, they almost always say the same thing. Their first times sucked. They don't remember it well, and the way they felt after was...cold. Like they didn't mean anything to the other person.

I didn't feel like that last night. I was nervous, but I was sure. Like he had only ever seen me.

Now, it just feels like it was all a lie, because it was all just a race. Like the truck they were supposed to share but was only ever really Kade's.

Point Hunter. Score's tied. The tears keep falling.

A motorbike comes whirring down the lane, the engine audible before the bike is even visible. In my peripheral, I see it speed in, sliding right and into our driveway, and I know it's Noah without looking up.

I sit there, hoping he won't see me. The tree's leaves are sparse. I'm not as invisible this time of year.

But in a moment, his helmet is off and he's peeking his head around the house. I look back down, not waving.

He walks over, one hand in his pocket, and the other clutching a clear plastic bag of what looks like cotton candy. He stops underneath the tree and looks up, but when I don't say anything, he just jumps up to me.

Climbing the branches, he plops down on the thick one that stretches over to my room and faces me.

My voice is gravelly. "I don't want to talk."

"That's okay," he tells me. "I'm used to being the chatty one."

I actually meant 'I want to be alone,' but I can't be rude to Noah.

You'd think he'd want to move out and have his own space, but no, he loves living with a family. Even if he's constantly getting lectured in our effort to civilize him. My dad was about to pop a gasket when the cops came because Noah was burning trash in the backyard.

That's when he learned that we put garbage on the curb to be collected—just like families on TV.

And my mom screamed when she walked into the garage and saw Noah draining the blood out of a decapitated deer he'd bought off one his new friends who'd gone hunting that morning. He was going to make us stew or something.

She ran, about to puke. James just dove in and helped Noah.

He loves it here. He says he still needs to be raised.

He opens his bag, pinches off some cotton candy and holds the bag out to me.

I take some. Blue's my favorite.

I slip it into my mouth, the sugar breaking down to little granules as the taste of carnivals and festivals dissolves on my tongue. Hot sun hits my cheek for a second, and I almost smile. "That's good."

He nods, taking more bites and looking out at the street. He must've picked it up at the parade. Did he see the fight?

"I grew up surrounded by thousands of trees," he says. "I rarely ever climbed them."

He offers me the bag again, and I take a little more.

"People come to Chapel Peak for the mountains, the skiing in the winter, the hiking and off-roading in the summer, the scenery..."

I blink, a remaining tear spilling over. "Sounds pretty," I murmur.

"I hated it."

I dart my eyes up, and he chuckles.

"I like people." He shrugs, chewing and swallowing. "I wanted neighbors, noise, culture..."

Culture? I dig in my eyebrows, and he sees, rearing back and looking affronted. "Fuck you, I like plays and shit."

I finally smile a little.

He goes on, staring at the street again. "We were so isolated up there, and I don't remember a time when those majestic mountains didn't feel like walls."

I can't imagine seeing things like that every day gets boring, but I'm sure it does. We get used to anything.

And the seclusion would be hard. I'm like Noah. I like activity.

"When we did see anyone," he says, "it was the same old bullshit. You're rotating the same girls in and out of your bed, determined to live in the present, because the only thing getting you up in the morning is the thought of the beer you'll get to crack open at five o'clock, and who you're going to screw that night."

I watch him stare out at the street, my heart suddenly beating so fast. I've never heard him talk like this.

I'm not sure if I'm shocked, or if I appreciate someone in this house speaking to me like I'm not a child.

"But I kept doing it." His voice sounds strained. "Day after day, year after year, because I didn't know if I'd find what I wanted if I left, either." He pauses, breathing hard. "I don't think I ever would've left if she hadn't first."

"Who?"

Finally, he looks over at me. "Step-cousin, actually." He pulls out more cotton candy. "Same as you and Hunter and Kade."

He offers me more, but I forgot to eat what's in my hand. I stuff it in my mouth.

"I stayed miserable," he swallows, "because I was too afraid to leave and risk failing. Kaleb hadn't spoken a word since he was four. And my father had stopped knowing why he was alive. Fear was rotting us."

He's talked about Kaleb. His older brother.

"And one day," he says, pausing to smile, "she comes into our house and we start fighting for our lives again, because now, we have something we don't want to lose."

"She's not there anymore?"

"No."

He said she left first.

"She found what she wanted, but not what she needed." We both grab for more cotton candy. "So...this eighteen-year-old girl, desperately in love, breaks her own heart and walks away, because she's not wasting one more second on anyone who costs her her peace of mind."

My chest aches and swells, and my eyes water again, and I don't know why. My grandpa said the people you invite into your life should stay because they make it better. If they make it worse, then...

It's just hard when sometimes it feels so good.

Noah's eyes soften. "And I thought, if she could do it, so could I. And when she never came running back, my brother did what he had never done before and left Chapel Peak too. To find her."

To go after her.

So...

My eyes go wide. "You shared a girl with your brother?"

He stares at me for a second, then waves me off. "Mmm, not just my brother, but I'll tell you more when you're grown up."

Huh?

I blink, shaking my head. Never mind.

"My point is," he continues, "you're way ahead of the curve."

I hold his gaze. I am?

"You know exactly who you are and what you were built for."

He means unlike him.

"Don't forget it, and keep going."

I try to smile, but my chin is trembling too hard.

"There's no choice," he says.

Yeah, I know who I am. I like being who I am.

And I know exactly what I want.

My dad pulls up in one of the JT Racing trucks, two bikes and some gear tied to a trailer in the back. Noah crumbles up the empty cotton candy bag and gives me one last look before hopping down to join everyone.

James climbs out of the back seat, my uncle Jax from the other side, and my mom steps out of the front.

My dad moves to the tailgate, lifting up the cover and pulling out a cooler. They were all at the parade, but he doesn't bring work home. They must be heading out for an event.

I wipe my eyes and climb down, trying not to hide my hands in my pockets as I walk over, but I do anyway.

Dad looks over at me, stopping his work.

"Hi," I say.

He gazes at me for a few seconds, a smile in his eyes. "Hey, kid," he almost whispers.

Jax walks past, behind me. "Staying out of trouble?"

"Neverrr," I tease under my breath.

I blink, still feeling the tears. I know my eyes are red.

I tip my chin at the trailer with the bikes. "What's on the schedule today?"

"Air show," he tells me. "They'll have a hangar for displays, engineers—"

"Robotics," James chimes in.

I watch my little brother pass with a crate of gadgets and hand it to our dad.

"We texted and called," James adds. "To see if you wanted to come, but somebody doesn't like to answer their phone."

"Shhh," Dad tells him.

I don't tell them that my phone is sitting on a wet forest floor in Weston.

Which means Hunter can't reach me if he's trying, either. I'm okay with that right now.

I swallow, inching a little closer to my dad. "Need some help?"

He smiles a little, his shoulders visibly relaxing. "Yeah."

I crack, unable to look at his face, but I come in all the same, wrapping my arms around my dad's waist and planting my head against his chest. He immediately hugs me back.

I don't know if he's assuming I'm sad that we've been fighting, or if he saw the fight at the parade and knows something is up, but he simply asks, "Do you want to talk?"

"Not yet."

And he doesn't push it. Thankfully.

My mom steps over, removing a carrier from the front seat and handing me a strawberry milkshake.

I laugh, taking it.

"So that's why you wanted an extra one," my dad says to her.

"How'd you know I'd be here?" I ask her.

"Your dad and Jax installed some cameras." She points to one at the front door and one at the corner of the house. "We all have apps on our phones. He was sure someone was in the house the other night."

Hunter.

I suck on the straw, not saying anything though. If I tell them he snuck in, I'd have to tell them why.

Jax and James carry more gear, sliding it all into the bed of the truck.

"Do I have time for a quick shower?" I ask.

Dad nods. "I'll pack the cooler."

"I got the snacks!" James shouts.

But my mom stops him. "You only pack chips." She wraps an arm around his shoulder, walking him inside the house. "You can *help* me with the snacks, how about that?"

I just hear his disgusted sound as I follow.

"Mom, not even you want to eat the almonds and carrot sticks you pack," I tell her.

She argues over her shoulder, "But I still need to put that stuff in there to make it look like I'm a good parent."

Dad and Jax chuckle behind us.

Dad pulls into the Weston High School parking lot the next morning, dropping me off after I got to sleep in my own bed last night. I'm not sure if spending a day away from the Rebels constitutes a forfeit of the prisoner exchange, but they're free to kick me back to the Falls if they want. I have every intention of trying to finish the week.

Dad pulls his Mustang Dark Horse up to the curb, one hand on the wheel as he leans down and looks out through my window. Students trail into the building, some slowing and checking out his car as they pass.

"Are you sure you want to stay here?" he asks me.

I open the door. "It's only a few more nights," I say, climbing out. "I'll see you Friday."

"Got our tickets," he calls out.

I draw in a long breath. *The game.* I wasn't sure which side I was sitting on yet. Guess I know now.

I bend over, peering into the car and smiling at my dad. We didn't talk about racing yesterday or anything that we still need to hash out, but I wasn't looking to anyway. I just wanted to go home.

Noah helped a lot.

"Love you," I say.

"Love you too."

He shifts into gear, and I slam the door shut, twisting and walking up the stairs.

Students pass, giving me a nod or smile, and I walk into the school, spotting Coral. She's wearing my jacket now.

"Hey." She falls in at my side, Mace and Codi following. "Where'd you go off to? Where's Hunter?"

"What do you mean?"

"He disappeared yesterday, same as you." She looks around to her friends. "No one's seen him since."

He doesn't have his phone, either. I saw it on the ground when the Pirates tried to take me Saturday night. I think that's what he threw at Kade's truck.

"I spent time with my family," I tell them. "I haven't seen him."

His parents were at the parade. They'd know about the fight. If there was something to worry about, we'd know by now.

"Are you okay?" Coral asks.

"Yeah."

I'm not sure how much they saw or heard, but I'm not talking about it either way. I glance at Coral. "You know I'm getting that jacket back?"

She makes a face, and I laugh.

"Well, she looks better in it."

But the voice wasn't Mace's. I turn my eyes over my shoulder, looking at Codi. "Well, look at you, using your words."

She beams, glancing at her friends.

She talked to me.

I turn around, all of us heading into class. I'm fine if I never get the jacket back as long as I can see her in it once.

"Essays, please," Mr. Bastien calls out as we enter.

I dig into the satchel, pulling out two pieces of crisp paper stapled together. I don't often have homework done on time, but I got a sudden burst of energy after we got home from the air show last night. I wanted to walk back in this school with some paint on my nails and my book report done like I hadn't missed a step.

"You know," I say, setting my essay down on the pile, "most teachers in the digital age ask us to submit assignments online. Saves trees."

He picks up the stack, sifting through. "Any idea how many more hydrocarbons, carbon monoxide, and nitrogen your motorcycle pumps out than my car?"

I turn away. "Whatever."

I hear him snort behind me as I walk to my seat.

Sliding in my chair, I drop my bag to the floor.

"Did you see Kade Caruthers's post?" Mace whispers next to me.

I dig out the class text that we've been discussing. "No."

"He's having a pool party this week," she tells me "Both teams and their dates are invited."

"No fights allowed." Coral leans over my shoulder. "He promised."

Well, I'm not going to be Kade's bait to get Hunter there. That's what the party is really about.

But I look out the window as the bell rings and the football team runs outside, a quick jolt to my nerves when I still don't see Hunter. Farrow is there. His guys too. They laugh and joke in the parking lot as they make their way to the field, and I start to worry. Like I think I'll never see him again.

Bastien comes around the front of his desk and sits on the edge. "So..." He gives a tight smile. "The parade was fun."

A round of laughter goes off, everyone who wasn't there at least hearing about the fight by this point.

"Oh, come on, the kids will remember that one, at least," a guy in the back calls out.

The teacher nods in agreement. "They will."

He unzips his dark blue pullover, revealing a thick vein underneath a tan neck. His Kelly green T-shirt peeks out, and I hear Coral inhale behind me, almost whimpering. I shake with a laugh, knowing my father would never let my mom have a parent-teacher conference alone with this guy.

Of course, she's obsessed with my dad, but he still gets jealous.

"And I'm sure the Falls High alumni will remember it, as well," Bastien informs us. "They'll remember it, reinforcing their continued assessment that thugs like us should never win."

Someone tsks behind me, while others make aggravated sounds.

He goes on, "So they'll write more checks, pumping more money into equipment, extra training, physical therapy, away games, hotels, and buses with bathrooms." He pauses, looking around his room of seniors. "You made their coach very happy yesterday."

I'd love to say that he's not right, but that's exactly the narrative about Weston in my town. Of course, we know better, but it pumps us up and increases our enjoyment of the rivalry to talk shit like every single one of them is trouble-loving, rude, and has no regard for personal property.

Just like they assume we never work for anything, have never experienced loss, and have never had a deep thought in our heads.

"And for what?" Bastien asks. "Why do we do it? Put on our colors and march down the street to represent our towns?"

And one by one, students throw out answers.

"Community pride?"

"Solidarity for our shared history?"

"Supporting the hard work of our athletes?" Mace offers.

"What about the hard work of the students?" someone else asks. "We don't have parades for Honor Roll."

"Stadiums for science fairs," I add.

People laugh, and the teacher nods, liking the questions we're asking.

Competition is fun. The prospect of winning brings people together. That's easy enough to figure out.

But why just football?

"Take out your phones," he says.

He walks to the board and picks up his marker.

"Email me a letter." He writes down his email address. "Dylan Trent wants us to save trees today."

"Haha," Coral jokes behind me.

Haha.

"Write to a Shelburne Falls Pirate parent," he continues. "Mom or Dad. It doesn't matter." He turns and recaps the marker. "Tell them what you think of all of this, what you want them to know about you, *and* what you hope for them. Five-hundred words."

386

Hmm, boring. Sounds like he doesn't want to teach today.

"If you don't have your phone, paper is fine," he calls out.

I take out paper and a pencil, and he raises his eyebrows. I roll my eyes. What am I supposed to do? I don't have my phone.

"Does Dylan just write to her own parents then?" someone asks, followed by a round of snickers.

I put my name on my paper and try to think of a witty comeback, but I'm honestly not sure who I'm going to write to.

"Are we sending these to the parents?" Coral asks.

Bastien doesn't reply, simply plays some downtempo on his computer while most of the class starts typing away on their phones, a few of us, including Codi and me, writing on paper.

Next week at this time I'll be sitting in computer science, my class right before financial literacy. They didn't have either of those options on my schedule here.

The classes are better at home, but still, it'll be hard to leave Weston. I like Bastien. He talks to us like adults, and gives us more questions than answers. I don't like people who think they know everything.

I mean, I understand the significance of learning programming and why my credit score matters and how the stock market works. I know new jobs are being invented every day, taxes help society function, and we're being groomed to be useful parts in the massive machine, and hey, I don't even mind all that much. I love helping the economy. I like shopping.

But I don't love those classes. They're not fun, and I never feel like I'm discovering anything.

Since coming to Weston, I've discovered one new thing about myself. I might be a Shelburne Falls parent someday, but I can't say I want the jacket back anymore. Not really.

We turn in our assignments, and I go through the day, keeping my eyes forward.

Even when I feel him.

I thought maybe he wouldn't come when I didn't see him with the team during first period. Hunter has a habit of walking away. This is his third school in a little over a year, after leaving Falls High and St. Matthew's.

But I head down the hallway, knowing when I pass him and his friends standing by a set of lockers, and he watches me.

I don't look.

I draw in a long breath and release it, the weight of caring disappearing.

I talk to Codi at lunch, the others with the pack at the football players' table, and I stay after school, helping Mr. Bastien print off all the letters that students emailed today.

He doesn't read them before he asks me to stuff them in envelopes, including the one I wrote, writing the person's name who wrote it on the front. He tells me to seal them.

"Are you mailing them?" I burst out.

He can't. I don't want this going to my house.

He shakes his head. "No. Just trust me."

I cock an eyebrow and continue my task.

After I leave, the parking lot is empty, but instead of going to Knock Hill, I walk down to the mill district, seeing my bike still parked in front of the abandoned insurance business.

The hair on the back of my neck rises, though, and I pop my head up, looking around. Leaves blow across the street, workers jump off a tugboat down the street at the dock, and

I see a mom carrying a bag of groceries, a small boy walking at her side.

No one is watching me, although it feels like there is.

I head up Phelan's Throat, making runs around and around again for the next two hours. I shouldn't be without supervision, I should be in more protective clothes, and I shouldn't push it this fast, but I shove everything out of my head as my heart drops into my stomach and I just go. I have to.

I race up the hill, swerving around potholes and the *Road Closed* sign. I fly up to the top and jerk the handlebars right, skidding down the throat just like Farrow taught. My knee catches on the ground, and I can feel the sting as it shreds my jeans, but I'm okay. I speed down and back up again, over the bend, and back to the finish.

The sun sets, darkness seeping in, and the eyes I felt before are in the woods, behind me, up ahead, all around now. I race back up the Throat one more time, headlights appearing far behind.

A car.

Cars don't come up here. Road closed and all. I'm not even supposed to be up here.

It gains on me, but not close enough to threaten. All the same, though, I slow down and cruise around the Throat, taking it easy before speeding up again and dashing back to Knock Hill. It follows me the whole way, and I cruise up to the curb in front of my place, skidding to a halt.

The car, an old, black BMW with rust around the grill stops on the other side of the street, in front of Fletcher's.

Constin climbs out. He's alone.

"What are you doing?" I ask, but my eyes are stern.

He walks over to me, glancing up at my house.

"Farrow told me to keep an eye on you," he says. "For your safety."

"Farrow told you that?"

I get off my bike and remove my helmet.

Farrow would ask Hunter. Of course, that doesn't mean Hunter would do it.

He closes the distance between us, stopping on the sidewalk in front of me. "I need to check the house."

"What for?"

"There's someone in there," he says.

I turn my head, looking up the stairs. What?

"I saw movement through the window just now."

Oh, bullshit. "Give me a break."

I jog up the steps, away from him. He's just trying to get inside. That was plain enough when he asked me to homecoming. I told Hunter I was thinking about it, and that's what I told Constin, but only because I couldn't think of a reason to say no fast enough. As if I need a reason.

I just don't get asked out a lot, and turning people down makes me feel badly.

He catches up to me, pulling me around by the arm. "You're still a prisoner," he says. "I don't have to ask."

"No, you do," I correct him. "And I can say no."

It's my house for the rest of the week.

He stares down at me, his expression softening a little. "Let me in," he whispers.

I know what he wants to happen if he does come in. Is Hunter watching right now? I glance behind Constin, to Hunter and Farrow's place. I don't see any sign of life in the house.

"Let me in," he presses again.

He brushes my chin with his fingers, and I snap to, shoving him away.

I run inside, slam the door, and race up to my room to the phone Hawke left me.

I throw open my door and see Hunter, sitting in my desk chair, leaning his elbows on his knees.

A new Android phone sits on my desk, still in the box.

He looks at me, his brow etched with pain.

He shouldn't be in my room without my permission.

I walk in and drop my bag, heading to the nightstand and pulling out the cell Hawke gave me. "I have homework to do."

He immediately rises to his feet. "Dylan, please let me apologize."

I turn on the phone, waiting for it to start. "I appreciate it." I look at him and nod, doing a good job of ignoring how beautiful he looks in black. I love the jacket. "But you don't need to," I tell him. "I forgave you almost immediately."

I walk to the door, holding it open for him. He just stands there.

"You're a part of me," I say, not looking at him again. "Like Kade, Hawke, Quinn...I'll always be there for you, Hunter."

His spine straightens, and he grows another inch taller. "I'm not Kade," he growls. "Or Hawke. Or Quinn."

He approaches me, and I breathe shallow, my skin on fire the closer he gets.

"I..." I swallow. "I have work to do, Hunter."

"I'm obsessed with you," he gasps, grabbing my head in his hands, threading his fingers through my hair, and pressing me into the wall next to my door. "I've been obsessed with you since we were kids."

Everything hurts. My eyes sting, and my mouth falls open, everything below my fucking waist coming alive at just the feel of his body pressing into mine.

I pant but then quickly clench my teeth. His chest rises and falls hard against mine as he stares at my mouth.

"I'll always care about you," I say. "You're a part of me."

"Stop saying that."

His forehead presses into mine, his lips hovering, and I hate him. I hate him so much.

"Hit me," he whispers. "Hit me, bite me, make me pay, but don't fucking tell me you care about me."

A fist clenches around my heart.

"Show me you hate me instead," he hisses. "Show me how much you fucking hate me."

I shove him in the chest, forcing his ass back, and then dive down, lifting his shirt and sinking my teeth into his stomach.

"Ah," he groans, holding my head against his body as he leans a hand on the wall behind me.

I hold his flesh between my teeth, hearing my pulse race in my ears. I take another bite and then another, the feel of him in my mouth so fucking good.

And then...I come up and kiss him hard on the mouth, groaning as I feed, because this is what he deserves. He wraps his arms around my waist, and I shove my hands in his chest at the same time I'm nibbling his mouth.

It means nothing.

"It was a mistake," I tell him, tugging on his bottom lip with my teeth.

"Fine." He pulls my shirt over my head and yanks my bra down, taking me in his arms again. "It was a fucking mistake."

He lifts me up, and I wrap my legs around his waist as his mouth covers a breast.

"Just one more time," he pants.

I shove him in the shoulders as he bites my flesh. "I hate you."

"I hate you too."

Gripping the back of his head, I force his mouth up to mine and kiss him, unable to eat enough.

He drops me back to my feet, our lips glued as we shove down my pants, breaking only when we pull off his T-shirt.

Picking me up again, he carries me to my bed, throwing me down on it and coming down between my legs.

I suck in a breath as his mouth covers my clit, and I grip his hair as he licks.

He eats hard, not slowing down as a groan escapes his throat while he sucks my clit like a straw. "Ah," I moan, squirming underneath him. My legs bend, my thighs widening, and I feel his fingers move from my waist to my ass and then around my thighs.

"Constin is outside," I taunt. "I could scream."

He kisses and licks, sliding a finger, then two, inside me. I whimper, arching my back and rolling my hips into his mouth.

"Fuckin' scream, then," he says, his voice breathy.

He sucks, flicking my clit with his tongue.

"Scream," he tells me.

I moan louder and louder, his tongue teasing me over and over until I feel the orgasm rise.

I squeeze my eyes shut, fuck his mouth, and cry out, not caring how loud I am.

His fingers glide in and out, in and out, in and out, and my whole body tightens as I gasp.

The orgasm flows through me, but he doesn't stop. Rising back up to his knees, he clutches my thighs and flips me over. I blink, startled.

"Up on your knees."

And he grabs my hips, pulling me up. I stand on all fours, on top of my bed, feeling him unfasten his jeans behind me.

"Hunter," I gasp.

He positions himself at my entrance, and I tremble as the head of his cock starts to stretch me.

"Disappearing for more than a fucking day," he whispers.

He thrusts, burying himself inside me, and I shut my eyes again, holding my breath. "Oh my God..."

So deep.

He slides out, and then in, and before I know it, he's fucking me hard and fast.

"I go to your parents' house," he growls, yanking my hips back on his dick. "I wait here..."

He did?

I grab onto the headboard, pushing myself up and arching my back.

He hits deeper, and I grind the wooden railing in my hands, holding on.

"And you don't even have the decency to look me in the fucking face at school," he murmurs.

He slams into my ass, filling me—the ache of his cock stretching me so fucking good.

He grips my hair, tugging me back to whisper in my ear. "Is this the last time you want to touch me?" he pants.

I nod. "Yeah."

I can't tell him the truth.

"I put your plastic dick underneath your pillow," he says, and I hear him wet his lips. "Ride it really good in the morning, okay."

"Okay," I whimper.

"Put it inside you."

"I will," I tell him.

He releases my hair and grips my hips tightly as I hang on. The headboard hits the wall, and I back up into him, meeting him pound for pound.

"Oh my God," he groans. "Fuck, baby."

And I smile, loving that he loves this. A vibrator can't give me that.

CHAPTER TWENTY-TWO

"These Pirates..." Deacon laughs, rubbing his temple as we listen to the Pirate and the Rebel go at it upstairs, above our heads. "Frickin' rabbits," he says, a lit cigarette between his fingers. "Just like her."

Her.

He looks at me as I sit in one of our cushioned chairs in the living room, the headboard above banging against the wall.

We were standing in the kitchen when she ran in. We heard footfalls on the stairs, muffled talking, arguing, a sense of a struggle, so we stayed close, but then there were moans.

And something like screams, but they were the good kind. The kind men love to hear because they're doing something right and not something bad.

We should leave now.

Dylan Trent cries out again, and I close my eyes, almost remembering the taste of moans like that. Almost.

Winslet MacCreary didn't deserve the fun she had in this house.

"Just...like...her," Deacon coos, smiling at me. "It was so dark in that room, I don't think she knew which one of us was which most of the time."

He looks away from Deacon, remembering the first time he and Winslet were in that very same room together where Dylan and Hunter are right now.

She knew which one was which. She always knew.

He descends the attic stairs, pushing the door open into the upstairs hallway.

Deacon sits up against the wall to the right, between the bathroom and our parents' old room. He wears Army green cargo pants and no shirt, hanging one arm over his bent knee.

He rests his head back against the wall and grins at me. The house is dark, the storm killing the electricity and the streetlights outside. The moon doesn't even pierce the clouds.

I jerk my chin, telling him to take a walk. It's my turn now.

His smile widens, and he skips down the stairs, but he doesn't leave the house. He wants to hear it.

I stop at her door, having only seen glimpses of her since she was traded to us in the prisoner exchange a few days ago. She knows I'm here, but I wanted him to have his fun first. He deserves it.

Opening the door, I stand in the frame, seeing her sit up in bed.

"Deacon?" she asks.

The night is so black, the rain can't even find a speck of light to spread. It hits her window, and I make out my brother's desk and bed. His pictures on the wall, and his nice curtains. He always took the most initiative with the house and making it look nice. His room is comfortable. She shouldn't have it.

I walk in, pushing the door shut behind me, and stop at the bottom of the bed. I take her sheet and gently tug at it.

She lets it go, and I make out the shapes of her naked breasts, tummy, and the barest hint of panties in the dark.

I see her chest cave as realization hits. I'm bigger than my brother. "You," she says.

She steps out of bed, but I'm there in an instant, grabbing the flashlight and tossing it behind me, into the fucking wall.

She covers herself with her arms. She doesn't cover herself with Deacon. They're both the same. Their hearts stopped working or maybe hers never did, but now that she's old enough to pay for her crimes, no one holds her accountable.

I will. She'll be destroyed when she leaves me.

Lifting her chin, she gazes up at me. "Everyone knows about you," she taunts. "Your brain's not right, is it? You used to be in a hospital? My dad said."

I clench my jaw so fucking hard it hurts.

She steps around me, forcing me to turn.

"Everyone whispers about you like you're a vampire or something," she says, "But I think you're probably just a little dumb. Can you talk, huh?"

I grab her arms and press her into the wall, bearing down.

She drops her hands, brushing a tit with her thumb. "Is this what you want?" she coos. "You want to make it with me? You didn't have many girls in the psycho ward, did you?"

Fucking bitch.

I reach to the left of her head and grab the bookshelf, yanking it away from the wall. My brother's books spill, the furniture toppling over.

I punch the door on her right and spin around, whipping the nightstand across the room.

"Oh, there's the man of the house now," she sings. "What a big man, you are."

I charge her, holding her fucking little head in my hands, and all I have to do is twist.

"Come on," she goads, but I can feel the shaking in her body. "Get it over with. Hurt me! I know you both want to. Hurt me!"

"I don't want this to hurt," I growl in her face. "I want this to be over for you very quickly, in fact."

I don't notice her hands are hooked around my biceps until she curls her fingers deeper.

We hold each other, and I wait for her to beg. To cry. To explain.

To apologize for what she did to him because the Falls always thinks that we're shit to be dumped on and discounted.

But as I hold her and she holds me, I can feel it in her body. The heartbeat. The pain. And a head full of secrets, just like the rest of us.

But her pride, her ego, and her fucking mouth...

Why did my brother love her?

"How could anyone love someone so ugly?" I ask her.

She goes still, and when she speaks I hear the sadness in her voice. "They don't."

She doesn't cry, and I almost drop my forehead to hers.

No, they'd don't. No one wants damaged people.

I lower my hand, fisting the hem of her panties, and

she doesn't pull away. Her breasts graze my chest, and I curl my other hand into her hair, wanting her upstairs. In the attic. Tied in my bed.

But I kiss her forehead and release her. "Go to sleep."

I walk out of the room, slamming the door behind me and leaving the house to stand in the rain.

"Did you see the blonde here the other night?" Deacon asks. "Quinn, they called her?"

The headboard upstairs has gone silent, but no door opens yet.

"I thought it was her from a distance," Deacon says.

But it's a joke because he knows it wasn't Winslet.

I take his cigarette and suck off a drag. "She owns that bakery connected to Carnival Tower."

I blow out the smoke and walk to the kitchen, extinguishing it under the faucet. I throw the butt into the trash can and see coffee grounds in the bag. She's using the groceries I bought for her.

"She'll be home again in May," he says, knowing Frosted is only open in the summers.

I avoid his eyes, opening the stairwell door and pressing the panel to reveal the basement stairs.

"I want to get involved in this," he begs, like he has a monkey on his back. "I want to play."

"She's too young."

"Not as young as Winslet," he points out, "and you had her crawling into your bed before school and after."

"That's enough," I bite out.

We hear a door close upstairs, both of us staring at the ceiling as footsteps cross the hall and close another door.

"It's not enough." He lowers his voice. "I want more. And more. And more."

I grab him by the collar.

"Our story's not over," he pleads, pushing me back.

I plant my hand over his mouth and wrap my arms around him, pressing him into the wall to shut him up.

Goddammit.

I listen for Dylan and the boy, not hearing anything coming down the stairs.

I stare at Deacon.

I've been able to keep him in check, but these fucking kids are opening up all of our boxes. It was kind of fun when Hawke found the tower. It was even nostalgic to see Weston get a girl in the exchange, especially with the kids here carrying on the legend. Like Winslet will live forever.

But...

Deacon wants to lurk. He wants to dial it up, and he wants to be seen.

He hums behind my hand, bobbing his head back into the wall. I release him and pull him away, so he stops.

He stands there, eyes locked with mine, and I notice his middle finger is threaded through the shackle of a padlock as he buttons his suit jacket. A chill climbs my skin, and I watch as the snake of a smile curls his lips.

"*On Knock Hill, there goes a knocking, knocking,*" he sings in a whisper, "*and in the attic a rocking, rocking...*"

He climbs down the basement stairs, his words drifting up as he goes and reminding me that this is all my fault, and once set in motion, Deacon will never stop.

"*On the wind does bring a chill, the ghost of the girl... you did kill.*"

I close my eyes, and I see her face. Always.

REBELS

CHAPTER TWENTY-THREE

Hunter

She fucking kicked me out. After I gave her two orgasms. She's spent more time with my friends this week than me. If she's not training with Mace or Farrow, she's staying after school to help Codi and Coral make pep rally posters in the Art room. I've barely spoken to her since we went at it in her room on Monday.

I stand in front of the mirror, gripping the bar in both hands and curling at my elbows. I lift the barbell to my chest again and again.

I can't go another night without her.

Farrow settles on the bench next to me, starting crunches with a medicine ball. "You're coming tonight."

"I know," I reply.

There aren't many people whom I'd let tell me what I'm doing or where I'm going, but I won't hide from Kade's party.

"Are you bringing her?" he asks.

"That's up to her."

"That's a Caruthers answer." He sits up, twists side to side, and leans back down. "Give me a Pierce one."

"Fuck you."

He grins. "That's more like it."

It's also not an answer. I don't have one. Dylan knows about the pool party tonight. Players and their dates. I've tried to corner her, but she doesn't deserve to be subjected to another fight between Kade and me, and I'm pretty sure she doesn't want that either.

"You know, I've learned a lot from your grandpa," Farrow tells me, barely out of breath as he keeps going. "And one of the most important things is that anything that matters should never be left up to anyone else."

"What do I do?" I roll my shoulders, starting another set. "Bring her against her will?"

"Yeah."

"Her pride won't allow surrender," I tell him. "That's not how I earn her."

"And that's what you need to understand about someone who's in love with you, Hunter." He drops the ball and sits up. "She wants you. She wants you badly, but she's mad and you probably deserve it, so to make her feel like she's not giving up any power, you're gonna have to fight her." He grabs his towel, wiping the sweat off his forehead. "And I promise, she wants you to. Don't be afraid of the fight, man. Let her be mad. She can be mad *at* the party. I don't give a shit."

He grabs a barbell, fixes on some weights, and lays back down on the bench, doing skull-crushers.

Someone who's in love with you...

Is he right? Monday afternoon in her room wasn't sweet. It was almost hate-fucking. We were both mad and fed up and frustrated and frenzied, and she was even a little violent. The biting, Jesus.

But she couldn't get enough, either.

I throw Farrow a glance. "I never really know if you're actually wise or just say things with so much confidence that it makes me believe you."

He grunts, raising the bar over and over. "If you go to bed alone tonight, I guess we'll know."

A chuckle escapes. "So who are you bringing?"

"Are you kidding?" he raises his voice so the whole cage can hear. "The Pirates will all have dates. The question is 'which one am I taking?'"

The guys howl and laugh, Calvin pounding his fist against the chain-link.

I want to call my parents to make sure they know what they're in for, but I half-suspect Kade is throwing the party on a Wednesday night because they'll just happen to be out of town. He posted the invite on his secret account, after all, so they wouldn't see.

It would be a dick move to sabotage it, and I don't want him to think I'm afraid to show up.

I shower in the locker room, the extra afternoon workout our last before the game. Coach wants us to rest up until Friday. I pass by the Art room, seeing that it's empty, and when I go out to the parking lot, Dylan's bike is gone, as well as Coral's car. They must've finished the posters.

I drive home, Farrow's advice spinning inside my head.

I love her. She's social. I'm not. She loves crowds and noise. I don't. She hates school, and I could keep going forever. She'd risk her life just to feel a rush, while I consider my choices too much. She's so much like Kade, but she fits my heart like she was cut from it. It's always been hers.

I pull up to the curb in front of the house. Her bike is parked next door, and I climb out, debating.

I have four more nights with her. I'm not fighting again.

Fletcher wipes down the windows of the garage door that acts as the wall in his shop, and I stroll over. Stepping inside, I run my hand through my hair, giving him a nod.

"Missed you on Monday," he says, dropping his cloth and cleaner.

"Girl trouble."

He smiles. "That's good trouble to have."

If you say so.

He gestures. "Got a haircut, I see."

"No offense." I take a seat in his barber chair. "Moms, you know? Could use a shave, though."

Not that I even come close to growing a full beard yet, but I could use a touch up before tonight.

The chair reclines back, me with it, and I close my eyes as he wraps a hot towel around my face.

This may be my last time coming here. I only have four more nights, too, before I return home, like I promised my parents.

I could still return every week, though, couldn't I? My dad would love to do this with me. It could be our weekly hang-out time.

The heat sinks into my cheeks, making it feel like something is pulling the hair on my arms under my skin, but in the best way. I hear Samson remove his tools from the Barbicide and dry them off before coming in and pressing the hot towel deeper into my face.

Would Kade like to come here? I can't picture him sitting still for a shave. He seems to slow down even less than I do.

In a minute the towel comes off, the warm shaving cream is smoothed onto my skin, and Samson drags the straight razor up my neck as I tip my head back.

I stare at the pictures on the wall.

"My grandpa was in here a lot back in the day?" I ask.

"He was." Samson glides the razor up my throat. "He still stops in once in a while."

"Why would he let this town go to shit if he loved it here so much?"

Samson concentrates on his task, wiping the razor on the cloth hanging over his shoulder before he brings it back to my face. "He's not God, Hunter."

I know that, but look at what my family—and Dylan's family—have done for Shelburne Falls in the same amount of time. The Falls wasn't considered an affluent area when my dad was growing up. Our house was one of the first of its size when it was built, and now there's a whole neighborhood of them. With Jax running the track and the summer camp, Jared and JT Racing, and my dad bringing in new businesses, the town is a destination. My grandfather is just as smart and just as invested. He kept a home here, after all.

I need to know why he'd let it fall into Green Street's hands, especially with...

I let out a long breath as the razor slides up my cheek. "You know Farrow is my grandfather's son, right?"

Samson doesn't falter, wiping off the razor and scraping it up my skin again. "You know she's not alone in that house, right?"

I curl my fingers around the armrests, all thoughts of my grandpa and Farrow gone.

I haven't seen a single person whom I didn't know come or go from that house.

But...

It also never felt truly abandoned, either. Someone still owns it.

Fletcher finishes, and I pay him, heading across the street to Dylan's house.

I lift my hand to knock, hesitating a moment.

A Caruthers would end it now. They would throw her over their shoulder, regardless of how much she kicked and screamed.

A Pierce knows they'll get what they want—eventually—so enjoy the foreplay.

I knock, and within a few seconds, Dylan answers.

"I need your help tonight," I tell her.

We cruise to the party, only fashionably late. The team didn't want to be on time and appear like we had nothing better to do tonight, but my brother isn't stupid. If we waited an hour to arrive, he'd just post about how scared we were to be on their turf.

Instead, we all pull into my parents' driveway—Constin, Farrow, Dylan, and Mace on bikes, the rest of us in cars and trucks—at eight-thirty, and according to Farrow, we're leaving by ten.

Dylan climbs off her bike and removes her helmet, the red leather jacket doing a shitty job of protecting her from anything. I see the outline of her bikini underneath, her naked waist calling to me like a fucking magnet.

She removes her backpack and takes out a container of brownies she must've picked up at Frosted on the way. She said Quinn left treats.

We all stroll to the house, and I open the door, leading everyone inside.

"Welcome," Kade calls.

He strolls through the foyer in swim shorts, no shirt or shoes, and a drink in his hand like this is my first time here too. Stoli and Dirk flank him, and I hear people in the kitchen. Others move around the pool through the double doors on the back patio, steam rising from the water.

Kade stops in front of me. "Keys in the bowl," he says, pointing to his friend next to him who holds a glass dish. "Stoli will be in charge of the sober check when you leave."

The bowl already has a dozen or more sets of keys.

Farrow looks around to his people, announcing, "A guy named *Stoli* will be checking if *we're* sober enough to drive. Did you hear that, everyone?"

Chuckles and snickers go off, because Stolichnaya earned his nickname by always being the first one *not* sober. His real name is Josh.

Mace steps forward, holding out her open backpack. "I'll hold ours."

One by one we all dump our keys into her bag as Kade and I lock eyes, and I see the faded purple bruising under his eye and the scratch along his jaw. His gaze, heavy with tension, tells me he'd offer no argument if I wanted to finish that fight. All someone has to do is light the match tonight.

I glance down, catching sight of the triple triangle tattoo on his torso that matches our mother's.

"There's a bathroom in the pool house," Kade tells everyone, "one off the kitchen, and another in the basement. Don't go upstairs, and if you have sex in my house, leave no trace. Not even your condoms."

Coral hands him a cardboard carrier by the handles.

He takes it. "What's this?"

He peers inside, seeing the three bottles of El Tesoro that Farrow probably swiped from Green Street's private stash.

Kade smiles, handing it to Dirk. "We can use that," he tells Farrow. "I half-expected it to be drugs."

"Not before the game," my friend retorts. "We want to beat you fairly."

Kade laughs and then turns his attention to our group. "Ladies, the legal age of consent in this state is seventeen. Anyone younger than that?"

"Kade, shut up." Dylan drives forward, shoving the container of brownies into his chest. "You're being a tool on purpose."

And she heads past him into the party.

Kade turns as we all follow her. "Oh, you missed me," he coos. "You know you did."

We head through the kitchen, my parents and sister nowhere in sight, everyone ripping off their hoodies, jackets, and shirts as we step onto the pool deck.

"Turn it up!" Kade shouts.

All of the Pirates—the players and their dates—turn, see us, and howl as "HONEY" by Luna Aura blasts over the speakers loud enough for the neighbors a quarter of a mile away to hear.

Dylan takes Mace, Coral, and a few others over to Aro, and the girls strip down to swimsuits, stepping into the pool. Dylan wears a light blue bikini, the ties thin across her back, and I don't know why, but I glance at the pool house. There's a couch inside. The door locks too. I take a drink from my cup to hide my smile.

She stands waist deep in the heated water, laughing at something Mace says, but then I look up to see Kade standing on the other side of the pool, his gaze on her too. Then it rises to me.

With his eyes gleaming, he takes a step and drops into the pool. Walking to Dylan and the girls, he slips a drink around her waist and into her hand, the plastic cup in my own grip cracking. I stop squeezing before I break it. *All part of the plan...* I tell myself.

I turn to Constin, trying to look busy while Dylan does her thing and I make an effort to look like I'm not keeping an eye out for her.

A girl named Ava stares at Constin, and I remember her from when I went to school here. She stands in a pinstriped bikini with a group of people on the deck, playing with one of her braids as she looks at him.

I lift the cup to my mouth. "She's interested."

"I'm not."

I glance at him and then quickly at Dylan, seeing Kade press into their group and force her back away from them, back to the pool wall. He doesn't touch, and her lips move calmly as she speaks.

"You can't have Dylan," I say to Constin.

He looks around the party, still avoiding my eyes. "If you ever figure out what I like about Dylan Trent, you'll finally understand me."

"You won't tell me?"

He hesitates, raising his cup to his lips. "No."

I look at Ava and then Dylan, wondering what the difference is. Both are beautiful, and I didn't know Ava well, but she was always nice. Maybe a little more pink going on, with her swimsuit and the bandana tied in her hair... Definitely more makeup.

But if he hasn't spoken to her yet, I have no idea what he finds in one that he's not seeing in the other.

"You can't have Dylan," I say again.

He takes another drink, casting his eyes from lawn chair to lawn chair and face to face. A guy films his friend jumping into the pool, while two others funnel a beer. A group of young women film themselves dancing, and a guy in Crocs urinates on the tree my dad planted with my mom right before Kade and I were born. Food, liquor, and music overflow, everyone wears sunglasses even though it's night, and none of the keys they had in that bowl when we arrived were for cars that were used, stolen, or paid for out of the drivers' own pockets. They were supplied by doting moms and dads.

"You know, I thought I understood you," Constin tells me. "Some rich kid slumming it for kicks or under some misguided notion that it makes you noble to reject the comforts that not everyone gets to enjoy."

I glance at Dylan to see her lift her chin as she talks to Kade.

"But it was all bullshit, of course," Constin continues, "because you're never really suffering if you know that you can run back to the mansion at any time." He still doesn't look at me, just studies the party. "But now, I think I misunderstood you. I see all this, the house you grew up in, the fuckin' laze and people choking on their own egos, and I think no wonder you came looking for us."

I go still, a little glad and a little sad. He sees what I saw. The boredom of people who value nothing, but...it doesn't mean I was right, either. It just means I didn't see it, and I wasn't finding what I needed here.

He walks away, leaving me alone, and it finally occurs to me why my grandpa might've left Weston to fend for itself. *Hard times make strong people.*

He says it all the time.

Of course, Weston loves a good party as much as we do. They love to drink and fight and go to bed with people who make them feel good, but the difference is Weston doesn't trust anyone easily. If you're their friend, you earned it.

I don't want to leave my school there.

"What the fuck is he doing?" Farrow grits out suddenly at my side.

I follow his gaze, seeing Kade fall in behind Dylan as she leads the way out of the pool. He takes her hand, both of them disappearing into the house.

I tip my head back and close my eyes.

"Hunter," he says.

I hand him my drink and walk away. "Don't follow me."

"What?"

But I'm gone.

I follow Dylan and Kade into the house, and I don't see her take him down to the basement, but I know that's where they went. Through the entertainment room, past the bar and the people playing a video game, down the hall, and into the liquor storage room way at the end.

"I can't," I hear Dylan say.

I pause, listening by the cracked door.

"Sit," he tells her.

"No."

"Are you fucking him?"

I draw in a breath, pushing open the door. Kade turns his head, looking at me over his shoulder.

Cases of liquor and two kegs of beer sit against the wall to my left, while several barrels of my dad's homemade whiskey are stacked to my right.

I step in, meeting Dylan's eyes as she stands with her back to the wine racks. "Thanks," I tell her.

She just looks away and starts to walk past me, but I catch her. "Stay."

"I'm no longer interested."

"I need you here," I tell her.

She looks away, but she stays.

Kade sighs, crossing his arms over his chest, realizing Dylan wanted to get him alone. For me.

I close the door, the party far away, and if there's shouting, no one will hear. "Where are Mom and Dad?" I ask him.

"In Springfield. Back tomorrow."

A.J.'s either with Jared and Tate or Jax and Juliet, or she went with them. They wouldn't trust Kade to get her and himself to school on time.

I clear my throat. "One Saturday morning, when we were fourteen—"

He starts to leave. "I need to play host, Hunter."

I step in front of him, stopping him. "I told you I wanted to take Dylan to the new *Fast* movie," I go on. "I was going to ask her and then ask Dad to drive us. Do you remember that?"

"Jesus," he scoffs.

He moves around me again, but I shove him in the chest and advance quickly into him as he stumbles back.

Fire ignites in his eyes, but he stands tall.

He doesn't push back, though. Dylan is still.

"Do you remember that day?" I bite out.

He smirks. "I remember going with her."

I nod, smiling, but it's a bitter one. *Yeah, me too.* He found an earlier showing, told Dad I didn't want to come, and they were out of the house before I even knew what happened.

I swallow, squaring my shoulders. "When we were fifteen in JV, and it was the last game of the year, and our grandparents were in the stands, and so was Dylan, and you called the play where I run a lead block, but you threw the ball to me instead." I remember it like it was yesterday. "I

414

missed it. In front of our grandparents and Dylan and the whole stadium. You remember that?"

"I seem to remember you making a lot of mistakes in football."

Yeah. He changed the play on me. I wasn't supposed to receive the ball.

"And when we were sixteen,"

"Fuuuuck," he gripes.

"And you brought a girl into my room while I was asleep one night," I tell him. "I wake up, she's taking her clothes off, and you're standing behind her... What did you say?" I search my brain, trying to remember his exact words. "You slapped her on the ass and said, 'He doesn't talk cool, but tell him to keep his mouth shut and you won't even know the difference, honey. Our dicks are identical too.'"

He starts laughing.

I bite the corner of my mouth. Hard. "You might've been drunk," I finally say, "but do you remember that at all?"

He beams. "I honestly don't, but it sounds like me."

I shake my head. Is that something he'd do to A.J.? No, because he gives a shit about our kid sister. Would he have purposely humiliated Hawke at a game? No. He loves Hawke.

And to my knowledge, he has never moved in on a girl one of his friends was interested in. He treats me like garbage.

"Why don't you like me?"

"Oh, give me a fucking break, Hunter. They were jokes!" he yells. "You're too sensitive."

"You knew how those things, and the hundred other things you did, would make me feel!" I try to lower my voice, but I can't. "You wanted me to feel like shit! Why?"

"Because I wanted you away from her!"

I stand there, staring at him, his eyes piercing me.

Dylan doesn't move, but I see her chest rise and fall in heavy breaths out of the corner of my eyes.

I stand up straight. "So, you were jealous?"

"Let's get one thing straight, Hunter." He sneers at me. "I will never be jealous of you."

"So why all the bullshit?" I ask. "Why not just tell me the truth?"

"Would you have given her up?" He cocks his head, challenging me. "Huh?"

Give her up? And let them be together?

I look over at Dylan, and I notice tears hanging in her eyes, about to fall. *No.* It would've fucking hurt too much. I can't...

I can't get the words out for a few seconds.

"If..." I blink, dropping my head. "If you made her happy..." I whisper. "If she was happy, then yeah."

If she didn't want me, I would never want to be someone who made her miserable.

I dig in my eyebrows, trying to get my fucking vision to clear. "Fuck."

I twist around, but I feel a hand grab me. "No, no..." Dylan says, pulling me into her arms. "You don't walk away. Come here."

She pops up on her tiptoes, holding my face in her hands as she kisses me.

It only takes a second, and I wrap her in my arms and kiss her back.

Kade brushes past me and leaves, but it doesn't even register to stop him.

She wants me.

Me.

"I love you," I whisper.

"I know." She presses her forehead to mine. "And he's lying."

"About what?"

"About something."

She wipes the tears off her face and takes a step back. "I didn't know I was coming between you—"

I grab her back. "You don't come between us. He's the problem, not you."

"And we love him," she says, and it almost sounds like a plea. "I won't come between you two anymore."

She wraps her arms around my neck, holding onto me for dear life before she lets me go.

"I can't," she says.

She leaves the room, and I slam my hand into the back of the door.

Goddamn him.

PIRATES

CHAPTER TWENTY-FOUR

Dylan

My Hunter.

He was always my Hunter, wasn't he?

I can't be his, though, and walk into this house with the weight of Kade's anger and act like we'll be able to be happy at barbecues, birthdays, and Christmas. We won't.

I yank open one of the French doors and charge onto the pool deck.

"You're a fucking liar," I say to Kade's back, and I don't give a shit who hears me.

He pours a drink. "Among other things…"

"You don't want me," I growl. "He wasn't here for a year. I was. Just the two of us. Why are you putting everyone through hell?"

He bounces from one girl to the other and never asked me out or even wanted me alone.

He turns and faces me, a lazy smile on his lips.

I can't stop myself. I slam the drink out of his hand, and it goes flying to my left.

"Ohh..." someone mumbles as more people take notice and watch us.

Kade cocks an eyebrow, moving closer to me. "If I'd made a move, what would've happened?"

He pins me a knowing look, and I harden my jaw.

"Would you have let me keep going?" he presses. "You would've, wouldn't you?"

I narrow my eyes, balling my fists.

"Yeah, I think you would have. Maybe Hunter should know that," he taunts. "That he's just a consolation prize, Dylan."

I whip my hand, slapping him across the face. His head jerks to the side as fire spreads through my palm, but I don't regret it. The way he talks about Hunter...

I close the distance, speaking low. "There were no girls around me who liked doing the things I liked doing," I tell him, my voice shaking. "Riding ATVs or motorcycles. None of them were into cars. I had you, and I had Hunter." I look at him, his face still turned to the side and his eyes down. "I looked up to you. Especially you when we were younger, because you took up entire rooms, and you truly did not give a shit what people thought." Tears stream down my face. "I would watch you, and I learned that your trick wasn't to be yourself. It was to love being yourself. If I could find that, then...there was nothing to worry about. Nothing to worry about that I could control anyway."

Kade used to be so impressive. I didn't want him. I idolized him.

"You stood up for me when we were kids," I whisper, holding back my sobs. "You were strong, and you always win."

Always. I think his force will rival his father's someday in working a crowd, closing a deal, or spreading his influence.

I shrug. "You win."

His brow creases, and I see his jaw flex.

"I'll be home in a few days," I tell him, "and I'll leave next summer, either for college or training, and Hunter will be alone. And I'll be alone, but it was worth it." I pause, trying to hold back the sadness. "I'm glad it was him."

I take my clothes and backpack off the table and leave, walking back through the house and out the front door.

Once my clothes are on, I climb on the bike and speed out of the driveway before Aro or anyone tries to catch me.

As I turn onto the highway, I catch Hunter in my rearview mirror walking out the front door and watching me go.

I cry behind the helmet, tears blurring my vision so much I have to pull over. I remove my helmet and let the tears fall.

And then I smile through the sobs.

How instinctual it was in that moment. In a single moment when he admitted he would do what hurt him most if it meant I was happy.

It was that quickly I knew... He's the one I grabbed. Not Kade.

I never wanted to let Hunter go.

Hours later, thunder cracks across the sky, and I open my eyes, unsure if I got to sleep or when. My head pounds behind my right eye and courses up my forehead, over my scalp, and down the right side of my neck. I sit up, still fully dressed, even in my jacket and shoes as I look at the rain pattering the window through puffy eyes. The drops are small but constant.

The rocking chair above swings slowly with the wind, and I look to see my door still closed.

Standing up, I wince and rub the back of my neck as I walk to the window. Hunter's bedroom is dark, and I don't see his car on the street. Granted, I can't see much of the street from this vantage point.

Walking to the desk, I grab my new phone that Hunter got me and press the button, seeing that it's almost midnight. I forgot to put it on the charger.

I start to walk back to my bedside table, but I see something on my desk and stop.

Turning on the desk lamp, I scan the little folded-up pieces of paper, some in intricate triangles and squares like the kind we passed in class when we were younger, before we got a phone.

These weren't here this morning. Were they here when I got in tonight? I squeeze my eyes shut against the pain in my head. *I don't remember*. I was still crying a little, avoiding calls from Hunter, Aro, and Coral. I laid down on the bed, awake for a long time, running through endless scenarios in my head of how I might be able to be with Hunter and be happy, despite Kade hating us for it.

I look around, finding the room empty and nothing changed.

Someone was in here, though, and I hope it was while I was gone and not while I was asleep.

I open one of the notes, seeing it's written in blue ink.

Library. After school. 2nd floor. -D

Deacon? The brothers were Conor and Deacon. It could be him.

I drop it to the desk and open another.

Lift your skirt up.

I raise my eyebrows. Wow.
And then he writes, *More.*

It's the same penmanship, like Hawke's, Hunter's, and Kade's. Block letters, a little ragged, as if written quickly. I picture them in class, her taunting him.

I take another note and open it.

Feel me licking it right now. I know you can feel me.

Licking it? An image of Hunter in the back seat of his car flashes in my head. I swallow, scanning the rest of the note.

I want you so bad, they write again.

It's the same writing. Same blue ink. The messages aren't signed, but it looks like the same person. D.

You're not going to kill me? someone replies underneath in black cursive.

Not tonight, D replies.

My heart starts beating faster. It has to be Winslet MacCreary and Deacon Doran. They were in school, and he was writing these to her. Did she fear him? Was this a game for them?

I open another.

You know, I jerk off when he comes at you at night? He waits until I'm in bed before he descends from the attic like some nightcrawler to feed on you. As if I won't hear your headboard pounding against the other side of my wall at one o'clock in the morning.

I glance at the wall behind my headboard, imagining Deacon in the room on the other side. Chills climb my spine, all the way up to my neck. Who was she in here with when he was over there?

I love listening and stroking it," he writes. *He had you on your hands and knees last night. I can tell because everything makes noise. The springs in the bed, the headboard, and you. Does he come inside you? Tonight, I'm going to come in right after he's done and fuck you too. -D*

Mr. Bastien said Conor was dead. Maybe he wasn't. Maybe it was him in here with her? Maybe it was just like what Hawke thought. That Conor made people think he jumped off the bridge. Maybe a body was never found and the story Bastien told me is just a narrative that became the truth to people.

I bet if I bend you over right now and spread your ass apart, he'll drip out.

Leave me alone! Winslet writes in her dark cursive.

You love it when I don't, he replies.

I breathe harder, wincing a little. She's not playing along with it anymore. She's angry. Or scared. Hurriedly, I pick up another and open it.

I'm sorry. I just got carried away last night. I thought you were liking it. You were. I just lost my head. I'll be gentler next time. I promise you'll like it.

It's Deacon's writing.

When I open the last one, it's a drawing in blue pen that takes up half the sheet of lined school paper. It's the top half of a woman, breasts bare, a hundred tiny circles carved on top of each other onto the paper with his blue pen for her nipples, a rope around her neck. Head thrown back, spine arched, mouth open, and if not for the rope, she might look...euphoric.

With the rope, though, it looks like torture.

You like it, the caption reads.

They don't talk about the other one who comes down from the attic again. Did he write her notes, too? I look at the desk again, having opened all that were left.

I don't realize my fists are clenched around the last note until my hands ache. I relax, setting it on the desk with the others.

Both brothers whirling around her, one quiet and one very threatening. How did these get here? The chair above rocks faster, and everything in my gut tightens like a coil. I grab my phone and bolt from the room.

As soon as I land in the foyer, though, I see Calvin and Coral rolling out sleeping bags, Coral on the couch and Calvin on the floor.

I halt, glancing to the door, into the kitchen, and then up the stairs.

I don't see anyone else.

"What...what are you guys doing?" I ask, a little breathless.

They each have a bag, and Calvin plops down in the chair with a beer in one hand and four more hanging from a six-pack ring in the other.

"Relax," he says, yawning. "We're going to take turns every night until we return hostages. Farrow doesn't want you to be alone."

That's odd timing. Does he think someone's coming into the house, too, like I'm starting to wonder?

"For my safety?" I ask.

"He thinks you'd like company," Coral replies, fluffing her pillow.

Calvin brings the beer to his mouth. "And maybe a buffer, in case you don't want other visitors."

Like Hunter or Kade?

Maybe Farrow is doing it for the team. Keeping Hunter mad and horny until he's ready to let him loose to kill.

My nerves ease a little, though, grateful. I've been fine for over a week. I don't know if I should be that scared of anyone sneaking in.

And the notes could totally be a prank. "Did you guys leave the notes on my desk?"

Calvin pinches his brow together in confusion. "Huh?"

Coral looks at me.

I shake my head. "Never mind." I take a seat at the end of the couch and let out a sigh. "So where is Farrow?"

"Tending to needs," Coral says.

Calvin laughs, still in his swim shorts, sneakers, and a hoodie.

Coral opens a pizza box on the floor, and I see steam rise into the air. "Want some?" she asks me.

I take a slice of cheese, folding it the long way, but I stop before I take a bite.

I glance at both of them, getting an idea. "Are you guys tired at all?"

Calvin holds up his cans. "I will be in four beers."

I reach over and snatch the pack away from him. "Give me that."

"Hey."

"You can drink after the game."

I toss the pack to Coral, who dumps them in her backpack.

"Plus, I need your help." I shoot to my feet, taking a bite of pizza as I leave the room. "Let's go!"

"Where?" he calls out behind me.

But I just walk for the door, waiting for them to follow.

Ten minutes later, we're climbing out of Coral's car, as she runs to the trunk to grab a couple of flashlights. I look out at Esplanade Street Cemetery, the rain light, headstones peeking out of the tall grass.

I turn to Calvin, continuing our discussion. "How do you not know where Conor Doran's grave is?"

It's local folklore. The town's youth doesn't have some tradition of making a pilgrimage or offering to it or something?

But he just waves his hand. "Look at this shithole."

I bring up the light on my phone, Coral and Calvin taking the flashlights.

"I mean, how do you expect to find anything here?" Calvin goes on.

We head through the narrow opening in the short rock wall around the old graveyard, the overgrown landscape almost swallowing any sign of what's buried underneath.

I flash the light around, seeing sporadic markers peeking out of the tall grass. "Yeah, it's pretty awful."

I shuffle through the brush, finding a row and holding up my light to the names.

Cool rain wets my face, and I gaze over at the wooded area to my left, dense and dark.

"Spread out," I tell them. "I'll take this section." I point to Coral. "You sweep the bottom." Then I nod to Calvin, gesturing to the hill above us. "You go over there."

"What are we getting for this?" Coral grumbles.

I stand up straight and let me head fall back. "I can't believe I have to pay friends."

"Oh, you'll get used to it," Calvin points out. "Last week I had to pay Farrow gas money for a ride he was already making anyway."

Hustlers. I cock my eyebrow, looking to Coral.

She crosses her arms over her chest. "I want season access to the raceway next summer."

"To compete?"

"To watch, dipshit," she retorts.

I shoot a glare at Calvin.

"A hundred-dollar gift card to Frosted," he says.

I turn away. "Fine."

We spread out, Calvin working through the headstones above and Coral below. There are tall monuments, groups of similar stones for husbands and wives, and once in a while, I step on one planted in the ground.

This cemetery feels like it should be bigger. Next to seaside towns, river towns are the next most settled areas. Weston has to be over a hundred years old. Maybe there's another cemetery?

But Bastien said it was Esplanade Street.

I squint at a white marble marker. "Can you guys see the names okay?"

"Some of these markers are old," Coral calls out.

I rise up, realizing. "Yeah, his won't be."

Conor only died twenty-two years ago. I can ignore the ones that look like they're from the Prohibition.

"I got nothing!" Calvin shouts.

If we come up empty, then Bastien was mistaken. The twins, Conor and Deacon, are probably alive.

"Do people get buried here a lot?" I ask.

"No." Coral moves to another row, flashing her light. "We don't have the population anymore, and when someone does die, it's often off to the crematory."

It's the same in the Falls. Mausoleums are more popular too. Whatever's cheaper.

"Dylan?" Coral says.

I turn my head, seeing her staring at a block of stone in the middle of the last row.

I run over, hearing Calvin trail in behind me.

Rushing to her side, I look down to where she flashes her light and see a marble bench with a bottle of liquor sitting between the two support posts.

She picks it up. "I would've missed it, if not for this."

I take her light and read the name in black letters on the front of the stone slab. *Conor Doran*

The birth date is listed before the name and the date of his death after. Twenty-two years ago.

I take the bottle from Coral, flashing the light on it. "Chimney Wind," I read, swiping the grime off the faded and wet label.

Calvin takes it, tossing it up and catching it, the liquid inside sloshing against the brown glass. "It's been here a while."

"Not that long," Coral chimes in.

I glance at her. "What?"

She scrolls her phone, droplets of water landing on her screen. "The brand's been in the works for a decade, but it looks like they didn't bottle their first batch until two years ago," she says, showing me the website. "It's made in New Orleans."

Only two years.

My light catches a glint of something silver, and I bend over, picking up a tiny skeleton key off the bottom of the bench, next to where the bottle sat. I lift it up, searching for markings or numbers, but there's nothing. It looks like a key to an old padlock.

Something cracks next to me, and I look over to see Calvin twisting the cap off the bottle.

Coral flashes her light at him. "What are you doing?"

He lifts the bottle, smiling. "Waste not."

Tipping the bottle back, he gulps down a swallow, and I shake my head.

But immediately, he pulls the bottle away and coughs.

"What?" I ask.

"It's not whiskey." He laughs, clearing his throat. "It's cognac. And it's fucking good too."

He gulps down some more as I pull up my camera and snap the pics Hawke requested.

Tucking my phone away, I lead Coral and Calvin back to the car. Calvin holds out the bottle to me.

"No," I tell him.

He offers it to Coral, but she damn near runs away from him. "No, that's bad luck," she scolds. "You don't steal from the dead. Didn't you ever see *The Mummy*?"

I laugh, but yeah, she's right. I'm not that brave.

"That wasn't us!" she shouts to whoever is listening, making a big show of pointing at Calvin. "If anyone is listening, that was him!"

We reach the car, and she growls at him. "Put it back."

"Fuck, no." He opens the door. "It's free."

We climb in, turning off our flashlights, and we're gone before I realize I still have the key in my hand.

REBELS

CHAPTER TWENTY-FIVE

Hunter

If she loved me, she'd hold out hope. She would try. Yeah, holidays and parties will suck with Kade pissed off—and I don't want him to be hurt—but those events won't be any less awkward now. Every time I see her, I'll want her, and she'll know it.

I close my eyes, rolling my neck as I move to the chest press. I blow out a long breath, trying to get her out of my head.

Coach told us to stay out of the gym and rest, but we leave for the game in a few hours, and I don't want to be home with Farrow. Best to stay busy.

I hear cars through the auto shop door peeling out of the parking lot, classes today were a mess as no one's mind was on anything other than the game. The cheer team and band are eating sandwiches catered by a few of the parents up in the gym, and my team is carb-loading at Fletcher's, whose wife helped him make the guys breakfast for dinner. Eggs, rice, oatmeal, turkey bacon, and potatoes.

I should be with them. It would distract me, at least. Dylan hasn't spoken to me since the pool party Wednesday night, and I haven't pushed her, either.

Two days.

She didn't tell me she loved me back.

I'm not going to say it again, and I'm not going to force into her space like I did Monday after school every time I want to fuck. It's not enough.

I sit on the bench and start the presses, wishing it was tomorrow already. I'll wake up, knowing we already won, and I'll start working on my application to Chicago again, gearing up to start my life at the end of the year. There are other girls out there for me.

"Kade won't be tiring himself out before the game."

I pause, hearing Dylan's voice behind me. She came in through the auto shop.

I continue moving my arms up and down, tightening every muscle. "Just warming up," I tell her.

I hear her footsteps on the padded floor before she's coming around my side to face me. I stare ahead, but I can tell she's still wearing what she wore to school today. High-waisted jeans with a vintage brown and pink Sukajan jacket, crop top underneath. She hasn't gone home yet. I imagine she'll be changing into Pirate gear for the game.

She stares down at me. "If you win, what happens?"

I grunt, pushing the bar up. "We'll feel good."

"You will?"

I don't meet her eyes. Yeah, it'll feel good. It'll actually feel great to shut him up.

She slides her hands into her pockets. "If you lose, what happens?"

I drop my hands, hearing the bar clang back into place. I shoot my eyes up to her as I rise. "Get out."

I grab my towel and move toward the rowing machine.

"If he wins..." she says, following me. "Did you even think? After the game? What happens then? If he wins?"

I slam my towel down on the floor and turn to glare down at her.

"What are you going to do when you're standing on the field, sweat dripping down your face, out of breath, watching him celebrate with his team?"

I lock my jaw so hard my teeth ache.

"He's going to feed off that high for years," she goes on.

No. I refuse to wake up tomorrow, knowing I lost.

"He might win," she continues, "and I'm going to go home, and what will you do then? Keep running, thinking your happiness is out there somewhere, and always feeling second place, because you learned nothing? Because you thought winning a game would beat him."

"Stop."

"Because you wrapped all of your value into proving something to someone who never loses, even when he does."

"Stop," I grit out.

"Because doing this for the wrong reasons will make me see you as less than a man."

Motherfucker...

I spin away from her, grab a barbell, and throw it into the mirrored wall, glass splintering and cracks spreading two feet long.

I shake, still seeing her behind me, calm and watching.

Less than a man...

I'm not doing this for the wrong reasons. Everyone needs to prove themselves at some point. I don't...

It's not wrong to want to succeed and have him see that and then watch me walk off the field without a backward glance, like it all meant nothing.

But I hesitate as she stands there, and I feel a trickle of sweat glide down the back of my neck.

It does mean something.

For a year, it's meant everything.

What *if* he wins?

Will I still go home Sunday?

I can't fucking walk in that house in no better position than when I left. With him knowing he won everything. Him knowing that he beat me at *everything*.

I stand there, my shallow breathing hard and fast as it pours in and out of my nose.

Eyes burning, I turn to her and take her face, brushing her cheek with my thumb. "You still have two more nights in Weston. We're not done."

I leave, the warning still hanging in the air as I dive into the locker room to shower.

He's going to win...

Second place...

Does she think that?

I blink long and hard as I stand under the spray, pushing it out of my mind. I have to clear my head, stay in the moment, and do my job.

This is about a game. It's my turn.

My brain drifts back to the doubt minutes later when I'm dressing, and I shove it away again.

It arises still when some of us climb into our cars and some of us into the bus as we head to Helm's Field.

We'll push them back.

Every time.

We'll win.

But the more I try to talk myself up, the emptier I feel, and I have to force my breathing to slow down as we dress in one of their locker rooms, and I feel the walls start closing in as we run onto the field.

If we lose, what then?

I twist my head, cracking my neck as the stadium fills and people walk to their seats with drinks and popcorn.

What then?

"It's not the last game of the season," the announcer booms over the loudspeaker, "but it's certainly our favorite! Welcome one and all to Friday Night Football! This game is sponsored by..."

"Are your parents here?" Farrow asks next to me.

I look around, scanning the Pirate sideline and then the fifty-yard line seats across from me. My dad will want to have the best view.

"They wouldn't miss it," I tell him, still not finding them, though.

"Well, at least Ciaran's on your side," he says.

I follow his gaze behind us to my grandfather sitting in the front row, tapping away on his phone.

My grandfather wouldn't choose sides with his grandchildren.

He'd show up to support his son, though. I dart my gaze to Farrow and then the field.

I pull on my helmet, finding Kade across the field surrounded by his teammates as they listen to their coach's instructions.

Just then, he shoots his arm in the air, looking to the end zone as if waving. I glance, finally seeing our parents. They sit on top of the flat roof of the pavilion that houses a couple of picnic tables beyond the field goal posts and the chain-link fence. I smile, making out my parents and A.J., as well as Jared, Jax, and their families. A couple of extra kids sit with them, and I think they must be Aro's brother and sister that Jax and Juliet foster.

Hawke and Aro are present, too, and everyone sits on camp chairs with a couple of coolers around.

They found a way to watch without picking sides.

Some are dressed in Pirate colors, while a few—like Jared—don't go in for things like team pride. My dad wears an orange and black T-shirt, but a wolf's head hat. I shake with laughter at the long-ass snout protruding off his forehead, because he's supporting both of his sons and doesn't give a shit about looking ridiculous.

I study each form from a distance, not seeing Dylan among them at all.

Not with Aro. Not with her parents.

I look behind me, not spotting her with Mace or Coral, and I don't find her on the other side, either. She could be here. It's a lot of people.

I'm not paying attention to the announcer, and only know it's time for the coin toss when Farrow whips his hand at my stomach. "Let's go."

With our helmets on, Constin, Farrow, Calvin, and I head to the middle of the field, Kade and his crew walking to meet us.

"Good evening, gentlemen," the referee says. "Let's have a fun, clean game—"

But Kade is speaking before he's done. "Switched sides, huh?" he asks me. "I was hoping to see you running after me."

I turn my eyes to the referee.

"Heads." He shows us the coin and then flips it. "Tails." He points to us. "You're the visitors. Call it in the air, please."

He tosses it up, and I hear Farrow say, "Tails."

It lands on the turf below, the referee leaning over to read it. "And it's tails."

"We'll take the ball," I announce.

My guys start to leave, and Kade's do as well.

Kade stares at me. "I promised a nice, crisp fifty-dollar bill every time they sack you," he tells me. "Try not to let it happen too much."

He grins and walks away, and I turn, Farrow at my side.

"What a fucking asshole," he grumbles.

But I just look up in the stands for Dylan.

Why isn't she here?

Is she that certain I'll lose?

Huh?

Spinning around, I pace back and forth as the coach gives direction, but I'm barely listening.

She's not here.

The whistle goes off, we take the field, and I feel Kade. He's on my left, watching me from the sidelines, and I look over the faces of his team. Stoli, Dirk, and all the rest.

"Relax, boys," Stoli tells his team. "Hunter plays like shit."

Heat courses down my arms, my chest swells with ire, and I fucking growl, "Two-seventy!" She doesn't need to be here. I can do this without her. "Two-seventy!"

Luca hikes the ball, and I catch it, my offense charging ahead. Constin runs, Dirk chasing after him, and I see the Pirates pushing past my line and coming for me.

I jerk my head left, then right, Constin the only option. I hesitate and then...I launch the ball, watching it fly ten yards—then twenty—before a body crashes into me, dragging me to the ground.

My knee twists out, and I wince, holding back my howl as a Pirate—then two—pile on top of me.

The crowd cheers, but I can't tell which side, or if Constin caught the fucking ball.

"It's going to be a long night for you, traitor," someone says, shoving their knee into my gut as they rise.

I roll over, breathing hard and straightening out my leg.

I don't wait. I'm not giving him the satisfaction. Pushing myself up, I walk and then run to the twenty-yard line, getting back in formation as my team celebrates the completed pass.

"You okay?" Calvin asks.

I don't reply. I look to the coach, watching his signals, and then shout to the team. "Blue forty-two! Blue forty-two, set, hit!"

The ball snaps, I catch it, and everyone floods each other, my guys pushing back against their defense. I pass the ball to Calvin, he passes it back to me, and I rear back to throw it to Constin, but someone barrels into me, and I'm gone. On the ground, the crowd losing their minds as Pirates jump on me, crushing my ribs into the football between me and the ground.

I groan as more weight crushes me, and I can barely fucking breathe. What the fuck?

The whistle goes off, and the weight lessens. Someone reaches down to help me, but I shove them away, still clutching the football.

Constin and Stoli push each other, part of the crowd cheering and part of them booing, and I refrain from looking over at my brother.

"What a shitshow," I grit out.

I can't look at my parents.

Calvin walks back with me, still on the first set of downs. "I don't think your brother will be happy until something is broken," he says.

No shit. Two plays, and I've already lost him a hundred dollars.

The clock runs, I get into position and call the play. The ball shoots to my hands, and I throw, but the pass is incomplete.

"Whoo!" the Pirates cheer, Dirk shoving me in the chest. "Again! Again!"

Constin thrusts him back. "Fuck you," he says.

They get into each other's faces, Luca pushes a Pirate, and I step in. "Enough!"

We go again, Constin charges to the end zone, and I dig the toe of my shoe into the grass, throwing the ball. He catches it, running into the end zone, and I almost have time to smile before I'm tackled into the grass again.

Pain splits my side, and I grunt, feeling something knock against my ear, inside the helmet, as another body topples on top of me.

Fuck... Where's the fucking foul?

Pirates peel off me, and my guys are there, flipping me over.

"You okay?" Calvin asks.

"Help me up."

They pull me to my feet, and I flinch at the pain in my body. Rebels party in the stands, the guys chatter excitedly, and we get into position for the extra point. *Where's Dylan?*

Where would she be if she's not here?

Extra point goes on the board, offense moves to the sideline, and Farrow steps on with defense as Kade takes the field.

He gets into position, points at me, and I slip off my helmet, but I can't watch. I stare at the ground, knowing every time he gains yardage, moving closer and closer to the end zone. Guys roll to the ground, and I hear curses and insults, and I still don't look at my family.

I don't have to look at them to know that they hate what they're watching.

I don't have to look at them to know Dylan's not here.

We may or may not win, but I'll wake up alone tomorrow.

She's done with us. That's why she's not here. She doesn't care about the game. She can't watch us do this.

Kade scores a touchdown, our offense steps on the field, then them again, and by the end of the second half, it's seventeen to seven, Pirates.

The band marches, people leave their seats for the bathroom or food, and the teams drift into the locker room.

"Hunter, half time," Dewitt calls.

I turn my head, just enough so he'll hear me over my shoulder. "I'm staying here."

"Now!"

"I'm staying here!"

They leave, and I don't sit. I stand there and hydrate and fume, but shit fills my head like a bucket, pouring in until it overflows, and all of a sudden, my head falls back and my shoulders sink.

I don't even like football that much. I never did.

I played, because I knew Dad loved his kids in sports, and if Dylan was at the games, then I wanted her to watch me as much as she did Kade.

I laugh with no one there to hear.

"Do you love your brother?" a voice asks next to me.

I look over to see my mom.

I stare at her a while, and I don't want to lie to her, but God, it's been so long since Kade was my brother. I forget what it feels like. "I want to," I tell her.

She nods. "It's just a game, Hunter. It won't solve anything. It won't humble him to lose. Why are you really here?"

I stare down into her eyes, the tears not falling, and I hate to think of how my family is seeing this.

"I want to face him."

She shakes her head. "You're so much better than that. Why are you here?"

I turn away, swallowing through the needles in my throat.

"Anger happens," she says, "but you can't let it be your entire identity."

It never used to be. Having Dylan close showed me how good it felt to be happy. I want that every fucking day.

"For the team," I tell her. "I want this for Farrow and the guys. They need it."

She gives me a small smile, looking proud of me finally. "That's what I thought."

She heads back to my dad, and the teams walk out, the referees take up position, and the second half starts.

Running up to the guys on the field, I pull on my helmet. "Spot left. Twenty-five dive."

They gape at me. "Are you sure?" Calvin asks.

I look to Constin. "Spot left. Twenty-five dive."

He smiles.

"Ready?" I ask.

They clap. "Ready."

We line up, facing the Pirate defense, and Ozzy Ozborne plays over the speakers of the stadium.

I look left to right. "Yellow thirty-two!" I shout. "Yellow thirty-two!"

Luca snaps the ball, and all in slow motion I see the Pirates charge ahead. Constin runs behind me, and I twist, passing off the ball. He barrels through the shit, leaping over the players, and just fucking runs, and by the time the Pirates know who has the ball, he's already ten yards ahead. Digging in, he races as Dirk comes in for me. I twist out of his way, watching and holding my breath, fists tight and body charged until...

Constin flies over a Pirate trying to tackle him and rolls right into the end zone.

"Yes!" I howl, jumping and pumping my fists with my team. I look over the field goal, seeing my parents standing and cheering, and I see my dad's smile from here.

Kade takes the field, struggling for yards, but he makes first down, and a touchdown with a pitch from the five-yard line. The score is twenty-four to fourteen. It's our turn again, but we're unable to get past their defense. We manage to make a field goal, bringing us up to seventeen.

The fourth quarter moves in, and Farrow and I walk down the line, pumping up the players. "They're going to bed pissed tonight!" Farrow shouts. "We're not giving up another yard!"

"Not one more!" I yell.

Farrow runs into position, and Dewitt grabs my arm. "Take tackle."

"What?"

"Keep that little shit from scoring one more time," he grits out.

He means my brother, and I almost feel a stab of pride for Kade. I nod.

Running into the lineup, I stare at Kade as he notices me too. "Grew a pair, huh?" he taunts. "This is going to be fun!"

I look to Farrow, nodding once, and Kade throws a glare at my friend and then back to me.

He calls out his play, catches the ball, and just as Farrow and I predicted, he fakes passing and runs it instead.

But I'm already there, on his tail, chasing him hard. The wind blows past me, players run at each other, and I dig in, pursuing him hard. Almost there, almost there, and then...I take him to the ground before he reaches the end zone.

The ball spills out of his hands, and all at once, everyone scrambles. Farrow grabs the ball, spins around, and I flip over, watching everyone charge after him as he barrels back the other direction.

"Fucking son of a bitch!" Kade bellows at me.

I grin, out of breath as I lie on the ground. "Hey now, that's your mom too," I tease.

Farrow scores a touchdown, and Kade screams, "Fuck!"

I laugh, but only because after the extra point, we're tied, and Weston might not deserve this any more than the Falls, but they'll appreciate it more.

The stadium fills with thunder as the crowd pounds their feet.

I rise up next to Kade, watching my team celebrate and memorizing the image for the years to come. I don't need to fucking beat Kade. I don't know what the hell I've been thinking, but this feels a hell of a lot better than some validation from him that was never going to come no matter how many games I win.

"You pushed the ball out of my hands!" he growls.

I cock an eyebrow. I didn't touch his hands.

I walk away, but he shoves me to the ground, and before I know it, he's on top of me, I'm laughing, and the referee is blowing his whistle as the teams run in to join in the fun.

"Ah, shit." I wince, peeling off my jersey, pads, and undershirt.

The locker room practically vibrates, excited chatter, laughter, and energy bouncing off the walls as people rush around and celebrate.

We won. By one touchdown.

And while the Falls will spin some narrative over bad calls or something, we wouldn't have wanted to earn it easily. I'm glad it was close.

"You sure you didn't break a rib?" Farrow asks.

"No, I'm not sure, actually."

It was worth it, though. Every family in Weston will be smiling this weekend, even the ones who don't give a shit about football.

"Everyone smile!" Calvin shouts.

I look over, players crowding together as Farrow hangs over my shoulder and cups a hand around his mouth, howling. I grin, Calvin snapping a picture.

Everyone moves away, and I lift my arm, checking my ribs for bruising. It fucking hurts.

But still, I'd scoop up my Pirate girl and let her wrap her legs around my battered body if she were outside waiting right now.

She skipped the game, because she knew what I didn't. She knew what my mom knew. There's no victory in doing anything for the wrong reasons.

I did it for my friends.

Coach Dewitt comes in, carrying the game ball, guys crowding around.

"You won!" he calls out, followed by a round of cheers as people bang on their lockers. "I couldn't be prouder, and you know what got you here? Not luck, not muscle, and not even hard work!" He looks around, meeting everyone's eyes. "Willpower. You are capable of everything, and *never* forget that!"

"Whoo! Whoo!" the guys shout.

"You will get distracted in life," he goes on, "and you will make mistakes, but you can always come back to this moment and remember it was *you* that got you here."

I drop my eyes. I know the words aren't for me. He's not worried about me.

"Game ball goes to Hunter Caruthers," he shouts.

He moves in, holding out the ball as someone grabs my shoulders from behind and shakes me in congratulations.

I smile, taking it and absolutely wanting to keep it, but...

It wouldn't be right to take it with me when I go.

"Thanks," I say to everyone. "Especially for not beating the Knight and Pirate secrets out of me at practice."

They laugh, someone yelling. "We're gonna beat the Knights fair and square too!"

A round of cheers goes off, everyone excited for next week's game that I'm not sure I'll be here for.

I hold up the ball. "But this stays in Weston," I tell them. "Everyone signs it. Come on."

I grab the Sharpie off Dewitt's lanyard and pass it off to Farrow with the ball, letting him sign first.

I stuff my pads, shirt, and jersey into my locker, but before I can get to the shower, I hear my name.

"Hunter..."

I look around.

"Hunter!" someone calls.

I see Luca pushing through all the bodies to get to me. "Kade took your car!" he says.

"What?"

He shrugs. "Mace just grabbed me outside. She said he told her you'd 'know where to find him.'"

How the hell did he take my car? He doesn't have keys...

But then I stop, realizing. I have a spare set in my desk drawer, and he was in my fucking room last week.

Christ. I slam my locker shut and spin, Farrow already slapping his bike keys into my palm and handing me his helmet.

I give him a nod and shoot off, dashing out of the locker room.

"You want us to come?" Luca shouts.

But I'm already gone. I run outside, still in my pants and shoes as the chilly air hits my chest, and I feel the dirt on my fingers as I grind my fists.

I'd know where to find him?

I stand outside, people filling the parking lot as they make their way to their cars.

We didn't have a place where just the two of us hung out. I have no idea...

Then, I stop.

Dylan.

He would go to Dylan to take the only other thing from me that he can.

Climbing on Farrow's bike, I head the short distance to Fallstown, forcing myself to not speed, and determined not to fight. At least in front of her.

I pull onto the empty country road, not driving long before I see the long driveway into the race park. I coast down, trees on both sides, and spot my car dead ahead, at the end of the lane, just before the track. A parking lot sits to my right, and I see a blue and black motorbike race around the bend, continuing on around the Loop.

Kade leans against my hood, only the back of his head visible as he watches Dylan.

Parking the bike next to my car, I climb off and remove the helmet, hanging it on a handlebar.

I walk to his side and lean against the car.

He draws in a breath. "I'm sure she thought I was you from a distance and yet, she ignores me." He glances over at me. "She mad at you?"

I give a small smile, watching Dylan lean into the far turn. No one is here, which is odd for a Friday night, but with the game, I guess Jared gave the crews the night off.

"She's busy," I tell him. "And you and I have drained enough of her time."

I can't remember the last time we stood so close and didn't yell.

I hold out my hand. "Give me my keys."

Watching Dylan train on the otherwise deserted track, he drops the keys in my hand. "You didn't win anything, you know?" he says. "In a week, they'll be spinning a story about how we gave it to Weston out of pity."

I nod, running down the narrative they'll likely spin. "The fumble looked so real... Kade's just so amazing, selling it as well as he did.... So self-sacrificing," I coo. "Let's all go suck his cock."

He smiles and stands up straight, turning to face me. I do the same.

Darting out his hands, he shoves me in the chest. "Are you coming home now?"

I stumble, laughing under my breath. "I might."

He shoves me again, and I stop the grunt of pain before it escapes fully.

He gets in my face. "Is that a yes or a no?" he bites out.

I hear Dylan's bike close in again. I keep my hands to myself.

"I like it across the river," I tell him. "The teachers are cool, and Farrow's a fucking slob, but he has my back."

Kade's glare sharpens because he's never backed me up.

"T.C., Anders, Luca, Calvin, Constin, Mace, Coral..." I list off all the other friends I'm lucky to have. "Yeah, I like it there."

He grabs me by the back of the neck and yanks me to the ground, the pavement cutting into my back. I growl as he straddles me and squeezes my throat in his fist, hitting me across the face.

"Guys, stop!" I hear Dylan somewhere off to my left.

But Kade doesn't. "You don't give a shit about our parents!" he screams at me. "They want you home!"

"Stop, or I'll call the police!" Dylan yells.

I shove Kade to the side and leap to my feet, facing him as he rises.

Dylan takes a couple steps toward us. "Enough!"

I only stare at Kade, though. "I like it there, so it works out for everyone. I can stay in Weston, then there's nothing standing in your way," I finish explaining. "Because she won't have me like this. She doesn't love me!"

"Hunter..." Her voice cracks.

"But maybe..." I say, no longer yelling, because sadness swells in my fucking throat. "Maybe, eventually, she'll love you, and maybe you'll be happy, and you'll get off my fucking back!"

I don't know what the hell he wants!

"She doesn't love me," I tell him again. "There's no reason to hate me or to be jealous of me—"

"I wasn't jealous of you!" he bellows. "I was jealous of her!"

I go still, Dylan and I falling silent as tears shake in Kade's bloodshot eyes, threatening to spill.

His breathing is hard and heavy, and I turn the words over in my head, trying to understand. Jealous of her?

"What?" I ask, confused.

What does she have that he wants?

He turns a little, hiding his face as a bitter laugh that sounds almost like a sob leaves his throat. "Fuck..."

We all stand there as the anger dissipates, Kade calms, and he inhales and exhales deeply.

Turning to me, he says, "Do you remember us getting a dog when were eight?" He doesn't wait for me to answer, though. "And we were supposed to take care of it together and train it together, and we'd pull him up into our treehouse with a bucket." He holds my eyes for a second before going on. "And then you took Sith to sleep over at Dylan's house one night and left him there when we went out of town the next week, and then he was bonded to you two, and you were the ones feeding him and playing with him and holding him." He starts yelling. "It was our fucking dog, dude! Yours and mine!"

I stand there, speechless. I remember the dog, but I don't remember Kade having a problem with...

"You didn't tell me you—"

"Well, what was I supposed to do?" he growls, cutting me off. "Force him to love me again?"

Dylan remains quiet, and I try to put myself in Kade's shoes and imagine how that probably felt.

But he keeps going. "And the time we were camping out in the backyard," he says, "but you told Dylan to stay and camp with us, without asking me, so instead of you and me, it's you helping her bait her hook, and you helping her get wood for the fire, and you helping her make a fucking s'more..." His brow etches with pain. "And we were going to do laser tag, but we couldn't because there were only two guns. We were earning patches, Hunter! It was supposed to be you and me!"

I open my mouth, but I can't talk. My heart aches, remembering that night.

"And the time I was drunk," he continues, tearing up again, "and I don't even remember the girl I lost my virginity to, and I wanted to talk to you, because I was feeling..." He looks away, his jaw flexing so hard, because he's trying to keep his emotions in check. "I was kind of feeling like shit about it, but you two looked so happy, blowing up balloons for A.J.'s birthday, and I decided to keep my mouth shut because..."

My chin shakes. *Because he didn't trust me enough to be vulnerable with me.*

I turn away, closing my eyes and letting the tears spill over. *Goddamn.*

He doesn't continue, but I'm sure there a lot more instances—as many as the ones I remember where he was the villain in my story.

"So," Dylan says quietly. "Everything—all the fighting—for the past ten years was because you...missed him?"

"I'm not..." Kade stammers. "I'm not...so good...about communication."

"Noooo shit." I turn around. "Wow. Jesus Christ, Kade." He couldn't talk to me?

"I always knew you loved her," he blurts out, almost begging, "so I was mean to her at first. I wanted it just to be us sometimes, all right? I was a fucking kid!"

All the times he was mean to her when we were little. Telling her to leave us alone and...

I clench my fists.

"And then later," he goes on, "she turned out pretty cool, and I genuinely loved her—I mean, like a cousin-love." He throws her a look. "I don't want to fuck you." He looks back at me. "So I just started doing shit to keep you guys apart for a little while. Just a little while."

I glare. "To make me shrink—"

"Because I knew..." He just keeps going. "I knew you loved her, and whenever you finally...made love to her, it would be over for me. You'd be hers for the rest of your life."

I hook the back of his neck and slam him down on the hood of my car. "You put us through all of that! What the hell?"

"It got out of hand, okay?" He doesn't fight back or try to escape my hold. "Way out of hand! I was fucking pissed, and I just got angrier and angrier—"

"You mean your ego just couldn't handle it!" I shout. "You fucked with her head. You deliberately confused her for years! That's why you didn't make your move while I was gone. You had what you wanted! Us apart."

"I didn't think you were going to fucking leave!"

I shove away from him, backing up. "So, you doubled-down instead of stopping me and talking to me?"

I mean, shit! All this time? He never wanted Dylan. He wanted...

I shake my head, running my hands through my hair.

He just wanted his brother back?

I bow my head, locking my fingers behind my neck and try to slow my breathing.

I can understand being a kid and not knowing how to express yourself, but was I supposed to read his damn mind? I was a kid too. I had no idea he was mad when I wanted to include Dylan. She was family and our age. Why wouldn't I?

But yeah, that dog thing was shitty. I didn't realize I was doing anything wrong, but I can see how that hurt.

The years just piled on, and after a while neither one of us could swallow our pride and be open with the other. Feeling so alone, I left, and he perpetuated the only interaction with me he knew how to do anymore, because, at least, he stayed important that way.

We stand there, and I have no idea what the next move is, but I'm not mad anymore. I love Dylan, and I really want my brother back.

"I love you guys," Dylan whispers, exhaling hard as she backs away. "Please, go get drunk, make that tent, and have a good weekend."

I watch her climb on her bike, fasten her helmet, and drive away, her taillights visible until she pulls onto the highway.

I drop down in front of my car, leaning back on the chrome bumper and hanging my forearms over my bent knees.

And Dylan's gone from me again...

I half-suspect this was Kade's plot, but I laugh to myself, because I don't think he could've predicted any of this.

He moves to the driver's side and disappears for a moment before he's next to me, sinking down on the ground at my side.

He uncaps a flask and takes a swig. Tears slowly dry on his face.

He doesn't look at me as he passes the alcohol.

I take it, swallowing a hefty mouthful. Our dad's homemade Irish-style whiskey. I can tell, because the Irish make it with barley. He works hard to try to impress my mom's very Irish father, to no avail.

The old man drinks the hell out of the whiskey, though.

I hand it back.

"Was your..." Kade broaches. "Was your first time okay?"

I smile a little, because I didn't realize I wanted to share it with someone until he asked.

I nod, looking over at him. "Yeah, it was good. It was amazing."

"She treated you right?" he asks softly.

My chest swells, remembering making love to her in the back of this car and knowing I'll never sell the thing. Ever.

"Yeah," I tell him.

We sit there for a minute, and I know there are things to talk about—first and foremost being if he's going to be okay with me and Dylan together if I can win her again, because it's too late to go back.

And then there's school and his friends and coming home...

But before I can worry too much, he twists the cap back on the flask and looks over at me. "Why don't you take me to a Weston party?"

PIRATES

CHAPTER TWENTY-SIX

Dylan

Weston is alive tonight.

There isn't a single street without people on it and barely a house on Knock Hill not pumping light and music into the neighborhood.

I barely see any of it, though.

Parking up the lane, which is as close as I could get to the house, I slide through the crowd, between bodies, overflowing cups, and an impromptu game of football in the middle of the street. "Slip to the Void" blasts from the speakers sitting in the windows of Hunter and Farrow's house, and I don't know if anyone is doing the car-vibrating-sex thing, but there are plenty of people making out.

Entering the house, I hear laughter and quickly dry my eyes as I step toward the living room. Blankets and pillows sit in a pile on the chair as Codi and Mace rest on the couch, laughing at something on Mace's phone. Codi wears my jacket.

Their jacket now, since the Pirates lost.

I lean on the wall. "My babysitters tonight?"

But Farrow comes out from the kitchen, shoving a drink in my hand. "Come on, we're getting lit," he tells me. "Weston won. Time to celebrate."

I blow out a breath, looking down at the yellow-brown drink with ice in it.

"You don't care, do you?" Farrow teases.

"I do," I tell him. "I'm happy Weston won."

I take a drink, tasting rum and juice.

"We're going to be sorry to see you go," Farrow tells me, moving to the windows to look outside.

"I have till Sunday." I swallow another gulp. "You guys still have time to make me into a ghost."

Farrow chuckles, and I plop down on the arm of the couch, grabbing a handful of Cheez-Its from the box.

"What are you going to do next year?" Farrow asks me. "College?"

I sigh, hating this question. They want our senior quotes and future plans for our captions in the yearbook at Falls High, and of course, I know what I want. I just don't know how to say it in a way that doesn't sound like *Unemployed* or *Moving to L.A. to be an actress!* Everyone will assume I'll be living at home for the rest of my life.

"If I go to college," I say, "it'll be because I'm scared not to. I know what I want to do with my life, and I don't need a degree."

"It's gotta be nice, though," Mace chimes in. "Having time to figure stuff out. My dad got kicked out when he graduated from high school, and I have to start paying half the rent when I do." She flashes me a smile. "But at least he's not kicking me out."

I sit there, silent. I whine because I have choices? Everyone should be so lucky.

Cheers go off in the street, and I rise, taking my drink with me.

"Seriously, you guys go party," I tell them. "Go have fun. I'll be right here. Upstairs asleep."

Farrow just watches me.

"Are you sure?" Mace asks as Codi looks up at me.

"I'm exhausted," I say. "I'll see you all tomorrow."

I head upstairs, away from their stares, and close myself off in my room. In a minute, I hear the door shut downstairs as they hopefully join the crowd. I slip off my clothes, except for my T-shirt and underwear, plug in my phone, and cast a look to Hunter's dark bedroom window before I climb into bed.

But my head is working overtime, and I can't calm down. Minutes pass, and then an hour passes, and I wish I knew what happened after I left Hunter and Kade. Did they start fighting again? Did they go home to their parents?

All I know is that I was right. I was coming between them.

I was the problem.

I know I wasn't doing anything wrong, but it's hard not to feel like I should've been more invisible. Should've disappeared more. Should've taken up less space.

Like I feel people want me to do at school, on the track, and...even at home sometimes.

Hunter and Kade need each other, because love may or not last, but blood does, and they'll always be connected. I want Hunter to have him back.

I turn on my side, hugging the pillow under my head as tears fall and more time passes. "He said he loved me..." I whisper to myself.

I squeeze my eyes shut. I don't want to go home without him. I should've kissed him more the last time we were here, in bed. I should've let him stay and smiled at him and snuck downstairs for snacks with him in the middle of the night. I should've loved him more and slower and harder.

The party continues, another hour goes by, music beats, tires peel, and Weston howls their victory. I smile.

I'm glad I came.

And I'm glad I'll leave something here when I go—just as Farrow said I would.

Maybe someday Hunter and I will come together again. When the bad blood with Kade is gone and everything's okay.

I just hope he's the same.

"Dylan..." I hear my name in a low hum somewhere in the house.

I freeze as the door slams downstairs and footfalls hit the steps.

I rise up, staring at the light under the door.

"Dylan..." a deep voice drones on.

I look up to my ceiling, thinking about the weird dude in the attic from those notes.

But the sounds aren't coming from there.

I shoot my gaze to the door again, seeing a shadow fall over the light.

"Shhh," someone hisses outside.

"You shhh," the other one says.

I clench the blanket, looking around for a pencil or something to stab with. Who the hell is in my house?

Then, all of a sudden, my door swings open, and I scream.

"Shhh, Dylan." Kade swats the air, his brother and him hanging onto each other. "Shhh...shhh... You're going to wake me up!" he whisper-yells.

They stumble into the room, Hunter bare chested and

dressed in jeans, and Kade in the same jeans and T-shirt he wore earlier. I smell the beer from here.

They lumber across the room, both of them toppling onto my bed.

I growl, kicking at both of them. They're wasted.

"What are you guys doing?" I yell.

They crawl up by me, one on each side. "We're just gonna sleep," Hunter says.

"Not in here," I cry.

Kade lays in the spot where I was trying to rest, Hunter pulling me on top of him to save room.

Kade lays an arm over my back. "Dylan, we love you so much."

I shove his hand away. "You're all wet." I try to push off Hunter. "Both of you are soaking wet!"

The water from Hunter's jeans drips to my legs.

"They brought out the hoses downstairs," Hunter mumbles, already drifting.

I pry myself out of his hold, and push myself up. "Go sleep downstairs," I yell at both them.

Kade pulls off his shirt.

I look between the two of them. "I'm going to push you both on the floor."

Kade drops his shirt, lying back down. "He used to sneak in and sleep over with you, and I never did that, and I feel you didn't have the full experience."

"I don't think I need it," I reply flatly.

But Kade yawns. "Everyone should get to sleep with me once."

He pulls me back down between them, but Hunter grabs me away and pulls me on top of him again. "Dude, that's mine."

"Dylan, we just love you so much," Kade says again.

Hunter throws his brother's hand off his face. "Man, that's me."

They both lie under me, and I flip over, staring at the ceiling, two men and me in my dinky twin bed. "I don't believe this."

I won't get any sleep.

But then Kade shifts to my left, and he holds up something over his head. "Is this what I think it is?"

I look over, seeing my vibrator in the moonlight. "Oh my God!"

I grab it and throw it across the room, seeing it land just by my open bedroom door as Kade chuckles.

"Someone's not doing their job right," he teases.

I turn back over, burying my face in Hunter's chest.

His hand touches my hair, and I look up, seeing him looking down at me. "Yes, he does," I whisper.

He quirks a little smile, and so do I.

We don't sleep well.

At first.

The bed is too small, so we find that we can all fit if we sleep on our sides, but then Hunter found that he didn't want to spoon me with his brother, but they also didn't want to spoon each other, so Kade stayed sleeping on his side while I just fell asleep on top of Hunter.

They drift off between maneuvers to get comfortable, but I don't think I actually fall asleep for another hour.

When I wake, I'm almost entirely sprawled on top of Hunter, Kade's arm around both of us.

I blink, tilting my head back to look up at Hunter. With his head laying to the side, he breathes peacefully, his hair resting over his closed eyes.

The heat of his body soaks into my skin, and I can't stop staring at his hair. So many shades of blond, strands of almost light brown mixed in as if on purpose with the lighter tones. I never noticed that before.

Reaching up, I trace the ridge of his nose, touching him with just the tip of my finger, but the contact makes the hair on my arm rise.

His brow pinches together as he starts to stir, and I run the back of my fingers lightly over his eyelids. I drag the pads of my fingers down his face, something swelling in my chest so big that I feel like the air is being sucked out of the room.

I cup his jaw, running my thumb over his mouth.

He opens his eyes, immediately locking gazes with me. "I love you," he says.

I smile, teeth and everything, this amazing feeling like I want to cry because I'm so excited taking me over.

I open my mouth, but a sound behind me stops me in my tracks.

I twist my head, Hunter lifting his, and Kade jerking awake.

My father stands in the open doorway, a tray of two to-go coffees laying on the floor where he dropped them.

Rage fills his eyes, making them look like lit sticks of dynamite, and his chest rises and falls faster and faster.

"What the fuck?" he growls.

I suddenly become aware that I am only wearing a T-shirt and underwear, and Kade and Hunter are both half-naked.

I scramble, trying to climb out of all the arms and legs. "Dad," I gasp.

"Oh, shit," Kade groans, rolling onto the floor and rising to his feet.

I scurry, Hunter quickly throwing the sheet over me and leaping over to my desk, grabbing my jeans. He tosses them to me, and I hurriedly slip them on under the bedding.

I keep my eyes locked on my father.

But he's not looking at me. He stares at the floor, takes two steps, and picks up something off the ground. When he holds up the vibrator, I whimper, my eyes rounding in terror.

"It's not what it looks like!" I scream. "I promise."

When he raises his eyes, he glares at Kade, then Hunter. His hand is visibly shaking, and my palm shoots to my mouth.

"Oh, no," Hunter mumbles.

"Yeah." Kade nods, throwing on his shirt. "He's about to fucking explode." He growls at his brother, "Go!"

Kade rushes for the door, flying past my father as my dad turns, looking like he's about to grab him. Hunter twists toward me. I jump out of the bed, fastening my jeans.

"Just go!" I tell him, pushing.

He shakes his head. "I'm not leaving you to face this—"

I kiss him, feeling his groan as I quickly pull away. "Just go," I bark. "Please!"

My father moves in, Hunter looks at me, in turmoil, and I push him. "Please!" I cry. "I'll handle it."

My mom appears at the door with my brother, takes one look at my scared face and Hunter and sends my brother away.

"Hunter!" Kade yells from downstairs.

"It's not what you think," I say to my dad, and then look to my mom. "Mom, nothing happened!"

"Hunter!" Kade bellows again.

Dad charges, and I push Hunter. "Go!"

"Dylan, no," he argues.

"You being here won't help," I beg.

He bares his teeth, frustrated, and charges out of the room, getting his brother out of here.

"Did they coerce you?" my dad asks. "Get you drunk?"

I look at him like he's crazy. What? "Dad, you practically helped raise them! How can you ask that?"

He holds up the sex toy, and I snatch it back, hiding it behind me as I hear Hunter's car outside start up. "Nothing happened!"

"You're lying!" he yells, and I startle.

He's never yelled like that before.

"You're lying to me," he bites out.

My mom flies in, putting herself between us. "Enough."

"I won't have it!" he cries. "You don't sleep in a bed in your fucking underwear with two guys and say nothing happened."

"Kade has never touched me!" I yell.

Air pours in and out of his mouth as he seethes, but his voice is a level quieter when he asks, "And Hunter?"

I close my mouth, swallowing through my parched throat.

His glower pounds me into the floor, but I square my shoulders and don't look away. "I'm eighteen, and I'd like my privacy."

He rears back, a whole new look in his eyes as if that's not the stance I want to be taking right now. His eyes light up with the challenge, but instead of fighting me more, he starts to back up and leave the room.

"Where are you going?" my mom asks, sounding nervous.

He spins around, stepping through the door.

"Jared?" she calls.

"I'm just going to talk to their father," he says as he disappears around the corner and pounds down the stairs. "Bring her home!"

Talk to their father...

I shoot a glance to my mom. "Mom," I beg.

"Get your shoes," she tells me. "Hurry."

In less than a minute, I have my sneakers on, and I'm running down the stairs, tying my hair up into a ponytail. My stomach growls at the scent of eggs and bacon, but I don't stop to think where it's coming from.

My mom leads the way out the door, followed by my brother, and I see my car parked at the curb. I guess they thought I might like it for my last night here?

But then I climb in the passenger side as my mom drives, and it hits me...the dance.

And the coffees my dad showed up with. They probably brought breakfast for the fake family I'm staying with as a thank you for hosting me.

Shit.

And my mom probably wanted to see if I wanted to go shopping for tonight.

Son of a bitch. My shoulders slump as my brother and I fasten our seatbelts, my mom peeling out of the neighborhood. I don't see anyone on the street, but it's early, and Farrow is undoubtedly sleeping off his hangover.

I'd kind of love for him to be awake right now. It's going to take an army to keep my dad in line.

My mom shifts into third, then fourth, cutting a sharp right and descending into the mill district. She races down River Road, and I glance at my brother in the backseat. His AirPods are in as he plays a game on his tablet.

I keep my voice low. "I promise nothing happened last night," I tell her. "We all just slept."

She throws me a look. "Dylan..."

And I can see that it's as hard for her to believe as it was for my dad.

I know it looked bad. A situation like that where no one touched each other just wouldn't happen.

But....

"Mom, I love Hunter," I say.

And that's all I tell her. It's enough. I'm an open-minded person, and like I told Hunter, I absolutely believe that we're all capable of a lot, given the right motivation and circumstances.

But I don't want anyone else.

She glances at me once—then again—and I see her purse her lips as she races onto the bridge and kicks it up a gear. "And he's loved you forever."

She sighs, and I know she believes me.

"You could tell?" I ask.

She simply chuckles under her breath, speeding into Shelburne Falls. "Everyone could."

So even though Kade was overreacting, he wasn't wrong. He knew ten years ago.

"What's Dad going to do?" I ask.

"Something that will ruin our day, I'm sure."

I fold my arms over my chest, balling my fists and tensing every muscle, far too anxious. We need to get there.

All I can say is I'm glad I fell for a guy more like Madoc than like my dad or Jax. Those kinds of tempers aren't conducive to my personality. Whoever falls in love with Kade will either need to be a saint or have a temper that rivals his.

We fly through town, but not fast enough. I'm tapping my foot, and not at all hiding the fact that I'm checking her speed the whole way there.

She's only going five miles over the speed limit. "Ugh."

She shoots me a look but continues at the same pace.

As soon as we pull into Madoc's driveway, I see everyone in front of the house—Kade, Hunter, Fallon, Madoc, A.J., and my dad. My dad's car door hangs open, the parking lights lit up.

"Oh, God," I groan. He didn't even take a split-second to turn off his car?

Mom speeds in, skidding to a halt, and she and I hop out of the vehicle. I hear their raised voices as we run over. Hunter casts me a worried look.

"What the hell happened?" Madoc shouts, dressed only in sleep pants. Fallon is, thankfully, dressed in jeans and a fitted gray Pirate hoodie. She wears her glasses with her hair swept up into a messy bun as she stands in front of her twin sons.

"I want them both gone." My dad sticks his finger in Madoc's face. "You send them to wherever your people send rich kids for school. You understand?"

"Don't talk to me about what to do with my own kids," Madoc retorts and then looks around. "Someone tell me what the hell is going on!"

"He found us in bed with Dylan," Kade tells him.

Madoc's eyes go round.

"Nothing happened," Hunter rushes to add.

"They were practically naked!" Dad growls.

"None of us were naked," Kade says.

"Dad, nothing happened," Hunter explains. "There was a party in Weston, Kade and I were drinking, and we were teasing Dylan. We never meant to fall asleep."

Madoc looks at them over his shoulder. "You guys were drinking?" His tone is light, surprised. "Together?"

He sounds so happy that they were together, he doesn't give a shit they were drinking underage.

My dad exhales hard. "No parent in their right mind would believe that story."

"Everyone's telling you the same story," I say, moving in.

"I never touched her," Kade states.

My dad looks at Hunter. "And you?"

Hunter's gaze flashes to me, and I see his jaw twitch with a smile, but he remains silent.

Madoc turns when his son doesn't answer and sees the truth in Hunter's eyes.

"Were you careful?" my dad barks at him.

Hunter inhales a deep breath, meets my eyes again, and I open my mouth, but my dad's not going to like that answer, either.

"Dude..." Kade scolds his brother when he doesn't reply.

But my dad is already charging Hunter. Fallon and my mom lurch to intervene, but Madoc is already there, his hands on my dad's chest, keeping him at bay. Madoc's chest shakes with laughter.

My dad snarls. "You're laughing?"

"Man, we knew it was going to happen," he says. "Come on!"

"And you should have raised your sons to wrap it up!"

"Now you're pissing me off!" Madoc points a finger back in my dad's face. "I raised my kids right!"

My dad grabs his stepbrother in a headlock, Madoc's arms flying as he tries to swat at my dad wherever he can reach.

The moms rush in, Kade keeling over with laughter as A.J. just looks disgusted, and I think my brother is happily still checked out with his video game in the back of my car.

Madoc tries to stomp on my dad's foot, which is a mistake, because Madoc's foot is bare, while my dad's is booted. Dad stomps back, and I just tip my head back sighing.

I...

Yeah.

No.

I breeze past everyone into the house.

REBELS

CHAPTER TWENTY-SEVEN

Hunter

"**J**erk."

"Jackass."

Our dads try to keep their language clean in front of the kids, and Kade and I move in, trying to pry them apart.

My dad wraps his arms around Jared's waist and pulls him to the ground. Both of them slide out of our grasp. They wrestle, grunting and growling. *Jesus.*

Mom snaps, "Stop it right now! Both of you!"

"Jared!" Tate barks.

I stand there and look to Kade for what to do, but he already has his phone out, filming.

I look around. *Where's Dylan?*

"You talk about my parenting," Dad grits through his teeth as he fixes Jared into some UFC hold. "Your mom raised a *dickhead*."

I glance at Dylan's car that Tate drove in, only seeing James in the back seat.

"Guess she likes them!" Jared fires back. "She married your dad, after all!"

Dad tightens his arms and legs. "Asswipe!"

I roll my eyes and spin around, leaving the adults to it. I head into the house, still half-naked and with no idea at what point I lost my shirt last night.

I run upstairs to look for Dylan. Maybe she crawled into my bed to hide, and if so, I'm hiding with her.

Kade let me take him into Weston yesterday. I smile despite the headache and churning in my stomach from the alcohol, remembering how good it felt to have him at my side. Like he cared, never stopped caring, and we hadn't missed a step.

We drove onto Knock Hill last night, ignoring the eyes of everyone partying in the street as I brought him inside the house, so I could shower and change. I had every intention of going next door to find Dylan, but by the time I was out of the bathroom, Kade had found Farrow's tequila stash and was asking about the Ray Bradbury collection that Grandpa left in the curio cabinet. I kept my answers short because he was only asking to make conversation. Trying to find a common ground, but we sat down for a minute, and before I knew it, we were three shots and a beer in when Farrow and everyone dragged us outside for a game of football in the street.

I almost thought it was a bad idea. Constin played rough. Kade's nose was bleeding in less than a minute, and I thought for sure Weston was going to force a fight with my brother on our turf, but Farrow stepped in before more happened. He pushed Constin back.

Because Kade is Farrow's blood, too.

We played football for a long time, and no matter that Weston was more brutal than necessary, or how many times

Kade was shoved onto the pavement, he kept getting up, and we were side by side the whole time, trying to protect each other.

We drank more, the firehoses came out, and we stumbled into Dylan's house to bring her out to play, but then we were just ready to pass out.

I want to wake up to her again. It's going to be damn near impossible with her dad as angry as he is, and seven months still left of school before we're on our own. But my parents always go up to our cabin in Wisconsin for a weekend in November to do a little belated celebration for their anniversary after the leaf peeper traffic is gone. They usually send A.J. off to one of our grandparents.

An image of me and Kade with the house to ourselves floats into my head, him waking up with his girlfriend in his room, and me with my girlfriend in my room. I groan, thinking about the early mornings, her crawling on top of me without a word...

I was born for her.

She's not in my room, and the bathroom is empty. I head through Kade's room, peering out the window, and see her in the pool below. Alone. In her clothes. Light sprinkles of rain hit the surface of the water.

She has to be freezing. I didn't check the temperature, but the pool isn't typically heated unless for a party. My dad will be covering it altogether in a matter of weeks, in preparation for the snow to start.

I spin around, passing the three green lockers that my brother now has in his room, and make my way downstairs. I cross the kitchen and open one of the doors, stepping out and closing it behind me.

Her sneakers lay next to the pool, small drops of rain hitting my chest and shoulders as I walk into the water, coming up behind her.

Teeth sink into my skin at the feel of the icy pool, and I see her shiver as I approach. Her hair is slicked back over her head, and her clothes are drenched, sticking to her body.

I close the distance, she turns, and I take her in my arms, pressing her chest to mine to cover her breasts through the wet fabric.

Everyone's still in the driveway, and I kiss her, digging my fingers into her body.

She pulls her mouth away. "Not here."

"Do you love me?" I ask.

That's all I need to know. I don't want to ask. I've waited for her to say it, but if she loves me, then I know she's mine no matter how long I have to wait.

She just looks up at me, brow pinched in pain. "I think you and Kade need to rebuild things."

I shake her. "Do you love me?"

It's not for her to worry about Kade and me. My brother and I will fix it.

I gaze into the storm in her blues, trying not to be angry with him all over again. Now she thinks she interrupted our bonding as kids, and we need to make up for lost time.

No. Not now when I finally have her. Kade and I are grown. *We'll fix it.*

But she just shakes her head. "It'll be too much," she whispers.

Pushing away, she climbs out of the pool, and I see her face split with a silent cry as she dives into the pool house.

I don't stand there more than two seconds. Swimming for the edge, I leap out of the pool, water sloshing onto the deck as I hear loud chatter in the house and doors slamming.

I slip into the dark pool house.

She twists around, and I grab her, her arms circling me too. "Hunter," she cries softly. Tears wet her face.

"Fuck them," I say. "I love my brother, and I love your dad, but fuck everyone who makes you feel like you should be smaller. Like you should fade. It's *our* turn, Dylan."

I kiss her, and she kisses me back, clutching onto the back of my neck for dear life.

"And when you go away to college?" she argues. "Huh? Everything is going to be so much harder than you think it is. You're living in a dream."

I peel off her shirt, unfasten her jeans, and slide my hands inside, gripping her ass. "Then let's just fuck then," I pant over her mouth. "You up for that?"

A whimper escapes right before she can't hold back any more. Opening her lips, she comes in, sliding her tongue into my mouth, and I grip the back of her hair as she pushes off my jeans and then hers.

I pick her up, pulling her legs around me, and throw us both down on the couch.

I reach between us, guiding my cock into her.

"They're gonna look for us," she breathes out.

But she nibbles my lips, rolling her body underneath me and not asking me to stop. I slide myself inside and glide my hand down her thigh, thrusting deep.

"Ah," she moans.

I lower my mouth to hover over hers, gripping the arm of the sofa above her head as I pump fast and hard.

"I'm going to start sneaking into your room again, but you're not getting any sleep when I do." I take her lip between my teeth for a second before letting it go. "I'm going to fuck you quietly when you're not at home alone, and we're going to have some fun when you are."

A smile lifts the corners of her mouth.

"You're going to fuck me over the phone when I'm far away in my dorm room," I pant. "And every time someone asks you out, you're just going to want me. I'm gonna wake up to you sucking on me in the morning, you'll be mine that badly."

She growls, pushing me back, and I fall to the other end of the couch, grabbing her as she climbs on top.

But she pivots instead.

Turning around, she straddles me backward and looks at me over her shoulder as she rides.

I gaze at her ass as it moves. "Oh, God."

I'm never going to not love her, am I?

She rises up and lowers herself slowly, over and over again, taking me inside her. "Oh," she whimpers. "Oh, Hunter."

I squeeze her ass in both hands, her moans getting louder.

"Shhh," I murmur softly.

"It feels so good," she moans, her orgasm building.

I hear the patio door slam shut.

Fuck.

My cock throbs, filling with blood. "You have to be quiet, baby."

But God, she fucking rides me, rolling her hips, her ass taunting me as she slides me in and out, in and out.

"Dylan..." I arch my neck back, about to come. "God, you're so tight."

Chatter goes off outside, she moans, and I start to come. "They're coming." I breathe hard. "They're coming."

"You want me to stop?"

"Fuck," I grunt.

I pump her from the bottom, and she lets her head fall back, both of us convulsing as our orgasms rock through us.

"God, your dick feels so good," she breathes.

I run my hand up her back, feeling the pool water or her

sweat, but we stay there for only a moment before she slides off me, and we quickly dress.

"Dylan!" Tate calls.

Dylan casts a worried look to the door, and I grab her and kiss her.

"I'll meet you at the dance tonight," she tells me.

And that's all she has to say before she leaves.

A half hour later, I'm showered again and dressed, and I'm still not sure what I'm going to wear tonight. We have hours yet, though. I walk to my window, seeing the rain has ended yet the clouds hang low, and my grandfather's car is in the driveway. He must've just arrived.

Dylan's car is still here, too, and I smile a little, relieved that she didn't run.

Heading to Kade's room to search for a suit, I open his closet door and my eyebrows immediately nosedive, seeing the shit all over his floor. A pile of shoes and junk that I can't even make sense out of. That's him, all right. I laugh, shaking my head. When told to clean his room, he just hides the mess.

I sift through his clothes, veering for the back where the garment bags hang. There are a ton. He's kept every suit he's ever owned. I go for the last one out of the bigger ones and unzip the bag, seeing a navy-blue three-piece. I inspect it closer, checking the size of the pants.

It's the right size.

And I like the color.

But it's fitted, and I don't need anyone but Dylan seeing my dick.

I open another, seeing a black single-breasted coat with pants, and I check the size. Thirty-two. That works.

I close his closet door and lay the bag on his bed. I'll ask him first. I don't think he'll say no, but I won't deny him the opportunity to give me shit about finally taking advantage of his superior fashion sense.

I start to leave, but I spot the three tall, green lockers, side-by-side and anchored to his wall next to his closet. I look around, seeing he still has the two dressers he always had. Did he need more storage space for something?

I check his door, making sure no one's coming, and reach out, picking up the combination padlock hanging from one of the lockers. All three doors have one, and I tug on it just a little, but of course, the door is secured. Is my dad not worried he's keeping something he shouldn't in here? Each one's not big enough to fit a body but definitely liquor or drugs.

Not that I've ever known Kade to smoke, snort, or swallow anything illegal other than alcohol, but the need to lock up whatever's in here makes me wonder. Who would care if it was anything else?

I head downstairs, stopping in the foyer and pulling on my hoodie.

Maybe Dylan knows why Kade has the lockers. Unfortunately, she's seen him a lot more than his own brother has over the past year.

And it's her last night with me tonight.

Maybe.

I don't know if I'm coming home, nor do I know if Jared will even let her stay in Weston this evening. He's pretty fucking upset.

But as I head toward the kitchen, I hear soft talking and I slow, in case I don't want to intrude.

Hanging back near the doorway, I peer in, seeing my grandfather, Ciaran, sitting at the island, mixing pancake batter. Jared and my dad hover around the stove, making eggs, bacon, and toast, and I'm guessing Tate and Fallon put them to work, making breakfast for the family.

"People tell you that you never stop worrying about your kids," Ciaran tells them, rising and removing his jacket and rolling up his sleeves, "but in a way, you kind of do. When they're about thirty."

"Thirty?" Dad gripes.

"After that they seem to settle down," Ciarin tells the two younger fathers as he whisks the pancake mix. "They calm, make better decisions, and the only thing you're worrying about is them dying before you do." He looks down at the bowl, and I can tell a memory of my mom when she was younger plays in his head. "After a certain point, they're going to do what they want to do, and all you can do is make sure they know they can still come home when they're ready. If you lose the relationship, you've lost it all."

I glance over at Jared, seeing his jaw flex as he blinks away whatever's in his eye.

They continue cooking, my grandpa sees me, giving me a reassuring nod.

"Thanks," I mouth.

My dad said Jared loved becoming a father, but I can imagine it's hard not to feel as if you're just like the parents who raised you when your kid makes decisions that scare you. His father was a monster, but now he's learning how bad you can make it when you hang on too tightly too.

My dad opens and closes his fist, and I see his knuckles are battered. "That really hurt," he bitches at Jared through clenched teeth.

"Then don't bite next time," Jared whispers, dropping bacon onto a plate lined with a paper towel. "Idiot."

He steps out of the room, and I quickly follow him.

My dad glances as I pass by but doesn't try to stop me.

Jared stands in front of the mirror over the credenza in the dining room, running his hands through his hair. I move in behind him, leaning back on the table and meeting his eyes in our reflection.

"It's only been me," I tell him. "And there's only been her. For as long as I can remember."

He drops his eyes and draws in a deep breath, and I can tell he's trying to grow. Like super fast so he doesn't alienate his wife and daughter any more today.

"I have loved that kid so much," he says, "and I'm grateful she's stubborn. I hate when she's stubborn with me, but I'm proud of her."

He turns and faces me. "But I was scared to have a daughter, Hunter. I know how young guys look at women, and what they think they're good for, because I used to be one of them. I treated women like shit before Tate." And then he quickly adds, "I treated Tate like shit."

I get it. Young guys haven't really changed. Kade's exploits aren't a secret. But I will say, he doesn't think women are toys so much as he looks for ones who hopefully think of him as no more than a toy too.

Jared shakes his head. "I walked into that room this morning and thought she'd been..."

"Used," I say when he trails off.

He nods.

"Kade's never touched her," I tell him once more. "Not like that anyway."

His shoulders stay squared, he exhales, and he has to know that Dylan would've gotten into a relationship at some point. I don't know if that's what we have, but Jared knows—and I think he's always known—I want everything from his daughter.

"But you know, women enjoy sex too," I state matter-of-factly as I stand up straight. "Threesomes are fun for everyone."

He raises a glare to me. "You trying to stay alive right now?"

I laugh, enjoying teasing him, because I'm more like my dad than I guess I knew.

I let my smile fall and look at him without faltering. "She owns me."

He grips my shoulder and yanks me in next to him as we walk back to the kitchen. "I know what that's like."

I step back into the kitchen, seeing Kade popping some ibuprofen and chugging Gatorade.

Dad hands me a plate, and my stomach growls.

"Make it into a sandwich," Kade tells me, downing some more of his drink. "I want to show you something. Come on."

I look around for Dylan, but I don't see her. A.J. and James are nowhere to be found, either. They must be playing video games downstairs.

Kade walks out of the kitchen, and I throw some egg and bacon on the toast, grabbing the napkin my dad hands me as I fold everything in the bread and stuff a bite into my mouth.

We pull on shoes, climb into his truck, and I set my food on the center console as I tap out a text to Dylan.

Running an errand with Kade, I type and reiterate, *Meet you at the dance.*

I want to pick her up, like a date is supposed to do, but she specifically told me she'd meet me there. Probably because she always wants her own wheels, in case she needs to escape.

Kade speeds into town, and he tries to snatch the rest of my sandwich, but I grab it back, spilling scrambled egg into his lap.

By the time he pulls into the alleyway behind Quinn's shop, we're already fighting.

"Always, always, always wear a fucking condom," he scolds.

"I will! I'm going to!"

"No, you're not," he retorts, slamming his door and finding his key to the backdoor of our aunt's shop. "Not after you had her without one now. You act like Dad didn't show us every TV movie on teen pregnancy or YouTube video on STDs."

I don't bother telling him that she's on birth control, and we were both virgins, because he already knows.

"Get yourself in love," I tell him. "And in a monogamous relationship, and you can have fun just like me."

"Monog..." He gags. "Relationship." Another gag followed by a whine, "Dad, he's using four-syllable words again. Make him stop."

I chuckle as he unlocks the door, and I follow him inside.

He leads me through the kitchen, to the front of the shop, and walks toward the mirror. He reaches up, behind the frame, and looks at me. I watch as he pulls something, and the mirror clicks open, swinging inward like a door.

My stomach flips. He's showing me where Dylan escaped to the night the Rebels vandalized the school. The place Hawke talked about when he came to see me.

Kade steps inside, and I touch behind the mirror in the same spot, finding the tiny lever. I follow him, and he leaves the mirror open as I look down the long hallway with black walls. There's light ahead—daylight, I think—and I can smell the water and the subtle subterranean chill that basements and caves have.

We walk in, and he doesn't speak as I look around and absorb. A hallway appears to my right, and I think I see more doorways—more rooms—before we descend a few steps and the hideout opens up to a great room. Dim light spills through windows high above, and I see Latin in massive white letters written on the wall ahead.

Vivamus, moriendum est.

I type it into my search bar, but Kade translates before I can finish. "Let us live, since we must die," he tells me.

There's a couch, an entertainment center with a TV, and I spot game controllers on the coffee table. To my left, there's a small kitchen—fridge, stove, sink, and a counter with a couple of stools.

Kade moves to the door beyond, and I follow him down another hallway, seeing another floor-length mirror ahead and kitchen staff moving through Rivertown, preparing to open for lunch.

"Damn," I say.

They hustle in and out of the kitchen, a guy with a mop and bucket moving toward us but not seeing us.

"What is this place?" I ask, looking around and drifting back to the great room.

"Hawke found it," he says. "Quinn doesn't know about it yet. We wanted to wait for everyone to turn eighteen."

I stand next to the couch, taking it all in, and yeah, I'm thinking I shouldn't tell Farrow about this anytime soon. He could try to take it, given it could be quite an asset to his career path. I'm not sure why Hawke or anyone else needs it, but I might find out myself soon enough.

Kade leans against the kitchen counter, watching me. "I'm...sorry about everything," he says.

I look over at him, appreciating the sincerity in his eyes. He didn't need to say it. Maybe last night, but I think we understand each other now. I'm just glad to move on from it.

"Me too." I sigh. "I'm sorry. I never meant—"

"I know."

He nods, not needing to relive it again. I never wanted him to feel like a third wheel when we were kids.

"I'll get your Chicago application reinstated."

I smirk. "You mean you'll have Dad make a call?"

"No," he interrupts. "I'll call one of our grandfathers. Dad will kill me if he finds out what I did."

I laugh, but then it finally occurs to me. "You got me into Clarke because that's where you're going."

He doesn't reply. He just looks away.

It's pretty impressive, actually. He got me into a college. I thought for sure someone was going to have to get *him* into college. I need to read that essay that admissions guy gushed about. Maybe someone else wrote it.

"We think Rivertown was a home—a townhouse— some years ago," he explains. "This was a secret hideout. A speakeasy or something."

He tells me about Winslet, the twins, and the possible suicide of one or maybe not. How Weston started the prisoner exchange to get the same Pirate girl across the river where they exacted revenge but no one is sure on how. We only know she disappeared from there. All that I knew, but what I didn't know about was Grudge Night and how they came for her in this place first. Or the cell phones they left here.

Maybe they were going to end it that night. And maybe they realized they wanted to carry the fun on a little longer.

I look at Kade, and he looks at me, and I don't think it escapes either of our attentions the parallels between their story to ours. One brother in love and one angry. Losing each other and whatever remained being half-alive—in limbo— because of it. You don't share a womb with someone and not have a bond made of iron. Sometimes that iron makes a shield. Sometimes it makes manacles. It can feel great, and it can hurt, but it's always strong.

If Winslet's really dead, the brothers know it, and they're quite possibly still alive.

Someone in Weston must know where to find them.

I follow Kade out, back into Frosted. "You know who else spent time in Weston twenty years ago?" I ask, not waiting for an answer. "Ciaran."

PIRATES

CHAPTER TWENTY-EIGHT

Dylan

"Thanks for helping," I tell Aro.

I sit in a chair at my house in Weston—in the room Winslet slept in—and gaze up at Aro in the reflection of the makeup mirror she brought that sits on the desk. She stands behind me, fixing some waves in my hair with her curling iron.

She meets my eyes for just a moment. "It sucks around school without you."

"I'm sure you're the only one who thinks so."

She shrugs. "They'll get over it."

I'm sure a few people miss me in classes, but there might be a grudge or two, despite Kade assuring me that everyone will know that it wasn't me who vandalized the school.

It was me who stole the locker, and set off the fireworks. He hasn't brought up either.

"You are coming back, right?" Aro asks, but it sounds more like a statement. "You can't leave me there on my own."

I laugh a little, fiddling with her lipsticks in the tote of stuff she brought. "My parents would never let me transfer my senior year."

"Would you?"

I glance up at her and then back down, thinking. I convinced my parents to let me sleep here my last night, despite the fact that they know there was no adult supervision over the last two weeks, as long as I have a girls' sleepover. Mace, Coral, and Codi happily agreed, so they'll be staying here after the dance tonight. Hunter isn't allowed in my room.

I had to leave his house before he and Kade made it back this morning, so I haven't seen him. Mom and I went shopping for a dress, and then Aro and I came back here.

After my dad calmed down and he, Madoc, and Ciaran made us all breakfast, Dad just hugged me. He didn't apologize for going ape shit, but he didn't punish me, either, for lying about staying with a host family. I think no matter where I go or who I meet in life, I will always have met my match most with my dad. He needs to come to terms in his own time, like me. We can't be forced.

"Actually, no," I finally reply to Aro. "I mean, I wouldn't hate it here, but I want to go back to the Falls and stand my ground."

I'm ready to walk back into that school, and my house, and have the best year.

I suck in a long breath and look up at her as she crafts my hair into beautiful locks. "Where'd you learn how to do all this?"

My desk is covered in makeup and hair product. When I met her, she looked like a teenage guy starting his first metal band.

But she just smiles. "I always knew how to do all this. But when you steal cars and fence tech for a living, it's best not to be noticed by people who consider women just as much of a commodity."

"Right," I murmur. Her lips are a dark pink, and her eyeliner make her eyes almost look like a cat's. She's gorgeous, and I can imagine she was around a lot of people whose attention she didn't want.

She doesn't talk about her life here in Weston much, but like Noah, she's made big changes to chase the life she wants.

"Your first time..." I broach. "Was it okay?"

She releases a lock of hair and takes another in the clip of the curling iron. "I was fourteen."

I narrow my eyes. "Did he..."

I don't want to say it.

But she quickly adds, "He would've stopped if I'd asked him to."

I release a breath.

"I was just too young to understand what I was agreeing to," she points out.

"Do you regret it?"

"Regret is pointless," she tells me. "I can't change anything."

She should tell that to my dad. He regrets so much, and I think he knows he projects it. He thinks I'll regret racing and not going to college if I decide not to.

"But it was bad," she goes on. "And the way he treated me afterward was bad. The feelings I have about it are bad. Sometimes I wish I didn't have those memories." She looks at me in the mirror. "Other times, I know they're the reason that I realize exactly what I have in Hawke. He's my love."

I smile at that. My cousin deserves her too. He's good to her.

"Were you scared, moving to the Falls and everything changing?" I ask.

"Yeah. But I was scared all the time before that too," she explains. "You gotta choose which scared you want to be. Love or fear, remember?"

I nod. Love or fear. If I choose to back off racing, it won't be because I love my parents. It would be because I'm afraid of making them unhappy. Or because I'm afraid of getting injured.

She finishes my hair and covers it with hairspray. I look at my makeup in the mirror, my dress laying on the bed.

"You okay?" she asks me a question next.

I nod. "Yeah."

"Anything you want to talk about?"

Mischief gleams in her eyes, and I laugh, knowing she wants to talk about sex now that I'm having it too. "You mean, do I need advice on the most optimal position for reaching multiple climaxes?"

"Let me know when you're ready. I have an answer for that."

I stand up, my cheeks warming. "I think I'd like to figure it out on my own."

I dress in a backless, black dress with spaghetti straps and a slit for cleavage that trails halfway down my stomach. The waist is tight and then flows out in a wide skirt that falls to mid-thigh. I slide on some black high-top sneakers, and thirty minutes later, we're walking out the front door.

A whistle cuts through the air, and I see Coral, Mace, and Codi standing around Coral's car.

Codi is in jeans and a hoodie, and Mace is in her usual black jeans and leather jacket. But her eyes are done and her lips are red, and she wears a fun, gothic white blouse that leaves half her tummy bare.

Coral is dressed in a tight, short black dress with long sleeves and strategically placed holes, the hems frayed at her thighs and looking very apocalyptic.

"Back at ya," I say.

I meet them at the bottom of the steps, sliding my phone into the small purse that hangs from my wrist.

"You should come," Coral tells Aro. "We can scrounge you up a dress if you like, but really, that's fine too." She gestures to Aro's black shorts that you can barely see, because they're nearly swallowed up by her huge black hoodie. Her long legs and toned thighs look gorgeous all the way down to her black, heeled ankle boots. "There are some people who'd love to see you."

But Aro is tapping away on her phone. She glances up. "Maybe prom." She sighs, looking at me. "There's apparently a huge race in the Falls tonight. Jax and Jared need me there, and Hawke's already on his way. I gotta go."

"A race?"

"Yeah, some team from L.A. is coming through on their way to Pittsburgh?" she explains what they must've just texted her. "Your dad just found out, so he's letting them make a special appearance. He's running a superbike race, endurance tests, and Van der Berg's on the dirt."

Superbikes...

And all of a sudden, I feel it. All the people, the lights, the sounds of the motors filling the air... I don't want to miss it.

But she touches my arm and starts to leave. "Have fun," she says.

"Bye," I say, barely audible. In a moment, she's gone and Mace is opening one of the car doors. "Let's go," she calls out.

We slide in, Codi and me in the back and Mace and Coral in the front. We speed off toward the dance.

But it only takes a few seconds before I realize that's not where I belong. I want to see the race.

"Wait," I blurt out. "Stop."

Coral slams on the brakes, she and Mace looking around like we were about to hit something.

"What's wrong?" Mace asks.

I don't know. I just know I can't pretend that I don't know exactly where I want to be.

I'm about to tell them I need to turn around when my phone rings.

I dig it out of my little purse and see my dad calling.

"Dad?" I answer.

"There's a Motocross Special at seven," he tells me. "And a superbike exhibition just after. I can have your bike here."

I stop breathing, tears filling my eyes.

"You want in?" he asks me.

"You mean it?"

"I think so?" he says like he's scared.

I laugh a little and wipe my nose. He's inviting me to race...a motorcycle. "I'm on my way," I tell him.

We hang up, and I look at Mace and Coral. "Turn around."

"What?"

"Please," I beg Coral. "I have to go to the track."

She pauses for a moment and then hits the gas, spinning the wheel to make a U-turn. We charge back down Knock Hill.

But we pass the house. "I can take the bike," I blurt out.

"No, we'll drive you," she says.

"You want to change?" Mace looks at me then to Coral.

494

But we've already passed the house. I look to Codi. "Give me your clothes."

Her brow wrinkles as her eyebrows damn-near touch her hairline.

She starts removing her clothes, and in minutes I'm in her jeans and she's in my dress. I pull her hoodie over my head. "I'm not sure if Hunter has a phone," I tell whoever's listening. "Can you text someone at the dance. Ask them to tell him I'll be really late?"

Mace gets on her cell, typing away.

Cruising into Fallstown, we can barely maneuver around traffic, whether it's vehicles or people on foot. Coral just ends up pulling as far ahead as she can and parking.

"Thanks, guys." I hop out. "Sorry to drag you here!"

I start to run, but then I notice Coral turning off the car and everyone climbing out. They walk up to me, fixing their clothes. "You're going to need a ride back," she says.

"I can find one," I tell her. "Are you sure?"

But just then, Mace's face lights up. Or it lights up to about as amused as I think she ever gets. "Holy shit." She looks around at the track, the crowd, and the bikes racing by. "I've never been here."

Codi's wide-eyed, chewing her gum, and I smile. "Come on," I tell them.

We stroll in, bypassing the metal detectors, and I nod to Pax, one of the security guys dressed in a black polo.

"Hey, Dylan," he says.

"They're with me," I tell him, gesturing to my friends.

He lets us pass, and I lead them to the stands. "Concessions are over there." I point to my left and then wave my hand to the seats. "Sit anywhere."

Superbikes race to my left, while I hear a motocross race going far in the distance, over the hills, on a track deep in the field. People are spread all over the place, standing on the sidelines, watching, and some sitting in their own chairs they brought. Beer flows, and I smell the food trucks serving burgers, sandwiches, and pretzels.

My brother sits in the media booth, a pair of binoculars around his neck that he's not using, because he's playing games on my dad's phone.

I run up, jumping onto the edge of the booth and swinging my legs over. I slip his binoculars over his head.

"Hey!" he blurts outs.

But he doesn't put up a fight.

I look through, spying Noah in his green and gray uniform flying over the hill, into the air, and setting back down with ease. He's not even close to first place. "Come on..."

"Van der Berg standing tall, feet on the pegs, powering through the ruts," Shane Benchly tells the crowd.

"Sinclair, Fahl, and Weisman climbing high," the other one whose last name, I think, is Dubois adds. "Richter falling back to fifth."

"And here were go, last lap..."

I watch Noah put his foot down, speeding faster and faster.

"Stuart closing back in," Dubois says. "We saw Weisman wobble there, back tire caught in a rut, and Van der Berg trimming four seconds off Sinclair's lead..."

My dad is down in the pit, his headset on, probably talking to Jax in the tower.

"And Van der Berg pulls ahead!" Benchley shouts. "Coming in fast!"

Noah sails through the finish line, and I exhale, smiling wide.

"Borrrrring," my brother groans.

I laugh, handing his binoculars back. Not that he'll use them.

Jumping back down, I run over to Dad. He stands next to my bike, all the mud from the last time I rode gone.

"Your mom's still at the hospital," he tells me, handing me my gear.

I open the bag, bypassing the pants and pulling off Codi's hoodie as I grab the jacket.

Zipping up, I climb on, taking my helmet from him.

"Now, you haven't been on a bike in a couple of weeks," he says.

I flinch. I can tell him that's not exactly true, but I'll wait until after I win.

"These guys—"

But I interject. "Athletes, racers..."

There are a ton of other words he can use that include me.

"Athletes," he corrects himself, "are on their way to Pittsburgh to qualify for the championship." He pins me with a stern look. "Six laps. It's a display. That's it. You ride, you learn, you keep up. Nothing more. Understand?"

I smile, but my knees shake.

My stomach swims, and I feel like my heart is floating in my throat.

I'm scared.

But I remember Aro's words. *Love or fear.*

I tip my head to my dad. "I can do it."

He helps me into my helmet as I fit in an earbud, and I hear the other bikes approach. They move past, one looking at me until he passes so far that he can't stare anymore. I breathe harder, fasten my strap, and pull on my gloves.

Dad looks at me, and I meet his eyes.

He looks like he's holding his breath. "I didn't tell your mother I was letting you do this, so..."

"I won't die."

He laughs, kisses my helmet, and hesitates like he wants to change his mind.

He doesn't, though.

"I love you," he says.

He moves back, and I start the bike, shouting, "I love you too!"

I move to the starting line, fitting in among the other drivers, all men and all far more experienced, which I kind of blame my dad for, but hey, I'm also younger.

My chin trembles, and I squeeze the handlebars, trying to get my hands to work. Everything is hot with adrenaline, and my limbs feel weak.

Do you love me?

I hear Hunter's voice as if I'm tasting it.

Do you love me?

My teeth chatter twice before I stop them, and for some reason, tears fill my eyes. It's the excitement. That's all.

Do you love me?

I look around for him.

I didn't tell him. I should've tried to call.

I close the visor and say the words as I see his face in my head. "I love you," I whisper.

Taking out my phone, I go to my app, but then I remember I still haven't redownloaded anything onto my new phone.

But as soon as I open it, I see a playlist ready to go.

It's called *Pirate Girl*.

I grin wide, but no one can see.

He made me a mixtape.

I scan the songs, few of which I recognize, but I see one of my mom's favorites from when I was a kid. I haven't heard this in forever, but we would rage scream it in the car when it was just the two of us.

I press play, turning up the volume as the announcer introduces our race, and "The Collapse" by Adelitas Way starts playing in my ear.

Men rev their engines around me, getting louder and louder, and some of my father's guys move around us, taking pictures while I'm sure others are filming to research the footage later.

The purr of the bikes quickens, and my heart pumps as I watch the signal lights. They turn green, and I suck in a breath, all of us darting off at the same time as my feet find the footrests.

Bikes fly past at my side, the music blasts in my ear, and I see arms shoot up in the crowd as people cheer. Some of them know me by my dad, but I don't know if it was announced that I was on the track too.

Either way, I am. Tightening into nearly a ball, I fall in behind everyone, struggling just to keep up, much less get ahead. The world zooms by in a blur, the wind barreling into me, and my heart races, feeling like I'm on a tight rope, and it's not a matter of if I'll fall, but when. Any second.

I can't... It's too fast.

"Come on, come on, come on!" I yell, firing it with more gas. I pull up, head-to-head with the racer in last place, all of us leaning left, hugging the curve as we race around.

A real superbike race can be over two-hundred miles long. The same massive lap a handful of times. Fallstown can't accommodate that, and probably never will, but this allows my dad and his competitors to measure against each other. A "fun" exhibit of their designs.

Billy Waters, a racer out of Texas, swerves in front of me, and I tremble, jerking my handlebars. He looks over his shoulder at me as the guy next to me, whom I don't know, skims his eyes behind his visor down my body and back up again. He jerks his wheel, faking me out, and my hands shake.

Fuck...

I let off the gas, starting to fall behind again. They keep staring at me.

Like I'm a novelty and not really here.

That's how it always is. If I win, it's because they let me. If I lose, then of course I did. Nothing I earn will be deserved to them.

And it makes you feel like the hill doesn't have a peak. It'll never end.

As we finish the third lap, I catch sight of my dad, standing with his arms crossed and watching. I start to face forward again, but I see Hunter.

At least, I think it was him.

He stood in front of the media booth, and it was quick, but he wore a black suit and white shirt, and his hands were in his pockets.

He watched me fly by, and I hear his words in my head again. *Maybe the only way to beat him was to stay.*

To know what we can control and what we can't. To know my own mind, and that I don't need permission or validation, especially from people I don't know or love.

The chorus in my ear charges my arms and legs, and I tighten my fists around the handlebars, zooming around the bend, and then another, and skimming the curves just like Farrow taught me.

I blast past the guy in last place, then Billy Waters, and slide around a black bike with red accents. I cruise into the middle, ramping up my speed a little more and a little more, and find myself creeping up onto the lead guys.

Their speed increases, and I push it faster, finding them accelerating more. I smile behind my helmet, my heart swelling in my throat.

We fly around and around, and I sink into the curves, holding my own as we race. The finish line approaches, and I find myself pushing it just a little harder, until...

We charge past, blowing through the finish line and the flag and cruising around again, slowly decelerating. *Third*.

I think I was in third place.

I shake with laughter as I ride around to the start again and pull up to the side. I don't look at the other guys, and I won't worry about what they say.

We're going to do that again someday. Mark my words.

Dad rushes up, followed by Hawke, Aro, Mace, Codi, and Coral.

I beam. "It was so much fun," I say to my dad.

He fixes me with a look like I went far faster than was the plan, but I see

a smile peek out as he helps remove my helmet and I take off my gloves.

"You've been racing," he says. "Who taught you how to do that?"

I flash him a big, toothy smile, but I don't unclench my teeth, and he knows he won't find out the answer to that tonight. Maybe someday I'll tell him about Farrow when I'm sure my dad won't kill him.

Hell, if I can be coached by my dad, and mentored by Farrow *and* Noah, nothing will be able to stop me, much less catch me. Farrow and Noah have very different styles, though. I don't think they'd work well together.

"Tuesdays and Thursdays, four to six," Dad says. "Here at the track, you got it?"

I nod quickly. He's training me?

He hands off my helmet to Aro. "And I'm setting you up with a personal trainer at Astrophysics," he tells me.

I wince. "Exercise?"

He narrows his eyes, and I remove the expression from my face immediately. "I'm sorry, yes."

All of his racers go to a trainer. It's part of the program, and in this, he's my coach. Not my dad.

He smiles a little and comes in, kissing my hair.

And then he back away, making room for my friends.

The girls rush in. "That was awesome," Coral blurts out.

"You were going so fast, I thought I was going to die," Mace laughs.

I hug Aro and then look around. "Where's Hunter?"

Aro shrugs. "I didn't see him."

I look to the others, and they shake their heads, having no idea.

But he was here.

REBELS

CHAPTER TWENTY-NINE

Hunter

Kade drives us back to Weston, and I don't know why I let him drive my car. I don't even know why he asked. He hates old things.

"Is this an actual fucking radio?" He presses each knob, the dial darting left to right as he searches for music. "Not like a satellite radio or anything?"

He looks at me with an expression somewhere between confusion and pain etched on his brow. I shake with a quiet laugh and look out the window.

"Bench seats are useful, though," he adds with a playful tone.

Yes, they are.

We drive back through town and cruise down High Street, toward the river.

"Why didn't you wait for her?" he asks.

"She's going to be celebrating." I take out my phone and start scrolling. "Her friends and family are there."

"You're her friend," he points out the obvious, "and her family."

I turn to face him. "I wasn't invited."

"Her boyfriend doesn't need an invitation."

"I'm not her boyfriend."

I don't mean to sound defeatist, but she didn't send anyone with a message, telling me to meet her at Fallstown. She said she'd be late. That's it. It was me who decided I wanted to be there for her. She didn't ask.

"Hunter..." he chides.

But I cut him off. "Look, I know, all right? But I also know I've told her I loved her twice, and she hasn't said it back. Whatever the hell we're doing is confusing for her or some shit. I'll fight with her another day. Not tonight. She's feeling too good."

She looked incredible on that track.

But if she felt the same way I do, she would've said so.

"Girls don't like to be the one chasing a guy," he mumbles. "That's all I'm saying."

I rub my forehead and then exhale. "Why are you coming back with me?"

I sound aggravated, and I'm hoping he notices.

But he just grins. "What's her name? Arlet?"

Oh, fuck no.

"We need to talk about that," I say in a hard voice.

But he just laughs. "I didn't mean to do it in your bed."

"Bullshit."

"She started getting handsy," he tells me, "and when she found out I wasn't you, she didn't seem to care, and hey, neither did I."

"So you decided to screw in my room on the off chance Dylan would see."

It's not a question.

He just kind of shrugs and winces at the same time. "You know I don't think," he explains. "I won't do it again?"

Damn right, you won't. *Asshole.*

But...the confrontation with Dylan about it ended pretty great, so I can't complain too much. I see her in the back seat of my car again, feeling myself sliding all the way into her for the first time. The way her breathing shook against my body...

I'll fucking take that one memory to my grave with me. I'm never letting it go.

It's good to know that Kade is on my side. He wants me to love her.

We head down Frontage Road, toward the bridge, and I see an email pop up on my phone from Robert Cartridge from Clarke University.

I open the attachment, the essay Kade submitted loading on my phone.

I knew Cartridge would be confused about why I didn't have it when I sent him an email, asking for a copy, so I gave him a story about being hacked. I hoped he didn't need more detail.

The essay Kade submitted appears in my screen, and I almost download it and save it for later, but the first line catches my attention.

He's put me in a new prison.

I glance at Kade, then back to my phone as he turns up the music.

That's what he does with all of us, the essay reads. *Hides us. Locks us up. All of his little treasures.*

And there are so many of us. He's grabbed, shoved, squeezed, bent, torn, and even bitten us, but he's done that to me more than most, because I'm his favorite.

Or I used to be.

I narrow my eyes, unsure if I want to read more. This sounds a little creepy. Did he write this?

I remember the feel, you know? Watching him lick his fingers and slide them up my skin, touching me, turning me, and gazing at me for hours. Smiling while he chewed his lips and looked at me with wonder in his eyes.

I took him away. Far away to places he can only visit in his mind, but he got to go there, and that was enough.

And I wasn't his just once, either. He picked me a lot. Out of all of them, I was the one he hid in his sheets the most after a long night and he got too tired to let me go. He mended my tears. Stitched my spine. Wrapped me in a band to keep me together. He loved me. Ever scar he left me was proof of that.

It didn't last, of course. New becomes old. Familiar becomes boring. He started trapping me in dark places with no room to move. Did he know I needed air? Time passed and I started to rot, but I'd see glimpses of him from time to time. When he flipped the lid on the case. When he opened the door. Light would spill in, cool air caressed me, and he'd run his hands over all of us, searching for whatever would feed his appetite. He never picked me again, though.

"What are you reading?" Kade asks.

I see him look over at me out of the corner of my eye, and it takes a minute to dislodge the lump in my throat.

"Uh, this study on Gingko trees and their effect on—"

"Never mind," he groans. "Jesus."
I keep reading.

I didn't see him at all for a long time.

I'd hear him, though. Laughter, shouts, music, and fighting... My boy's life carried on, and even though his voice got deeper, I knew he hadn't left me. A fact, I confirmed when one day, he pulled us all out of his closet, and I thought, maybe he was going to let us go. Maybe he was going to give us to someone new or take us to another part of the house.

This is written from the perspective of an object, not a person. I exhale a little.

But he didn't take us to a new room. He put us in a new cage—steel, cold, and hard—but strangely enough, it wasn't worse.

I could see him for a while through the vents as he laid on his bed and held a phone in his hand. I liked watching him. He found a new way to enjoy us that no one would know about. He'd scroll, I'd watch, he never smiled, and I'd stare at his thumb moving up the screen again and again and again.

Over and over and over.

He didn't smile. He didn't laugh. He didn't fight. He just tapped.

Tap, tap, tap.

Summer came, and I could smell flowers through the vent in my prison. He opened a window, and a fly buzzed in. The others and me loved the warmth and the glimpses of sun. He was gone a lot, but sometimes there was music outside, and sometimes he didn't come home at all, but we listened to the world, even as his little sister came in and set some new T-shirts on his bed. She left. We stayed. The fly stayed.

Buzz, buzz, buzz.

It's the lockers in his room. Cold, steel, hard. *Vents.* Whatever's in the lockers is telling the story.

He filled my cage with more little secrets, locked the door, and started piling more of us that he wanted to hide in the cage next to mine. I heard screams—rips and tears— and he'd curse, angry. The cage door would slam, he'd hit our box, growling, and then he'd charge out of the room. Where's the one who looks like him? The one he fought with? I haven't seen him in so long.

Football games played on his T.V. Friends would laugh and talk with him in his room. They'd howl and clap, a savory scent filling the air and reminding me of the same scent I had on a piece of me once. Pizza. He still doesn't laugh, but he likes football.

Clap, clap, clap.

It's cold now. So dark. I smell snow. He comes in late, crashes against my cage, and I'm scared. Is he hurt? Will he hurt me? He breathes hard, whimpers a little. Punches my cage. Slits of his face appear through the vent, and he looks like he's in pain. He's so big now. Grown. I missed everything. Why is he so sad? I can help. I'm here. I don't see blood. He drinks from the bottle like he's so thirsty.

Gulp, gulp, gulp.

I harden my jaw, trying to fight back the tears as I read.

Spring again. He has new friends. Lots of friends. He

seems happy, and I smell and listen, because their scent is pretty and they sound soft, and he touches them too. Licks, bites, grabs, and bends. They don't talk much. They play on his bed, the steady banging of the headboard against the wall.

Bang, bang, bang.

The summer goes on. All the same, all the time. Sometimes our doors open and some of us disappear and we don't return. Where does he take us? Some of us stay. I lose sight of him, but I hear him drink and crash on his bed, and every once in a while, I hear the banging against the wall.

Gulp, gulp, crash.

Bang, gulp, crash.

Gulp, bang, bang.

Gulp, bang, crash.

He doesn't love me anymore. I want to be loved. I want to go. Travel. Be in backpacks on a train. On a shelf in a sidewalk bookstore. On a picnic blanket in Central Park. Why doesn't he release me? I can't bear to watch him forget how close he is to being happy if he just opens my door.

And then...

He does.

It's a book, I realize. He keeps books in those lockers.

It's night, the house is quiet, and the cage swings open. He pushes all of us into a bag, pulls it closed, and carries us downstairs and outside. I smell the fresh-cut grass, hear fireworks in the distance, and feel the sighs of the others in the bag with me. They're happy to be remembered.

Where is he taking us?

When the bag opens again, he's reaching in and removing stacks of us, stuffing us into shelves.

Shelves! We'll see people walking by. They'll look at us, and even if they don't ever touch us again, I long to be part of the world. To be seen. Considered.

One of us tears, pages spilling onto the grass. We're still outside. What kind of shelf is this?

He puts us in, closes the door, and I see him through the glass. I don't like the way he's looking at us. Like it hurts for him. Why?

If he loves me, why did he hide me? Why was he ashamed? Is this goodbye?

He disappears, and moments later, someone else comes and picks a book out. They take it and leave one in its place, and I realize this is a place to trade stories.

But my boy didn't take any of the books that were already here. He didn't take anything new. Why?

Then, suddenly, he's there. Again. He opens up the glass door, pulls me back out—just me—and I know I'm not new for him. He's been rough with me, marked me, and bent me, but he's remembering how he loved me. How he can't give me up, and how I taught him so many things.

Like how mind-boggling big space is. Vastly! Hugely!

How dolphins are the second most intelligent species on Earth, second only to mice.

How digital watches are really pretty neat.

How the answer to the meaning of life is forty-two, and how a towel is really the most useful thing any interstellar space traveler will own.

I laugh, meeting Kade's eyes as he looks at me like I'm crazy.

"Gingko trees are a trip," he mumbles.

It's *The Hitchhiker's Guide to the Galaxy*. That's the book that's talking in the essay. I think our dad would agree that a towel is always useful.

I'm a part of him, and he can't say goodbye just yet.

Maybe it wouldn't have been better to stay on the free library shelf. To sit on someone's coffee table for three months, collecting the smell of cigarettes and watching reruns of Friends, *while issues of* Cosmo *and* Golf Digest *scatter around me.*

But perhaps I would've gone to Africa or Paris or on a ship at sea, so I'm grateful some of us stayed on the little bookshelf, and I wish them well on their journeys.

My boy still needs me, though. My travels can wait, because I will live much longer than him.

He folds me in his fist, and once in a while I feel a drop of water from his face as we go back home.

Drip, drip, drip.

I turn my face out the window, so he can't see my eyes. He submitted this with my application. *Mine.* Not his. He didn't want anyone to know this about him. I raise my thumb to the corner of my eye, wiping away the wet.

I don't need him to explain anything to me, but I'm glad I read this. He hides so much that I get used to thinking he's not complicated, or that he never feels pain. He'll blow it off if I bring it up, but I'm glad I know this. We don't have to talk about it. Not yet anyway.

"Who is that?" he says.

I look ahead as he cruises across the bridge and see a girl standing up on the ledge. They need a damn fence. Most bridges have one.

The white hair flies in the breeze.

"It's the Dietrich kid," I tell him. "Stop for a second."

He draws in a breath, impatient, but he cruises up to the side and stops.

"Thomasin," I call.

She doesn't turn, just stares down at the water dressed in jean shorts, black leggings underneath, and a big, yellow hoodie.

"Tommy," I say her nickname instead.

She turns and looks at us over her shoulder. Her expression doesn't change.

"What are you doing?" I ask.

She doesn't reply, just stares at us.

"Do you need a ride?" I press.

She doesn't respond, and I try to see if she has earbuds in, but then I hear Kade next to me.

"Get. Down," he bites out slowly.

And very quietly.

I look over at him, his gaze only slightly turned toward her, but it's stern.

I glance back at her, and she starts to spin, but then she wobbles. I grab the door handle, and I feel Kade jolt, but then she throws out her arms, twirls, and drops back down to the street next to my car.

I breathe hard, my pulse racing. She quirks a smile and walks back the way we just came, toward the Falls.

"Shit," I grumble, laughing under my breath.

I look over at Kade, but he's not smiling. Eyes flat, he shifts into *Drive* and hits the gas, any sign that he's in a good mood now gone.

Reaching into the glovebox, I take out a coin and flip it over the bridge as we head into Weston.

By the time we get to school, the parking lot is packed. Most people have been here for a couple of hours already, and we stroll in, finding the gym crowded. People dance, surrounded by tables and balloons and whatever else parents were able to donate, and I spot Farrow and Constin hanging by the drinks.

Surprisingly, they're in suits, which concerns me more than I would ever admit. They don't look like students anymore.

A year from now, they'll be far from it if Dewitt is correct.

Constin's outfit is black, including his shirt, while Farrow's shirt is white like mine. None of us wear ties.

I approach, and they eye my brother at my side. I realize that having him over here last night might've been okay, but maybe not twice.

In any case, Kade holds out his hand to Farrow, all of us sober now.

"No hard feelings," Kade says.

Farrow quirks a smile and shakes hands with him. "Oh, there are lots of hard feelings, but...not tonight. Be our guest."

Kade's happy with that and spots Arlet off to our right, moving to join her, while Constin heads to the dance floor.

"So, what happens Monday?" Farrow asks me when we're alone.

I move in closer. "I think I have to go home." I stare out at the crowd with him. "I'm missing my little sister grow up. And I'm going to need my brother."

Now that I know he wants me close to him and has always wanted that, I need to make up for lost time.

I try to tamp down my grin. "Of course, I'll miss having you as a roommate...and a..."

I look to him, and he chuckles. "Don't you fucking call me uncle."

We laugh, the truth finally out. He's Ciaran's son. I'm guessing my grandfather didn't know until Farrow was older, otherwise he would've raised him and Farrow would've been in our lives from the beginning.

"When did you know that I knew?" I ask him.

"Every damn time you looked at that picture too closely."

"The resemblance is severe," I admit, remembering the photo at the barber shop. "You think if we just invite you to dinner my mother will figure it out?"

He smiles, looking amused, but then his face falls a little, looking serious. "Don't tell her."

I stare at him.

Someone has to tell her.

"It's not my place," I point out. "It's yours and Ciaran's, but she needs to know."

My mom grew up largely alone. She'd love to find out she has a sibling. I can't keep something like that from her forever.

But Farrow shakes his head. "Knowing me won't make her life better."

I watch him, how his expression changes from serious to solemn, and I know he doesn't want to complicate her life. He thinks he'll be a burden, and it's not an unreasonable concern, given how he makes money. Given that he's following in their father's footsteps.

But he should let my mom decide that. She knows how to say no to things she doesn't want.

Just then, Farrow tips his chin, and I follow his gaze, seeing Dylan walk through the gym doors.

My whole body vibrates under my skin, and whatever we were talking about is suddenly forgotten.

She steps in, Coral, Mace, and Codi drifting in behind her. They move into the dance, but she stays close to the entrance, smoothing out the lumps in her hair, the remnants of curls still visible.

Wide-eyed, she looks around, fiddling with the little purse on her wrist, and when she sees me, she smiles.

My chest aches.

The dress leaves little to the imagination, showing off the curves of her breasts as they sit in tight fabric, her cleavage deep and wide. I can tell her back is nearly bare, and her legs are long and toned, and I smile at her feet in high-tops.

She moves her gaze to my left, and I look to see who she's watching.

Kade stands with Arlet, leaning into her as he grins.

Dylan doesn't move toward me.

She walks to him.

I breathe calm and slow—so slowly—as I watch her reach up and squeeze his shoulder. He turns, looking surprised, and I watch her lean in to whisper in his ear.

I lock my jaw.

He smiles and takes her hand, leading her to the dance floor.

"I'm about to take her over my knee," Farrow grumbles through his teeth.

I watch them dance, my brother holding her, her arms around him, and she whispers in his ear again, this time for longer, and a wide smile spreads across his face.

I take a step, about to walk over, but then they move, she's taking his hand and leading him out the other set of doors.

What the fuck just happened?

They disappear, the doors close, and Farrow sets down his cup. "Okay, tonight's for fucking him up."

I plant my hand on his chest, stopping him. "Stand by."

Leaving him where he stands, I shoot off, charging after Dylan and my brother. I'm sick of this shit. This morning, she's sitting on my dick, and now she's ignoring me. I push through the doors, look both ways, and see the stairwell door to my left closing.

I run for it, shoving it open, and looking down the staircase, hearing another set of doors shut. Well, they're not leaving. What the hell are they doing down there?

I grind my teeth, feeling like I want to bite something.

I head down, opening the doors to the bottom floor and moving toward the auto shop to the left.

But just then, Kade steps out of the shop, into the hallway, and smiles as he walks toward me.

"What's going on?" I ask.

He doesn't answer. He just reaches into my breast pocket, searching for something.

"What are you doing?" I blurt out.

He pulls out my keys. "Borrowing your car for an hour," he says. "You're not leaving anytime soon."

His eyes flash to the room he just came out of—without Dylan—a mischievous grin on his face.

"I'll be back later," he tells me. "Have fun in there."

What?

He walks away, and I glance to the auto shop door.

Dylan's in there? For me?

I almost start to smile, but then realization hits at what he's going off to do while he leaves me here with her.

"Hey, don't have sex in my car!" I yell after him.

He pops his head back out the stairwell door. "Can I use your room then?"

I sigh hard, heading to the auto shop. "Have sex in my car."

"Thanks!"

I shake my head and step into the dark auto shop, looking around to the cars and over the desks, but not seeing Dylan. The bay doors are closed, but the door leading to the cage is wide open. A light flickers inside the dark space, and I drift toward the door, my lungs emptying as Dylan appears.

She's inside the cage, between the lat tower and the chest press, pressed into the chain-link fence with her wrists bound above her head. I gaze up at the handcuffs—my handcuffs that she must've snatched from my room tonight—and quietly approach our Pirate hostage for her last night here.

"Hunter?" she asks, sensing me.

Her hair spills down her back, and I look up to the fingers clenched around the fence. Her phone sits on the weight machine to my left, an app with candlelight running.

Kade saw her like this? *Tsk, tsk, tsk...*

Sliding my hands up her dress, I yank her ass into my body as I whisper in her ear. "What if someone else had found you?"

But I guess that's why she took Kade with her. To lure me to follow and to make sure no one else came in here before me.

I roam her body, seeing goosebumps break out on her arms as I caress the tiny fabric between her legs. Her naked hips are only covered by the thin string of her thong, and I keep going, gliding my hand up her bare back.

My cock strains against my pants. "Where's the key?"

She groans, letting her head fall back. "Somewhere on me."

Fuck.

I kneel, removing her shoes and tipping them to see if anything falls out. Leaving her barefoot, I leave little kisses as I move up and lick the backs of her thighs, touching every inch of her I can reach.

Rising, I slip my hands farther up her dress, over her stomach, before I slip my fingers up the back of her scalp. She breathes hard, and I close my fist around her hair, pulling her back and nibbling her mouth. I bite and kiss as I unzip the back of her dress with my other hand.

"Where's the fucking key, baby?" I murmur.

She just smiles.

I pull away from her mouth and slide my hands inside her dress, cupping her breasts.

She moans, and I look into her eyes and she looks into mine, and I hold them as I tear one of the spaghetti straps off her shoulder. Fire lights in her eyes, and I do the same fucking thing to the other one.

The dress falls, pooling on the floor at her feet, and I let my eyes glide up her body, trussed up in cuffs. My dick is throbbing.

"It's awfully dangerous," she taunts as I slide my finger inside the string of her thong. "Someone's going to come in."

"Then give me the key."

I tug her panties down over her ass.

All she says is, "You're so close."

I wind the string around my fingers and yank, ripping the thong clean off her body.

She shakes with a whimper, and I grab her hips, pulling her ass into my groin as I bite her earlobe and massage a breast.

Someone's going to fucking come in. This isn't funny. Not really. I know for a fact that members of the team like to bring their dates in here to screw around. Where's the goddamn key? She's naked. I just need her uncuffed, and

I'll take her into one of the cars in the auto shop, or into the locker room and one of the shower stalls.

I back away from her and leave the cage, taking in the view of her long brown hair falling down her back as it gives way to her beautiful waist and gorgeous ass.

Walking around, I come to the other side and face her, taking in her body and her wet lips.

She presses herself into the fence, her nipples peeking through the diamonds in the pattern.

"I like it here," she whispers. "My last chance to see it before you give me back tomorrow."

I lean down and lick her nipple before I catch it between my teeth. She gasps excitedly, clawing at the cage and pressing her body against the chain-link. I kiss her tits through the metal holes, sucking as I move from one breast to the other.

Squatting down, I slide my tongue inside of her, running the tip up and down her clit.

"Hunter," she moans.

I suck her little nub into my mouth, and I'm swelling and hard, about fucking ready to make her twist around so I can fuck her through the fence right now.

"I know where I didn't search yet," I tease, biting her flesh.

Standing up tall, I sink my fingers through the hole and into her pussy.

She grunts, pressing against the metal as I feed her long, slow strokes, and I keep going long after I realize there's no key there, either.

Thrusting against the fence, she rides my hand, and I can't take it anymore. I need my body on hers.

"You're so wet." I kiss and lick her mouth through the fence. "I think you like it here."

She bites her bottom lip, but I see the smile. Moving back around and into the cage, I strip off my jacket, rip open my shirt, and unfasten my belt.

Taking myself out, I look up to her fingers clutching the thick wires of the fence before I yank her ass back and turn out her thigh.

I nudge the head of my cock at her entrance. "How many times can I fuck you before I give you back tomorrow?"

I thrust—once, then twice—burying myself inside of her as I cover her mouth with mine.

Her head turned over her shoulder, she returns the kiss as I slide my tongue in slow, soft, and touching the sharp metal of the key.

Lips on her, I meet her eyes as I take it from her mouth and see her smile.

"I love you, Hunter," she says.

PIRATES

CHAPTER THIRTY

Dylan

Silly *boy.*
   If he'd acted like a romantic and kissed me deeply like he should've done first thing, he would've found the key immediately. But my man went straight under the skirt and couldn't help himself after that.

Not that I'm complaining.

"I love you so much," I tell him again.

He covers my mouth, kissing me rough and deep and moaning as he does.

"Fuck me hard," I whimper.

He presses me into the cage, and I arch my back as he fucks me, his fingers clenching the cage and his thumbs wrapped around my forearms, holding me.

His hands roam everywhere—up my neck, down my back, squeezing my breasts and then my ass. His grip lands in my hair, his cock hits deep inside, and I inhale sharp, quick breaths, holding each one for a few seconds.

"Right there," I moan over and over again. "Just like that."

He slides in and out of me, the cage rocking and clanging with the force, and I lean my head back, begging, "Rub me."

He slips a hand between my thighs, sliding his fingers in circles over my clit.

"Like that?" he asks in my ear.

I nod, my throat parched. I kiss his mouth again and again, my moans getting louder, and I really don't care who hears.

My pussy contracts, tightening on his cock, and he growls under his breath. "Baby..."

"You feel me coming?"

"Yeah."

My orgasm climbs higher until...I freeze, feeling it gather between my legs and low in my belly, raining down, unable to stop.

"Oh, Hunter!" I cry, hanging on as he thrusts faster and harder. "Fuck," he groans, squeezing my breasts.

The orgasm fills my whole body with tingles, and my knees almost give out as I hang by the handcuffs.

He brushes his thumbs over my nipples. "I need these in my mouth."

I can barely open my eyes as I feel him unlock me from the cuffs, spin me around, and lift me up, guiding my legs around his body.

He sits on the weight bench, and I straddle him, taking his dick in my hand and fitting it back inside of me.

I ride him, rolling my hips in and out in long smooth waves. Arching my back, feeling my hair graze my ass as he sucks on my breasts.

"Say it again," he whispers.

"I love you."

"Again."

I smile. "I love you, Hunter. I love you. I love you..."

He growls, pulling my head back up and snatching up my mouth.

I look over, seeing us fuck in the mirror on the wall. He follows my gaze, watching me ride him.

That's us. It was always going to be us.

"And I want to sleep in your bed tonight," I say.

He tips his head back. "Yeah..."

Sounds leave his throat, building and growing deeper and harder, and I move my body, letting him look and touch and have anything he wants.

His breathing stutters, every one of his muscles under my hands tightens, and he jerks again and again.

And again, finally letting out a long, single groan.

I lay my head on his chest, hearing his rapid heartbeat against my ear. "I love watching you come."

"And I love you," he says back.

I hold him, it hurting to think about being traded back tomorrow. I don't know if he's coming home yet, but it feels like we'll be a thousand miles away from each other. I've loved having him next door with no rules interfering.

And eventually, we'll be even farther away from each other.

"What?" he asks.

I look at us in the mirror, seeing him staring back at me in the reflection.

"Just already dreading next year," I tell him. "College."

"Oh, yeah. That." He runs his hand through his hair. "Kade made a mess with my University of Chicago application, so I need to sort that out."

I hold him tighter.

"I'm in love with you," he says, kissing my hair. "And I'm proud of you. You were beautiful on that track. Right where you belong."

I smile to myself. No matter what happens, it will be hard to be separated by even ten miles, but I'm going places, too, and that's a perk to be going home, I guess.

In any case, he's in love with me, and we have winter nights, spring rains, and summer heat to look forward to before next fall.

I try to swallow through the dryness in my mouth as pain hits my stomach. "Oh, God, I'm starving."

I haven't eaten anything since the dads' breakfast this morning.

"Breaker's?" he suggests.

I nod, and he comes up, wrapping his arms around me as we kiss.

I look over to a shelf, his lips still on mine. "Oh, yay. Towels," I chirp.

I need to clean up before we eat.

But he glances over to the rack with white gym towels for the football players and falls back against the bench again, laughing. I don't know why.

I turn around, taking in Winslet's bedroom one last time. I don't know if I'll ever sleep here again, but I know I'll be close. Hunter will still have his room next door, even though he's moving home. I'm already daydreaming of Sunday afternoons when it's raining and we want to disappear for a few hours some place that isn't a cramped back seat. I'll miss this house, though.

And I'll certainly miss that cage. Last night was incredible.

"Dylan, you ready?" Hunter calls downstairs.

Music plays out in the street—someone's car speakers— and people move in and out of the house, waiting to take me to the bridge and release me back to the Pirates.

"Almost!" I call out.

I swipe the notes off the desk, having saved those for last when I packed up all of my things. It feels wrong to remove them from the house. They're not mine, but Hawke will want to see them, and someone left them here for me to find anyway. I'll return them. Someday.

I stuff the notes into my backpack, making sure the window is closed, and scan the room once more as I turn off the light.

I close the door and leave, jogging down the stairs. Hunter catches me in his arms as I swing into the living room.

"I don't want to give you back," he whispers, hovering over my mouth.

I kiss him. "You'll be over at your parents," I say, kissing him again, "not across the river anymore."

"But he'll be here with us all day," Coral adds, walking past with the garbage bag to take out to the curb.

I sigh at Hunter as she heads out to the porch, and Mace and Codi drift in. "True."

He's not coming back to school. His team still has at least four more games, and he wants to be here. He's just not living here anymore, though. He's going home to his own room and will drive over here for school and practice.

"You sure you're okay with that decision?" he asks.

"It's the right one."

The Rebels fit him.

"Hunter!" Farrow shouts from the street.

Hunter looks toward the door and then back to me, kissing my hair. "Meet you outside."

I let him go, and Mace reaches out, handing me my phone. "Halloween party Friday after the game at the rink," she tells me. "We all put our numbers in."

"Great." I tuck my phone away. It makes it easier to leave knowing I'll be back for Hunter's game in five days.

"Want me to bring anything?" I ask. I doubt I can get a hold of liquor, but I'm great with pizza.

Coral enters the house again sans garbage bag. "You can bring your dad."

Mace and Codi laugh, and I wince. "Gross."

"Bring the gang," Coral says. "It'll be cool."

Codi removes my Pirate jacket and hands it to me. "I know we won, but..."

I shake my head. "Keep it," I tell her. "I like the idea of it staying here, actually." I look around to the three of them. "Pass it on to someone else when you're ready."

I slip my arms into my backpack and move into the kitchen, checking for anything else that's mine.

I point to the refrigerator. "There's some food left that I can't really take home, so go for it."

"Are you stealing a shirt?" Coral asks.

I stop, remembering the *No Fear* T-shirt I found in the closet. I open my jacket and look. "Is that okay? Did it belong to one of you?"

"It was here," someone else says, and I see Arlet step into the house. "The clothes have always been here."

She stops next to the others, and we didn't talk much while I was here. Hunter made sure I knew that she was fully aware it was Kade she was sleeping with.

"Something of hers should be in the Falls, too, I guess," Arlet tells me.

I smile, appreciating that. I still don't think I believe these were her clothes, but as long as they're no one else's, then we're good.

"Oh, I forgot my helmet." I spin around, heading to the kitchen table.

"I'll take this out," Mace tells me, grabbing my other bag.

"Thanks!"

They all drift outside, and I grab the helmet Noah brought for me, already having given Farrow back the keys to his bike. I move to the stairwell door, running through the list in my head. "Phones, helmet, vibrator..."

I start to swing the door closed, but I look up just in time.

Not to the left side with Deacon and Conor's measurements, though. I spot something on the door frame, but this time to the right. I open the door wide and take out my phone, bringing up my flashlight.

"Ready whenever you are," Hunter says, coming up to my side.

I scan the list of markings, same as on the left. Another record of measurements. Another sibling?

Hunter moves in. "What's this?"

"I think we missed something," I tell him.

I read the name in jagged, slanted script. "Manas?"

He studies it closer. "He was older."

"How do you know?"

"Extra layer of paint," he replies. "Or two. Look."

He takes my phone, pointing it lower in the inside of the frame, and I see the earlier markings look like they were barely dug into the wood, but the carving gets deeper and deeper the more Manas aged. I glance at Deacon and Conor's grooves that appear more pronounced. They have one or two less layers of paint covering them.

I look at Hunter. "*Three* brothers?"

He shakes his head. "Not necessarily. Could be a previous inhabitant."

But something starts unraveling in my head.

"You said 'them.'"
Bastien looked up at me.
"You said 'a few of us like to think she escaped them.'"
If Conor is really dead, and it's just Deacon, then who else...

I blink rapidly, staring at the kitchen floor as this feeling starts to puzzle itself together, and I'm not sure where my thoughts are leading, but I know it's right.

I drop my backpack and run upstairs with my phone.

"Dylan!" Hunter yells.

He runs after me, following as I open the attic door and race up the wooden steps, onto the third floor.

I don't look for a lamp or light switch, the sunny fall day outside streaming through the windows.

There's a bed—rather large, perfectly made with sheets, pillows, and a blanket, neatly tucked in under the mattress. I see the rocking chair near the window, the varnish on the wood long since worn away and faded, and the rope tied to a spoke on the back, the other end disappearing out the window.

There's a bedside table, and I walk over, opening it, but all I see is a padlock. The shackle is closed, and there's no key.

Remembering the key from the grave, I pull it out of my pocket and try the lock. It doesn't fit.

I stuff the key back into my jeans and drop the lock into the drawer.

There's nothing else in the attic.

No empty liquor bottles, no condoms, no pizza boxes, no graffiti. Aro was right. The Rebels don't disrespect this house.

A whine sounds behind me, and I look over my shoulder to see Hunter checking a window to make sure it's locked. The floorboard underneath him creaks again as he shifts on his feet.

I cross the room toward him. "Stop."

He faces me, and I nudge him back just a little as I squat down and lift up a floorboard. A newspaper sits inside, and I remove it, opening it up.

Pictures spill out, and Hunter dips down to grab them. I stand up, inspecting them with him.

Two brown-haired boys, one crying and one gazing at the camera with big blue eyes. Same age, same face. "Twins," Hunter whispers.

The other picture is of a woman at a picnic table outside. She wears a simple dress, and the table is covered with food. Deacon and Conor look about thirteen years old as they sit on the bench seat.

"Twins," I say, pointing to the boys and guessing Deacon is the one who looks pissed about something in this photo too. "Deacon. Conor." Then I point to an older boy propped on the edge of the table who looks about sixteen. Black hair, brown eyes. "Manas."

Manas wears the *No Fear* T-shirt on my body now.

"Oh my God," I breathe out. "There were two brothers here with her, but not the twins. Conor did die."

He did commit suicide.

I meet Hunter's eyes. "It wasn't Conor and Deacon texting on those phones. It was Deacon and Manas."

I don't know if Hawke or Kade filled Hunter in, but he doesn't ask me to explain.

The brothers who went after her were the twin who survived and the older brother.

I look at Manas in the picture. He's the one in the notes who comes down from the attic.

Something about the way he's perched on the edge of the table in the picture just like....

"Your parents were around?" I asked Bastien.

"No." He shook his head. "I still couldn't come and go as I liked, though. Siblings."

Younger siblings.

I study the newspaper, seeing the headline for the flood the night she probably disappeared.

A picture of water spilling onto the river banks and covering the streets in the mill district stares back up at me as images flood my head.

Resting on the edge of the table, just like...

Just like he leans on his desk at school.

"Oh my God," I whisper.

He lightened his hair to dark brown, and he's more than twenty-five years older than he was in this photo, but that's him.

"Can we stop at the school?" I ask Hunter.

He nods. "Yeah."

I snap a quick picture of the newspaper and the photos for Hawke and put everything back where I found it. The phones, the notes...someone is feeding us.

But they didn't give us these things. I'll leave them here.

We hurry to the school, Hunter getting me inside through the auto shop. The bay door is easy to maneuver open, and we slip inside, running immediately upstairs.

Hunter grabs my hand, taking the lead, and we stop at Bastien's classroom, the door wide open.

Before I even enter, though, I can see that nothing is right. We walk in, slowly absorbing the bare walls, the empty desk, and the clean whiteboard. No lamp. No container of markers or pens. No posters of student work on the walls.

As if the room has always been abandoned.

"He's gone," I say.

Did he know I would figure out who he was?

Or was he scared of something else?

"What are these?" Hunter asks.

I look as he holds up an envelope from my desk in the front row. I walk over and notice all of the desks have envelopes on them.

I take the one in Hunter's hand, seeing it has my name and my address at home.

"Letters," I tell him. "Letters we wrote to parents...that we never intended to mail."

He looks at the front of it again, then turns it over. "Open in twenty-two years," he reads.

I stare at the inscription that I didn't write written on the back flap. *Twenty-two years?*

He moves between the desks, picking up a few others. "They all say that."

I look around, hoping to find some other clue. Why did he leave? Is he guilty?

Is Deacon with him?

They must've left the cognac on Conor's grave. *New Orleans.*

Hunter comes to my side again. "Open the letter now."

"I know what it says," I tell him. "I wrote it."

"So why does he want to open it again in twenty-two years?"

I think back to his lectures on the rivalry and discussions on community pride and what we perpetuate generation after generation.

"Because we weren't writing them to our parents," I finally say, understanding. "We were writing them to *us* as parents. Because we change."

Like my parents and his parents probably have. My dad was a lot like me. Now, the idea scares him.

"Why not twenty years, though?" he presses. "Why twenty-two?"

"Because he..." I swallow and shake my head. "Because he lost her twenty-two years ago."

He wants us to be in our forties, like he is now.

I fold up the envelope and slide it into my pocket, leaving the classroom for the last time.

Hunter takes my hands as we stroll down the hallway. "You think he'll be back?" he asks.

"I hope not."

But I say it with a little smile. If he is guilty of something, I'd like to know more before I wish him caught.

And if he is guilty of her disappearance—or death—he and Deacon are dangerous. Better gone than near us.

I think I'll miss Mr. Bastien a little.

I'm not sure I would like Manas Doran, though.

Hunter wraps his arms around me and picks me up, walking us down the hall. "You need Rebel gear for my game Friday."

I groan. "Oh, are you sure?"

Maybe Aro has a T-shirt I can borrow, but still...

He laughs, pressing his forehead to mine. "I'll make it worth it."

Flutters hit my stomach as I think about the costume I can change into for the Halloween party afterward. Win or lose, he's going to have such a good night.

PIRATES

EPILOGUE

Dylan

Seven Months Later

Damn, the water's cold.

I let myself have one good shiver before I kick my legs, dragging the lane rope from one dock to the next. It's early June, but the waterfalls feed Blackhawk Lake. I have to remember some of this water was snow in Canada a week ago.

My teeth chatter, keeping faith. The sun will beat the cold into submission by July. Unfortunately, the kids arriving to the camp in a week will still suffer a little while longer.

"Need help?"

I look over at Hunter, standing on the dock in his shorts and nothing else. His triple triangle tattoo on the left side of his torso, same as Kade's, has completely healed since his brother took him to get it a month ago. They surprised Fallon. Three intersecting triangles: mind, body, and spirit. Mother, brother, son.

Kade and Hawke pass behind him, each carrying the blowup water equipment on their shoulders. "You only slow her down," Hawke gripes.

"Oh, don't sell Hunter short," Kade says. "I'm sure he can be unbelievably quick."

Hunter shoves the folded-up turbo water slide off his brother's shoulders, Kade spinning around and both of them laughing as they wrestle each other.

Hawke turns, still holding what looks like the inflatable bongo bouncer. "Guys, come on!" he barks.

I keep swimming.

Hawke must be planning to take over his parents' summer camp someday. He doesn't let anyone on staff have any fun. Even me, and I'm his favorite.

Well, other than Aro.

I shout over to Kade. "At least my man has a repeat customer."

He works his head out of Hunter's hold, backing away. "I only need one date to do everything I could possibly want to do with someone."

I roll my eyes.

He stands at the edge of the dock, looking out at me. "You remember opening up new toys on Christmas? It only took five minutes to push all the buttons..." He curls two fingers. "And twist all the knobs..." He holds his hands, splaying his fingers like he's squeezing boobs. "And take the new wheels for a little spin." He balls his fists and jerks his elbows back twice, thrusting. "Before you got bored? Same thing."

It takes a minute to realize my mouth is hanging open. *Oh my God.*

But Hawke and Hunter are laughing, Hunter grabs his brother in a headlock again and both of them fall into the water.

They crash onto my line, jerking it out of my hand, and I slap the lake with both hands. "Thanks!"

They resurface, splashing water at each other and still smiling.

"Y'all are being useless!" Hawke growls.

"Your dad will still pay us, because we're family," I tell him.

He scowls, continuing on down the dock as Kade scales the ladder to get out of the water. They're supposed to inflate all of the water toys, make sure they're ready for the campers, but Hawke knows Kade will need to play on everything for a while first.

Hunter swims the lane rope back over to me, and I take it.

"You have thirty minutes!" Juliet shouts from the shore.

We look over to see her standing on the beautiful lawn, the main lodge in the background and the flag whipping in the wind.

"Counselor meeting in the Astronomy Tower," she reminds us. "Quinn dropped off pastries. Bring your tablets!"

I hook the rope onto the next dock. "Yes, I'm starving."

Hunter comes in, wrapping an arm around my waist, both of us with one hand on the dock.

"Twenty-five minutes to finish this," Kade goes on. "Four minutes to change and get over to the lodge, and one minute of you on her. You can do it."

Hunter chuckles, kissing me as I circle his waist with my legs.

I'm so excited for this summer. Sun, splash, and steamy nights.

"You're smiling," he whispers, coming in to kiss me again and again. "Happy?"

I nod, moving my arms around his neck. "Quinn is finishing her four-year degree in three, so after she graduates next May, we'll have pastries year-round."

He snorts. He thought I was happy about working with him this summer. Psh-please.

Actually, I am happy. So happy. I love Blackhawk Camp, I like working with kids, and my boyfriend will only be a cabin away.

He kisses me again, and I deepen it, grinding into him and taking full advantage that no kids have arrived yet. I hope we can sneak in some night swimming this summer.

Shouting hits our ears, and we pull away a little, recognizing his sister's voice. We both look over, watching her bark at people to get off her obstacle course. She's personally designing one for the Color Powder War on the Fourth of July.

"A.J.'s already set to be a counselor-in-training," he says. Then he looks at me. "Where's James?"

We forgot that two kids actually are on the premises today.

I jerk my chin to Chimney Lock Island, out beyond the docks. It's not much land, only about an acre or so. I see my brother's canoe on the shore. "Making that altar to Jason Voorhees's mother's head from *Friday the 13th Part II*."

Hunter's face falls, and he looks at me. "He's not."

"Oh, it's brilliant." I grin big, pressing my finger to my lips. "Don't tell anyone."

We laugh, because everyone is scared of that island. It's part of the camp fun. The veteran campers pass around stories to the new ones, and every summer, Jax catches at least one batch of kids trying to sneak out there in the middle of the night.

I hold Hunter close. "You're smiling," I say back. "Happy?"

"Yeah."

But I draw in a long breath. "I feel like you should still go to the University of Chicago."

It was his dream, and I feel like he's sacrificing it for me. I could never get in there, but he did.

But he simply says, "There's always graduate school."

But...

"I'm excited I'm not leaving," he tells me before I can protest more. "Kade and me in the dorms at Clarke, my family close, and I get to fulfill the fantasy of climbing that tree and sneaking into your room right under your dad's nose."

He kisses me again, and tingles spread over my body.

I know he's happy to stay and keep building his relationship with his brother. And I know he feels he owes it to his parents to stay close for a little longer since he thinks he cheated them of taking part in his life for more than a year.

"I just don't want you to miss what you were meant for," I say.

"My family—and you—" he says, "are what I'll need through every hard thing that ever happens in my life. This is where I want to be right now. Home."

I hug him tightly. He's right. Chicago has graduate school.

I pull back, pouting a little, though. "I should be in the dorms too."

"You will," he says. "Between classes."

And he grins, full of plans for us this fall, already. It's not enough, though. I need my freedom if I'm going to be forced to continue my education.

It was the deal I made with my parents, though. Dad agreed to continue training me *and* sponsoring me if I committed to going to Clarke University for one year.

Their hope is that I'll love it and keep going. We'll see.

If I do, then I'm moving into the dorms my sophomore year. I'm pretty sure they'll agree to that if I continue college.

I'm not all that excited about quickies in Hunter's dorm room, though, with guys shouting down the halls.

"I prefer our place in Weston," I tell him.

Knock Hill's trees are in bloom, and the air is so thick, you can drink it. I want to sweat in a house where we can be as noisy as we want.

"And I like it here." Excitement makes his eyes go big. "The Sports Shack, the Hobby Nook, the showers, the Swallow's Nest, the archery range, the boathouse, the barn…" he lists all the places to sneak away, and my pulse rises.

I bite his bottom lip. "The tents…"

He groans, wrapping his arms around me tighter and twirling us around in the water.

"I wish summer would last forever," I say.

"There are plenty of places to hide in the winter too." His lips trail to my neck. "As you remember."

His mouth runs over my skin, and I drop my head back, losing my breath. God, I love him.

"We're literally getting paid for this!" someone shouts at us.

I pop my head up, and he turns his, both of us seeing Aro standing on the dock in shorts and a bikini top. She glares.

Hawke passes behind her. "You tell 'em, baby."

We break into laughter, and I can't wait to catch them all over each other this summer like they're any different. They love the barn as much as we do.

Later that night, or maybe it's already early morning, Shelburne Falls is quiet and asleep, having their fucking sugarplum dreams, as someone stands on the bridge between the Falls and Weston.

She looks down into the river, her long white hair with blue tips wrapped up in a wild ponytail as locks whip across her face in the wind.

She had to wait for Dylan to graduate. And for the winter to end and the spring rains to slow. She didn't know if it was possible, but her chances were better with the water level lowered.

Today, the river stage measured seven feet.

That's manageable.

Of course, that doesn't mean this area of the river will only be seven feet, and she actually hopes it's not. She'll need more cushion to break the fall.

But she points her flashlight, seeing the outline of something below and she knows she's in the right place. She flips the light off and tosses it on the ground, next to her dad's tow truck.

He'll bluster and break things if he sees she took it, and he'll threaten to beat her ass, but he never does.

Clutching the rope wrapped around her hand, she lurches forward but stops, her heart jumping through her chest. She knew this would be hard. Water frightens her, but more so because she's alone and it's dark. She looks around, seeing no one on either bank, no boats coming, and no traffic. She may not get another chance.

Now.

She jumps, gasps, and instantly regrets it, but it's too late now. Inhaling a deep breath, she plummets down into the night river, her stomach rising past her diaphragm.

But she pushes the fear back down her throat and closes her eyes, hitting the water. She's engulfed, cold immediately seeping into her bones, but she squeezes her fist around the rope, pushes her arms, and kicks her legs.

Shooting through the surface, she looks around and then up, the rope stretching between her and the tow truck above. Pulling her head lamp out of her pocket, she wades as she fits the band around her skull and presses the button. The brown water around her lights up, and she sucks in a breath, diving quickly.

The light from her lamp illuminates the area around her, and she descends, kicking hard.

Things glint, like shiny rocks below, and it takes a second for her to realize it's the coins that people toss when they cross.

And then... A straight line appears. Nature doesn't make straight lines.

She reaches out, touching the steel locker, caked in mud and slime. It sits almost upright, its back corner buried in the river floor. Working quickly, she pulls the rope, having left herself plenty of slack, and ties it around the middle, coming up for air only once before she dives back down to tie it again, head to foot.

She starts to swim up, but the light from her head lamp catches a patch of clear water about fifteen feet away.

She stops, seeing the driver's side of a vehicle come into view.

The car...

It's there.

And then a cloud of mud passes with the current, and the vehicle disappears again.

She thinks about swimming over but decides not to. Popping back up through the surface, she swims quickly for the Falls side of the river and climbs back up to the bridge, walking for the truck. Pushing the lever, she reels in the rope attached to the chain that's attached to the crane. Peering over the side of the bridge, she watches the old school locker rise from the river, spilling water from its cracks.

Bringing it in, she guides it onto the truck bed, rips off her head lamp, and picks up her flashlight. Getting into the truck, she makes a U-turn on the bridge and drives back into the Falls.

It doesn't take long. She's a planner. Accounts for all challenges. She knows which roads to take in order to avoid cops. She brought a rolling cart to load the locker onto. She knows which door in the senior hallway of Shelburne Falls High School doesn't lock.

She doesn't need help. Doesn't need pity.

And hour later, she stares at her mom's locker back in the display case where it belongs.

"Sorry, Dylan," Thomasin says, wiping off the water under her chin. "But I think I'll let Kade have his fun, after all."

She slides the glass door shut and walks away, letting out a long breath.

"I'll be fun, too, someday," she whispers.

THE END

Turn the page for a sneak peek at the
next installment in the Hellbent series,
Quiet Ones!

This will be Quinn's story!

Quinn

One Year Later

I peer out the little window in the kitchen door, seeing the man still finishing his coffee. He sits at the table in front of the big mirror, and he's been there for two hours. I hate kicking people out, but...

Oh, who am kidding? I've never kicked anyone out.

I usually rely on them seeing me switch the sign on the door and start cleaning up for them to get the hint that I'm closing.

Here I am, though, and dishes are done, counters cleaned, trash taken out, dough for tomorrow prepped, and floors swept and mopped. I only have to pack up the leftovers for the day and count out the register, which I refuse to do when I'm alone in the shop with a customer I don't know.

But as if he can hear my thoughts, he rises, buttons his suit jacket, and tucks in his chair. *Aw*. Nobody does that. I smile as he leaves the bakery, pushing through the door.

"See you soon," I say, smiling.

He doesn't reply, simply turns his head slightly, showing me the side of his face, and nods once.

I lock the door behind him and shut off the light, heading to his table and picking up his cup and saucer. I swipe up his napkin to find a phone sitting underneath it.

I look to the windows, then to the phone, grabbing it as I set the dishes down and run to the door.

I open it and peer out. "Sir?"

I look both directions, but all I see are diners at the outside tables of Rivertown Grill and some cars driving by. He's gone.

I lock the door again and inspect the phone, finally noticing how old it is. The gritty texture leaves patches of black on it, and I bring it to my nose, noticing the scent of fire. I flip it open, pressing buttons, but it's dead. No one uses these anymore. What a strange thing to even carry.

I shrug. He'll come back for it.

Swiping up the dishes again, I walk into the kitchen, set the phone on the counter, and place the dishes in the sink. I turn and move all the remaining pastries from the tray to a box.

But no sooner have I started than Dylan comes bursting through the swinging doors, from the front of the shop.

"No, no," she cries, running for the chocolate coconut donuts. "I need them!"

Hunter laughs, trailing in behind her, followed by Hawke and Aro.

Dylan barrels into me, and we take turns shoving each other with our hips for supremacy over the remaining baked goods.

I snatch one out of her hand before she takes a bite. "No, you need to take them to the senior center and help me out."

I'm doing a test run for the summer to see if I can be a bakery *and* do stuff for lunch too. Sandwiches, flatbread pizzas, soups....

I'm staying open way too late, though, and trying to be back here at three-thirty in the morning to bake is making it difficult to find time for exercising, my family, or any kind of sleep.

If I don't get into a groove soon, this trial will be a fail.

Hunter stands on the other side of the counter, plucking one off the tray and handing it to his girlfriend. "We'll take them," he tells me.

"How'd you guys get in?" I look around at them. "I locked the front door."

Aro won't meet my eyes, Hunter gives me a tight smile, and Dylan leans her elbows on the counter, shrugging. "No, you didn't."

Hawke snorts, pulling a chocolate milk out of the fridge. Hunter looks to him. "It's time to tell her, man."

"We'll tell her when she's ready to use it," Hawke replies.

Aro smiles at Dylan, the latter stuffing her mouth with chocolate donut as she looks up at me with glee.

I point my finger around the room. "You know I'm older than all of you, right?"

They all laugh, and they've been hinting about something—I don't know what—for a while now. I know there's some urban legend they're researching, and I know they're in here during closing hours and off season too. I gave them all keys because I might've needed any one of them to have access, in case a pipe burst while I was away at school, or if they were in need of extra space for holiday cooking.

But something is going on, and I don't press harder about it, because honestly, I don't want to know. If I know, then I'll feel like I have to be the responsible one, and I'd rather not ruin their fun.

I shouldn't feel like that, but it's like I'm inexperienced compared to them, and I don't know why, and it sucks.

I've got a college degree. My own business. I'm disciplined, punctual, and a taxpayer. Why do I feel younger than them?

"Come on, we've gotta get back." Hunter dusts off his hands. "Lights out in thirty minutes."

They're all working at Camp Blackhawk, like last summer. They get a couple of hours of free time while the kids have campfire jamboree at night.

I hand Hunter the two boxes to drop off at the senior center. "Where's Kade?"

"Tending to needs." Dylan cleans her teeth with her tongue. "Whatever that means."

"Even I know what that means," I say as I lead the way to the back door.

Kade would prefer to spend his summers doing one thing and one thing only, so suffice it to say, he makes the most out of his two hours of free time before lights out.

"Hey, what's this?" Dylan asks.

She picks up the phone that the customer left, turning it over in her hand.

"Someone left it on a table," I tell her. "I'm going to put it in Lost and Found."

"It looks like the one that was in my desk when I stayed in Weston," she explains. "I forgot about it."

A look passes between her and Hawke.

"Did you see who left it?" Hawke asks me.

"Some guy." I take the phone out of Dylan's hand and set it back down. "I didn't get a good look. Why?"

Hawke's quiet before he draws in a deep breath and shakes his head. "No reason. Just leave it in Lost and Found. Someone will come for it."

Aro throws him a look as I push open the back door, nudging them out. Not that I don't love them, but I have exactly two hours before I need to be in bed.

Dylan takes another bite, groaning. "Quinn, seriously. You should go global."

"Mm-hmm."

"At least Goldbelly!"

I smile, giving her a little shove.

But then she spins around. "Or enter that baking contest!"

"Right!" I feign enthusiasm. "The Shelburne Falls Festival of... Reindeer...Chestnut...Silly Sweater Dasher Dancer Ice Miracle Angel Fest!" I tease. "Will do!"

Hunter laughs his ass off because I'm a baker in a small town, and I've heard all of the Hallmark jokes.

They wave, Dylan blowing me a kiss, and I catch it, closing the door and locking it.

I adore them all. I love how happy they are. They deserve it.

It's just hard to be the odd one out in the group now. I don't feel lonely until they're around.

And Kade doesn't count. He loves his life the way it is.

I shake it off, growling at myself in the privacy of my shop. It's just the fatigue. It's making me cranky. Overworked, not enough me-time.

I need some fresh air. And my earbuds.

Changing in the bathroom, I don a pair of black leggings, sports bra, and white tank crop top with a black jacket over it. I sweep all of my hair to one side and fix it in a low braid, draping it over the left side of my chest. I pull on the faded blue Yankees cap, slip my ID and shop key into the pocket on my leg, and fit my earbuds into my ears. Tuning to my favorite list, I slide my phone into the pocket on my other thigh and leave through the back door, locking it behind me.

It's only after eight. Dark but not late. The streets will still be alive with activity. Especially on a beautiful summer night.

I leave the alley, heading onto First and turning onto High Street. I roll my shoulders, stretch my arms above my head, and let the cool breeze wash over my body as the scent of potted flowers on the sidewalks and the heat from the day holds the fuel from the cars in the air just a little.

I double-knot my tennis shoes and start jogging, passing my shop, Rivertown, and the bowling alley. I take a right, into the neighborhood, and feel a burst of energy in my legs, free at last. I sidestep trees and mailboxes, swerving around cars parked at the curb. Then, I cross the street and dive between houses.

Mr. Zellers sits on his back porch, and I wave as I descend the small grassy hill to the fenced-in community pool. I race past it, inhaling the chlorine and remembering the first and last time I swam here. I had a pool at home growing up—still do—but if you wanted to be seen as a teenager, this was the place.

I pound the pavement, sweating already and curving right onto Main Street.

A truck comes up behind me, passes, and I see the red of the paint and the JT Racing emblem on the tailgate. I hold my breath, dread setting in, but I keep running, even when I see his taillights brighten. *Oh, no.* The vehicle halts in the middle of the street and I square my shoulders, continuing on.

Jared steps out of the driver's side. I don't slow down. "Don't worry. I'm staying in lighted areas—"

But he swoops me up and throws me over his shoulder.

I grit my teeth together, but only kick my legs once in frustration. It's no use fighting more.

My brother carries me around the truck, and Jax, one of my other brothers, hops out of the passenger side, opening up the back door.

Jared deposits me inside, and I try to jump out, but Jax slams the door in my face. I yank out my earbuds and pound my fist against the window.

I don't believe this.

I kind of loved it when I was six. Started to resent it when I was eleven. I'm twenty-one years old now.

"Run in the morning," Jared says, climbing in the cab.

"My business is in the morning!" I'm louder than is helpful. "This is the only time I have."

He shifts the truck into gear and hits the gas.

"Shelburne Falls is a safe place," I point out.

"Until a traveler comes through one night and slaughters a family," Jax argues, "and people start saying 'it was such a safe town, we used to leave our doors unlocked...'"

I drop my head back, locking my hands on top. "I'm in prison."

"No." Jared turns down his music. "You're our little sister."

I meet his eyes in his rearview mirror and actually laugh. "Do you have any idea what your daughter," and then I point to Jax, "and your son, for that matter, are getting up to at that camp with their significant others?"

"Don't piss me off," Jared bites.

"Don't gross me out," Jax snaps.

This is a part of the reason I feel younger than my niece and nephews. Jared and Jax are well aware their children are in love—and acting upon it—but I'm too fragile to go out at night.

For a minute, I think he's driving me back to the bakery—or to my parents—where I still live since I just finished school and moved back and haven't had time to rent an apartment, but he stops a block over, in front of the new gym that popped up a couple of years ago.

Which I was interested in checking out, but again, haven't made time for.

They drag me inside, a young woman smiling at the counter. "Hey, welcome to Astrophysics. Can I help you?"

"Look, Quinn, a track." Jared points above, and I see runners circling the building on the second floor.

Jax slips his hands into his pockets, nodding in approval. "Indoor, cameras, proper lighting...loving it."

I give the girl a tight smile as Jared slaps down his credit card. "Set her up."

I should fight it, and I have every intention of being quite the handful for my brothers eventually, reminiscent of all the movie heroines I love, but I'm just too tired. It takes twenty minutes to fill out my information and sign some papers. I bypass the tour, schedule a fitness test, and grab a towel, heading through the lobby.

Jax works on his phone at a small round table near the doors. Jared sits with him, elbows on his knees as he peels a complimentary orange.

"You're just gonna sit there?" I ask. "The whole time?"

Like he doesn't trust me to get home on my own?

He just looks at me but says nothing, and I remove my jacket and head into the gym. I wish Madoc was here. He can get protective, but he's the brother who's a lot more reasonable.

Or like, reasonable at all, for that matter. He would get them to leave.

Sticking my earbuds back in, I restart my music, leaving my towel and jacket on a bench. I step on to the three-lane track, wait for another jogger to pass by, and quickly follow. An arrow on the wall dictates the direction we're running, accompanied by a sign letting runners know that eleven-and-a-half laps equals one mile. I dig in my heels, loving the slight cushion of the ground, easier than pavement, and I pass under a digital timer above our heads that keeps minutes and seconds if we want to pace ourselves.

I just want to go, though. There are mirrors on the

outside wall, sporadically interrupted with windows, the inside walls occasionally giving way for people to leave the track and head into the workout areas. Two-dozen weightlifting machines sit in the oval floor at the center of the track, and I look around, seeing a few women, but a lot of men. One huge guy with a long silver beard lifts a massive dumbbell over his head with one arm as he sits on a bench and watches himself in the mirror. Another props up his phone to film himself doing squats.

I float my eyes over the room, seeing a man in black track pants with a white hoodie doing pullups. Long, lean, broad... Blond.

A wall cuts off my view, and I blink, my heart suddenly pulsing a mile a minute.

I try to swallow, but I can't. The wall breaks again, and I jerk my head, looking back into the workout area. He keeps going, pulling his chin up over the bar, and I stare at the side of his face and the back of his head...but it's too far away to be sure. His hair is recently cut, but wet with sweat, and I see he has earbuds in like me.

I lose sight of him again. I can't get a look at his face. Another wall, and I enter the other side of the gym, a new workout area. I try not to, but I find my legs moving a little faster to circle around again.

It's been eight years. If he were back in town, Madoc and Fallon would've made a big deal about it. I would've heard.

The Yankees cap feels tight. I keep going, my braid bouncing over my chest, but when I come up on his weight room again, he's gone. Runners pass me, and I scan the room twice out of the corner of my eye.

Then...

There he is.

559

My stomach flips. He lays on a bench, holding a bar over his body before bringing it down and pumping it back up, again and again. His long legs are bent, his shoes on the ground, and even though he's wearing a lot more clothes than the other men here, I can't stop staring at everything but his face. Built chest under the hoodie. Narrow waist. Toned shoulders and strong arms. The muscle on the top of his thigh that bulges just a little under the black pants.

The wall separates us again, and when there's a break, I glance quickly, seeing him replace the bar and sit up. He rises, grabs his towel, and looks up, meeting my eyes.

My heart plummets into my stomach.

Lucas.

I look away, disappearing behind another wall and entering the other side of the gym.

Oh my God.

I can't breathe. I stop, tapping my earbud to pause the music as I step through the entrance to another workout area. I stagger a little over to the water fountains on the wall and bend over, pressing the button. I drink, wetting my parched throat.

How can he be here? How can he be here for even an hour without me hearing something?

But he's just working out like he's been here for days.

I stand upright, wiping off my mouth. Did he recognize me?

I should say 'hi,' I guess. I kind of grew up with him, even if I was way younger. He was Madoc's 'little brother' in the Big Brothers Big Sisters program. Lucas's dad had died when he was young, and Madoc became his older male influence, so Lucas was around our family a lot.

He went to college, became an architect with Fallon, and moved out of the country eight years ago, building skyscrapers in Dubai.

I was thirteen when he left.

I catch myself in the mirror behind the fountain, my hair's a mess, makeup's gone, and I'm sweating already. Thankfully, my tired eyes are hidden under the bill of the cap.

No, it'll be awkward. This isn't how I imagined seeing him again.

I walk to one of the Pelotons and climb on. Starting a Lanebreak workout, I mute the music and just follow the designated pacing and resistance while I absently read the headlines floating across the bottom of the TV screen above. Through my earbuds I hear barbells clanging and feet pounding the treadmills, and I almost settle into a pace until he passes behind me with a friend.

"Come on, cardio," his buddy says.

His friend jumps on the treadmill next to me, Lucas taking the one on his other side. I pedal hard, glancing at them both in the mirror on the wall in front of us. His friend glances over at me, short, dark hair, black shorts, and a gray sleeveless T-shirt with the sides cut out, showing off his tanned muscular arms and pecs.

He turns back to Lucas. "I fucking hate working out at night," he says. "What do you do with the endorphins when you leave?"

I keep facing forward, and it must be a rhetorical question, because Lucas doesn't reply.

"I need my wife," his friend with a smirk says as he jogs. "Thank God, I married a woman with as much energy as me."

"Girl," Lucas corrects him. "You married a girl ten years younger than you."

"I had to cast a wider net to find my soulmate."

I keep my smile to myself. They think my earbuds are on and I can't hear.

And if he's the same age as Lucas, his wife is older than me. That's not a girl.

His friend is right, though. I hate working out at night. It takes longer to calm down when I go home and try to sleep. I still have so much energy.

Lucas taps his earbud. "Lucas Morrow."

My stomach swims up to my heart, hearing him say his name. There's no mistake. It's him.

His friend continues to run next to me, Lucas listening to the other end of his call.

"I won't be away long," he tells whoever he's talking to. "Retrofitted? No. That boat's fifty years old. He's not paying for that."

Business call.

"He can have his dock outside his office building as long as the city sanctions it," Lucas says. "Blame the timeline on them."

His voice is deeper, and I try to see his eyes in the mirror, but they're cast down.

He nods. "Bye."

And he ends the call.

He jogs, taking a drink from his water bottle. His brow is pinched, and I don't like that he still has that look on his face. One he didn't have when he was in college, but developed a little while before he left eight years ago. It's still there. Like he's always on guard, ready to fight back.

"You should stay longer," his friend says.

"Come to Dubai more."

"They look at me funny when they search my luggage."

His friend grins over at him in the mirror, Lucas looks up, and I dart my eyes down.

"Stop traveling with handcuffs," Lucas says in a low voice.

My mouth falls open a little.

But then his friend asks, "And use rope instead?"

My mouth is dry again. What the hell?

His pal smiles at Lucas in the mirror. "I guess people don't get suspicious when they find it in your apartment."

I slow my pace, unsure whether he just means in general, or if he should use rope...like Lucas does. Rope for what? It's the knowing look he gives Lucas that makes it feel like the room is tilting a little.

Lucas's jaw flexes, and then he shifts his gaze, meeting mine in the mirror.

I lower them again.

"Lucas!" a familiar voice yells behind us. "Racquetball."

I glance up, seeing Madoc opening the door to a court, two rackets and a ball in his hand.

He doesn't seem to notice me yet.

Lucas hops off the treadmill, grabs his stuff, and whips his towel at his friend. "See you tomorrow."

The guy nods once. "Tomorrow."

Lucas and Madoc disappear into a court, and I don't even notice that the guy next to me is gone until my ride ends. I didn't pay attention to my speed or resistance at all. I was lost in thought the whole time.

He said on his call that he wouldn't be away long. Which means he's not staying.

I should've talked to him.

Maybe I would look into his eyes and see him smile at me, and all of a sudden, realize that my stupid childhood crush was better in my memory. Maybe then I'd be free from this idyllic fantasy I always had of him that was nothing more than idolatry.

I spend another half hour weight training before I drift to the snack bar for a smoothie. I can still see Jared and Jax out of the corner of my eye waiting, and I hold up my finger, telling them I'll only be a minute. I tie my jacket around my waist, pulling down my cap, but then I hear Madoc's voice. "Fallon is excited to see you."

I glance up and then back down, seeing Madoc and Lucas, showered and back in their suits as they stand in line in front of me.

Madoc swipes his card and hands Lucas a straw.

"Ran into her today at the office, actually," Lucas tells him. "She didn't tell you?"

"She told me to convince you to stay with us."

My heart starts pounding again. This would be the perfect time to speak up.

"That's nice." Lucas's voice doesn't sound right. "I'll think about it."

"You like your alone time now, huh?"

Lucas shrugs a little. "I'm used to it."

I could ask for my compass back. That was the deal, right? He had to come back, if nothing else to return my compass that I gave him before he left.

"Stay the summer," Madoc suggests. "She could use you here."

I see Lucas turn and glance over his shoulder at me. "Uh..." He turns back to Madoc. "Uh, I have to get back as soon as possible, actually."

No.

He turns a little again, and I know he's staring at me. I raise my eyes, meeting his.

"Sorry." He laughs at himself a little. "It's just... I used to have a cap like that."

I can't talk. I can't blink. I just peer up at him under the hat.

Madoc takes his drink. "You had that cap. That's Quinn, dude."

Lucas's face falls, Madoc hooks an arm around my neck and plants a kiss on the side of my head, and I can't seem to remember my own language, all of a sudden.

"Hey, guys," Madoc calls to Jared and Jax, leaving to go talk to them.

I stand there, managing a small smile.

Lucas blinks, and here—now—I know that nothing was better in my memory. I loved his longer hair as a young guy, and his lazy clothes when he loved rock climbing and being a lake bum, but I can see his blue eyes better now, striking with his hard jaw and sun-kissed skin. I drop my gaze to the crisp white shirt and tie wrapped tightly around his neck.

"I can't believe I didn't recognize you," he says.

I swallow. "It's been a...long time."

He breaks into a grin, shaking his head as he comes in. "My big brother's little sister." He hugs me. "How are you doing?"

I almost let my eyes fall closed. He smells like one of the stores my mom takes me to that has a dress code.

But I quickly pull away. "I'm...sweaty. Sorry."

I lick my lips, hearing my brothers chat, and I know he can see how nervous I am.

I clear my throat. "So, how long are you around?"

I know the answer. I heard him tell Madoc and someone on the phone.

But his smile drops, and he thins his eyes a little, gazing at me. "I don't know..."

The vein in his neck throbs steadily, and I take it back. I don't really like his suit. I liked him with messy hair and no shirt.

"Uh, how old are you now?" he asks. "Twenty-ish?"

"Twenty-one."

"In college then?" he presses.

I open my mouth, but then Madoc is there, with his arm around me.

"Our little Quinn finished at Notre Dame in three years," he says proudly. "Runs Frosted over on High Street."

Lucas looks from my brother to me. "The bakery."

"Yeah," I reply.

He smiles again. "I remember your pizza."

My whole body warms. It warms too much, and I'm boiling.

"You okay?" Madoc asks me.

"Yes," I say, but it comes out as more of a pant. "I need a ride home. Since I'm not allowed to ride my bike or run in the dark."

Madoc laughs and Jared and Jax walk up.

"We got you," Jax says.

Yes, I know.

I always know that. I love it, but I kind of hate it sometimes.

They start to walk out, and Lucas takes his drink but drops his straw. I bend down, but so does he, accidently hitting the cap off my head. The long pieces of hair not secured in my braid fall out, and we squat there, meeting each other's eyes. I look at him through the locks hanging over my face.

He's not smiling anymore, and I can't breathe again.

I pick up the cap. "Here. You said to hold it until you got back."

I hand it to him.

But he shakes his head, gently pushing the hat back to me. "Hang on to it for a little while longer. I'll get it before I leave."

So, I'm going to see him once more before he goes?

I rise and so does he. "Goodnight," I say.

I turn and leave, resisting the urge to look back at him, because my brothers are watching, and I already know what they'll think.

Lucas Morrow and I are too old to play together now.

Quiet Ones coming next!

MAIN CAST OF CHARACTERS

Dylan Trent – from Shelburne Falls, wants to race motorbikes, only woman in twenty years to be traded to Weston in prisoner exchange, Hunter and Kade's step-cousin

Hunter Caruthers – Dylan's step-cousin, left Shelburne Falls over a year ago to attend St. Matthew's but switches to Weston High School, on Weston football team, Kade's twin brother

Kade Caruthers – Dylan's step-cousin, Hunter's twin brother, lives in Shelburne Falls, quarterback of Falls High School football team, he and Hunter had a falling out over a year ago

Farrow Kelly – Hunter's friend, goes to Weston High School and plays on football team, works for Green Street—the local gang

Ciaran Pierce – Hunter's grandfather, ex-Irish mob, lives near Chicago, has connections to Weston

Aro Marquez – heroine from *Falls Boys* (Hellbent #1), Dylan's friend, former resident of Weston, lives in Shelburne Falls now with Jax and Juliet Trent

Hawken Trent – Aro's boyfriend, Dylan's cousin (blood related), son of Jax and Juliet from the Fall Away Series, first year Clarke University in Shelburne Falls

Constin, Luca, T.C., Anders, and Calvin – on the Weston football team, friends of Farrow and Hunter

Coral Lapinski, Arlet, and Mace – Weston crew, high school students, hang out with Farrow and friends

Stoli – Kade's friend, real name is Josh

Dirk – Kade's friend

Jared Trent – Dylan's father, hero from *Bully* (Fall Away #1), husband to Tate, runs JT Racing

Tatum Trent – Dylan's mother, heroine from Bully (Fall Away #1), wife of Jared, they live in same house she grew up in

James Trent – Dylan's little brother, ten years old

A.J. Caruthers – Hunter and Kade's little sister, nine years old

Quinn Caruthers – twenty years old, Dylan's aunt, but they grew up more like cousins, half-sister to Jared, Madoc, and Jax, attends the University of Notre Dame

Thomasin Dietrich – nicknamed Tommy, Falls High student, fourteen years old, hangs out in Weston

Codi Gundry – student at Weston High School, the crew watches out for her

Madoc Caruthers – mayor of Shelburne Falls, father to

Hunter, Kade, and A.J., step-brother to Dylan's dad, Jared, and Hawke's dad, Jax

Fallon Caruthers – architect, mother to Hunter, Kade, and A.J., daughter of Ciaran

Jaxon Trent – Jared's half-brother and Madoc's stepbrother, husband to Juliet, father to Hawke, guardian to Aro and her siblings, runs Fallstown

Juliet Trent – wife to Jax, mother to Hawke, novelist, guardian to Aro and her siblings, lives with family in Jared's old house next door to Tate's house

Mr. Bastien – Weston teacher

Samson Fletcher – runs the Weston barber shop

ACKNOWLEDGEMENTS

From book to book, my acknowledgments never really change. I've worked with most of the same people that I did when I started, and what I'm continually grateful for is that they accommodate the way I work. This isn't the norm in this industry. Everyone has a schedule. Everyone has a life of their own. Everyone has other obligations and other clients. I need to get my book done or my order in or I might lose my spot with that designer, formatter, or editor.

Unfortunately, I just can't. I never could. For someone who thrives off routine and being on time, deadlines are my Achilles' heel.

I know when I sit down and start thinking about how the conversations you just read between these characters are going to go that I will get them written down. I know the words *will* come.

I sit there.

See the characters in my head.

I've almost got it.

And then...

Yes. That's what I want her to say, and then he's going to say that next. And then I sit there again, trying to figure out what she says back.

Sure, I could type anything. I can keep the story going, type words, and finish the book, but I know if I think about it just a little bit longer, the heroine will say something that'll make me smile even more.

Some days, I sit at my desk for ten hours and actually only type for three of them. Some days, I'll type for five of those hours. Given that, it's impossible to predict when I'll finish until I'm about two-thirds of the way through the book when it's pretty much on auto-pilot from there.

I'm grateful when my formatter says, "Don't worry, I'll squeeze you in," when I tell her I need two more weeks. Or when my editor barely bats an eyelash that I'm late turning in a manuscript. Again.

Of course, everyone's time is valuable, and I do not expect anyone to drop what they're doing when I'm finally ready for them, but it's hard to anticipate needing extra time and having the freedom to take it when needed has made all the difference. I'm thankful that Bekke, Elaine, Chrissy, Ashlee, Marisa, Adrienne, and Lee appreciate that stories are a fucking hassle to write, but the end product is so worth it.

Thank you, as well, to all of the YouTube content creators who play nonstop in my office. Truly unsung heroes, helping us all live an aesthetically pleasing life. You inspire, nurture my mood, and surround me with whatever atmosphere I need to focus me. Thank you, especially to my favorite channels: Inner Academia, Regnum Umbrae, Chill Music Lab, Galaxy Waves, Outdoor Therapy, and SP Sounds Chill.

Also...

To Dystel, Goderich & Bourret LLC—thank you Jane, Lauren, and Gracie for being so readily available and helping me grow every day. And Nataly! I love getting emails from Nataly! We know why. LOL

To the PenDragons—love you! Excited to hear your theories on what's to come in the series!

To all of the book bloggers, bookstagrammers, and BookTok accounts—thank you, thank you, thank you. I've never believed authors are the best people to sell their own books. Readers are! You've changed the game. We can write and make a living, and you're helping the indie community thrive like never before. So much has come in throughout the past year, and I know I haven't nearly acknowledged every tag, but I want you to know you're appreciated. Your beautiful pictures, your hot (or funny) TikToks, your time writing reviews... I know it won't last forever, but I'll enjoy it for as long as I can. Thank you!

To every author and aspiring author—thank you for the stories you've shared, many of which have made me a happy reader in search of a wonderful escape and a better writer, trying to live up to your standards. Write and create, and don't ever stop. Your voice is important, and someone out there needs to hear it.